ARK

ARK

Stephen Baxter

A ROC BOOK

ROC
Published by New American Library, a division of
Penguin Group (USA) Inc., 375 Hudson Street,
New York, New York 10014, USA
Penguin Group (Canada), 90 Eglinton Avenue East, Suite 700, Toronto,
Ontario M4P 2Y3, Canada (a division of Pearson Penguin Canada Inc.)
Penguin Books Ltd., 80 Strand, London WC2R 0RL, England
Penguin Ireland, 25 St. Stephen's Green, Dublin 2,
Ireland (a division of Penguin Books Ltd.)
Penguin Group (Australia), 250 Camberwell Road, Camberwell, Victoria 3124,
Australia (a division of Pearson Australia Group Pty. Ltd.)
Penguin Books India Pvt. Ltd., 11 Community Center, Panchsheel Park,
New Delhi - 110 017, India
Penguin Group (NZ), 67 Apollo Drive, Rosedale, North Shore 0632,
New Zealand (a division of Pearson New Zealand Ltd.)
Penguin Books (South Africa) (Pty.) Ltd., 24 Sturdee Avenue,
Rosebank, Johannesburg 2196, South Africa
Penguin Books Ltd., Registered Offices:
80 Strand, London WC2R 0RL, England

Published by Roc, an imprint of New American Library, a division of Penguin Group (USA) Inc.
Previously published in a Gollancz hardcover edition. For information contact Gollancz, an imprint
of the Orion Pubishing Group, Orion House, 5 Upper St. Martin's Lane, London WC2H 9EA.

ROC REGISTERED TRADEMARK—MARCA REGISTRADA

ISBN 978-0-451-46331-9

Set in Bembo
Designed by Alissa Amell

Printed in the United States of America

PUBLISHER'S NOTE
This is a work of fiction. Names, characters, places, and incidents either are the product of the author's
imagination or are used fictitiously, and any resemblance to actual persons, living or dead, business
establishments, events, or locales is entirely coincidental.
     The publisher does not have any control over and does not assume any responsibility for author
or third-party Web sites or their content.

For Mary Jane Shepherd

1955–2009

ARK

One

2041

1

Gordo Alonzo and Thandie Jones had rustled up a helicopter to take the Ark Three party back to the ragged Colorado shore. All of them but Grace Gray, who wasn't going anywhere.

Grace, her arm held firmly by Gordo Alonzo, watched the bird come down over Cripple Creek, scattering some of the flimsier shanties that crowded the narrow streets. The town had once been a mining settlement, and then a tourist trap. Now, in the age of the flood, with the sea that had swept over the United States lapping at the Rockies, homeless were camped in the streets and parking lots and the forecourts of disused gas stations, and a shantytown of tents and shacks spread far beyond the core of the old settlement. The population didn't seem scared by the descent of the bird. They just cleared out of the way, dragging their blankets and sheets of cardboard.

Thandie led the Ark Three people aboard the chopper: Lily Brooke, Nathan Lammockson, and Grace's own husband, Hammond, Nathan's son, thirty-five years old, flabby and resentful. But Grace was staying behind with Gordo Alonzo to be taken away into Project Nimrod, into Ark One, whatever that meant. Hammond didn't even look back at her.

Gordo, though, spoke to her steadily. "You know, some parts of this drowning planet have gone back to the Stone Age. But this is the neighborhood of NORAD. One of the few places in the world where helicopters are still commonplace. That's why the people aren't spooked by them. And believe me we do a lot more exotic stuff than flying choppers. You'll see . . ." Maybe in his way he was trying to reassure her.

Gordon James Alonzo was a former astronaut. He was in his seventies now, and all his hair was gone, but he was just as upright and fit-looking and intimidating, his blue eyes still as bright, as ten years ago when he had shown up with Thandie Jones at a Walker City campsite, when Grace was just sixteen. Well, Gordo had been in a US army uniform then and now he was in the blue of the air force, but none of that was important to Grace. He was a relic of an age she had never known, as alien as the rich folk on Nathan's Ark-ship had always been to her.

Grace had spent most of her life on the road with Walker City, fifteen years walking with her home on her back, like a snail or a crab. The time before that, when she was younger than five years old and a pampered prisoner of her father's family in Saudi, was a blur, unreal, as were the years she had most recently spent as another kind of prisoner on Nathan's liner. Now here she was yet again passed from one stranger's hands to another.

Only the walking was real, she sometimes thought. Past, future, the vast cataclysm humanity was suffering—none of it mattered if all you could actually do in the world was put one foot in front of another, day after day, kilometer after kilometer. She could just walk away now. Walk off with nothing but the clothes on her back, just as it had been with Walker City. But she had her baby growing inside her, a baby she hadn't wanted by a "husband" she loathed, but hers nonetheless. She didn't want to manage the pregnancy on her own.

Gordo said, "They're lifting."

The wind from the rotors battered Grace's face. Lily Brooke leaned out of the chopper and stared down at Grace. She mouthed what looked like, "Forgive me." Then Thandie pulled her back into the machine, and the bird lifted smoothly.

"Are you OK?"

Grace was angry with herself for showing weakness, angry at Lily for her manipulation and abandonment. She snapped, "What do you think?"

Gordo shrugged. "They left you behind to give you a shot at getting into Ark One. A chance of a better life than any of them face now, especially if they're right that their boat has been sunk."

"I don't even know what Ark One is."

"You'll find out."

"I'll never see any of them again."

"I guess not."

"Once again I'm alone, with strangers."

He sighed, pushed back his peaked cap, and scratched his scalp. "So are we all. The whole world is screwed up, kid. At least here we got something to *do*." He looked around. The last dust from the chopper was settling now, and the homeless were pushing back to recolonize the space they had cleared, like water pooling in a dip. In a few minutes there would be no sign that a chopper had landed here at all. "Well, that's that. Come on, let's get you out of here." He released her arm and set off back through the town, toward the waiting cars.

She followed, having no choice.

2

They clambered aboard a jeep, and the convoy moved off with a soft whirr of electric engines. This small fleet of cars, emblazoned with Homeland Security and US military logos, had brought the Ark crew here from the coast. The convoy soon broke up, cars peeling off, leaving Gordo's jeep and one other heading steadily north out of town, skirting the flanks of Pikes Peak.

Gordo sat with Grace behind the young uniformed woman who drove the jeep. He pointed ahead; the road was a good track through the mountains. "The drive will take a few hours. This is mountain country, the Rockies. We're following the old state highway up to US 24 at Divide, where we'll head west. We'll turn north at Hartsel and make for Fairplay, and then you're only a few miles from Alma, which is south of the Hoosier Pass."

"Is that where we're going? Alma?"

"It's just a little town, an old mining place. Or was. I don't know if any of these names mean anything to you."

"We never walked this way."

"Right, with your okie army."

"Walker City. We had maps from the old days. But on Ark Three there were computer maps. Up to date." The ship's computers generated maps that showed the consequences of a flood that now approached eighteen hundred meters above the old sea level, maps of the archipelago that was the surviving remnant of the Rocky Mountain states. "The flooding started just about when I was born. I don't remember the country the way it used to be." You always had to explain that to older people, who clung in their heads to images of what had been.

Divide, when they reached it, was just another small town. Whatever it had once been before the flood it was now overwhelmed by eye-dees, IDPs, Internal Displaced Persons, as was everywhere else. The road was fenced off by rabbit wire. As the little convoy passed through people came out of their shacks and tents to watch. Grace saw how the troopers in the lead jeep cradled weapons.

The two jeeps drove steadily west, through Ute Pass that Gordo said was above nine thousand feet. Everything seemed to be feet, inches, miles with Gordo the astronaut. Gary Boyle, the scientist who had raised her, had taught Grace to measure her world in meters and kilometers.

The mountains had a bare, brown look. It hadn't snowed here for years. As they passed through a tiny community called Florrisant, Gordo talked about a park of fossil beds nearby, full of petrified redwood thirty-five million years old. Now, he said, it held more people than fossils.

Then, at Wilkerson Pass, views of a high-elevation meadow called South Park opened up, and the road seemed to sail off into the air.

"God," Gordo said suddenly, "*look* at that view. You know, it's just not reasonable that all this can be drowned beneath a mile of fucking seawater. I guess this is why I work so hard at Nimrod—trying to save something of it, the essence anyhow. Bobbing around on some crumbling raft just won't be the same."

Grace stared at him. The driver kept her eyes fixed firmly on the road, as if she hadn't heard this outburst.

Gordo relaxed, and laughed at himself. "Sorry. Am I coming over like a tourist guide?"

She frowned. "I'm not sure what a tourist is."

"OK. I'm told you used to be a princess."

"My mother, in captivity, was raped by a Saudi prince. Does that count? If so I still am a princess. You used to be an astronaut."

He nodded his bullet head. "I guess I still am, following your logic. Flew in space once, to ISS."

"To what?"

"The space station." He pointed up. "But after that my own career got fucked over by the flood. Well, grounded I may be, but I found something worthwhile to do here."

"It's got nothing to do with me. And I didn't ask for it."

"Maybe not. But we didn't ask for you either. Look, there's a selection process for newcomers to the project. Like Thandie said back in Cripple Creek, you're actually a better candidate than your husband would have been, in terms of Nimrod's criteria. You've shown independent survival skills. I saw that for myself. How old are you?"

"Twenty-six."

"Well, if you make it you'll be one of the oldest on the crew. Any religious affiliation?"

"Walker City had priests, rabbis, imams—"

"I didn't ask about Walker City. I asked about you."

"No. I'm not religious."

"Good. The social engineers are trying to make the crew an entirely secular society. Lessens the chance of factionalization and conflict, they think. Well, we'll see about that. And Thandie was right that the selectors currently like pregnant women, by the way. With a pregnant woman aboard you're getting two sets of genes in one package. You'll be an easier sell."

"Lily Brooke planned it that way," Grace said, the bitterness welling up again. She had figured all this out in the hours since Lily had delivered her into the hands of Gordo, had reevaluated everything that had happened to her over the last months and years on Ark Three. All of it had been the product of manipulation by Lily. "She set up my relationship with Hammond so Nathan would favor me. She even timed my pregnancy, I think, so I'd tick another box on your chart."

"And she did this because—"

"Lily was in captivity with my mother. In Barcelona, Spain. I was born there, in some cellar, with my mother manacled to a radiator. Lily feels obligated to me because of that."

"You're not entirely grateful."

"Lily just controls me. Who would want that?"

He waved a hand. "Well, none of that matters now. You'll never see Lily again. Here you are, here's the situation you face, however you got here. The only question is where you go from here."

"And if I choose not to go along with your project?"

Gordo said bleakly, "Then you'll have no place with us. You or your kid. We can't feed you."

3

They drove through one last town, Fairplay, where an open-air museum of old wooden structures from the mining camps had been colonized by refugees. Gordo said the museum had once been much more extensive, but wood to burn was precious.

Then they followed the signs for Hoosier Pass, driving along a well-maintained highway, and came at last into Alma. The place was overlooked by a broad peak called Mount Bross, on whose flanks sprawled a pine forest, much scarred by logging. The original town was little more than a handful of blocky buildings to either side of the road, clustered between rusting speed-limit signs. But newer, more extensive facilities had accreted around the old stock, blocks of glass and unpainted concrete.

The cars pulled off the road onto a dirt track, and stopped before one anonymous block. A slogan was neatly painted over a heavy steel door: "Genesis 11:6: NOW NOTHING WILL BE RESTRAINED FROM THEM, WHICH THEY HAVE IMAGINED TO DO." Oddly, a child's swing, metal and bright plastic, stood before the door.

Their driver got out and opened the door for Gordo, saluting him briskly.

Gordo had a cell phone clamped to his ear. "Hey, Holle? Glad I caught you. Would you mind coming out front? There's somebody I want you to meet." He put away the phone. "Doesn't look like much, does it? But we retrieved a lot of facilities from the NASA sites in Houston. Control, comms, training centers. There's even a small nuke reactor. We brought all this stuff all the way up to Alma, some little bitty miners' town. And you know why? Because Alma, ten thousand, three hundred and sixty-one feet above the old sea level, is the highest incorporated municipality in the United States."

The driver, a woman no older than Grace, said, "Actually, sir, that's not quite true. My mother was born around here, and she said it lost out to Winter Park—"

Gordo waved that away. "All Winter Park has above Alma's elevation are ski lifts, so the hell with that, Cooper."

"Sorry, sir."

"Grace, at times government works in simple ways. The decision-makers wanted this facility to survive as long as possible, no matter how bad the flood gets. So where do you build? You go to the record books for the highest town in America, and that's why a significant chunk of the single most expensive federal project since the decampment to Denver was unloaded on this little mountain town of two hundred souls. Look, I live over there—see the block in back of the Stone Church? Some of us pray in there, come Sundays."

"*What* facility? What is this place?"

The door opened. A young woman emerged, slim, not tall, pale, her red hair shaved short. She wore a lurid red and blue jumpsuit, with phones and other gadgets stuck in pockets. She was young, twenty-one, twenty-two. Blinking in the daylight she looked warily at Grace.

"Grace, this is Holle Groundwater, one of our most promising Candidates. Not that that's saying much. Holle, meet Grace Gray—and Gray junior," he said, clumsily pointing to Grace's belly. "Here for selection. Maybe you could show her the ropes."

"Sure." Holle smiled at Grace, and offered a hand to shake. But Grace could see the smile was forced.

"You aren't glad to see me," Grace said bluntly.

Holle raised thin eyebrows over sea blue eyes. "It's just we've got enough competition for places already, and there are only a few months left. The last thing we need is more applicants." Her accent was soft, lilting, British maybe, unfamiliar to Grace. Then she grinned. "Of course that's not your fault."

"Places? Places on what?"

But there was no reply. Evidently secrecy was habitual. Holle was well fed, earnest, bright. Grace remembered how she had been at Holle's age, still on the road, feet like leather and not a gram of fat on her body, everything she owned in a faded pack on her back.

Maybe Gordo sensed the tension between the women. He took off his cap and ran a hand over his grizzled scalp. "Listen, Grace. You're going to need some way to prove your capabilities. Let me give you an assignment. Just now we have a crime we need solving here."

"What kind of crime?"

"A murder," Gordo said simply.

The word shocked Grace. She looked blankly at the block, the biblical slogan, Holle's intent, competent-looking face. "I don't know anything about investigating crimes. We had cops in Walker City, and on the Ark Nathan's guards—"

"You can start by talking to Holle, here. Find out how it all started for her. I mean, you've been in the program since you were six years old—right, kid?"

Holle smiled. "According to my father, since I was conceived."

"It will be a way for you to figure out what we're up to here." Gordo grinned. "Yeah. Solve the crime, and earn your place. Two birds with one stone. I don't often have ideas, but when I do they're generally doozies. Now I got work to do, not least organizing the retrieval of Nathan Lammockson's seed cache from his sinking ship. But before I go—" Gordo fished in a jacket pocket, and produced a key ring with a bauble pendant. "I hand these out to the government suits, and anybody else I think needs some inspiration. What we're working toward." He put the little artifact in Grace's hand.

She raised the key ring. The pendant was a translucent sphere, bluish, maybe a centimeter across. Embedded within it were two silver splinters, connected by a bit of thread. "What is it?"

"Ask Holle. Catch you later, Groundwater." He strode off back toward the cars, and once more Grace was abandoned with a stranger.

"This way—Grace, is it?" Holle led Grace into the building.

Inside, the block was corridors and offices and computer rooms, suffused by a hum of air-conditioning. It reminded Grace of facilities aboard Lammockson's Ark Three, the bridge, the engine room.

The two of them didn't meet anybody else until the corridor opened out into a glass-fronted room with banks of chairs, microphones, screens. Through the glass Grace saw a larger chamber, dug some way into the ground so that she was looking down on rows of people before consoles, where screens glowed brightly, text and images flowing. Before them the front wall was covered by two huge screens. One showed a map of the world—continents outlined in blue, surviving high ground glowing bright green—with pathways traced over it. On the second screen concentric circles surrounded a glowing pinpoint, each circle labeled with a disc. Gary's amateur education program had always heavily favored science. Grace understood that she was looking at a map of the solar system.

Holle was watching her curiously. Grace felt utterly out of place in this technological cave, still in the clothes she had put on that morning on the Ark, with her pitiful collection of belongings lost forever.

"This is at the heart of what we do," Holle said.

"What is this place?"

"Mission Control. We're running a simulation right now—"

"And this?" Grace held up the key ring globe.

"Our spaceship." Holle smiled, a basic humanity shining through the competitiveness. "Come on. You look like you need a coffee. We'll talk about how Harry Smith got killed. And I'll tell you how we got started here."

Two

2025–2041

4

June 2025

t was raining in Denver, a steady, unrelenting downpour that fell from a gray lid of sky. It pinged off the wings of the plane that brought Patrick Groundwater and his daughter in over the city, and glistened on the runways and sculpted roofs of the terminal buildings as he carried six-year-old Holle through the international airport, discreetly tailed by Alice Sylvan and the rest of her security team, and hammered on the roofs of the cars that drove them through kilometers of suburban sprawl, crowded with IDP camps and welfare facilities, toward downtown. Under rusting junction signs the interstate was deserted save for police and government vehicles, and only a handful of private cars. To the west the mountain line was entirely invisible.

Patrick had visited Denver long ago, in his early teens, on his way to go skiing at Aspen. This was before the turn of the millennium, maybe fifteen years before the inception of the flood. He remembered the breathlessness, and today the air felt just as thin. Back then it hadn't rained at all, save for a couple of intense storms which had been kind of fun, nothing like this steady, relentless downpour. But since those days the sea had risen two hundred meters from where it used to be, the air was full of heat and moisture, and you couldn't expect to escape the rain even in the mile-high city. Well, Thandie Jones would tell Patrick and the other assembled mega-rich folk of LaRei all about that tomorrow.

All Thandie's words wouldn't deflect a single raindrop from his daughter's head. But in Denver he hoped to meet people who intended to do something about it.

At the hotel they were met by smiling porters in galoshes and wielding umbrellas.

Patrick was reassured by his first impression of the Brown Palace. Set on a peculiar triangular lot where two street layout systems collided, it reminded him oddly of an ocean liner wrought of red granite and sandstone. Inside, an atrium towered up eight stories. While Alice completed the check-in formalities, Holle ran around the polished floor, pointing at the golden onyx pillars and lifting up her little face to peer wide-eyed at the filigree rails and the stained-glass ceiling far above, from which hung an immense Stars and Stripes. In a world that was slowly breaking down, you could rely on a church-like Victorian-vintage pile like the Brown to stand solid and comfortable where newer confections of glass and reinforced concrete were crumbling. Besides, it was only a few hundred meters from Denver's civic center, where in the morning he was due to meet Nathan Lammockson and the rest of the LaRei people.

The suite Patrick was given had everything he needed to keep Holle happy, including a kid-friendly mini-bar, a net sack of books and toys, and screens with a variety of entertainments. There were tough notices about conserving water. Denver's weather had always come from rain on the Rockies, and although the climate was a lot wetter now, the disruption to the rainfall patterns and the increased population made the freshwater supply chancy.

One TV screen was tuned permanently to a news channel, put out by the Rocky Mountain News, a defunct old print outlet revived as a broadcaster. Over a rolling tickertape of more or less dismal headlines, the channel showed images of the latest disaster, in this case a kind of limited civil war that had broken out around Alice Springs, Australia, as the residents resisted attempts by the federal government to relocate refugees from flooded-out Victoria, New South Wales and South Australia.

Holle played before the TV, investigating the toys. She seemed immune to the bombardment of horrors on the news, just as the world's various disasters had seemed unreal to Patrick when he was a kid in the long-lost twentieth century. Best not to hide stuff from her, he had decided. Holle's life was liable to be shaped by bad news. He liked to think Linda would have backed up this intuition, but he was never going to know.

That evening he took Holle down to dinner in one of the hotel's fancy restaurants. The waiters made a fuss of her as they elegantly served her a kiddie version of paella. It was a special request from Patrick, a kind of comfort food, a dish her mother used to make for her. Afterward, back in the suite, he played card games with her, and let her watch a couple of episodes of *Friends* on TV, and read to her until she slept.

Then he opened up his laptop and checked his e-mails.

The big construction projects up on the Great Plains were proceeding well, although disgruntled refugees being settled there bitterly called them "Friedmanburgs." He referred that to his PR department for guidance.

Patrick was also involved in the furiously paced open-cast mining of the Athabasca Oil Sands in Alberta. Oil, coal, gas and oil shale were already being intensively mined in Colorado, all over the Western Slope. The Alberta grab was on a different scale. It was supposedly sanctioned by the relocated Canadian government in Edmonton, but that was a fig-leaf fiction. The US federal government in Denver intended to extract as many of the hundreds of billions of barrels of oil available from the bitumen as possible before the seas closed over it all, in not many years from now if the gloomier experts were right. The government's purpose was to secure its own position in the short term, and have a basis for national recovery in the longed-for day when the flood started to recede. The damage already done to the ecology and environment and so forth was ruinous. But rich men in the right place, like Patrick Groundwater, were getting even richer. Patrick had never imagined he would find himself in such a role. But somebody had to do it, and he tried to fulfill what he saw as his responsibilities conscientiously. Such was the way of the world.

A gentle snoring told him Holle was sleeping deeply. He checked on

her, covering her with her blanket a little more tightly, and made sure her
Angel was switched off.

Then he went back to work.

In the morning Holle woke him up at six a.m., as usual. To his huge relief
it wasn't raining, and the summer sun was trying to break through towering clouds. By eight they had finished their room-service breakfast.

Despite Alice Sylvan's protestations, he decided they were going to
walk and see the sights; they had a couple of hours to spare before he was
due to meet Nathan Lammockson at the city's public library. Holle had
spent most of her young life in gated communities. It would be enriching
for her to see something resembling a functioning city. So he packed a
bag with child-type essentials, tissues, a book, a couple of toys, Holle's
Angel, a water bottle. Holle wore a summer dress, and with sunblock on
her arms and face and a pink hat on her head they were ready to go.

They set off with Alice's team scattered around them, pushing through
the early morning crowds down Tremont Place toward the 16th Street
Mall. The buildings were marred by cracked glass panes and peeling paint,
the green spaces given over to crops like potatoes and beans, and the trees
had long ago been cut down for firewood. Few cars moved on the wide
avenues—you saw tanks or armored vehicles more than cars—but the
roads were full of pedestrians and cycles and rickshaws, pushing past long-
disconnected traffic lights.

The Mall itself was a straight-line strip of shops, once a pedestrian
precinct, with rusting tram lines and tree stumps. The shoppers' trolley-
buses no longer ran, but heavy vehicles from the Sheriff's office and the
police passed slowly along the road, occasionally barking instructions from
bullhorns. Patrick was struck by how many military and security operative
types he was seeing. He suspected that the Mall was being used as a control corridor, stretching through the Central Business District and maybe
up to Lower Downtown.

The walking turned out to be relatively easy, with only a fringe of homeless camped under heaps of blankets and cardboard in the doorways, some families with children. Cops and Homeland Security on foot were checking the permit papers and biometric ID markers of the unresisting IDPs, making sure no more illegals had slipped into the city during the night. Aid workers handed out cups of beans, rice and hot water.

Some of the shops were still functioning. The food stores and restaurants sold local produce almost exclusively. In the other windows you saw rebuilt and repaired electronics, clothes and accessories, shoes and coats, even books, everything recycled or reclaimed from drowned cities. Patrick found the existence of the shops comforting, a sign that he was in a functioning city, a contrast to the chaos prevailing over much of the surviving country. But if any of the original character of Denver had lasted into the twenty-first century, anything of its origins as a western trading post, nothing had survived the great erasure of the refugee flows. Without buying anything, they walked on.

They came to California Street, and cut down to the Colorado Convention Center on 14th. This had been turned into a refugee processing camp, and long lines wound through the streets around it. The IDPs, from a distance, were gray clumps of misery, as they always were. The time for the meeting was approaching and, following Alice's lead, they turned down 14th toward the civic center park. As they tried to cross Colfax Avenue, the main east-west artery through the city, they had to get through a cordon around the civic center, manned by police and military detachments.

Patrick led his daughter past the monumental buildings set around the park: the US Mint, the curving frontage of the City and County Building, and the public library where Thandie Jones was due to give her briefing. The Art Museum was particularly striking, and Holle stared at its angular geometric forms, like the abandoned origami experiments of a giant. But the thin metal panels were streaked and corroded, the windows boarded up, the billboards empty. The coming of the flood had frozen all Earth's great cities at around 2015, save for emergency construction to cope with refugee flows, where it hadn't drowned them altogether. That was a decade ago, and buildings like the Museum, neglected or co-opted for purposes for which they had never been designed, were showing their age.

Denver, as the largest city for a thousand kilometers around and a key junction for transport and communications, had been a significant federal center long before the flood. Since the capital had decamped here after Washington had flooded six years before, properties around the city had been requisitioned by the great departments of government. President Vasquez herself, the first three-term president since Roosevelt, had moved into the governor's mansion. Patrick happened to know that much of the government's business was run out of a more secure location, an old FEMA regional command center, a two-story bunker refurbished and revamped for the purpose. There were even embassies here, some from drowned nations, their flags hanging limp in the morning air. These struck Patrick as pitiful relics.

In this civic center, however, you had the sense of a great capital, the way Patrick remembered DC in the old days. People in suits bustled everywhere, many of them speaking into the air or with the characteristically absent expression of Angel users. Patrick imagined they were lobbyists and bureaucrats and staffers of all stripes, maybe even congressmen and senators. Patrick had a sense of the vast resources being poured into this place, that the city was the focus of huge energies and determination, a new refuge for the spirit of America and a base for the recovery to come. The President herself was in Denver. If you weren't safe here, then where?

A brace of helicopters swept low overhead with a great clatter of noise. Holle squealed and jumped, excited.

Holle was enchanted by the State Capitol, an eighteen-story structure with Greek columns and rotunda and golden dome, gleaming in the watery morning sunlight. She skipped up the Capitol's stone steps, counting them until she got to the eighteenth. Here the step was engraved, and she read with painstaking care: "'One mile above sea level.' Is that right, Dad?"

"That's so, sweets. One mile up, right here."

A gruff voice broke in. "Well, a mile less six hundred feet or so. They ought to make that plaque dynamic. Hey, George, we should get Axys-Corp to pitch for the business . . ." A burly man, short, aged maybe mid-fifties, was coming down the steps toward them. His gray-flecked hair was shaved short to the scalp, and his fleshy nose and double chin were bright with sweat. His accent was British, London or Essex maybe. He was trailed by a couple of other men, one tall, composed, black, the other shorter, agitated. "Patrick Groundwater, you old dog. Good to see you again." He stuck out a hand. "Nathan Lammockson."

5

olle stood in the middle of the circle of the four men, peering up.

Nathan introduced his companions. "George Camden, one of my senior guys in AxysCorp." Camden, black, was slim, confident, apparently competent; he returned Patrick's gaze. He wore a coverall in AxysCorp blue, with the corporation's famous logo, the Earth cradled in a cupped hand, emblazoned on his chest. Like Patrick's own Alice, he stayed silent and stood back, watchful.

"And Jerzy Glemp."

Glemp, tubby, his greasy black hair speckled with gray, and with heavy old-fashioned spectacles perched on a thin nose, was nervous, intense, his palm damp. He wore a stuffy-looking suit. "Mr. Groundwater. I am pleased to meet you." His accent was heavy, east European or Russian. When he smiled his jowls crumpled, stubbly. "I learned your name through Nathan. How you were one of those who expressed concern at the reaction of the 2018 IPCC in New York."

2018, when maverick oceanographer Thandie Jones had presented her conclusions on the state of the world to the Intergovernmental Panel on Climate Change, to be met by what struck Patrick as unjustified skepticism by the scientists, and then denial and evasion by their political masters in the months and years that followed. "Yes, I was there—that's where we first met, right, Nathan?"

Nathan grinned and clapped Patrick's shoulder. "After the session I made sure I got him locked into LaRei there and then. Hell, I could see right off that here was a man with resources and vision—the kind of man who sees through the bullshit and false hope and thinks about the long term, and deals with it. And I was right, wasn't I, Patrick? It was after that meeting that you started buying up all that land on the Plains, and what a smart move that was. And that's what I intend to come out of today— what we all intend. A fresh new direction."

"So you're based in Peru now?"

"Yeah. You'd think I'd be used to the sun." He wiped sweat from his fleshy brow. "I should have glopped up. Some days you almost miss the rain. But it rains like Manchester even up in the Andes."

Jerzy Glemp said, "Mr. Groundwater, you're originally Scottish, aren't you?"

"Is my accent still so strong?" But Glemp would know all about him from Nathan's files. "Born and bred in Orkney, from an old family there. We took Holle there once. Let her crawl around in the Ring of Brodgar, just so she could say she's been where her ancestors grew up. She was only six months old. But now the place is drowned, every last island. So we're rootless."

Glemp said, "As are so many of us. And your wife—"

"A local girl," Patrick said. "Lost her a year ago, to cancer." They looked uncomfortable. "It's OK. Holle knows all about it."

Holle stared up at Glemp. "Where's he from?"

Glemp laughed. "We've been ignoring you, haven't we? She has your color," he said to Patrick. "And your charming accent. I myself am from Poland."

"Where's that?"

Patrick began to try to explain, but Glemp cut him off. "It is nowhere now. Under the sea. A place for the fishes to play."

"You're funny."

"Well, thank you. Today, you know, we are going to try to make sure that when you are grown up, your children will have a place to play."

"Instead of the fishes?"

"Instead of the fishes. Quite so."

"You're funny."

Nathan said to Patrick, "He works for Eschatology, Inc. He's always like this. Got to love him. Well, let's hope he's right."

The public library was a collision of eras, a sandstone and glass block from the 1950s cemented to a redbrick block from the 90s: another aging structure that hadn't been refurbished for a decade or more. They had to get through another layer of security to enter, this one operated by LaRei and a lot tougher than the police and military cordons elsewhere.

An open area on the ground floor of the library had been set out for a conference, just rows of fold-out chairs set up before a podium. It was a homely setting, Patrick thought, as if they were here for a town meeting to discuss planning applications. But shadowy figures sat at the back of the block of chairs, like Alice and Camden, guards and minders. And maybe twenty of the fifty or so chairs were already occupied, by men and women many of whose faces Patrick immediately recognized from news media and conferencing and some face-to-face contact. There were people in this room who could have bought and sold Patrick and even Nathan Lammockson a dozen times over.

This was LaRei, a secretive and exclusive society, established in the years before the flooding as a source of contacts for good schools and exclusive vacation resorts and fabulously expensive merchandise like watches and jewelery, now become a kind of survivalist network of the superrich. LaRei, where a net worth of a billion bucks wouldn't even get you in the door; without Nathan's sponsorship Patrick wouldn't be here.

And at the front of the room, by the podium, stood a slim black woman of about forty, wearing a battered coverall that might once have been AxysCorp blue. She was setting up a crystal ball, a big three-dimensional projection system that showed an image of the turning Earth. Patrick recognized Thandie Jones.

Holle was distracted by the pretty Earth globe, whose blue light cast highlights from the library's polished wood panels and the rows of books on the shelves. But she quickly grew bored, as Patrick had expected. He let her wriggle to the floor and explore the contents of his shoulder bag, pulling out books. When she got her Angel started up, before she got the gadget settled, a few bars of music wafted through Patrick's own head. Right now Paul Simon's "Graceland" was her favorite. Nobody was making new music now, but that made no difference to Holle; she was developing her own tastes, and was working her way through Patrick's own collection, all of it as fresh to her as if it had been written yesterday.

Then she became aware of another child, a blond little girl of about her age, sitting on the other side of the room. They stared at each other as if the adults around them were as remote and irrelevant as clouds.

6

A portly man, white, maybe sixty, his head hairless, his face round and pale, stood up before Thandie. "You're ready to go, Dr. Jones?" He turned to face the audience. "You all know me, I think. I'm Edward Kenzie, chair of LaRei." His accent was a harsh Chicagoan. He spoke without amplification, but so small was the group, so quiet the empty library, Patrick had no trouble hearing him. "You may not know my little girl, Kelly." He pointed to the kid who was playing with Holle. "But in a sense she's the reason we are here today." His fingers were fat and soft, Patrick noticed, and the tips were stained yellow with nicotine, a strange, atavistic sight.

Kenzie went on, "Many of us heard Dr. Jones speak to the IPCC seven years ago. Well, as a fellow Chicagoan I've followed her career since then, and the reports and papers she's been filing, and I can tell you that every prediction she made then has come true, near as damn it, and every prediction many of *us* made about the inaction of our governments has dismayingly come true also. Now we've asked her to speak to us again, to give us an update on her IPCC talk, so to speak. And then I want to suggest a way forward for us, as we move on from this point. Dr. Jones." And he sat down with arms folded, his expression intent.

Thandie glanced around the room. She looked hardy, weather-beaten, a field scientist. "Thanks. I'm Thandie Jones. My specialisms are oceanography and climatology. Formally I'm attached to the NOAA, the National

Oceanic and Atmospheric Administration, which fortuitously has an office in Boulder, Colorado, so still above the rising sea. I was present at one of the initial high-profile flooding events, London 2016, and since then I've witnessed a few more of the dramatic events that have followed—many of them hydrological catastrophes without precedent in historical times . . ."

She spoke of a worldwide community of climatologists and other specialists observing the rapidly evolving events. There was still formal publication, of a sort, still seminars, still something resembling the scientific process going on. But mostly all they could do was log the Earth's huge convulsion as it happened, and try to guess what would come next.

"What I'm paid to do is produce predictive models of the ocean and the climate, to assist the Denver government in its planning for the future. What I'm notorious for, as I guess you know, is my speculation as to the cause of the global flooding event, and its eventual outcome."

She turned to her spinning crystal ball, the turning, three-dimensional Earth, a fool-the-eye illusion wrought by spinning screens, lenses and mirrors, and multiple projectors. Patrick remembered she had used a similar display back in 2018, and he wondered if this was the very same piece of equipment. Quite likely it was. "Here's the Earth as we knew it before the inception of the flooding, back in 2012." It was an image of a cloudless world, with the familiar shapes of the continents brown-gray against a blue ocean. "And here's where we live now." She pressed a control.

The seas glimmered and rose, and the land melted away. The water erased swathes of China, and washed across northern Europe deep into Russia, and in South America took a bite into Amazonia. Patrick's eye was drawn to Britain, from which much of southern England had been lost, and the rest of the country reduced to an archipelago of highlands.

In North America the relentless sea had deleted Florida, and had swept inland to cover the east coast states as far as Maine, and the Gulf states as far north as Kentucky. In the west the ocean had pushed deep into the valleys of California. Great cities had been lost, abandoned: New York,

Boston, New Orleans, even Washington DC. And with so much lost of the old United States east of the Ozarks there had been a massive population displacement. America was so terribly young, Patrick thought. It wasn't much more than two centuries since the continent had been first crossed by the European settlers, and not much less since the great western migrations in search of land and gold. Now another vast flight to the west was under way.

Thandie went on, "I don't need to detail for this group the economic dislocation that has unfolded, nor the tremendous human tragedy. A few months back I myself visited a huge refugee camp outside Amarillo, Texas. But I do want to point out how all this illustrates the accuracy of my modeling. When I spoke to the IPCC in 2018 the flooding had reached a mere thirteen meters above the old sea level datum, on average. At that time the scientific consensus was that the flooding couldn't exceed eighty meters or so, because that was the upper bound from ice-cap melting. Well, just as my models predicted then, we have now reached a rise of around two hundred meters. The incremental rise is currently around thirty meters a year, and is following an exponential curve upwards. It seems clear the worst is yet to come, despite the denials of the scientific community and the governments. Regarding the source of the rise we have continued to gather data, and again every new piece of data has confirmed my tentative 2018 modeling."

Thandie had established that the sea level rise was fueled not by melting ice but by ejections from subterranean seas, from lodes of water stored within the Earth. She produced images taken from undersea explorations of vast, turbulent, underwater fountains, places where hot, mineral-laden water was forcing its way out of the substrate, up from the depths of the rocky Earth itself.

Nobody knew why it should be just now that the deep reservoirs broke open. There had been dramatic and abrupt changes in Earth's climatic state in the past. Maybe this was just another of those dramatic but natural transitions. Or maybe it was humanity's fault.

"But in a real sense the cause doesn't matter," Thandie said, "and it's futile to assign blame. Whatever the cause, we have to deal with the consequences. And from this point on those consequences are unknown. Up to now we have had some precedents to guide us. In the Cretaceous era, for instance, when the dinosaurs were still kicking around, Earth was warmer and wetter, and sea levels were much higher. Now we're passing such precedents. We'll soon be in an era when seas will be higher than at any time since the formation of the continents over two billion years ago.

"I'm aware that the federal government and other agencies continue to plan on the basis of the flood receding, of the possibility of recovery. Various departments are working on plans for the orderly recolonization of formerly drowned regions, for instance. I have to say I see no reason why the flooding should stop any time soon. Indeed we're finding it hard to put an outer limit on the ultimate sea level rise. My best guess is that if the subsurface chambers we've discovered release all their water, we'll end up with oceans five times the volume they had in 2010. All Earth's land area will be lost long before that limit is reached, of course." She let silence linger after that blunt statement.

Edward Kenzie nodded. "So, Dr. Jones, what do you think we should do?"

She shrugged. "You've three choices, as I see it. You plan for a life on the sea. Or under it. Or away from the Earth entirely." Patrick found himself nodding at that last. "Oh," Thandie said, "and you've around fifteen years to choose which, and implement your plan."

"Why fifteen years?"

"Because in fifteen years Denver will be flooding." She glanced around at the old library, the dusty calm, the sunlit air. "The water will be here. I guess whatever you're going to do, you need to start now. Any more questions?"

After fifteen minutes of reasonably informed questions from the LaRei members, the presentation was over, and Thandie began to pack away her gear.

"One more question," Patrick said. "What are your own future plans, Dr. Jones?"

She smiled. "To continue to observe. Events are unfolding which nobody has ever seen before, nor ever will again. I can't have children. I have no stake in the future. But the present is rich enough for me."

7

Once more Edward Kenzie stood up. "There you have it, ladies and gentlemen, as authoritative a picture as you're going to get. Just like New York 2018 all over again, right? Now we get to the crux of the meeting. Since New York, thanks to the incompetence, denial and buck-passing of our governments, we've already wasted seven years. The resources the federal government has put into dealing with the worst case, a continued sea level rise, have been minimal compared to what's been spent on the fanciful plans for recovery and recolonization to which Dr. Jones alluded. Well, I for one am not going to sit around dreaming while the rising sea obliterates my wealth and property and turns my family into drowned rats. Some of us are going to try and do something."

There was a rumbling of support for that.

Kenzie held up his hands. "I, with the help of Nathan Lammockson and others, have brought here experts in a number of fields. Now's your chance to talk to them, to start the seeds of your thinking about what you intend to do. What we need to consider is meaningful options for the worst case. I hope that out of this session will come a number of projects—a number of ark designs, if you will—that can proceed more or less independently of each other. That seems the way to maximize our chances of success. This is the inception of a program, not any one single project.

"But we're going to have to proceed with extreme caution. Think about it. The Earth is drowning. Tell the world you're building an ark, and every hapless IDP and his brood will be fighting for a place aboard." He glared around at them, his face pinched and calculating. "I'm hoping we're going to support each other in years to come. But we must work discreetly. We must keep our secrets—*even from each other.* We should each know only what we need to know about what the other guy is doing, like terrorist cells. Maybe that doesn't sound very American. But we suffered enough from those terrorist assholes with their pinprick attacks ever since 2001. We may as well learn a few lessons from the way they operate, right?"

He'd clearly worked all this out. And yet Patrick could see the sense in what he was saying. He'd seen for himself how every attempt made by the federal government to alleviate the crisis was soon overwhelmed by the sheer scale of the unfolding disaster. While it was hardly democratic, secrecy might indeed be the only way forward, to deny the multitude to give a few a chance.

As the session broke up, Patrick had to tap Holle on the shoulder to get her to turn off her Angel. She glanced around, looking for Thandie's spinning Earth, and was disappointed it had been switched off.

Outside the library, Jerzy Glemp approached Patrick and drew him away from the knots of conversation that were forming. "I saw you nod," he said, his voice a conspiratorial whisper.

"You did?"

"When Dr. Jones was summarizing. When she said we should seek refuge off the Earth." He looked up at the sky.

"I guess it struck a chord."

"Is the logic not inevitable? This Earth is doomed; that much is obvious. In a hundred years it will be a world for fishes. Just as Poland is already gone. The only hope for mankind will be to find some new place to live, out among the planets and the stars."

"You're talking about some kind of spaceship?"

"Of course." He glanced around. "Look at the others. Nathan Lammock-son is talking of building mighty oceangoing ships, like Noah. Others dream of submarines and undersea colonies. You and I know, Mr. Ground-water, that space is the only salvation. And you and I, Mr. Groundwater, here and now, in this very conversation, are laying the first foundation stone in the project that will save mankind. I have the qualifications. I studied astronautics in Poznan, before the flooding came. I contributed to European space missions. I have a doctorate in the writings of Tsiolkovsky. With your resources, and my vision—yes, we will build a spaceship, a spacegoing ark."

Patrick felt railroaded. "I believe you're manipulating me, Dr. Glemp. You're so sure I share your dream?"

"I know you do." Glemp glanced down at Holle. "I asked Nathan about you. Your daughter was born in 2019; she must have been con-ceived shortly *after* you heard Dr. Thandie Jones outline the end of the world to the IPCC. She was conceived in hope."

Patrick felt his face redden. But the odd little man was right. After he and Linda had listened to Thandie, and seen the dispiriting response of her audience—and even after they had been forced to flee the hurricane that had so suddenly struck Manhattan afterward—they had gone back to their home in Newburgh, New Jersey, along with other refugees from New York City, and had shared a meal and a bottle of wine, and thrown out their contraceptives. Holle had indeed been conceived in hope, in defiance of the blackness of the future as it had seemed then. She had even been named for the role he and Linda had imagined she might have to play.

"So come," Jerzy Glemp said. "We have much to do. It is time for lunch. You may buy me a drink, and we must start to plan how we will save mankind, and spend your money in the process." He led the way out into the street.

Patrick picked up a sleepy Holle and followed, wondering what the hell he was getting himself into.

8

The next morning a courier arrived at the Brown Palace bearing a handwritten note addressed to Patrick Groundwater: "Personal—Your Eyes Only—Do Not Disclose Contents."

The courier was just a kid, a boy aged about fourteen, in an anonymous AxysCorp—brand coverall. In a world full of hungry refugees, you didn't have to be too rich to afford a runner. But even so, in a world that was almost paper-free, it was an unusual way to receive a message. Patrick had Alice Sylvan tip the kid and sent him away. Then, as Holle was eating her room-service breakfast in the suite's main living room, Patrick, following the spirit of the note, took it to the bathroom, huddled in a corner he thought had to be free of prying surveillance cameras, and opened it.

The note was from Edward Kenzie. Handwritten like its envelope, it invited him to come to the Auraria campus at ten a.m. that morning, "to attend the launch of a new project." Feeling mildly foolish, Patrick ripped the note into shreds and flushed them down the lavatory.

Then he went back to the living room, gulped another coffee, and helped Holle get ready for her day.

It was a morning of sun and scattered cloud. The warmth and light lifted everybody's mood, and Holle skipped as they made their way across town, cutting southwest down Larimer Street to the bridge over Cherry Creek to the campus. Alice Sylvan, nightstick in her left hand and her right resting on her gun holster, smiled as Holle peered into the concreted-in creek. From here, Patrick could see the shoulders of the Rockies to the west, and the quartz splinters of Denver's small downtown to the east.

They reached the campus. Patrick had attended Yale and Oxford. Auraria, shared by three colleges, must once have been like a redbrick movie-set mock-up of a traditional campus, he thought, with broad leafy avenues set amid acres of car parks. Some of the academic buildings still functioned; in a federal capital there was still a need for college-level educated. But many of the buildings had been abandoned to housing and the athletics fields plowed up for crops.

The note directed Patrick and his party to the campus library and media center. This was a box of glass and white-painted steel shutters. Outside, they were met by a sober-suited man whose jacket barely concealed the bulge of his own weaponry. He waved a wand to check them over—even Holle, even the day bag with her toys and orange juice bottles—then led them into the aircon-cooled building. The interior space was wide and open, the floors connected by skeletal staircases. They were led down a short corridor to a small conference room.

Gathered around a table with inset touchscreens were Edward Kenzie, Jerzy Glemp, and a slim young man, perhaps Chinese, who Patrick didn't recognize. Alice joined a couple of security men on seats by the wall. The air was full of the aroma of coffee from a percolator on a table in one corner, and Patrick thought he detected a stale whiff of cigarette smoke.

In one corner a couple of kids, both about Holle's age, were playing with plastic toys. Patrick recognized Kelly, the bright blond daughter of Edward Kenzie, from the session yesterday. The other was a boy, a pretty kid with thick black hair. A young man sat on the floor with the kids, smiling, watching them play. Patrick released Holle's hand and let her walk tentatively over.

Kenzie came up to Patrick and handed him a mug of coffee.

"Edward," Patrick said. "So you decided to hook up with Jerzy too?"

Kenzie snapped, "I've got other irons in the fire, frankly. But after what Thandie Jones had to say, isn't the right course obvious? We got to get off this submerging planet. Besides it was Glemp's contacts through Eschatology, Inc. that set up the session in the first place."

"I hope you don't mind me bringing my daughter."

"She is welcome," Jerzy Glemp put in. "There is my own little boy, Zane. Say hello, Zane!" The boy, who with his thick dark hair and Slavic looks only faintly resembled Glemp, gave Patrick a shy nod. Jerzy said, "Of course our children should be with us—even now they may be old enough to understand something of what is said here. And after all, the project is *for* them and *of* them. In the year 2040, we will need crew."

Crew. The word thrilled Patrick.

Jerzy Glemp rubbed his hands. He looked excited, delighted, as if he'd been waiting his whole life for this moment, and perhaps he had, Patrick thought. "So shall we begin?"

9

The doors were locked, the walls swept. "We're sealed in tight as a mouse's ass," Kenzie said. He tapped a screen to begin recording. "As you can see we got a bunch of blank screens here. We've got secure access to the university servers through these things, and we can look wider if we want. We got reference sources, everything we need to find answers to the questions we'll raise. All right, let's start. And you can begin by introducing this gentleman you've brought in, Jerzy."

Glemp beckoned, and the slim young man stepped forward. "My name is Liu Zheng. I am Chinese. I am twenty-nine years old; I am an engineer."

"I found him in IDP processing in the Pepsi Center, right here in Denver," Jerzy Glemp said with a gleam of satisfaction. "It's astounding the talent you can filter out of the flood of displaced. Anything you want."

Edward nodded. "And what talent have you got that's so valuable, Liu?"

The Chinese, his face blank, said, "My father trained as a taikonaut. To fly in space. I design spaceships."

There was a long pause. Patrick asked, "What exactly are we talking about building here?"

Liu Zheng said, "A means to send a viable population away from the Earth."

Jerzy said, "An ark."

"No less than Ark One, damn it," Kenzie said. "I made sure we secured *that* little honor from Nathan Lammockson and those other assholes." He clapped Patrick on the shoulder. "Did you never see *When Worlds Collide*? Let's get on with it. What's the first question we need to address, Jerzy?"

Glemp smiled. "Where are we going?"

The man sitting on the floor with his legs crossed wore black trousers and a black jumper. He might have been younger than Dad, but Holle wasn't sure. He smiled at her. "My name is Harry. Harry Smith. I'm a teacher. But it's not a school day today! I'm just here to make sure we're all OK together. Your name is Holle, right? Look, this is Kelly, and Zane."

The two children eyed her warily. Kelly was the little girl she had met yesterday in that other place full of books, the big dusty room where the lady had the crystal ball. The boy, Zane, looked a bit younger than Holle was, and he had thick black hair and big eyes. He looked shy, but she kind of liked him. He looked like a doll.

"Look, we've got neat toys," Harry said. "You can play with us. See the fort? These guys are knights. Look, they have horses."

Kelly and Zane were playing with a kind of fort that you put together, and plastic people that you lined up inside. The fort had circular towers and walls that you set up on a base, and a drawbridge that you could let down, and little buildings inside. But the fort looked crooked, there were gaps between the wall panels, and Holle could see that the drawbridge was stuck. Maybe it hadn't been put together right. She didn't go near the toy, not yet. Kelly hung onto the little people she'd been playing with, and Zane copied her. They weren't sure about Holle, not sure enough to share.

Harry said smoothly, "Have you got your own toys? What did you bring in your bag?"

"I've got my handheld and my Angel." She dug them out of the bag, shoving aside the box of tissues and the drinks bottles.

"Oh, wow, that's neat."

Holle looked at him. "You say 'neat.'"

"That's how I was brought up to talk, I guess. I'm American. You're English, aren't you?"

"Scottish. Neat. Neat, neat, neat!"

The other children laughed.

Impulsively she held out the Angel to Harry. "Do you want to listen? It's got good songs on."

"Why, thank you, Holle, that's very kind." He held the heavy black gadget in his hand, and thumbed through the menu of choices. "Oh, you've got 'Phone.' Always liked that one." He pressed to select, and nodded as the music played inside his head, murmuring the words: "'I love you more than my phone / You're my Angel, you're my TV . . .'"

Zane and Kelly were watching Holle, not doing anything, just holding onto their toy people.

"I've got a handheld." Holle showed them.

"I've got one of those," Kelly said.

"It's got a camera."

"So has mine."

"We could film the toy, the fort. We could make the people attack, like a war, and film it."

That enthused them, and Kelly immediately took control. "Look, Zane, I could be in charge of the army inside and you're the army outside."

He looked doubtful. "Why can't I be inside?"

She snorted. "Because if you're outside you're an eye-dee, and I don't want to be one of *them*."

Harry smiled, still listening to the song. "An IDP is an internal displaced person, Kelly. An American who's become a refugee. That word you used isn't nice. It's OK, Zane. Look, this polished floor can be the sea, the flood. And you can make a raft out of the box the fort came in. See?"

Zane started experimenting with the box, skimming it back and forth over the polished wooden floor with his people inside. Kelly marched her little men and women up and down in front of the fort, calling out orders, readying them to repel the hordes of flood-driven refugees.

Now she was let into the circle, Holle put down her handheld and got hold of the fort itself. The pieces were plastic that fit onto molds on the base. She saw she'd been right, that two towers by the gate had been jammed onto the wrong sockets. If she swapped them over the gate should work better. But it was going to take an effort to dislodge the towers from the sockets.

She looked at Harry to see if she could ask him to help. But Harry was working with Zane. As the boy crouched down and pushed his cardboard-box-lid raft around the floor, Harry leaned right over him, so his belly touched Zane's back, and he ruffled the boy's thick hair. That looked funny, and she didn't like to watch.

Holle glanced up at the other grown-ups, who were all sitting around the table and drinking coffee, talking in deep rumbles. Dad had his back to her, but he wasn't far away.

Glemp's question hung heavy in the air over the table.

Liu Zheng spoke first. "If I may—" He tapped a blank screen to image up a keypad, and started listing headings. "I would suggest we have two broad categories of destination. Category One, the solar system. Category Two, beyond."

Patrick already felt out of his depth. "Beyond? What's beyond the solar system? *The stars*? You're talking about going to the stars?"

Jerzy grinned. "Only if we have to."

"Category One," Liu said, methodically typing out labels. "We can list various subcategories of destination. Earth orbit—we could imagine a permanent settlement something like the International Space Station. Or such a settlement in space beyond Earth orbit. Or we can imagine a planet or moon as destination—a colony there—Earth's moon or Mars seem the most obvious choices, or the ice moon of a giant planet. Europa, perhaps. Or we could imagine exploiting an asteroid or a comet."

Jerzy Glemp nodded, his eyes apparently unfocused. "You list old dreams. O'Neill cylinders. Domes on the moon and Mars. Comet ice blown into great bubbles, where people swim in the air."

Liu Zheng said smoothly, "We are poor at building closed life-support systems—that is, systems which do not suffer losses as they operate. We have to assume that in this scenario supplies from the ground won't be forthcoming—"

"Because there won't be any fucking ground," Kenzie said. He glanced at the kids again.

Patrick nodded. He tapped his own screen, and inserted red crosses beside some of Liu's categories. "So no space stations, no free-flying colonies. We need somewhere we can mine resources."

"The moon is closest," Kenzie said. "And we've been there, we know we can operate there."

Glemp shook his head. "There have been studies of how you could mine the moon for metals, various minerals, even oxygen. But the moon is a ferociously hostile environment—fourteen days of unfiltered sun followed by fourteen days of dark, no shielding from solar flares and cosmic rays. Crucially, the moon has only a trace of water. Apollo proved that. Water is the key resource for human life. Find water and you have solved most of your problems."

Liu said, "The asteroids and comets are a possibility. Some of them are rocky, some composed of water ice and other volatiles. Some of them are even rich in organic compounds. Similarly the ice moons of Jupiter and Saturn are balls of frozen water. One would not so much land on an asteroid as dock with it. The gravity is very low . . ."

Kenzie pulled his face. "Let's cut the Buck Rogers shit. All we ever did in space, in the end, was send a few guys to the moon for a few days at a time. Right? That and send them up to space stations in Earth orbit that were resupplied from the ground. So let's go for the obvious options, missions we know we can achieve. What's wrong with Mars? Mars has got water, hasn't it? All those scrubby little probes NASA sent there found signs of water."

"Of course," Liu Zheng said. "There are probably aquifers, certainly permafrost. We could land near the polar caps, where water is exposed at the surface. Mars has other resources, such as carbon compounds—the air is mostly carbon dioxide."

"Mars is no paradise," Glemp said. "The air is too thin to allow you to venture outside without a pressure suit. It doesn't even offer a significant shield against solar ultraviolet—the upper layers of soil are thought to be effectively sterilized because of that."

Kenzie growled, "OK. But compared to swimming with the asteroids, Mars is a picture I can understand."

Patrick raised a finger. "But we, our crew, would be living under domes? Would the domes include farms? What if the domes wore out, or collapsed? How many would you need for safety? I mean, I imagine you're talking decades here—centuries—living under those domes forever . . ."

Glemp nodded. "A domed colony on Mars would have to contain everything needed to sustain a technological human civilization, which means farms, water systems, air recycling, factories, resource extraction and processing plants. It would have access to local resources outside itself, but would otherwise be much like a habitat adrift in space. A closed, finite system, ever at risk of complex and catastrophic failure. You could imagine running such a thing for a few years, but how long?"

They talked on, each of them coming up with examples of long-term technological continuity, such as the Dutch managing land reclaimed from the sea for centuries. But Glemp's point was well made, Patrick thought. It was hard to imagine maintaining a machine as complex as a space station or a domed ecosphere over more than a few lifetimes.

Glemp said, "What we humans need is *room*. A world like Earth, big enough that it is effectively infinite in terms of resources. If Mars were Earth-like—"

"But Mars isn't Earth-like," Kenzie said. "Even *Earth* won't be Earth-like in a few more years. So what are you saying, Jerzy? That we ought to *make* Mars Earth-like?"

"The word," Jerzy Glemp said, smiling, "is terraforming. To make a world like the Earth."

And they talked about that. Once again there were studies by NASA and various earlier thinkers on how Mars could be made into a smaller sibling of Earth, with air thick enough to breathe, and an ocean pooling in the great basin of Hellas, and pine trees braving the flanks of Mons Olympus. It quickly emerged that to build such a new world you would have to import most of the "volatiles," in Jerzy's term, that Mars was lacking right now. There were schemes to do that, such as by deflecting comets and crashing them into Mars's surface . . .

This time it was Patrick who put a stop to the discussion. "You're describing a program of engineering that would span the solar system, and would take centuries."

"Millennia, probably," Glemp murmured.

Kenzie thumped his fist onto the table. "It would be easier to terraform *Earth*."

"And that," Jerzy Glemp said enigmatically, "has been considered. Ask the Russians."

Kenzie shook his head. "Let's not go into *that*."

Patrick had heard something about mysterious behavior by the Russians in space. In the summer of the previous year, 2024, the year Moscow was abandoned, there had been a brief flurry of ICBM launches from the Russian heartlands. US intelligence analysts had triggered an alert. But the missiles had flown into space, never touching down. Some analysts thought the Russians had simply dumped their weapons stock before the flood reached it. Others had developed elaborate and exotic conspiracy theories. If anybody in the American administration knew the truth—if anybody in this room knew—they weren't sharing it with Patrick.

Kenzie leaned back and locked his fleshy fingers behind his head. "We're stuck, aren't we? We agree we need a new Earth. But there are no new Earths in the solar system. We've exhausted our options."

Liu Zheng said patiently, "We have exhausted Category One. Category Two remains."

Jerzy Glemp grinned. "The stars."

Kenzie pushed his chair back. "Christ, before we get to that I need a cigarette. I know, I know. But I quit quitting after I lost my first thousand acres of seafront property to the flood. Hey, Joe, can you rustle up more coffee?"

As they broke, Kenzie went out to smoke and the others milled around the refreshed coffeepot.

Patrick approached Liu Zheng, who stood alone, politely waiting for the coffee. "You're a long way from home," Patrick said tentatively.

"As are many of us," Liu said, but he smiled.

"How did you come to be in the US?"

"When the floods came, my family was driven from our home in Shanghai. I was twenty. We lived in a refugee colony in Zhejiang province. I was able to pursue a career. Then came the draft."

"The draft?"

"For the coming war with the Russians and Indians, over the high ground of central Asia. I did not wish to fight in such a futile and wasteful conflict. My family paid for me to come to America. I was fortunate that, thanks to the aptitude tests administered in the processing center, I came to the attention of Dr. Glemp."

"You're more than a commodity, man. More than a set of skills."

"Am I? None of us is anything without land, Mr. Groundwater. Room to stand, a place to lie. If you have that, and I do not, you can do what you like with me. So it is here, just as at home."

"Well, maybe." But Patrick felt a new determination burn in him that that fate was not going to befall Holle. "So you have a wife at home, kids?"

"A wife," he said. "When I fled I had to leave her. Her family would not release her to come with me. I am not sure if she wanted to anyway. Fleeing is shameful."

"Is it? More shameful than sitting there until you're drowned out?"

"China is different, Mr. Groundwater. We have a cultural continuity going back to what is known in Britain as the Bronze Age. We, our ancestors, have survived many calamities before, fire, flood, plague, invasion. Always the essence of China has endured. Many cannot believe that it will not be so this time, that the flood is a terminus."

"But you think it is."

"I am an engineer, not a climatologist. But I understand enough of the science to believe that, yes, this is the end of China, and of the world. So here I am."

Kenzie came bustling back into the room.

As they walked back to the table Patrick asked Liu, "Do you still hope to bring your wife here someday?"

"It is a dream. But to find her in the great chaos of the flood, even if she survives, and to bring her here—it may be easier to fly to the stars, Mr. Groundwater."

10

Liu opened the discussion of his "Category Two." He brought up graphs and tables and artists' renderings of exotic worlds.

Liu said, "Like many other programs, the work of 'planet-finding' was pretty much curtailed by the flood. That is, using advanced telescopic and photographic techniques, including telescopes in space, to detect and study the planets of other stars. Nevertheless several hundred such 'exoplanets' were found before the flood came, and more have been found since. And of these, several dozen are like Earth. They have masses similar to Earth's, and appear to have water oceans—"

"Some of them have life," Jerzy Glemp said, grinning. "We know that from atmospheric signatures—oxygen, methane. Spectroscopic records of photosynthetic chemicals."

Patrick was stunned. "We found life on other planets? I didn't know that."

Kenzie said dryly, "These days the news agenda tends to be dominated by domestic issues."

"Think of the irony," Jerzy said. "We finally discovered life beyond Earth just as we are becoming extinct on Earth itself."

Liu said, "These worlds are 'Earthlike' only in as much as they are more like Earth than Mars is, say. Nevertheless—"

"Nevertheless," Kenzie said, "if one of them was floating around the solar system we'd fire our kids over there like a shot. Correct? So how far away are these things?"

Jerzy Glemp shrugged. "Well, there's the rub. The nearest star system is Alpha Centauri—four light-years away. That's a distance hard to grasp. It's around forty *trillion* kilometers. A hundred *million* times further away than the moon is from Earth."

Kenzie waved that away. "And the nearest Earth-like world? How far to that?"

Liu said, "The nearest reasonable candidate is sixteen light-years away."

"Oh, that all? OK, so how do we get there? I'd guess from our previous discussion about the domes on Mars that you guys wouldn't think we could run a space mission, unsupported, of more than a few years. A decade, tops. So that's the timescale. Have I got that right? So how do we get to the stars in a decade? I take it chemical rockets, the shuttle and the Saturn, are out. If it took three days for Apollo to fly to the moon—"

Patrick grinned. "Only three million years to Earth II!"

Glemp said, "An alternative is to use electricity to throw ions, charged atoms, out the back as your exhaust. A much higher exhaust velocity gives you a better performance . . ."

But Liu quickly dug out a whiskery study that suggested that even an ion rocket would need the equivalent of a hundred million supertankers of fuel to reach Alpha Centauri in a century or less.

"Nuclear engines, then," Glemp went on. "Back in the 60s NASA developed a ground-based test bed of a fission engine—hydrogen heated up by being passed through a hot nuclear fission pile and squirted out the back . . ." NERVA had worked. But again, as they paged through theoretical studies from the archives, they quickly found that the fuel demands for an interstellar mission on the timescales they required were impossibly large. They did find some useful material, such as a NASA study on lightweight nuclear engines meant to power a generation of unmanned explorers of Jupiter's moons, probes that never got built; Glemp and Liu flagged such material for further study.

Glemp said, "Look—you don't actually need any fuel *at all* to reach the stars. You can use a solar sail . . ." A sail kilometers across, made of some wispy, resilient substance that would gather in the gentle, unrelenting pressure of sunlight, of solar photons bouncing off a mirrored surface. "Such a craft would take mere centuries to reach the stars."

"Too long!" Kenzie snapped. "We're drifting here, guys." He pushed back his chair and walked around the room. He paused briefly by the kids, who, with Harry patiently filming them, were acting out a siege of their plastic fort. Kenzie said, "Captain Kirk never had this trouble. Where's a warp drive when you need one?"

They laughed, all save Liu, and Patrick wondered if that was because he'd never heard of *Star Trek*. But the Chinese said, "That of course would be the solution. A faster-than-light drive."

"No such thing exists," said Kenzie.

Jerzy Glemp said firmly, "No such thing *can* exist. According to Einstein the speed of light is an absolute upper limit on velocity within the spacetime of our universe."

"True," Liu said. "But spacetime itself is not a fixed frame. That is the essence of general relativity. In the early moments of the universe, all of spacetime went through a vast expansion. During the interval known as inflation, that expansion was actually faster than light."

Patrick was lost, but Jerzy Glemp was intent. "What are you suggesting? That we ride a bubble of inflating spacetime?"

"I don't know," Liu Zheng said. "I have a faint memory, of a study long ago . . . May I check it out?" Kenzie waved his permission, and Liu began to scroll through screens of references and citations.

Kenzie said, "You know, maybe we need to step aside from the core problem for a minute. We are after all talking about starting up a space program here in Colorado. However we travel to the stars we're going to need launch facilities to get to orbit in the first place: gantries, blast pits, liquid oxygen factories, communications, a Mission Control, the whole

Cape Canaveral thing. Jerzy, we need to find ourselves some space engineers. And some real-life astronauts, to train our guys. Got to be some of them around."

"Canaveral itself is long drowned," Patrick said. "Went under with Florida. There was an alternate launch facility in the west."

"Vandenberg," Kenzie said. "Run by the air force. Must be flooded too, but maybe more recently. If we have to salvage equipment from one or other of these places, Vandenberg might be the better choice."

"But that's a huge commitment," Patrick said. "A whole new space program! At such a time of crisis, how can you expect to get the government to back you?"

Kenzie smiled. "There's always national defense. Look—one effect of the flood has been to knock out our national war-making capabilities. Oh, we've been moving nuke-tipped ICBMs out of flooded silos in Kansas. But the basic infrastructure has been hit too. NORAD in Cheyenne Mountain is still operating, not far from here. But all Cheyenne did was gather data and feed warnings to Raven Rock on the Pennsylvania-Maryland border, the Pentagon's deep-bunker control hub, which has now been lost. Meanwhile our satellites are degrading one by one. Even our deep-defense radar systems are failing, now that the bases in Britain and Canada are flooded out. And you have warlike noises coming out of China and Russia and India. What if those guys decide they need a bit of *lebensraum* over here in the US of A? What are we going to do about it? I think the federal government could be sold the need for a space launch facility, here on the high ground, to give us the means to launch recon sats and to retaliate in case of any strike against us."

"Isn't that kind of cynical?"

Kenzie just grinned. "The space program has always run off the back of the military programs. The first astronauts rode honest-to-God ICBMs to orbit. And anyhow, isn't it for a good cause? Joe—make a note. Start working on fixing me an appointment with the President as soon as we have a reasonable shopping list—"

Liu spoke softly. "I have it."

He read, "'The warp drive: hyper-fast travel within general relativity.' A 1994 paper. I am no specialist in relativity but I recognize the soundness of the idea. It is only a theoretical concept, but there are a number of citations . . .'"

Jerzy quickly brought up a copy of the paper and skimmed it. "My God, Liu. Riding a wave of spacetime at superluminal speeds. This is it."

"The engineering details are entirely absent. And the energy requirements are daunting—"

"But we have the concept." Jerzy grinned at Kenzie. "We must start work immediately."

Kenzie looked from one to the other, openmouthed. "If this isn't bullshit—all right. Tell me the first thing you need."

Jerzy considered. "Mathematicians. Physicists. Computer scientists. Anybody who had contact with predecessor studies, like the old NASA Breakthrough Propulsion program of the 1990s. And, by the way, if we are serious about planning for a long-duration spaceflight we will need life-support experts, biologists, doctors, sociologists, anthropologists."

Liu said, "Also an artificial intelligence suite, equipped with symbolic manipulator tools."

"A what-now?"

"We will build a warp bubble. This will be a designer metric." He mimed a bubble with his hand. "A piece of spacetime, molded to our purposes. To design such a thing we will need a computer system that can solve Einstein's relativity equations."

"Make a list."

Patrick, feeling lost again, shook his head. "Are we serious? Are we really going to try to build a warp drive?"

Jerzy shrugged. "Compared to terraforming a planet, or trying to run a spaceflight lasting centuries to thousands of years, it is a relatively easy option."

"Fine. So we have something to work on. Meeting adjourned!" Kenzie slammed his palm down on the desk, and toasted them in cold coffee. "Here's to Ark One, born today. Hey, Joe, make a note of the date and time."

As the meeting broke up, Patrick went over to collect Holle. The kids were watching a playback of their movie on Holle's handheld. The teacher, Harry, was cuddling Zane; he moved away, smiling, as Patrick approached.

Holle ran to her father and hugged his knees. "Dad! Did you see what we did?"

"The fort and everything? Some of it. We were busy over there. But you can show me later."

She looked up at him, her face round and serious. "And did you have a good morning, Dad?"

Which was a question Linda had always asked. He ruffled her hair and said, "Yes, I think so. I hope so. We got stuck for a bit. You know what I always say, sweets. If the answer's not the one you want, maybe you're asking the wrong question. I think maybe we asked the right question in the end."

"That's good. Is it lunchtime now?"

"Yes, it's lunchtime. Let's get out of here."

11

Holle was late on her first morning at the Academy, at the very start of the new term.

She'd meant to cut through the City Park, on her way to the Academy which had been set up in the old Museum of Nature and Science on the park's east side. But the park had been turned into a mixture of farm and refugee camp, and overnight there had been trouble as mid-process eye-dees had protested over being forced to work on biofuel crops. Her father always said it was simply dumb to make mothers with hungry babies work on anything other than food crops. So this morning the whole park was closed off, and Holle, eleven years old and alone, had to skirt south along 17th Avenue, hurrying past cordons of Denver PD cops and Homeland Security, with their advisers from the Office of Emergency Management and homeless–IDP welfare agencies.

It wasn't a pleasant walk. It had been snowing, not so much as it used to in January according to long-term residents, but enough to leave a covering on the fields and slush in the gutters that she tried to walk around. And the air was foul. She kept her mouth clamped shut against the smoke and tear gas. There was an irony. Her father told her the air was cleaner than it had been when he was Holle's age, despite a global injection of volcanic products. Not this morning. Some days, everything sort of piled up to make life harder.

Denver wasn't as much fun as it had seemed when they had first come here six years ago. It was growing shabbier every day, and was increasingly cluttered up with eye-dees and everything that came with them—including diseases like tuberculosis, now that the capability to manufacture antibiotics was breaking down. The city itself was being transformed, in anticipation of a tougher future. Flood walls and storm drains were extended. Wherever possible hard paved surfaces were being ripped up to expose earth where crops could be grown and, more importantly, flood water allowed to soak away. Meanwhile the last year had been a record for tornadoes hitting the city, another outcome of the flood-induced global warming. The big sirens in downtown had wailed over and over, scarily, and buildings had been left battered and glassless, barely habitable. Even if you went driving out of the city, as her father sometimes took her out on the scrubland beyond Denver's urban sprawl, you couldn't escape it. You saw nothing but eye-dees walking in from the drowned eastern states and just setting down where they could. When no shelter was provided for them they built huts of bricks cut from sod, as the pioneers had once done a hundred and fifty years earlier, and started planting potatoes and raising pigs.

Sometimes she missed the gated community in New York State where she'd lived when she was small, with its clean apartments and swimming pools, and the tall whitewashed wall that excluded the rest of the world. And no floods or tornadoes or eye-dees in sight.

She was relieved to reach Colorado Boulevard and cut down to the museum. Though stained with age now, the museum was a big block of brick and glass set on a slight rise overlooking the sweep of the park to the west, toward downtown, and beyond that the Rockies. From here the park looked like a medieval village, packed with smallholdings and shabby huts, and threads of smoke rising up from dung fires. But the museum on its rise was fortified.

She had to show her Candidate's pass and submit to three biometric ID inspections before she was allowed into the main entrance. By the time she got through everybody else had already gone in—everybody save Zane Glemp, who was waiting for her by the door.

———

"I'm sorry," she said, breathless.

"It's not me you'll have to apologize to. Come *on*." He led her inside the building, through an echoing ticket hall and toward the stairs behind the closed-up museum shop. This was a bright tall open space, and overhead the dusty skeletons of marine dinosaurs from Colorado's vanished Cretaceous sea still swam in the air.

She felt a rush of affection for Zane. He was a skinny kid, and at ten he was a year younger than she was. But he had his father's brains, and had been allowed into the Academy a whole two terms ahead of her. This first morning he had promised to meet her and show her around, and he was keeping that promise even at the risk of making himself late as well. "Thanks for waiting for me."

"I was here already." That was true; he had his own room in the Academy, that he used when his father was away.

"It wasn't my fault I was late. There was a riot in the park, and I—"

"Save it. They don't accept excuses here."

"Well said, Mr. Glemp." By the elevator shaft, Harry Smith was hauling a small trolley laden with books. He stepped toward them and folded his arms. "Late on your first day, Groundwater? *Not* a good start." He was being teacher-strict, nothing more, and that was sort of reassuring to Holle as she tried to get her bearings. But he was standing very close to them. Something about him always made her uneasy.

"I won't let it happen again."

He nodded. "Good answer."

"I've got my assignment." She dug her handheld out of her bag, and tried to show him her study of the ecological disaster unfolding up in the Rockies, of how the tree line had already ascended so far that the old regions of montane forest and shrubland, with their ponderosa pines and cactuses, were withering, whole ecozones disappearing.

But Harry waved that away. "You've both made yourselves late for Dr. Zheng's class, haven't you? Pop quiz."

Zane fretted, and shuffled from one foot to another. "Can't we just go to class? A quiz will make us even later."

"Then you'll just have to make up that much more work, won't you? OK. Overnight the Ark executive announced they've finally made their decision on where to locate the space launch center—at Gunnison, Colorado. Why there?"

Holle glanced at Zane. "I didn't know about Gunnison. I listened to the news. But it wasn't in the bulletin I saw—"

Harry said, "Of course not. You know as well as I do about the secrecy around the project. You can't keep a space center under wraps, and there will be an official announcement later today. But both your fathers are at the center of the project. *You* both are. You should know everything they know." He dug into the pile of books on the trolley, found an atlas, and threw it at Holle; it was a big, heavy, pre-flood volume, and she had trouble catching hold of it. "Why Gunnison? Work it out. I'll give you five minutes. Otherwise, another question." And he walked away, towing his trolley.

The two of them kneeled on the floor and spread out the atlas, looking for the right map. "What an asshole," Holle murmured.

"He's our pastoral tutor," Zane said. "Looking after our overall personal development, while the specialist teachers—hey, look, here it is. Colorado."

They peered at the map, a splash of yellow and green laced across with roads marked in orange and blue. Denver showed up as a knot of development where major highways intersected. The map was pre-flood, but the shoreline of the great inland sea that had washed across the eastern United States, now reaching as far as a line from the Dakotas down to the Gulf, was still too far east to have shown up on this map.

Zane looked at her doubtfully. "So why would you build a space center in Colorado at all?"

"The government would need to keep it close to Denver to make sure it was safe." Her father talked this sort of thing through with her. As the flood bit away at the remaining land area, more roads and rail routes were cut, more people joined the homeless throngs that washed back and forth across the high ground, and the government's political control was weakening. The news bulletins were full of growing tension over a would-be separatist Mormon state in Utah; there was even talk of war. "Somewhere in Colorado. But where?"

"High up enough that it won't flood before 2040."

"But that still leaves a lot of choice." She thought about where Cape Canaveral had been situated—on the Atlantic shore, the eastern coastline of America. Why there? For safety reasons, she remembered. You always launched rockets eastward, to get a boost from Earth's own rotation. Launching from Canaveral had meant that any failure would result in a rocket, flying east, falling harmlessly into the sea. Now the same principle surely applied. "Look," she said, stabbing a finger at the map. "Gunnison. Twenty-three hundred meters above the old sea level. In 2040 it will be close to the eastern coast of the surviving land. A safe place to launch east." What else? She dug her handheld out of her bag and quickly interrogated it. "The town's on a valley bottom, so plenty of flatland. There's an airport nearby, so you have transport links, and this reservoir, the Blue Mesa, can provide water. And it's a college town, so there's a population of workers already in place—"

Harry Smith approached them. "Actually that took you only four minutes. Yes, that's why Gunnison, Colorado, is going to host the world's latest, and maybe last, space launch facility. Twenty years ago you'd never have believed it. Good bit of deduction, Ms. Groundwater. OK, you're free to go."

They got to their feet, handed back the atlas, and ran for the stairs.

"And, Ms. Groundwater—*don't be late again.* Next time you might find somebody else sitting in your seat . . ."

12

When they got to the classroom, in the back of a large, emptied-out chamber labeled "Edge of the Wild" on the museum's second floor, Liu Zheng was in full flow. He stood before an interactive whiteboard, rapidly assembling and erasing graphics, and allowing annotated equations to scroll by. "The essence of an Alcubierre warp bubble is simple," he said. "Conceptually at any rate. You have an isolated region of spacetime." This was marked as a circle on his two-dimensional diagrams, but he mimed a sphere with closed hands. "Your spaceship is in this zone here . . ."

As he talked, a dozen kids all about Holle's age sat at tables before him, and worked at handhelds and laptops, muttering and murmuring in pairs and threes. Zane led Holle to an empty table. As she passed, the students glanced at her indifferently and looked away.

Holle recognized a few of the kids in here, including Kelly Kenzie, a friend or maybe rival since they were little. Kelly was locked in intense conversation with a red-haired boy who looked a bit older. There were Cora Robles and Susan Frasier working in a huddle, two bright, pretty girls together. And Thomas Windrup and Elle Strekalov, sitting so close they might have been conjoined twins, as they had been all the way through grade school. Elle was a lot better-looking than Thomas, and the class gossips didn't know why they stayed together. There was a lot of noise in here, and among the noisiest were Joe Antoniadi and Mike Wetherbee. Joe, an Italian-American whose family had fled New York, was likable, friendly, easy to impress. Even as Zheng talked, Mike was cracking jokes in his broad Australian accent and making Joe laugh. Mike's family were refugees from an almost entirely abandoned continent.

They reached their table. Zane had a laptop, and Holle dug her hand-held out of her bag.

If the students had been indifferent to Holle, Liu Zheng didn't so much as register her presence. He just carried on with what he was saying. "So how do you fly to the stars? Well, you engineer the space-time metric. You arrange it for spacetime to expand behind you, mimicking the inflationary conditions of the early universe. And you make spacetime collapse ahead of you, mimicking a black hole, say. Thus your spacetime bubble is pulled and pushed, driven ahead across the manifold. You are riding a propagating wave in spacetime."

"Like surfing!"

"Yes, Mr. Meisel. Though I myself have never surfed."

Holle thought she understood. The spacecraft would be embedded in spacetime like a toy insect in a block of glass. You didn't transport the ship itself, but a whole chunk of the spacetime around it.

"This is the essence of the warp bubble. The transported spacetime must be large enough to keep you away from the regions of heavy curvature associated with the warp bubble itself—which would manifest, of course, like strong gravity fields. But what of travel faster than light? Einstein tells us that it is impossible to move faster than light-speed *as measured against local landmarks.*" He emphasized the words heavily. "The trick is to carry those landmarks with you. The ship itself is not traveling at all relative to the spacetime bubble around it. It is the bubble itself that propagates at multiples of light speed, as desired. *You* are not traveling faster than light, because you are carrying the light with you . . ."

Zane was already working, paging through notes on his laptop. Holle arranged for the board's contents to be downloaded to her handheld, and she made notes alongside Liu's diagrams and equations. All around her the students chatted, argued, joked, and scrolled through what looked like entirely disparate bits of work. This was not like the mostly calm, mostly studious atmosphere she had got used to at the grade schools in Denver.

"The warp bubble as a method of transportation has some paradoxical properties. Because the ship is stationary relative to local landmarks, there are none of the effects we associate with special relativity: no time dilation, no Lorentz-Fitzgerald contraction. Clocks aboard the ship stay synchronized with those at the starting point, and indeed at the destination. And there will be no inertial effects."

"What does that mean?" Holle whispered.

"You wouldn't feel any acceleration," Zane said. "The ship's not moving compared to the spacetime it's embedded in. So you don't get squished against the back wall of your cockpit when you turn on the warp drive."

"However, there are issues of control, for you run the risk of outrunning any signal sent forward to control your own bubble. Therefore, we think it likely that any piloted mission will have the parameters of bubble formation, propagation, dissipation and so on loaded by a remote station before launch; the crew of the starship inside the bubble will essentially be passengers."

Joe and Mike burst into gales of laughter over some private joke.

Holle leaned over to Zane. "Is it always like this?"

"Like what?"

"Noisy. Everybody messing around."

He shrugged. "There are no rules. They just put the material in front of you and expect you to make what you can of it."

"And if you can't cope with that," said the boy next to Kelly, twisting back, "you can go back to the kiddie schools and play with the plastic bricks. There's always somebody ready to take your place." He grinned. "Don Meisel. Who the hell are you?"

Holle found herself blushing as she told him her name. A year older than Holle, Kelly was growing into a tall, confident blonde, no great beauty but a leader. And this boy Don, who Holle hadn't met before, looked that bit older again. His eyes blue, his hair red, a stronger color than Holle's own pale strawberry, he looked relaxed in his own skin, lively, fearless.

"Your first day?" Don asked.

"Yes," said Holle. "It's great."

"Sure it is. That a Scotch accent?"

"Scottish, I—"

"You up to scratch on relativity?"

Her dad had gone through it with her. "Sure."

"Special relativity is trivial," Kelly said. "Nothing more than Pythagoras's theorem. So how are you on your Christoffel symbols?"

"On my what?"

Kelly and Don just laughed, and turned away.

Zane said, "They're teasing. They're talking about tensor calculus. The mathematics of general relativity. Which is what you need to describe how spacetime curves around a warp bubble . . ." He showed her some of Liu's equations. She recognized derivatives, but some of the symbols were strewn with superscripts and subscripts. "*That* is a tensor," Zane said. "A kind of multidimensional generalization of a vector, which is a quantity with both magnitude and direction—"

"I'm eleven years old," she said. "My dad has been cramming me since I was six, when he got attached to Ark One. But how am I supposed to know about tense—"

"Tensors?" He shrugged. "Liu's actually a good teacher, even if he never looks you in the eye. And if you don't learn—"

"I'll be out. I know."

"I'll help you."

"Thanks," she said sincerely. "So what's with those two? Kelly and Don. Are they going out?"

Zane just blinked. He didn't reply. That wasn't the sort of thing Zane ever took any notice of.

Holle said, "Kelly was always the boss at grade school. Maybe they'll drive each other on."

"Or they'll crash and burn together."

The lesson didn't get any easier.

"After five years of intensive study, we do now have a handle on how a warp bubble might be created," Liu Zheng was saying. He filled up his board with new kinds of diagrams, showing sheets and cylinders. "The expansion or contraction of spacetime locally reflects a change in Einstein's cosmological constant omega, which, as you know, describes vacuum energy, which is like an antigravity field that permeates spacetime—the engine of universal expansion.

"Now, we believe that our universe has a small extension in higher dimensions—higher, that is, than the three of space and one of time we experience. But those extra dimensions are small. Our universe is like a hosepipe, rolled up around the extra dimensions. The cosmological constant is inversely proportional to the fourth power of the characteristic radius of that hosepipe. *Inversely*. So the smaller that hosepipe radius, the higher the constant and the greater the expansive effect. Therefore, if you can change that radius locally, you can adjust the cosmological constant, and thus control the expansion of spacetime as you desire. To make a spacetime bubble you pinch the hosepipe.

"But *how* to pinch that hosepipe? On face value that would seem to require reaching *out* of the local three-dimensional plane of the universe itself . . ."

Now he spun off again, into "string theory," which described space as filled not with point particles like electrons and quarks and neutrinos, but with strings, tiny filaments whose characteristic vibrations determined the properties of the "particles" they defined, such as charge and mass. Holle had heard of these ideas. It was as if the whole universe was a symphony played on tiny violins.

But, Liu said, the strings could interact with those rolled-up extra dimensions of spacetime. In particular the strings could wrap around the extra dimensions, like spiderweb wisps around the hosepipe. That was how the dimensions stayed compact in the first place. And *that* meant—

"You can squeeze the hosepipe," Holle burst out, her imagination racing away.

Liu turned to her. "And how would you do that, Ms. Groundwater?"

"With a particle acce—" She stumbled over the word.

"Accelerator?"

"Yes. With an accelerator you're manipulating matter at its smallest levels. You can yank on the tiny strings."

Everybody was staring at her. Don and Kelly looked around, Don with amusement, Kelly with something more like resentment.

"I'm sorry," she said. "I was thinking out loud."

"Don't be sorry," Liu said. "You got it about right; that is what we're planning. We're setting up a hadron collider outside the city, based on scavenged components from accelerators in the US and overseas. Though we're still years away from even a ground test the energies required are ferocious . . ." He gestured at the board. "And can you see how that basic concept is expressed in my equations?"

"No," she said frankly.

Kelly laughed. "That figures."

But Liu was unperturbed. "That's not important. Intuition is the thing. But though we have a conceptual design for the creation of the warp bubble, we have a fundamental problem. The energy requirement is literally astronomical. A warp bubble is an artifact of curved space-time analogous in some ways to a black hole. Now, suppose we built a bubble a hundred meters in radius. That should be big enough to house a respectably sized spacecraft, shouldn't it? Give me an order of magnitude estimate of the mass-energy required."

The students huddled over their computers. Kelly muttered, "The radius of a black hole is twice the mass times the gravitational constant divided by speed of light squared . . ."

"Ten to power twenty-nine kilograms," Venus Jenning called out. She was a black girl whose family had come from Utah, fleeing the gathering Mormon uprising. As far as Holle could tell she'd figured that number out in her head. Even while she worked, she was reading a yellowing paperback book under her desk, a gaudy science fiction title.

"Give me that in English," Liu snapped back. "What does that number mean?"

Kelly said, "One-tenth the mass of the sun. You'd have to convert one-tenth of all the sun's mass to energy to be able to build a warp bubble of that size."

"Not exactly practical," Liu said. "And *that* remains our fundamental problem, after years of studying this concept. We just don't have the energy resources to build a warp bubble of the size we need." He drew a big red cross through the equations and diagrams on the board.

Again Holle found herself thinking out loud. "If the answer's not the one you want, maybe you're asking the wrong question."

Liu turned to her again.

"I'm sorry," she said. "It's something my dad always says."

"Then what *is* the right question?"

Zane said quietly, "Maybe, how big a warp bubble *can* we create?"

Liu thought that over. "OK. Let's run with that. What's the most energetic event humans can control?"

"Nuclear bombs," Thomas Windrup called. "Thermonuclear actually."

"Right," Liu said. "And the biggest blast of all was?"

That sent them scrambling to their computers, and whispering into search engines.

It was Susan Frasier who came up with the answer. "30th October 1961. A Russian test. Fifty-seven megatons, detonated at Novaya Zemlya." She smiled, always friendly, always eager to please.

"All right. And if that mass-energy was applied to creating a black hole?"

It took them a minute to find out how to convert energy measured in an equivalent tonnage of TNT into joules. This time Kelly made sure she was the first to come up with the final answer. "Its radius would be ten to minus twenty-seven meters."

Liu said, "Give me that—"

"In English," Don said. "Well, it's eight orders of magnitude above the Planck length, the smallest possible. But it's only one-thousandth of the radius of a one-mega-electron-volt neutrino! You couldn't even fit a *neutrino* in there, let alone a spaceship!"

There was a ripple of laughter, and Zane blushed.

But Liu just stood in silence, his eyes working as if chasing an elusive thought. "Class dismissed." Abruptly he walked out.

Grumbling, the students started packing away their stuff. Don said to Holle, "Now see what you've done. Liu's like that when he gets an idea. You better hope it's a good one or he'll rip your head off for wasting his time. Come on. I'll show you where to buy a soda."

13

olle was relieved to get home that night, to the apartment her father had rented in the same block as the Tattered Cover Book Store, a secondhand store that was still one of Denver's most thriving businesses as nobody was printing new books any more. She dumped her bag in the hall, fetched a glass of water and made her way to the big living room, where the wall-mounted TV was showing updates on the Rocky Mountain News channel.

Patrick didn't hear her come in. He was sitting on the floor, his back against the sofa, one arm over a cushion and the other hand cradling a glass of corn liquor. He had his shirt open at the neck, his shoes off, his black-socked feet crossed.

The news was uniformly awful, Holle saw as she glanced at the big multiscreen. In Denver the police were shaping up for another night of trouble from the itinerant agricultural workers in the City Park. Elsewhere diplomatic notes were being exchanged with Utah; Mormon leaders in Salt Lake City were now refusing to pay federal taxes. President Vasquez was going to make a statement about that. Seawater forcing its way up the Tennessee valley from Alabama was causing yet another evacuation crisis, producing yet more images of sodden, huddled people tramping along rain-spattered highways. The government was considering sending troops into the Friedmanburgs, the troubled new cities on the Great Plains, where residents were protesting against exploitation by the rich who had bought up the land and funded much of the development in the first place. Holle knew her dad had something to do with that. Surviving recon satellites reported what appeared to be nuclear detonations going off in Tibet, the flashpoint of friction between India, China and Russia.

Meanwhile there were more tsunamis and earthquakes and volcanoes as the Earth shuddered under the weight of the water that laid ever more heavily over the continents. These were reported against a summary map that showed that some forty percent of the world's pre-flood land area had been lost, some four billion people displaced.

Holle hated the news. All these shells of horror and misery and conflict, spreading out around the bubble of safety Holle had grown up in—which, she was coming to realize, was a very special place. And though sometimes there would be scientists talking about how the flood might be ending soon, the water receding, they never seemed to have much to go on, and her father never responded to the faint hopes they raised.

"Dad, can't we switch over to *Friends*?"

Patrick jumped. He hadn't known Holle was there. "Oh, hi, sweets." He snapped the TV over to a multiscreen conference call; Holle recognized Edward Kenzie, a suntanned Nathan Lammockson, and others. Their deep voices rumbled. He lifted his arm, making room for her. She got down on the carpet next to him and huddled in. He was hot, tired, sweating. His smell was immensely reassuring. "Sorry," he said, "I guess I was playing hooky. I'm supposed to be in this conference. *Friends* later, maybe. Well, it's on all day and all night."

Holle had grown up with the old pre-flood TV shows. They were comforting, set in a world as unreal to her as any fairy tale. "What's the conference about?"

"An astronomical survey going on at an observatory in Chile. Place called La Silla, very high up. It's South America, you know? Used to be owned by the Europeans, but now Nathan Lammockson, who's based in Peru, is supporting it for us. Not that he knows what we're doing up there specifically."

"Looking for planets, I bet."

"Well, that's the idea. Somewhere for the Ark to go. And once the new space center is up and running, there's a plan to run a starshade mission."

"A what?"

"I'm not sure I understand it, but it's interesting. You send up a giant sheet, spinning for stability. It looks like a flower, with petals. Then you have a conventional telescope—we're using the Hubble—thousands of kilometers away. The shade is supposed to block out the light of the star, allowing the telescope to see any planets. With that arrangement we should be able to image continents on an Earthlike planet, even out to thirty or forty light-years. It's a scheme that was championed years ago by an astronomer at the University of Colorado at Boulder, which is how we were able to dig it up."

"And this is your idea of taking a break, watching the news? It's always bad."

"I know."

"Everybody's frightened, I think sometimes." It was true: people were frightened of the flood, which was still remote from this place, and frightened of the waves of eye-dees for the dirt and disease and hunger they brought and the space they used up, and people were frightened of each other, for in the future there mightn't be room for everybody. Holle herself would have felt a lot safer if Alice Sylvan, who she'd grown up thinking of as a kind of honorary aunt, hadn't got herself taken out by a sniper in downtown.

"I know, I know." Patrick tousled her hair. "But there's no good in turning away. So how was the Academy?"

"Dad, it was awful. The kids are all bright and noisy and they compete like mad. There was only Zane who was friendly."

"Zane will be glad you're there."

"I'm not like Zane," she blurted. "And I'm not like Kelly Kenzie. I'm not tall and pretty and confident. Don't tell me those things aren't important, because they *are*. I know what they call the students. The Candidates.

You have to be special to be a Candidate, a star. I felt like Joey out of *Friends*."

He laughed, and sipped his drink. "OK. But, look—it's my money that's backed the Academy, as part of a consortium, among a lot of other initiatives related to Ark One. But the Academy is *not* a finishing school for little rich kids. If you weren't thought capable of justifying your place there, on your own abilities, you wouldn't be in there, no matter whose daughter you were. You deserve to be there, sweets." He kissed her head. "But if it's ever too tough for you, just come home."

"Oh, I won't give up."

The TV pinged, and filled up with a head-and-shoulders image of Liu Zheng.

Patrick said, "Liu? How can I help you?"

Liu grinned. It was a more human expression than any he'd adopted in class. "Actually it was Holle I hoped to speak to. Ms. Groundwater, you have a knack, I suspect, of asking the right questions."

"What right questions? You mean that discussion about the biggest warp bubble we could make? But the answer was teeny-tiny. Everybody laughed."

Liu said seriously, "Listen to me now. We are dealing with the engineering of spacetime, engineering in multiple dimensions. Everything we believe we know, all our intuition, is likely to be wrong. Inspired by that discussion, I returned to something I unturned in the literature during my earlier researches. A thirty-year-old piece of speculation by a worker in Belgium. Do you have your handheld? Try to follow the argument . . ."

And, as if Patrick weren't present, he slipped easily into his odd, absent-minded lecturing style and the big wall screen began to fill up with graphics and equations. Holle let the tensors flutter past her like falling leaves, and tried to follow the essence of what he was saying.

Liu said, "A warp bubble is a separate universe connected to our own, like a blister growing from a flaw in the wall of a toy balloon. The bubble wall, umm, *surrounds* this pocket universe. But 'surround' is a three-dimensional word, inadequate to describe the higher-dimensional reality. The bubble is actually the neck of the flaw connecting mother space-time to daughter. So it can be much smaller than the daughter universe itself."

"Smaller than the ship!"

"That's it. The warp bubble can be as small as you like." His grin widened. "Too small, on the face of it, even to fit in a single neutrino. There are other advantages. We have been concerned about the collision cross-section of our warp ship. Even dust grains, hitting the forward end of the warp bubble, would suffer enormous compression forces. There could be damage to the ship, and perhaps a loss of energy from the warp field. That danger is much reduced with this new geometry."

"My God," Patrick said. "I understand maybe five percent of what you've said. But I do know that the mass-energy issue has been the key stumbling block that's been holding up the design—"

"We are years behind any notional schedule," Liu said heavily. "This may be the conceptual breakthrough we have needed."

Patrick hugged his daughter. "All down to my little girl."

"Oh, *Dad*—"

"Of course that is not so," Liu said with unexpected sternness. "Can she handle the relativistic mathematics necessary to fully describe this new solution? Of course not. What she has contributed is an insightful question, which provoked an answer which may lead to an ultimate solution. Zane Glemp contributed more, actually. This is teamwork. At the Ark Academy we are not looking for the outstanding individual, Holle Groundwater. We are seeking to construct a team, a crew. Today you have shown you may have the potential to join that team. *May* have. It was a good first day. Now I suggest you sleep well, and make sure you are on time tomorrow." His image winked out, to be replaced by the muted talking heads of Lammockson, Kenzie and the others.

"Phew." Patrick let Holle go, and climbed stiffly to his feet. "I need another drink, and something to eat, in that order. Quite a day. A spaceship the size of a neutrino!"

"No, Dad," she said, following him. "A sub-neutrino-sized corridor to a pocket universe containing a spaceship."

"Whatever. Who's peeling the potatoes?"

14

May 2032

The day the government took over the project started like any other day in the Academy. Holle would never have guessed it was the last day of her old life, the end of the old regime, and the start of something new.

Magnus Howe liked to take his ethics classes on the old museum's Level Two, in the big hall devoted to North American Indian culture, with its dioramas and artifacts set behind glass walls in curving corridors. He said they were grounded here by the hall's association with the deep past of the landscape. Holle thought he was reminding them of other human cultures wiped out by earlier disasters, in the Amerinds' case a flood of greed and ignorance.

A dozen students of Holle's age cadre, twelve to fourteen, sat on the polished floor in a loose circle around Howe, who sat on the only chair in the room. They were mostly wearing their fancy new Candidates' costumes, robust one-piece Lycra uniforms in royal blue with crimson sleeves and rib panels. As usual, people were multitasking, breaking off in little huddles to discuss some assignment or other, or working through material on laptops and handhelds. Venus Jenning was walking around the book stacks, browsing; the room doubled as the Academy's library. Some students had the abstracted look that came from the murmuring of Angels in their heads. Thomas Windrup and Elle Strekalov were sharing the feed from an Angel. Thirteen years old, their hands intertwined, they rocked gently together.

The class was discussing why the Candidates and their families, those of a Christian background, had not been allowed to celebrate Easter.

"It was tough on my father," Holle said. "We could have done with a break." There was now an ambitious schedule in place which would see a fuel lode of antimatter, the key to the interstellar drive, being manufactured on the ground, and a long sequence of Ares boosters rising up from Gunnison to launch Ark modules to the space station, which was to be refurbished and used as a construction shack. All this to be done in just eight more years. But as milestone after milestone was missed the pressure was relentless on the senior people, including her father.

Magnus Howe said, "Easter is a vacation, yes. But what about the theology?"

Wilson Argent blew a raspberry. "It's got nothing to do with theology. It's politics. President Vasquez went to war with the Mormons. And then you have those New Covenant nutjobs who say that God is drowning the sinners. We're going secular in reaction." Dark, sharp, heavyset, Wilson was a recent recruit from the refugee camps, selected for his ferocious ability and tough personality. It seemed to Holle he was challenging Don and Kelly for the informal leadership of the cadre.

"You're forcing people into a choice," Kelly Kenzie said. "We lost some good people, whose parents chose the other way, chose God over your selection process."

"Well, it wasn't *my* process," Howe said. "The social engineers' theory was—"

"It's not the theory that matters," Venus Jenning said. She was flicking through a yellowing paperback. She was a slim, tall girl, calm and quiet, and, perhaps prompted by the chance of her name, fascinated by astronomy. And she liked science fiction, images of vanished futures. "Hey, look at this," she said now. Her book was called *The Door Into Summer*, by Robert Heinlein. "Denver gets to be the national capital in here too. After the Six Weeks War in 1970!"

Howe said evenly, "You were making a point about theory and practice, Ms. Jenning?"

"Oh, sure. Sorry. Look, because of the religious ban we lost Jews, Hindus, Muslims. Barry Eastman. Yuri Petrov. Miranda Nikolski! She was the best mathematician we had. She's a year younger than me, and she was teaching *me* interstellar navigation! You can't afford to lose people like that. Even Zane was almost pulled out."

The group focused on Zane Glemp. After three years in the Academy, twelve-year-old Zane was still among the shiest of the group, and he looked to the floor.

Magnus Howe prompted, "Zane?"

"Well, it's true. My father's ancestors were Jews. We don't practice ourselves. But my father didn't like the idea that we had to reject our tradition altogether. And I don't think he liked the social engineers meddling in *his* project."

Don Meisel snorted. "Jerzy Glemp was in at the start. But no matter what ideas he's been putting in, it's not *his* project. It's fueled by my father's money, and yours and yours and yours," he said, jabbing a finger around the room at children of the superrich: Kelly, Susan Frasier, Venus Jenning, Cora Robles, Joe Antoniadi, Holle. Cora, a rich kid who had grown up with attacks on her parents' wealth, just laughed prettily.

Magnus Howe prompted, "Zane? So why are you still here?"

Zane shrugged. "We wanted the Ark more, I guess. What use is faith if your family is extinct? Also Mr. Smith visited a few times. He urged my dad to keep me in the project."

There was an odd silence at that. Harry Smith, their pastoral tutor, loomed large in all their lives, big, bluff, complicated. He was close to his charges. He spent a lot of out-of-hours time with the Candidates. He had even taken to dressing like the students, in a version of their gaudy Lycra uniforms. And he had a heavy, hard-eyed, challenging way of looking at you sometimes. He looked that way especially at Zane Glemp. So it wasn't much of a surprise that Harry Smith had been there urging Zane's father to keep him in the project. Holle bet the others were thinking about this now. Nobody said anything, however. Nobody ever did. The Academy was a ferociously competitive place, and the Academy authorities were always looking for an excuse to dump you. Nobody went looking for trouble. If Harry Smith was a problem for Zane, it was up to Zane to sort it out.

If Magnus Howe was aware of any of this running around in his students' heads, he didn't show it. "Let's get to the point. Why do you think we're trying to exclude religion from this project?"

"To avoid conflict," Wilson said. "A starship is too small for jihads or crusades or pogroms. Maybe you could have a ship's crew that was entirely Christian, or Jewish, or Muslim—"

"Or Mormon," Don Meisel said.

Venus nodded. Her own family, though from Utah, had not been Mormons. "Or Mormon, yes. But a selection from any one faith would be limiting, and surely divisive politically."

"What about polytheism?" Susan Frasier asked. "Like the Hindu faith, for instance, or the old pagan religions. When you have many gods, not just one, you have flexibility, room for tolerance."

Miriam Brownlee said, "It worked for the Romans, their pantheon was roomy enough just to absorb all their provinces' gods—"

Mike Wetherbee said, "That came unstuck with Jehovah!"

Miriam laughed at his joke. A slim Texan, she had gravitated to Mike through a common interest in human biology and medicine.

"But even a single-faith group would be liable to splinter," said Elle Strekalov. "Think of Sunni versus Shia, Catholic versus Protestant—"

The conversation took off. The Candidates, growing interested, abandoned their other projects and started accessing social-dynamics software suites to study how different religious and social configurations might prosper in the enclosed environment of a starship—purely Christian or Muslim or Buddhist crews, or crews guided by an attic full of squabbling gods.

Magnus Howe let the explorations run for a while. Dark-haired, intense, he was quite young, under thirty. Rumor had it he'd once studied to become a Jesuit. He was actually a pretty good teacher, given the dry nature of his subject matter, and young enough to share his students' sheer pleasure in learning, in acquiring new knowledge.

Holle didn't join in. The engineering of the ship rather than its crew was her sphere of interest. But she felt a kind of warm gravity as she sat here with this group of smart, eager kids. It was heartbreaking to think that many of them were likely to be discarded long before the Ark ever got off the ground.

Magnus clapped his hands to bring them back together. He glanced down at his own laptop, on which he'd been monitoring their improvizations. "I can tell some good work's emerging here. Come back tomorrow with a presentation on your results." He didn't specify the assignment further; it would, as always, be up to the students to define their goals properly, to organize the work, to figure out how it would be reported and who by. "For now, let's concentrate again on the decision that's actually been made—to exclude anybody with strong religious convictions from the crew."

"What about atheists?" Wilson called.

"Including atheists."

Don Meisel said, "It'll be hard to police. You know how desperate people are to get their kids on the Ark. If it means covering up your faith for a few years, people will do it."

"You'd be found out," Zane Glemp said. He pointed to cameras mounted in the corners of the ceiling, silently watching as always.

Holle frowned. "And though we might exclude religion, we can't leave religiosity behind."

They seized on that new thread. Susan Frasier, small, plump, generous and popular, spoke up now. "Maybe that's true. Maybe we humans have a tendency for religious thinking programmed into us. It might be a consequence of our need to figure out cause and effect in the world around us."

"Don't forget theory of mind," Miriam Brownlee said.

"We'll take all that with us into space," Holle said. "Whatever else we leave behind we'll take the essence of our humanity."

Magnus Howe nodded his head. "That's a good contribution. All of you, all save Holle, are talking in the abstract—of how 'the crew' will react to various stimuli, or the lack of them. It's only Holle who says *we*. Only Holle who seems to be grasping, today, that you're not predicting the behavior of some bunch of victims in a psychological experiment. We're talking about *you*—some of you, at least, who might survive to board the Ark. How will *you* react? Look inwards."

That shut them up, briefly. Then Susan Frasier said, "Earth. I think no matter how far I travel, even light-years, I will always look back to Earth. As I look back to my mother."

"Yes," Magnus Howe said, nodding vigorously. "Earth, the planet that shaped its cargo of life for four billion years before any of us in this room were born. Surely none of you will ever shut her out of your mind and heart."

"But Earth has betrayed us," said Wilson Argent. "She may be our mother, but she's drowning us now."

"It's not a betrayal," said Susan. "Not necessarily. It's just a change, an evolution in Earth's own conditions. A transition from one climatic state to another."

Howe said, "This is a class in which we're discussing the discarding of religion. It wouldn't be appropriate to start deifying the Earth herself; Earth is surely a self-organizing system, but not a conscious entity. But there is a school of thought that we should simply accept the wisdom of the unconscious adjustment of Earth's biological and physical cycles."

Don Meisel leapt on that. "That's abider talk. Are you an abider, Mr. Howe?"

There was immediate tension. The loosely defined philosophy that had come to be known as "abider thinking" came from a biblical quotation: "One generation passeth away, and another generation cometh: but the Earth abideth forever"—Ecclesiastes 1:4. It was born of a kind of exhaustion, twenty years after the global flooding had first begun to interfere in human affairs. Maybe, some argued, humankind should just give in. The federal government saw such ideas as a reason not to pay your taxes, and cracked down hard.

And abider talk was frowned on in the Academy as the kind of thinking that could sabotage the project as surely as the actions of disaffected eye-dee terrorists. So Don's was a serious charge; Howe could lose his job.

Howe just smiled. "The question is, what is in your hearts—and what will be there in the future, when Earth is no more than a memory to you? You see—" His phone chimed. In class phones were supposed to be set to accept only the most high-priority calls. Howe frowned and dug the phone out of his pocket.

Then Kelly Kenzie's phone rang.

And Don's. And Wilson's. The screens of laptops and handhelds began to flash too.

And, at last, Holle's phone rang. It showed a simple text message from her father: she should come to the Capitol building right away, where President Vasquez was going to speak.

15

The crowd that had gathered around the clean obelisk of the veterans' monument, before the steps of the State Capitol, was smaller than Holle might have expected, only a couple of hundred. A selected group, but most of those close to the heart of the Ark project seemed to be there.

President Vasquez herself was already in place by the time the Candidates got there. She was a stocky woman in a dark blue suit, standing behind a lightweight podium bearing the presidential seal. She had a backing of military people, cops, city officials and suited security officers. Periodically checking her watch, Vasquez spoke to a man in a blue air force uniform. Stern-faced, tanned, very fit, he might have been sixty.

The day was dull, overcast, but warm, humid. Not a typical midsummer Colorado day, old-timers said, but then no day was typical any more. The Capitol looked the worse for wear, the pale stone streaked by years of dirty rain, but two big Stars and Stripes hung on poles to either side, stirring in the fitful breeze. Holle glanced back over the park, which was fenced off from the government buildings around it. Marble pavements had been dug up to reveal raw earth, and shabby residents worked on rows of potatoes. Potatoes were the Food of the Flood, according to official government advice.

Standing in the crowd, Holle felt self-conscious in her colorful uniform, aware of resentful glances from those around her. The Candidates were becoming celebrities, of a sort, even to their coworkers. Though hundreds worked on various aspects of the project, such as the huge construction sites out at Gunnison, few even knew that the whole idea was to build a starship. But even so it was clear the Candidates were being groomed for some great adventure. Not many in Denver were leading aspirational lives, and a lot of people liked to follow the Candidates' activities, their ups and downs, as if they were characters in some reality TV show. Some of the Candidates played up to it. Kelly and Don competed over hits on their blogs. But the downside was resentment and envy.

Holle recognized a lot of the faces around her, including the rich men and women of LaRei, some of them parents of Academy students themselves. The parents, huddled in little knots talking seriously, were mostly men, fathers. The Candidates had observed that many of their number came from families without a mother, like Holle, Kelly, Zane. Maybe only fathers dreamed of shooting their children off into space. Edward Kenzie, Kelly's father, wasn't here, however. Holle had heard rumors that he was spending a lot of time at Yellowstone Park, pursuing a different Ark project—Ark Two, maybe. But if Kelly knew anything about that she wasn't saying. Secrecy was everywhere, endemic.

Holle's father found her. He gave her a brief hug. "Hi, sweets." He looked tired, edgy. But then he always looked tired and edgy.

"Any idea what's going on, Dad?"

"I just got called out of a meeting, and then called you."

"If something's going on you should know about it."

Patrick shook his head. There was movement on the podium. "I guess we're about to find out."

Suddenly this was a key day, an exceptional moment. Holle felt a knot in her stomach tighten. As a Candidate, always aware of the possibility of expulsion, you lived with an edge of anxiety, and you didn't like surprises.

A suited aide stepped up to the podium. "Ladies and gentlemen," he said simply, "the President of the United States."

———

Linda Vasquez stepped forward, pocketing a phone and checking her watch as she did so. She glanced at the military man to her right. "The cordon is complete, Gordo? I can speak freely?"

"Correct, ma'am."

"All right." She glared around. She was a heavyset woman; she looked strong, ageless to Holle. She had held the presidency for four full terms, almost, three years longer than Holle had even been alive. Rumor had it she was planning to run for a fifth come the elections in the autumn. Holle found it difficult to imagine anybody else in her role. When Vasquez spoke, her voice still carried the lilt of the New York Alphabet City slums where she'd grown up, and which had slumped under the waters in the days of her first administration.

"I guess you know who I am. And, looking around, I know who you are. This is Ark One, right? You are the group who are intending to fly an honest-to-God starship right out of here, out of Colorado. And for this reason, this remarkable, wonderful, hopeful goal, my administration has been happy to back you. And also because of the synergy. The nation will need a space launch capability in the event of any meaningful recovery program in the future.

"But now things are changing. The flood doesn't let up, in case you haven't noticed. In the last year alone the water rose another seventy meters. Seventy meters! And that vertical rise translates into much more lost territory as the water pushes inland across the continents." She shook her head. "Sometimes I get out of bed in the morning, and I look at my daily update, and I still can't believe what we're having to deal with."

Holle was amazed that a president should speak to them this way.

"However, deal with it we have to, as best we can. I continually review and revise my priorities. And as the flood keeps on pressing, what were once outlandish options for the worst case slowly become more realistic, more vital. Because in the end those extreme options might be all we have left.

"Which brings me to Ark One." Unexpectedly, she slammed the podium with her fist; there was a blare of feedback that made Holle jump. "And what's been going on here is simply not acceptable. Chaotic organizational forms, lack of leadership, waste, infighting and general confusion are strangling this project. You've had seven years since the start-up meeting that kicked off the whole thing. Am I right? Seven years. I'm told it's only a couple of years since you even got together a feasible design—I say 'feasible'; my science adviser tells me that in this case that means a design that doesn't actually break the laws of physics. And you haven't flown so much as a Fourth of July rocket out of Gunnison yet. Seven years! The Second World War was won in four."

"Six," Patrick murmured to Holle in his soft Scottish brogue.

For a panicky instant Holle was convinced the President was going to cancel the Ark altogether.

But Vasquez said, "Things are going to change. As of now the civilian administration of Ark One is over. By presidential order I'm hereby requisitioning the project, its personnel and all its resources. From now on Ark One will be run under the auspices of the air force. Consultants from NASA and other agencies will be attached to the project as appropriate, but again under overall air force command. If you've been following the news you may observe that this isn't out of character for my administration. I took similar drastic action last year when I sent the army and the National Guard into those Friedmanburgs up in the Great Plain states. There will be a trade-off. I will lock in place the resources for you to complete the work, even if some other asshole is standing here addressing you a year from now, after the election. Let me begin that process by putting a personal stamp on the thing. 'Ark One' is kind of a dry name, isn't it? Numbers never got my heart beating too fast. From now on you're 'Project Nimrod.' You'll find out why."

Vasquez took a handkerchief from her pocket and dabbed her forehead; for a moment she looked like a weary old woman. Nobody spoke; there wasn't a sound, save for a breeze that sang softly in the cords of the twin flags.

"You may wonder why I don't just shut you down. Some lobby for more resources to be devoted to potential recovery projects, rather than last-resort options like this. Even among the pessimists there are those who argue I should turn over what's left of our infrastructure to more practical activities, like building rafts. I still believe we are capable of more than that." She paused, and looked around at her audience. Holle felt a peculiar thrill when it seemed the President looked directly at her. Vasquez said, "I'm no John Kennedy. If you want to hear the speech he gave on 25th May 1961, go find it. But the mandate I'm giving you now is similar. You have a challenge to fulfill that is immeasurably harder than flying to the moon, yet immeasurably more important. Your starship must be ready to fly by 2040, or all our futures may be lost. I guess that's all. Do good work." And she stepped back from the podium.

The crowd broke up into humming discussions.

Holle saw LaRei big beasts stalking Jerzy Glemp. "Jerzy, you bastard, you sold us out. All the fucking money I pumped into this—it's my ship, damn it . . ." Jerzy backed off, his hands spread defensively.

Patrick murmured, "So Jerzy engineered this takeover. Can't say I'm surprised. We needed the resources, the leadership. But I wonder what kind of deal he struck for himself. He'll have made enemies today."

Holle didn't care about the politicking. She tugged Patrick's sleeve. "Gee, Dad. That was historic, wasn't it? Wow. The President! But what do we do now?"

"I guess we're going to find out." He didn't seem excited or enthused. He just looked more tired than ever.

Both their phones sounded.

16

olle's call was a summons back to the Academy. By the time she got there, the students were lining up in the big North Atrium on the museum's ground floor, an open space of three stories of brickwork and a glass roof, where the museum's café had once been housed.

And here was the big, upright sixty-year-old military man who had stood by the President at her podium, his uniform air force blue. With a handful of aides at his side, he climbed on a step, facing the students. A couple of youngsters in uniforms, unknown to Holle, stood beside him, standing military fashion, legs apart, hands behind their backs. The Academy staff lined up nervously by one wall, before a whiteboard.

The officer began to speak while the latecomers were still filing into the room.

"My name is Gordon James Alonzo. My friends call me Gordo. To you I'm the Colonel. If you want to know who I am and what I've done, Google me. Do you little assholes still say 'Google'? Whatever. You'll learn I was air force trained, and flew shuttles with NASA. And now, at the President's request, here I am back in air force blue, and taking on this fucking shambles of a space project. That includes turning this kindergarten into something that resembles a crew training academy." He glared at the Candidates, some of whom were as young as eleven. "I'm not going to spare you, by the way. I'm sure your language is a lot filthier than mine.

And anyhow, if your performance records are anything to go by, most of you aren't going to be around here long enough for my foul mouth to make a difference one way or another.

"I looked over the records of the classes that were going on here just this morning. Sociology! Ethics! Jesus Christ. And I'll tell you one thing." He looked at the staff. "There'll be no more treasonous abider bullshit here. Is that clear? From now on things are going to change. Your training, those of you who survive the cull, will be wholly based on aspects of the actual project you're working on. Ship's systems—propulsion, comms, environment control, life support, G&N, that's guidance and navigation, pressure suits, cockpit integration. Oh, and general relativity and all that horseshit. Also wider aspects of the project, planet-finding, recovery systems, mission planning, training programs. If you're smart you'll pick a specialism and dive into it. Make yourself indispensable to the program— indispensable to *me*. Don't try to hide. If you do, you'll be out.

"Everything will be purposeful. Even your recreation time will be focused on the physical aspects of the mission. No more fucking softball. Ben, make a note," he said, turning to an aide. "We ought to get a centrifuge up here. And we need to get some flight training, or anyhow flight experience. How about a Vomit Comet? At least we could rig up a zero-G table. And so on and so forth." He glared at the Candidates. "Any questions?"

There was a long, stunned silence. Then, to her own surprise, Holle found herself raising a hand. "Colonel—why 'Project Nimrod'?"

His eyes narrowed. "Fair question. I guess you don't major on Bible studies here. Genesis 10, verses 8 to 10: 'And Cush begat Nimrod: he began to be a mighty one in the earth . . . And the beginning of his kingdom was Babel, and Erech, and Accad . . .' This is only generations after the Flood of Noah, and there is Nimrod, already King of Babel. I guess you know what happened in Babel, right? Chapter 11, verse 4. 'And they said, Go to, let us build us a city and a tower, whose top may reach unto heaven.'"

Wilson Argent put his hand up. "But, Colonel—are you comparing Ark One to Babel? God punished them when they built the tower."

"So He did. But why? Genesis 11:6. 'Now nothing will be restrained from them, which they have imagined to do.' God feared us. And that's why we're calling ourselves after Nimrod."

"Wow," Wilson said. "You're challenging God? Sir."

"Why the hell not? It was the President's idea." He glanced over at the staff members lined up before a whiteboard. He pointed at Harry Smith, who flinched. "You! Write it up on that board. Yes, now. 'Nothing will be restrained from them, which they have imagined to do.'"

Harry found a stylus and wrote up the words, which were translated into a bold font by the board's character-recognition software.

Alonzo put his hands on his hips. "And as for you pampered little ass-holes, I want to make it clear to you right from the git-go that things are going to be different around here. Daddy's money got you in here. It won't keep you here—not unless you prove you're more valuable than the competition. And here's the start of that competition." He looked over his shoulder. "Come forward, you two."

The two youngsters behind him stepped up, looking uncertain. One wore air force blue, the other a kind of police uniform. They snapped to attention, straight and tall.

Alonzo glared at the students. "You kids in this pansy palace don't know the half of what's going on out there in the real world. Well, these two are no older than many of you, but they've been out there. Mel Belbruno here is what I used to be, an air force brat. But he's been in a cadet corps since he was ten, and has gotten himself experience with what's left of NASA. He's a real life space cadet, and he's precisely the kind of student that ought to be working on this mission.

"And this here is Matt Weiss. Matt's in a police cadet corps with Denver PD. You want to know where Matt cut his teeth? Out on the front line, on the coastline of what's left of America, a coast that recedes every day. Matt has been out there helping senior DPD officers choose whose children get to land and whose don't, and implementing those choices. Which of you has experience to compare with that?"

Kelly Kenzie put her hand up. "Colonel Alonzo, I don't deny the validity of what you say. But there's no room here, on the course. We've all been training specifically for this mission for years. If these two are to join—"

"Good point, blondie. I'll have to make room," he said with a cold brutality. His gaze swept along the row.

Holle saw people cringe back as if from a laser beam. She told herself to stand tall.

Alonzo stared at Kelly, who'd asked him the question. And then he pointed at Don Meisel, who stood beside her. "You. Redhead. Pack your bags. As of now you're filling Matt's place with DPD."

Don was shaking. "Me? You don't know anything about me. You don't even know my name! And I didn't say anything—"

"Exactly. Kid next to you had the guts to speak out." When Don didn't move, he spoke with an ominous calm. "You still here?"

Don turned and walked. He pushed past Holle, his face red, eyes burning with humiliation and anger.

"And in the morning," Alonzo said, "I'll pick the second ejectee. Now go to work." He turned on his heel and walked out.

All Holle felt was a cold horror. Since the day she'd joined the group, Don Meisel had been one of the obvious leaders. She'd even imagined he might make captain. And now he was gone, just like that. If Don Meisel could lose his place so arbitrarily, then who might go tomorrow?

17

Less than thirty minutes after Gordo Alonzo's speech, Don Meisel was delivered to the door of the Denver police department head-quarters on Delaware Street.

He walked into a crowded hall full of cops coming and going, in shabby uniforms or plain clothes, some shouting into the air or listening absently to Angels. Heavy security doors, all closed, led off deeper into the building. Many of the cops carried paper cups of coffee; the smell of the stuff was strong in the air. The fluorescent lights seemed dim, the paint on the walls a muddy yellow. With the noise and the murky light, it felt like walking into a cave. None of it seemed real, in fact. He couldn't believe he was here. One man, a heavyset Latino, sat on a plastic chair, his hands cuffed before him. His nose looked flattened, the nostrils plugged with bloody tissue. He stared at Don in his gaudy Candidate's uniform and sneered, showing a mouth full of broken teeth. Don shrank, self-conscious.

A uniformed cop came up to Don. She was maybe fifty, with thick graying hair tied back in a bun behind her head. Her face was a mask, the wrinkles around her mouth and small nose chiseled deep, and her eyes were shadowed with fatigue. She had a small scar on her right cheek, maybe inflicted by a punch by ringed fingers. She was carrying a clipboard and handheld. "You're Don Meisel, from the Academy?" She didn't look at him as she said this.

He stayed silent.

That made her look up at him. "Don Meisel," she said more firmly.

"Yes."

"Yes, ma'am." She looked at him more closely, focusing on his face. "Defiant cuss, are we? You won't find that goes down well here. OK, Meisel, we don't want you here."

"And I don't want to be here."

"Then we're equal. Equal in mutual loathing." There was a flicker of humor in her eyes. "Look, I'll give you a once-only head's-up about how your life is going to be from now on. After that you're on your own. OK?"

He nodded stiffly.

"I can imagine how you're feeling. Really I can. Getting thrown out of your cushy berth, the wonderful expensive program they're running back there. Thrown down into the pit, here on Delaware. That's how it feels, right? And I know what you think your life will be like now. Policing food riots and battling eye-dees with TB.

"But it's not all like that. This is still a city, it's still populated by American citizens who are still preyed on by corner boys and touts and pimps and drug slingers and all the rest. And we're still professional cops. I'm talking about ordinary, old-fashioned policing, of which the challenges have only got worse as wave after wave of refugees have washed over this town of ours." She looked deep into his eyes, challenging him. "Think you might find some satisfaction in that kind of work? You're a smart kid, I can tell by the files they sent over from the Academy. It's still possible to build a career in this department. Just focus on the job and we'll see how you prosper."

Don said nothing.

"OK, Meisel, your training starts as of now. Down the hall to the left, ask for Officer Bundy. I asked him to find you a berth in the squad for the first couple of days, and a partner. He'll show you where to get a cadet badge and pick up a uniform. You seriously need to get out of the Spider-Man outfit."

"Thank you," he said. "Ma'am."

"Oh, and Meisel. Ask Bundy about lodging."

"I don't need lodging."

She sighed. "Yes, you do. You'll get no more support from the Academy. Look, it's not so bad. One time you had to be a Denver resident to be a cop here. Now it's switched around, if you serve as a cop you have a residency entitlement. A rookie cadet like you has a right to a quarter-share in a dorm room. Bundy will give you the paperwork. Go, go, get on with it."

He walked stiffly into the building, ignoring the stares and grins of the officers he encountered.

18

September 2036

The morning's class debate in the isolation camp was between Zane who had to defend the Ark's latest draft design model, and Mel Belbruno who argued for the tough engineering disciplines that had been brought into the project by veterans of NASA, the USAF and the Navy.

The Candidates were in the Cultural Center at Cortez, a small museum once run by the University of Colorado in this tiny little town in the southwest corner of the state, maybe five hundred kilometers from Denver. Within the walls of this hundred-year-old building, the Candidates in their gaudy scarlet-and-blue jumpsuits looked vivid against the drab background. Zane was on the stage, facing Mel, listening intently. Mel, though a fully fledged Candidate, had always been subtly excluded by the rest since being forced on the project by Gordo Alonzo four years back. But Zane knew Mel was no fool, and he had powerful allies.

Mel said forcefully, "In the Ark you're looking at a single machine big and complex enough to keep humans alive, that's going to have to function to something like its optimal parameters for years, decades even. In the military and aerospace we've been doing this for a long time. Look at the B52, fleets of which we kept flying for fifty years and more. Or the space shuttle, which lasted over three decades from first test to final operational flight, and which despite its problems had a safety record in terms of human flight hours per casualty that was second to none—"

"Poor examples," Wilson Argent snapped back. "B52 missions lasted hours, shuttle missions maybe weeks, and even then you had ground support for maintenance."

"But my point is that there are precedents of technologies being maintained for long periods—even across multiple generations, even centuries. We can look at these cases and abstract those features that enabled them to endure. A continuing purpose, for instance, as with medieval cathedrals in Europe—"

That earned him guffaws. Kelly said, "Are you seriously calling a cathedral a technology? Aqueducts are a better example of what you're talking about, engineering intended to *do* something. There were aqueducts built by the Romans and kept functioning in southern Europe until the flood finally washed them away."

Mel regrouped. "OK, I'll take that point. But what kept the aqueducts working? You need to ensure your machine has clarity of purpose and a compelling need to exist. You need to design on a basis of supreme reliability and low failure rates. And you need to build in ease of maintenance, redundancy, robustness of components. All of which argues against some of the fancier stuff you folks cook up. Nanotech. Self-replicating machines. Autonomous AIs, a ship that can run itself. These are things which we don't know how to do. The experience of decades of space missions is that you use stuff that's no more complex than it needs to be, and is proven in flight. No fancy, unproven technologies. No magic tricks."

And that, of course, was a jab directly at Zane and his father, and the whole warp-drive development effort. But more indirectly it dug into a split in the philosophy behind the whole project.

There were test pilots working on Nimrod now. If you were an ambitious American flyboy in the year 2036 there was really only one show in town, one place to be, and that was Nimrod. There had even been a test launch of an Ares booster from the new launch facility at Gunnison, a thrilling, startling sight, despite the surrounding perimeter fences against which resentful IDPs pressed their faces.

But as if in reaction to all this nuts-and-bolts work a whole raft of alternate schemes continued to be floated among the more fanciful thinkers. Maybe the whole project had started off in the wrong direction. If you took actual humans into space, lumpy bags of water, most of your ship's mass would necessarily be devoted to plumbing. But maybe there were ways to save weight. Kelly often loudly advocated taking just women and buckets of frozen sperm. Better yet, you could take frozen zygotes and let the first generation of colonists be raised by machine. All such schemes had eventually been ruled out, partly because of technical implausibility, and partly because there was something distancing about them for those who had to build the ship. The Ark was an expression of dreams, as much as logic; better to send a single living child than a million frozen geniuses.

But still the debate went on, and when Mel was done Zane was going to have to defend the fact that even the baseline design relied on at least one technological miracle, in the warp bubble.

Even as Mel spoke, Zane was aware of the muttering among the leaders: Kelly Kenzie, the big glamorous star of the Candidate corps, and Wilson Argent, brash, impatient, bossy, and sharp, intense Venus Jenning, and Holle Groundwater, unassuming, bright and loyal, who Wilson had labeled "the Mouse"—even soft, motherly Susan Frasier. Zane had heard enough to know what was going on. Kelly and some of the others were planning a breakout today, Day Fifty of their latest isolation exercise. Kelly's core group, bonded years ago, always dominated things. Once Don Meisel would have been in with them. Now, distanced, he sat away from the rest in his drab DPD coverall. Not for the first time Don had been called away from his regular duties and thrown back into a group from which he'd been arbitrarily excluded, to provide a minimum security cover while not disrupting the group's dynamics with strangers.

Whenever they put their pretty heads together like this, Zane felt a kind of deep panic. He was always left out of such discussions. Oh, Holle always took care of him, ever since her own first day at the Academy, when Zane had taken care of *her*. But that wasn't enough to give him a way into the core social network of this bunch of bright, attractive, intensely competitive sixteen- to eighteen-year-olds.

Nor was it much better for Zane in the outside world. His father was too deeply immersed in project politics and the intricacies of his own work on antimatter production to pay much attention to the adolescent angst of his son, save occasionally when he turned on Zane for some perceived failure or other. Zane did have the tutors, and in particular Harry Smith, but Zane was always uneasily aware of deeper levels to Harry's regard for him.

The nights were worst of all, when he lay in his bed in one of the big communal dorms, and heard the patter of feet and the giggling, and the soft parting of lips.

Zane was afraid, all the time. He felt as if his personality was nothing but a rag of bluffs and pretensions that at any moment could be torn aside like a rotten curtain to reveal the dark, miserable truth that he was no good at anything and of no value to anybody. Maybe *all* sixteen-year-olds felt like this at times, even when the world wasn't threatening to end. But if Holle or Kelly or Wilson had such doubts, they never betrayed them, not for a second that he could ever see. Only Zane, alone with his doubts and inadequacies and torments.

Mel had run down his argument, and it was Zane's turn to speak. He settled his laptop on his knees, brought up figures and notes, and focused his thoughts on what he was supposed to say.

"I hear your arguments, Mel, but it remains the case—" Ugh, he sounded like his father, like a fifty-year-old man, how he hated that in himself, but he couldn't help it. "It remains the case that we're going to have to rely on at least one brand-new technology, which is the Alcubierre drive. We haven't actually created a warp bubble yet, but we believe we're coming close."

He tapped his screen and fed their computers with images he'd taken from his father's files. They showed progress in building an atom-smasher in a suburb of Denver.

"We relied on scavenged equipment to build the thing, from the

CERN Large Hadron Collider in Switzerland, and Fermilab in Chicago." Divers had descended hundreds of meters to a seabed that had so recently been the Midwestern prairie, to bring up linear accelerators and superconducting magnets and X-ray sources, and tons of high-quality metals and cable. "We use a new technology, plasma accelerators, to deliver a comparable performance to the CERN LHC from a machine a fraction of the size. But unlike with the pre-flood colliders we're not interested in studying exotic products of high-speed proton collisions; we're not doing physics here, just trying to make antimatter. We accelerate protons to within a whisker of the speed of light, and smash them together, six hundred million collisions a second. The result is a trickle of antiprotons which are in turn stored in what we call the Antiproton Source, a magnetic bottle . . ."

If they came into contact, antimatter and matter enthusiastically annihilated. Only magnetic fields would do to keep the twin forms of matter entirely apart. But antimatter was worth the trouble. Fusion reactions typically turned only a few percent of the available fuel mass to energy; matter-antimatter reactions converted it *all*. As a result matter-antimatter was the most compact energy source known, yielding, as Jerzy liked to tell his son, as much energy from a gram or so as the Hiroshima bomb.

But the antimatter was only a step in the process. Once enough antimatter was created and stored it would be used to drive the even higher-energy collisions you needed to create a single point of such energy density that the fundamental string-fabric of matter and energy would be twanged and pulled tight, and spacetime's narrow hyperdimensional throat would be squeezed until it burst, and a warp bubble was born.

Zane spoke on about the engineering tweaks which his father had had to devise, and how he had labored to contain the costs.

Nobody was listening. You were *supposed* to listen. Here in Cortez, sealed off from the world, with their phones and net connections blocked, they were expected to feed themselves by working in a small indoor garden, to maintain the air-cycling system that mimicked the environment support of the ship, to figure out and divide up other essential chores—and, most importantly, to learn from each other. These isolation exercises were intended to help the Candidates develop the skills they would need when they faced the even deeper confinement of a long-duration spaceflight. So it paid to listen. Well, Don Meisel watched from his perch at the back of the room, and Mel Belbruno was assiduously making notes. But among the others the decision point was coming, something was passing between the core group in looks and nods and furtive grins. And now, like a breeze passing over a cornfield, a bunch of them unfolded their legs and stood up.

"We're going out," Kelly Kenzie announced. "Fifty days without sunlight is enough. Come if you want." She announced this to the outsiders, Mel, Zane. But she looked challengingly at Don.

Don folded his arms without standing up. "How will you do that?"

"We found the exit you blocked up."

"It's on the other side of the shop," Holle said with a laugh. "My father said that in places like this they always made you go out through the shop."

"Won't this count against you in terms of the exercise?"

"Not necessarily," Kelly said. "We're rewarded for initiative. I think Gordo Alonzo will be disappointed if we *don't* try busting out."

"My orders are to keep you safe," Don said. "Not to stop you making assholes of yourselves. Do what you want." His face was blank. It seemed to Zane that since being reassigned to DPD he had become very good at hiding his emotions, but he never spoke to the group about his experiences, what he had seen and done.

Kelly grinned. "Let's do it."

They all piled into the remains of the museum's small shop, with its bare shelves and faded labeling. Wilson had figured out where to break through the fake paneling that had been used to conceal the shop's main door, and he used a modified taser to disable the magnetic locks that held it shut. As the door swung open an alarm sounded, and they laughed nervously. But there was daylight beyond, a street, a slab of blue sky. It was irresistible.

They all hurried out, pushing and giggling in the doorway in their bright uniforms. Zane too was pleased to be out, to feel the sun on his face, and to breathe deeply of crisp uncirculated air.

"You look happy," Holle said with a grin. She linked her arm in his.

"I always feel more real out of doors."

"I know what you mean. But on the ship we'll be cooped up for years, not weeks. I sometimes wonder how we'll cope . . . Oh, that's my phone." She dug in her pocket.

All their phones were ringing. The museum's fabric had been laced with conductors to turn it into a Faraday cage, a block against transmissions. Cora Robles now had the largest fan base among the Candidates, or so she claimed, and she wasted no time, working her handheld with jabs of her thumb, replying to weeks of messages. Zane, vaguely guilty, turned his own phone off without looking at the screen.

He became aware of the people watching them.

The town of Cortez was a small place, once devoted to ranching and farming and catering for the tourists who had come to see the mountains and the river valleys and mesa tops where people had lived for thousands of years. Now the town was overwhelmed by the eye-dees' shelters and tents and shanties of cardboard and corrugated metal, crowding the sidewalks and every open space. And the people were everywhere, standing on doorsteps, or poking their heads out of tents, or walking the sidewalks and traffic-free streets, some dragging ancient supermarket carts, looking at the Candidates. But the Candidates, intent on their phones and handhelds, barely registered the staring locals.

A little girl came walking up to the Candidates. Aged maybe nine, she wore a faded adult T-shirt tied around her waist with a bit of old electrical flex. Don watched warily, his hand on the heft of the nightstick at his belt. She pointed at Kelly. "I know you. You're Kelly Kenzie."

With a smug glance at Cora, Kelly smiled. "How do you know that?"

"My dad works at Gunnison. He has a computer that lets you watch what you're all doing and read your blogs and stuff." She smiled. "I like watching you. I like the pretty colors you wear. I don't live here."

"You mean in Cortez? Where, then?"

"Mesa Verde. In the Cliff Palace."

Zane was amazed. He had seen the Cliff Palace, his father had once taken him there, dwellings built by ancestors of the Pueblo people and pecked into the rock. Now that precious, ancient place had become home to this little ragged little girl.

"There are lots of us," she said, matter-of-fact. "We have TV and stuff." She approached Kelly, holding out a precious bit of paper and a sliver of coal to write with. "Can I have your autograph?"

19

The question was, what to do with their liberty. They spent a few minutes consulting search engines. Then they settled on making for the Hawkins Preserve, a couple of kilometers away. This hundred-acre cultural park had been preserved by the city fathers, who had decided early that even the children of refugees needed a place to run and play ball.

So off they set, led by Kelly and Wilson, following interactive maps that took them south on North Market Street and then right onto West Main, then left down South Chestnut. Most of the Candidates stared into their screens rather than at the town around them, devouring news and mail, gossip and speculation.

Venus Jenning said, "They're still studying that detonation out in the Oort Cloud . . ." One deep space telescope, intent on exoplanet-spotting, had fortuitously caught a flash out in the halo of comet cores that drifted far beyond the orbits of the planets, cold and lightless. Later a handful of probes had reported anomalous traces of high-energy radiation and particles.

Zane asked, "So are they sure it's a nuclear explosion yet?"

Venus shrugged. "That's still the best fit to the data. Somebody lobbed a nuke out there and set it off, or a lot of nukes. But who? The Chinese, the Russians—"

"Could be the Americans," Wilson put in dryly. "Our whole project is a secret."

"OK," Venus said. "But why? The whole world's drowning. Why blow up a long-orbit comet? What's the point?"

None of them had an answer.

"Shit," Mike Wetherbee said. "The age-profile selection committee has handed down its recommendations." This was a lot more interesting, something that would affect them all. They crowded around him to see, and started downloading data to their own screens.

The social engineers had been devising ways to give the nominal crew, the target number now set at eighty, the best chance of social stability while maximizing genetic diversity. For instance, it had long been decided that families would not be taken, as they represented too many copies of the same genes. There would be no parents on the Ark, no siblings; each crew member, as genetically distinct from the rest as possible, would walk onto the Ark effectively alone.

But how *old* should the crew be? A uniform distribution of ages, matching the human world they had left behind, seemed the obvious choice. But such a distribution would leave any one individual with only a small number of possible mates of her own age. So, the social engineers had decided now, to maximize an individual's mating opportunities and to ensure the genetic diversity of the group as a whole, you had to have *everybody* on board about the same age: everybody would belong to a single "age-set echelon," in the demographers' term. The idea would be to wait for several years before having children—maybe even until after landfall on the destination planet—and then to produce another large cadre of children, all around the same age, who would follow their parents up the age graphs with a lag of twenty or twenty-five or thirty years. And, when they in turn came of age, they too would find they had a large choice of potential partners to choose from.

So that was the scheme. As it sank in, many of the Candidates looked troubled—Susan Frasier, for instance, who often spoke of her nephews and nieces, and her desire to have kids of her own, sooner rather than later.

Holle looked appalled. "My God, what a trip that's going to be. Just *us*, no grown-ups, no kids, going on and on and on."

Wilson grinned. "Can't face it, Mouse? You want to wash out, and stay here to teach your babies to swim?"

"Don't be an arsehole," Holle said, her long Scottish vowels rich.

Zane kept his own doubts to himself. Personally he couldn't care less about having kids or not, though if he made it into the crew it would be his duty to pass on his genes. But he was concerned about the age restriction. He was among the youngest in the group. What if he washed out just because his birthday lay just on the wrong side on some arbitrarily decreed limit? It was something else to fret about, another pointless, uncontrollable worry.

Something flickered in the corner of his eye.

He turned. It had been off to the north, like a distant lightning strike, or the reflection of the sun on a tilting window. Some of the others hesitated, distracted by the flash, or by reflections in the screens of their phones.

Now the phones started ringing again. Zane dug his own phone out of his pocket.

Holle covered his hand with hers. She had her own phone clamped to the side of her head. "Wait, Zane. Don't switch it on."

That eternal fear chewed deep into his belly. "What's wrong?"

"Harry Smith is coming. He'll tell you." She glanced around, and pushed a lock of hair from her eyes. "We need to get you back to the Center. Don, help me."

"Sure." Don stepped up, brisk and competent.

With Don on one side, Holle the other, both of them taller than he was, Zane found himself being marched along the street. The others watched him sympathetically. Everybody seemed to know what was happening except him. Even the heavy-handed care of Holle and Don felt like a humiliation. It was as if his worst fears were coming true. "What's going on? Has something happened to my father?"

"Wait for Harry," Holle said. She wouldn't look him in the eye.

And then he heard a rumble, as of distant thunder, coming from the north.

20

ack at the Cultural Center, Harry Smith was waiting, dressed in black sweater and slacks. He was over forty now, a big man, strong and physically direct, and his expression was grave. As soon as Zane walked in Harry put his arm around him, and led him away from the others to an office.

It took a long time of working the TV, computers and phones for Harry and Zane to unravel the news coming out of Denver, and for the reality of it to sink into Zane's bewildered consciousness. Through it all he kept remembering one glib phrase: *one gram of antimatter can give you a Hiroshima . . .*

The accident had happened at his father's collider facility at Byers. There had been a failure of an antiproton trap, a magnetic bottle. The amount of antimatter released had been a lot less than a Hiroshima gram. But it had been enough to devastate city blocks, to wreck the collider facility, to kill a dozen workers and injure a score more. The explosion had been the flash Zane had glimpsed; he had even heard it, the sound following the light flash through the air after long seconds.

It took the rescue workers minutes to find Jerzy Glemp, who had been working in the facility at the time. Sitting with Harry in the Cultural Center, following the operation on computer screens, far away, too far, Zane watched the paramedics ship his father's broken body to the hospital. Then they began the long wait for news of his condition.

After two hours Zane's strength was gone, and with it his self-control. Harry put his arm around him again. Zane resisted, but Harry was firm, and it was a comfort to rest his face against the black warmth of Harry's sweater.

Then he let Harry lead him to the infirmary the students had improvized, a small two-bed unit in another office, a place with more privacy than the big communal dormitories—a place where, just for tonight, Zane could weep, sleep, be alone. Harry offered him food, warm drinks. He ate only a little. When he took off his shoes and lay down on the cot he found his eyes closing, his thoughts scrambling. It was only around seven p.m. It made no sense for him to be sleepy, yet he was. He curled up, his legs against his chest. He was aware of Harry pulling a thin blanket over him, drawing the shade and turning out the light.

He dreamed, a dream in which he was very young, his father a figure that towered over him. He was in his room in the Academy building, the old Denver museum, where he felt as safe as he ever had anywhere in the world, safe with his books and toys and computers and his phone, waiting for that precious hour when his father came back from work and might play with him, if his mood wasn't for punishment.

He didn't know how long he slept. When he woke the room was dark.

There was somebody else on the bed, lying on top of the blanket, legs spooned behind his, a heavy, comforting arm across his hip. Somebody heavy. "Dad?" Of course it wasn't Dad.

"It's all right," Harry whispered. "I just wanted to make sure you're OK. I care for you, you know that." His breath was warm on the back of Zane's neck as he spoke.

"My father—"

"They'll have more news in the morning." Harry's arm moved up over Zane's hip, and his hand pressed Zane's chest, so Zane's body was pulled back against him.

Zane felt as if he couldn't move, as if he was trapped in a dream of immobility.

Harry whispered, "You poor kid."

"Why am I a poor kid?"

"Well, so much is up in the air now. Your father may not recover. Even if he does there is bound to be a rescoping of the project. People died, Zane." His hand moved, rubbing over Zane's chest and stomach through his shirt, tender but strong. "You can't be sure there will be a place for you after this. None of us can know that, not yet."

That black fear bubbled. "I hadn't thought that far."

Harry hushed him. "I know, I know." He pulled at the blanket so they both lay beneath it. Now Zane could feel the length of his body through his clothes, as they lay in the bed. Harry shifted and he passed his left arm under Zane's body, and worked that hand under his shirt. His fingers roamed over Zane's chest and belly, pushing down toward his groin. "Hush. Don't worry."

"But my father—"

"He fights with Edward Kenzie, you know. I don't think Edward ever forgave Jerzy for the way he helped the President sequester the project. What Edward wants is for Kelly to be on that ship. Now it's out of his hands. Oh, he's angry at your father for that. Angry at *you*." All this was whispered in Zane's ear. Harry's mouth was so close now that Zane could feel his stubble on the back of his neck, a soft scraping. Still he talked, steadily. "And then there's this strange crew demography they're planning, everybody the same age. As soon as I saw that I thought of you, Zane. You're an outlier in the age distribution. There's so much stacked against you, isn't there?" The words were harder now, the breath hot and percussive against Zane's neck.

With his right arm Harry reached over and grabbed Zane's hand in his own. Zane resisted, just for a second, but Harry was so much stronger, and he pulled the hand behind Zane's back, between their bodies.

"But I'm here." He pushed Zane's hand down. Zane felt a tangle of hair, and an erection, hot, the skin smooth. Harry made him close his fingers around the shaft, and Harry started thrusting, subtly. "I'll defend you," he said. "I'll keep you safe. Without me—without me—the others will get rid of you. But I'm here, and I'll always make sure . . ." It didn't last long. The words broke up in gasps and a shudder.

Harry released his hand, and Zane pulled his arm back. There was semen on his palm, hot and stringy. He wiped it on the sheet.

For long minutes Harry just lay there, his left arm still under Zane's body. Then he withdrew his arm and kissed Zane on the neck. "Sleep now." Zane felt the weight shift as Harry got out of the bed, and then a fumbling as he adjusted his clothes before walking out through the door.

Zane felt behind himself in the dark. The sheets where Harry had lain were a sticky mess, as were the back of Zane's own pants. Zane got out of the bed, and stripped off his pants and threw them to the floor. Then he pulled the blanket off the other bed, wrapped it around his shoulders, and huddled down in the corner of the room, facing the door. He sat there, sleepless until morning.

21

Three days after the accident Gordon James Alonzo hosted a preliminary inquiry in the Capitol building in Denver. To her surprise Holle was summoned, along with Kelly Kenzie and Mel Belbruno.

The walk across town, escorted by Don Meisel, was grim. The city was now surrounded by rings of defensive perimeters, and internally was sliced up into control zones, with barriers between Auraria and LoDo and the Central Business District. The civic center was like a fortress. Don was alert, wary. There was a fear that the Candidates could be a target.

Holle thought the mood was changing, generally. The rising flood had now passed the altitude of the lowest point in Colorado, a place called Holly in the valley of the Arkansas, a symbolic moment. The water was coming, and the inward flow of refugees was intensifying. Invesco Field and Coors Field and the Pepsi Center had become not so much processing as detention centers. A potato blight had drastically worsened the food situation. And now the Byers incident had raised tensions. As the flood went on and on, relentlessly rising, the waters seemed to be washing away any hope, any optimism that this vast convulsion would ever come to an end. For the first time the idea that this really was an end of the world was being taken seriously, absorbed imaginatively. That was what lay under all the stress, she thought. And that tension crackled across the dingy downtown.

———

Magnus Howe met them at the State Capitol. Once they were through the security barriers he escorted them to a meeting room, and showed where they should take their places at a big conference table.

Holle looked around warily. Gordo himself sat at the head of the table. Behind him was a big interactive whiteboard, and flipcharts summarizing the status of the project's various aspects. Screens and touch pads were set into the surface of the table before the attendees.

Down one side of the table sat senior air force, NASA and government people. The big names of the old civilian control of the project were lined up along the other side, including Holle's and Kelly's fathers. Liu Zheng and more of the technical team sat looking impatient, abashed. Some of the attendees had teams of assistants sitting behind their seniors, backs against the walls, so the room was filling up.

Holle's father caught her eye and smiled. She hadn't spoken to him face to face since the accident. Everybody had been running around too much, scrambling to cope with the accident's aftermath, preparing for reviews like this, and thinking about options for recovery and rescoping. But Holle knew that it was at Patrick's and Edward's insistence that the Candidates had representatives here at this crucial meeting. They might not be able to contribute much, but in a sense the whole exercise was *for* them; they ought to be here. "Even if," as Kelly had said gloomily, "it's only to hear the whole show is going to be canceled."

The air was already hot. The aircon was juddery, even here in the Capitol building. Everything was breaking down. Water jugs stood full on the table, glinting with dew, and Holle longed to pour herself a glass, but she didn't dare. As the attendees filed in there was silence save for a scraping of chairs, an occasional cough. Everybody seemed so *old*, save the Candidates and one or two aides.

At last only one space remained at the table, and there was a tense pause. Then the doors opened, held back by an air force orderly, and a paramedic in a bright orange coverall pushed in a wheelchair. Jerzy Glemp sat in the chair, his whole body swathed in a green blanket. A patch covered one eye.

As he was shoved into position at the table, Patrick leaned forward. "Jerzy, you shouldn't be here. The doctors insisted you stay in the hospital."

"Fooey. I wouldn't—" Jerzy broke up in coughing that jerked his body, and Holle could see the pain every movement caused him. The paramedic hovered with an oxygen mask, but Jerzy shook his head minutely, and she backed away. "I wouldn't miss this for the world." Jerzy looked around, his one good eye glinting. He found Holle. "How's my boy? They haven't let him see me."

"We thought that was for the best," Magnus Howe said.

Jerzy snapped, "I asked Miss Groundwater."

"Zane's fine," Holle said. "But—" She thought of Zane as he'd been in the hours since the accident, Zane who'd hardly spoken a word to anybody, Zane who seemed to cling to corners, to shadows, Zane pushed in on himself. She said at last, "He's working. His work is good."

"Ah. That's all one can ask, isn't it? Tell him I'll see him as soon as I can."

"I will."

"So we're all here," said Gordo Alonzo, rapping on the tabletop with a fat, old-fashioned fountain pen. Holle wondered vaguely where he got the ink. "I have to face President Vasquez herself later today, and make my recommendations about the future of Project Nimrod. I suspect that in my heart of hearts I'd rather just can this bull session right now, and go do something more productive. Because, you know why? I think I already know what recommendation I'm going to make, no matter what is said today. That we pull the plug on this whole fucking shambles."

"You don't have the authority for that," Patrick said heatedly. "In terms of the command and reporting structure—"

Gordo laughed. "Don't you guys get it? Command structure! At this minute that's me, pal. When your magnetic bottle went pop it took everything else down with it."

Kenzie said, "There's also the issue of hope, Colonel Alonzo. Of purpose. What would you have the administration do instead? Give the Homeland goons bigger sticks with which to beat back the refugees?"

Gordo said, "The sea is going to cover over us all in a few years or less whatever we do, buddy. I'm not sure if to give false hope is a worse sin than to give no hope at all." He turned to his charts and boards. "Let's get back to basics. Tell me how you think you're going to fly this dumbass mission in the year 2040. Which, let me remind you, is just four years from now." He stared around. "Who wants to lead off?"

Edward Kenzie spoke up again. "The basics are simple. We need to assemble a starship, with a crew of no less than eighty, in orbit." He got up stiffly. With age he was getting ever stouter, and according to Kelly he suffered badly from gout. He went to a flipchart and turned pages until he came to a construction schedule. "From scratch, we built a space launch center at Gunnison, Colorado." He tapped the whiteboard, and up came an image: a single launch gantry, blockhouses around it, mountains in the distance. He sat heavily in an empty seat by the board. "Intended to fly Ares I and V booster stacks, the launch technology designed to take humans back to the moon and to Mars, which of course never happened. We had to procure transport facilities. Fuel manufacture and storage—"

"Yadda yadda," said Gordo. "You flew one bird out of there so far, didn't you? One stick, one Ares I, unmanned, to orbit. How many launches you think you're going to need to assemble your 'starship in orbit'?"

Liu Zheng answered that. He tapped a touch pad, and the whiteboard lit up with graphics. "Fifteen launches, sir. Five of the heavy-lift Saturn V-class Ares V, unmanned, and ten of the human-rated Ares I sticks, each carrying eight or ten crew. The plan so far has been to reinhabit the abandoned ISS, the space station, and use that as a construction shack to—"

Gordo waved him silent. "Your deadline for completion of on-orbit assembly is still 2040. Right? You've managed one launch in the last four years. You imagine you'll get through *fifteen* in the next four. Fifteen launches, and that's without tests and failures, and you haven't flown a single Ares V out of Gunnison yet. *And* you're going to reoccupy the ISS, a station which has been mothballed for sixteen years. My God, at NASA we'd have looked at that alone as an activity that would likely take teams of trained astronauts years. It's down here as a milestone on your chart—no resources assigned to it—nothing. Who's gonna do that, the tooth fairy?"

Patrick steepled his fingers. "We're at a point at which our schedule is expected to accelerate, as significant mission milestones—"

"Bull," said Gordo simply. "This ain't the first fucked-up project I've been involved with, Mr. Groundwater, and I recognize all the symptoms, and I heard it all before. We screwed up, we missed all the milestones so far, but the future is bright! And you'll notice I haven't yet come to the issue of antimatter production. Remind me. How much antimatter are you going to need for your starship?"

Liu Zheng said, "We believe half a kilogram. That may not sound much but such is the energy density of the—"

"Yes, yes. Let's take a look at your production facility." Gordo tapped the chart, and brought up live images of the ongoing disaster in the Denver suburb of Byers. The accelerator site was a crater from which protruded odd bits of wall or the skeletal tangle of reinforcing steel cables. Smoke snaked up from a dozen fires, and rescue workers crawled in their bright orange gear through mounds of rubble. In one place a refugee camp had been destroyed, canvas tents blown flat. On the fringe of the disaster zone, ragged protesters faced a line of cops and soldiers and Homeland goons.

"There's your antimatter factory," Gordo said. "A hole in the ground, which it would have been a lot cheaper to produce by dropping a fucking nuke. Let me tell you something. No matter what else comes out of this disaster, I don't believe it's going to be acceptable to President Vasquez to go back to manufacturing this stuff in the middle of Colorado."

"Then we're screwed," said Jerzy Glemp, his damaged body twitching under his blanket. "Screwed. The whole point of the design is the warp bubble, Colonel. We can't fly without that. And we can't create a warp bubble without antimatter."

"I'm aware of that," Gordo snapped. "And I'm also aware of the short-cuts you took to get your precious atom-smasher up and running, Dr. Glemp."

Glemp grew more agitated. "I don't know what you mean."

"Like hell you don't. I've seen the documentation trail. The ass-coverers in your organization kept a record of every time you leaned on them to cut a test, disregard a safety precaution, push a design without a backup. If this was a court of law I'd have a case to prosecute you."

"It is rich for you to berate us for schedule delays then accuse me of negligence for my attempts to meet targets."

"*It was always out of your reach,*" Gordo said. "This dream of star flight. That's the truth, isn't it, Dr. Glemp? You always saw that more clearly than these others, and yet you pushed ahead anyhow, as far and as fast as you could, regardless of the risks—"

Edward Kenzie stood up again. "Colonel, it's four years since President Vasquez made her Nimrod speech, her Kennedy moment. *You* were in-volved then, and you're sure as hell involved now. But none of the prob-lems we've faced since have anything to do with you—is that what you're telling us?" He pointed a fat finger at Gordo. "Is that the game, Colonel? Blame?"

Jerzy struggled. "I want to say—oh, let me speak—" His voice broke up into a coughing jag that left him shaking.

Edward tried to speak again, and Patrick, and others joined in, and Gordo tried to shout them down. It was a room full of old people shout-ing at each other.

Holle tuned out. She felt stunned, emptied out. She hadn't suspected that the project was so far behind schedule, or that such risks were being taken to accelerate it. *And all for me.*

Something in Gordo's continual emphasis on the dates was working in her head. To her the flood had always been remote, something that happened to other people. Now she felt as if the world was closing in on her. In four years, when the flood waters would be lapping in this very room, she would be just twenty-one. Suddenly it wasn't some abstracted future version of herself who would have to cope with all this. It was *her* who would have to face the future, and if the Ark failed it was *her* who would have to deal with the ultimate nightmare, the washing away of the very ground under her feet. A deep fear bit into her belly, like a fear of falling. She glanced across at her father, wishing she was nearer to him.

Kelly was watching her. "Hey. It's OK. We'll get through this. We'll fly yet." And she turned back to listen to the arguments, serene, confident, strong. Just for a moment, rivalries put aside, Holle could see why she was so popular with the public who watched the Candidates' progress, their daily lives.

Gordo folded his arms, and silenced the room. "Then this is the crux. The way you have been progressing this project has led to delay and ultimately disaster. There's no way I'm going to endorse the kind of launch schedule you put together here. It was always a fucking joke, and it's certainly unachievable now. Unless you can come up with some new way forward, *now,* then the Ark don't fly. So who speaks next?"

"Holle Groundwater," said Liu Zheng.

22

Holle said, "What?"

Liu seemed quite calm. He even smiled. "Ms. Groundwater. Once, in my class, we were ruminating on a design problem that at the time seemed insuperable."

"I—"

"The size of the warp bubble."

"Yes. I remember."

"On that occasion, you raised a question. Not a solution, but it provoked a chain of thought that ultimately led to a solution. It was a good question. Perhaps that is your particular talent." His smile widened, encouraging. "Now would be a good time to ask that question again."

Patrick said, "What the hell are you doing, Liu? What kind of pressure is that to put on a seventeen-year-old kid?"

"It's OK, Dad," Holle said, though it wasn't OK, not at all. They were all staring at her, her father with anxiety and pride, Liu with intensity, Edward Kenzie with bafflement—Kelly with frank envy. She could feel her heart hammer, the blood sing in her ears. She thought she might faint. What a situation. Speak. Say the right thing. Or else in five years you'll either be dead, or starving on a raft made of plastic trash. "It's just something my father always said. If the answer's not the one you want, maybe you're asking the wrong question."

Liu Zheng closed his eyes and spoke rapidly. "Yes. OK. Now we have two apparently insuperable obstacles. First, the antimatter. We can't make what we need. Then what's the alternative to making it?"

Jerzy growled, "If you can't make it, go find it. Mine it from somewhere."

"Yes," Liu said, nodding. "The question is, where and how? And second, the multiple launches. We don't have the time to launch the Ark in fifteen pieces. Surely you are right about that, Colonel. Therefore we will have to send up a single package, a single launch, the whole Ark. Eighty people with everything to sustain them, *and* all the aspects of the ship's propulsion system. All to be launched at once. How do you launch so much to orbit, in one shot?" He opened his eyes and started to hammer at the keypad in the tabletop before him.

Jerzy was smiling, a twisted gesture under his covered eye. "I see what you mean. Those are good questions. And I think I know where you can mine antimatter."

Gordo had to grin. "Is this a setup? You old showboater."

"I am younger than *you,* Colonel."

"Where?"

And Jerzy said, "Jupiter and Io."

Jupiter, a monstrous world with the mass of three hundred Earths, so huge it was almost a star. And Io, moon of Jupiter, circling so close to its bloated parent that tidal forces kneaded it into continual volcanism. As Io circled through Jupiter's powerful magnetic field it created a "flux tube," an electric current connecting Io to Jupiter's upper atmosphere, a current that gathered up charged particles and caused them to slam into the Jovian air.

Kelly, racing through material retrieved to the screen before her, saw the point quickly. "The flux tube is a natural particle collider."

Jerzy said, "And as such it is a natural source of antimatter particles. Of course in nature such particles will annihilate with matter very quickly, but it is believed that some finish up in belts around Jupiter, analogous to Earth's Van Allen belts. And if they could be harvested—"

"How?" Gordo snapped.

"With some kind of superconducting magnetic scoop, possibly," Liu said. "A ship with magnetic sails that could waft through the flux tube and filter out antiprotons. The amount of antimatter is small—only three or four tons of antimatter per hour are created by such processes across the solar system—but the amount we will need to harness is small too . . ."

And the discussion spun on as the scientists, running with the idea, explored the resources available through their computers. Even Kelly and Mel joined in, exhilarated to be released from the closure and intensity of the post-accident discussion.

Holle just sat back, bewildered. She tried to follow the swirling discussion, the bare outlines of a new mission strategy emerging from the heated speculation. Jupiter's environment, saturated with radiation, was pretty lethal for humans. That plucky ramjet, swooping in around Io to filter out antiprotons, would have to be unmanned. But it might be controlled by a manned craft in a slow, remote orbit around Jupiter. So you would spend years in orbit, living in a tank, years in a place of huge, lethal energies where the sun was reduced to dimness, years waiting just to collect the antimatter needed to begin the mission proper. It seemed horrible to her, repellent, utterly inhuman. And yet, as the scientists talked, as Gordo let the discussion run on, this was the consensus that was emerging.

But how would you get to Jupiter in the first place?

For answer, Liu Zheng produced a video clip which he projected onto the big whiteboard at the front of the room. It was only half a minute long, and looped over and over. Scratchy, blurred, ghosted from having been copied across many formats, it showed an old man sitting in a rocking chair. He cradled some kind of model. It looked like an artillery shell, maybe a meter long, a third of a meter wide. The old man displayed the features of the gadget. That bullet-like cowl was made of fiberglass, and was pocked with holes where, it seemed, some kind of sensors had once been placed. At the base was a curved plate of aluminum, like a pie dish, or maybe an antenna. The dish was connected to the main body by a system of springs, a kind of suspension.

"This is how we may launch," Liu said.

Jerzy Glemp cackled. "In a Jules Verne spaceship?"

"It has nothing to do with Verne," said Liu. "But it is a spaceship—or a demonstration model of one." He froze the image. "It was driven by explosives. You set off a charge under your pusher plate, there. The plate is driven up into the suspension system, which in turn pushes the main body forward. And you set off another charge, and another." He mimed this with his hands, his curved left palm catching the imaginary detonations, the back of his hand pushing his right fist up in the air. "Boom, boom, boom. With this model, the charges were the size of golf balls."

Gordo covered his face with his big hands. "Oh, shit, I heard of this. My father showed me a scratchy old film, of this thing put-putting into the air . . . What was it called?"

Edward Kenzie said, "Are you suggesting this might be the way to launch our Ark? What kind of explosions would you need?"

"Thermonuclear," Liu said simply.

"Jesus Christ," Kenzie said, and he looked at his daughter, horrified. "You're seriously suggesting we load the last hope of mankind on top of a nuclear bomb?"

"Not just one bomb," Liu said, unperturbed. "Several. A whole stream of them, thrown behind the pusher plate and detonated—"

"Project Orion," Gordo snapped.

With that as the key, the others began digging into the electronic archives.

Holle quickly found that Orion had been run from 1957 to 1965 by General Atomic, a division of a company that had also built nuclear submarines and Atlas ICBMs. It was a time of extravagant dreams driven by the new technology of thermonuclear detonations, the energies of the sun brought down to Earth. One "dimensional analysis," pushing the idea as far as possible, predicted that it would be possible to have sent humans to Saturn by 1970. She flashed the report to the whiteboard.

"This is serious stuff," Kelly said, wondering. "They got support from Los Alamos, Livermore, Sandia. And look at all these technical papers: 'A

Survey of the Shock Absorber Problem.' 'Random Walk of Trajectory Due to Bomb Misplacement.' Some of these are still classified!"

Gordo said, "So would this have worked?"

"You bet," Mel Belbruno said. "I mean, you bet, sir. They never quite wrestled the technical details to the floor, as far as I can see. But the concept was surely sound. And they did fly a few demonstration models with conventional explosives."

"So why weren't we at Saturn by 1970?"

"Because," Liu Zheng said, "to get to Saturn, you must first leave the Earth."

Growing opposition to nuclear weapons through the 1960s caused the Orion concept to be viewed with suspicion. The final straw was an unwise presentation to President Kennedy of a model of a spaceborne Orion-technology battleship, bristling with nuclear missiles. Kennedy was disgusted.

"So the concept was mothballed. But it was never abandoned," Liu said. "You will see that NASA later developed a successor design called 'Extended Pulsed Plasma Propulsion,' with a greater distance from weapons technology."

"I guess it was always a good concept to have in the library," said Gordo. "If you ever needed to get something big off of the Earth quickly." He rubbed his eyes. "I think I remember a novel from when I was a kid. The aliens attack, and we use Orion to get at their mother ship. *Footfall*— something like that. Shame it isn't a bunch of aliens we got to beat now. Xenobaths or newts or aquaphibians. By comparison, that would be easy."

"There is, or was, a nuclear weapons plant close to Denver," Jerzy Glemp said. "At Rocky Flats."

Gordo laughed. "Why ain't I surprised you know that? But if President Vasquez won't back the idea of another antimatter factory in the middle of Denver, how do I get her to endorse building a whole fucking spaceship out of nuclear bombs?"

"And the fallout," Patrick said earnestly. "If such a thing is launched anywhere in what's left of the continental US—there is nowhere empty of people, certainly not in Colorado."

Jerzy said grimly, "If we launch in 2040, or 2041, or 2042, that will no longer matter, Mr. Groundwater. And nor, I am afraid, will those left behind."

The paramedic who monitored Jerzy had been following the discussion. Holle had never seen such bewilderment, such shock, on any human face, as they discussed spaceships driven by nuclear fire. Holle wondered if they had all gone insane.

23

olle had grown up with the flood. She had no memories of life before, how politics used to be. But even so she was surprised by the speed of President Vasquez's decision-making.

Just two days after Gordo's session, Vasquez appeared on TV and the web. Once the funerals and proper commemorations were done, she said, Project Nimrod would continue. The Ark would fly, if it was humanly possible to make that happen. That was her promise to the crew and those who were working on the project. And she promised further that there would be no repeat of the Byers accident, that the safety of the public would be paramount. ("Until launch day," Kelly Kenzie muttered cynically.)

But there was a price to pay. It seemed that the President had had to make considerable concessions to win over dissenters about Project Nimrod within her own administration. She, Vasquez, would not stand for a further reelection at that fall's election. It would have been her sixth term. She would step aside and endorse her vice president as a candidate.

And Jerzy Glemp would be removed from the project he had initiated, and face charges relating to his culpability for the Byers accident.

In the Academy, Holle was oblivious to the reaction of the students, their whooping celebrations, the way Harry Smith pushed through the crowd to get to a stunned Zane Glemp. All she could think was that the project was on, that the Ark would be built. That she might yet get to fly.

24

December 2038

After one last night in the Boulder training center they were bundled into the chunky biofueled bus that was to take them up into the Wilderness for the shuttle crash sim: Holle, Kelly, Susan, Venus, Mel, Zane, Matt, and DPD officer Don, here in his semi-regular role as unofficial shotgun. Don took his place up front, at the driver's position, though the bus was automated and knew its own way to the training site. Kelly sat up front beside Don.

Holle made her way to the back of the bus, where Mel was waiting for her. She shuffled down the bus, clumsy in her bright orange environment suit. They had already been in the suits for three days in the training center set up in the old National Center for Atmospheric Research, with hoods up and face masks and goggles in place throughout. They looked like medics heading for a plague zone, she thought vaguely. Even Don had volunteered to live in a suit for the duration of the exercise, even though he was never going to have to wear such a thing in anger. As she sat down Mel grinned and took her hand. His face was all but invisible behind his breathing mask and scuffed plastic goggles, and his human warmth didn't penetrate the glove layers.

The massive door closed with a hiss of hydraulics. The bus pulled out of the NCAR parking lot, flanked by a couple of light armored vehicles. Like most government vehicles, the heavy bus was plated with armor heavy enough to absorb a small artillery shell, and the bulletproof windows were so thick they turned the outside world blue.

The little convoy headed up Table Mesa Drive and turned left onto Broadway, the old Highway 93, past the refugee-processing center on the University of Colorado campus. Holle saw threads of campfire smoke lifting to the sky from the area of the Pearl Street Mall. Now nineteen years old, she sometimes wished she could have seen cities like this as they had been before she was born, the way they were in *Friends* and *Frasier.* They turned left again onto Arapahoe Avenue, heading west out of the city. Rough wire barriers, already rusting, had been thrown up along the sides of the main roads, for otherwise the highways, now little used by traffic, would have long ago been colonized by the lean-tos and tents of the dispossessed, and the city would have ground to a halt.

As they drove by, Holle saw people pressed up to the fences, rows of faces, children dressed in clothes faded to the color of the mud, or the gray of the overcast December sky. Kelly Kenzie had the nerve to wave a gloved hand. The Candidates were still celebrities. A couple of children waved back. But the adults stared back, as if the Candidates in their environment suits were visitors from some other star. Some held up improvised placards, a single name scrawled on bits of card or plastic or cloth: VASQUEZ. After withdrawing from the 2036 election former President Vasquez had become an outspoken champion of the nation's dispossessed. Conspiracy theories had been proliferating since Vasquez's assassination in her home, just a week ago.

There had recently been a new influx of eye-dees. When the sea-level rise had topped twelve hundred meters the flood had at last started to impinge on Colorado itself in a serious way. The waters had got as far as Burlington on the I-70 and Lamar on the I-50, and the great rivers, the South Platte and the Arkansas, were now tidal in their lower reaches. There was salt-poisoning in the aquifers, and, it was said, of some trees and crops even in Denver. A fresh, panicky relocation was going on, as eye-dees in the sod-house communities on the plains were moved up to the higher, poorer land of Monument Ridge or the Rockies. But anybody who could break out of the official corridors made for the sanctu-ary of the cities. And meanwhile, some of the Project Nimrod workers were drifting away, making an early claim for a place on the remnant high ground.

The result was all these faces, all anonymous, more and more all the time, and if you listened to their voices you could hear accents that hailed from across America and even from abroad, from South America, Europe, people from all over driven by the flood to wash up against these cold fences. Holle never forgot that if not for a chance of fate, if her father hadn't been smart or fortunate in the choices he'd made in his life, she could have been on the other side of the fences too. She was relieved when they passed out of the old town limits and the press of faces let up.

They rolled along Canyon Boulevard, a twisting, rock-rimmed track into the mountains. Maybe a dozen kilometers out they came to a com-munity called Boulder Falls, where a twenty-meter cascade spilled onto the rocks. Even here the IDP camps crowded the streets, right up to the hog-wire barrier that protected the road. Don said loudly that some of the eye-dees had to pitch their shanties so close to the waterfall they got sprayed on day and night. He laughed at this, and Kelly snapped at him. Don rarely spoke about his work, but Holle knew he had been reassigned from urban policing duties to border control and IDP processing, and she could guess what that was doing to his soul. But he never showed any bitterness, even when he was forced to spend so much time with the Candidate corps from which he'd been excluded. The bus with its escort rolled through the town without stopping.

The canyon opened out into a wider plain. They were heading for the town of Nederland, and would go further still, up into the mountain country of the Indian Peaks Wilderness.

Holle tried to concentrate on the country outside, and ignore the chafing of her suit. The idea of the sim was to get them used to how they might have to live and work in the first days and months after their land-ing on Earth II. Their yet-to-be-decided destination was expected to be Earthlike, otherwise there would be no point going there in the first place, enough that you would be able to walk around outdoors without a pressure suit. But you would almost certainly need a sealed environment suit. The partial pressure of oxygen might be too low or too high, there might be various toxins floating around, and even, conceivably, some biohazard that might target your utterly alien system.

But Holle detested her suit. Supposedly manufactured by AxysCorp in its high-tech base in the Andes before it was overrun by rebels, the suit was made of a smart material designed to let her skin sweat normally, while filtering out any pasties from the environment. The mask over her mouth secreted a moisturizer and mild anaesthetic to ease the friction with her skin. There were light packs on her chest and shoulders containing supplies for the suit scrubbers, and fresh water and food. Her goggles were self-cleaning and demisting, which was fine until they broke down.

She ought to be able to survive without replenishment sealed up in this thing for twenty-four hours, and with replenishment indefinitely—the manufacturers' lower limit was a month. She understood the necessity of learning how to live and work in such conditions. But after a few hours in the suit she always began to feel like a pale, desiccating worm, as the joints chafed and the thing filled up with her own stink. On sim days you had the additional irritation of medical sensors taped to your skin, and the unnerving presence of miniature cameras on your shoulder and helmet—even *inside* your helmet, so your face could be watched at all times.

Most of the Candidates didn't mind enclosure, or even the continual surveillance. They talked quietly, pulling absently at cramping folds in the suits. They had all been raised in enclosed, heavily monitored environments since they had joined the program, for most of them, for most of their lives. But Holle hoped that Earth II would be benign enough for her to be able to take her gloves and boots off, to soothe her feet in running water and run her fingers through alien soil, and maybe feel the breeze on an exposed cheek.

———

They passed through Nederland, an old mining camp that had become a hippyish tourist magnet, and then, like everywhere else, a camp and processing center for the dispossessed. They headed on west toward Brainard Lake. From here the views of the Wilderness mountains opened up, and the Candidates leaned toward the bus's small windows to see. The scenery was spectacular, and it was unusual to take in a view that had no humans in it; these rocky slopes were too steep for the most desperate of refugees to cling to. But the mountains were bare of life, safe for withering trees; the shifting climate zones had made the slopes unviable. Though it was December there was no snow save on the highest slopes. There had been no snow at all in Denver, not for a couple of years.

As they neared the sim site, Holle saw smoke climbing into the air, black and oily. At last they approached what looked like a tangle of wreckage, scattered across a rocky plain.

25

The bus pulled up and the doors hissed open. The Candidates filed off, and stepped down onto stony ground. They had nothing but the suits they stood up in, save for Don who carried a canvas bag.

The bus sealed itself up and pulled away, tailed by the other vehicles. Holle wondered where the surveillance eyes were. They would be watched constantly for security, and backup would never be far away.

The Candidates looked around at the wreckage that littered the ground, the twisted metal and plastic panels and the tangle of cables and pipes. Boxes of supplies, toughened to withstand impact, were strewn about. Somebody had started a fire where plastic popped and melted, creating that pillar of black smoke. Gruesomely, dummies dressed up in environment suits had been thrown over the ground, their plastic limbs broken back in unnatural angles. Some of them were children-sized, like seven- or eight-year-olds perhaps, and there were a couple of bright orange sacks, like holdalls, that were baby shelters. Children being an element of exercises like these was a new thing, and followed the social engineers' newest pronouncements about breeding and demography which had shaken everybody up.

Don pulled a plastic splint out of his pack, and beckoned to Zane. "Good news, buddy, you're a casualty." Resigned, Zane rested one hand on Don's back as he slipped his leg into the splint, which inflated rapidly.

Don stepped back, leaving Zane on the ground, his "bad" leg stuck out in front of him, and addressed the group. "OK. Your shuttle has crashed, here on Earth II. You can see your gear scattered around. You're far from the other shuttles and there are no comms; there's no rescue possible in the short term. Air pressure is normal, gravity is high, but the air is unbreathable—acidic. Keep your suits sealed up. You can see you had casualties, Zane here with a broken limb, some deaths. I was told that the rest of you ought to improvise injuries, and generally remember how beat-up you'd be after a crash."

Kelly nodded at that. "Sensible enough." Always eager, she bent down to one of the dummies, used a pocketknife to cut away a strip of environment-suit leg, and wrapped it around her upper body as a sling, improvising a broken arm.

Don said, "That's all I know. I'm not here. Exercise starts now."

"Suit integrity check," Kelly said immediately. "Double up."

They didn't need her to say it; the first priority was to keep the living alive. They quickly paired up, Holle with Mel, Kelly with Matt. Susan, Venus and Zane worked together, the two women huddled over Zane down on the ground.

Holle ran a quick visual inspection of Mel's suit, seeking obvious damage, and checked his chest display. For verisimilitude she slapped some sealant from a tube taken from her own leg pouch over a nonexistent rip at the back of his neck, and topped up his air-scrubber compounds with a sachet drawn from Mel's own backpack and dropped into a slot over his chest. Mel did the same for her; he faked a remedy for a suspected slow leak by tying off her suit just below the elbow on one arm.

Standing there with her arm in a sling, Kelly looked around, checking they were all done. She naturally assumed the role of leader in situations like this. "OK, so nobody else is going to die in the next ten seconds. Matt, will you take care of that fire? Now the injured. Susan, why don't you see what you can do for Zane? I see a first-aid pack over there, under that heap of blankets. The rest of you, let's take a look at the other casualties in the wreckage. Watch out for any injuries you've sustained yourself."

"Yes, mother," said Venus Jenning, and they laughed.

Holle clambered into the "wreckage" of the shuttle. She had to avoid the pockets of flame, and flinched back from the sharp edges that seemed to have been artfully positioned by the exercise designers to catch an unwary arm or leg. As the Candidates immersed themselves in this latest in a long line of puzzle-exercises Holle heard chatter, subdued laughter. But she found the experience oddly uncomfortable. Sometimes she thought she was plagued with an excess of imagination. She could envisage a scene like this being played out in the first few seconds after arrival on a hostile Earth II, under a lowering alien sky, with all of them badly shocked and loved ones lost, and knowing that death could be seconds away, the consequence of a single careless act. There would be none of the brisk confidence then, no muttered jokes.

She found the body of a woman, lying facedown, impaled on a shard of metal through the belly. Holle checked the woman's suit monitors, which were mostly functioning but showed no sign of life. She slipped off her outer glove, so that her hand was covered only by a delicate skin-tight inner glove with fine fingertip pads. She dug her fingers into a rip at the woman's suit neck; she could find no pulse. Then she pulled off the woman's own glove and tried feeling for a pulse at her wrist.

She stepped back, and tried to roll the woman on her back. The "body" was heavier than she had expected, maybe weighted to simulate the supposedly higher gravity. She dug her hands under the woman's torso, straightened her back and tried again. This time the woman rolled, and Holle had to jump back as the bit of metal on which the mannequin was impaled swung upwards. The twisted sliver of hull was thrust straight into an obviously pregnant belly. "Oh, Jesus." Just for one second she felt her throat tighten, a foul-tasting liquid push into the back of her mouth. But she swallowed hard. She took a pocketknife and slit open the suit over that pregnant belly. Then she pressed the palm of her bloodied underglove to the woman's undergarment and let the fingertip pads work as a stethoscope.

Kelly was beside her. "You OK?"

"Yeah. Got me for a second."

"Those sim designers are bastards, aren't they? Always trying to catch us out. But you seriously do *not* want to throw up in one of these face masks. I should know; I lost my breakfast yesterday morning, back in the NARC."

"You did? How so?"

Kelly shrugged. "I guess just something I ate. They shouldn't give us pregnant women to deal with. There won't be any pregnant women when we make planetfall."

Kelly was a stickler for the plan, whatever the plan was at a given moment. It was a strength or a weakness, depending on circumstances. Holle said, "No pregnancies *if* everybody obeys the rules."

"OK, OK, you sound like Harry. We have to train for all contingencies. You found a heartbeat in there?"

"No." And Holle was thankful they wouldn't have to go through the gruesome procedure of getting the body into a blowup shelter and performing an emergency Caesarean.

"Then you'd better give me a hand with this kid over here. My arm, you know, trust me to break the damn thing . . ." She led Holle over to another "victim," one of the child-sized mannequins.

Their exercises had begun to include children because the social engineers had suddenly decreed that women pregnant at launch time would be allowed on board the Ark. The idea was to increase genetic diversity at little additional cost in terms of volume, weight and life support at launch; the births could be handled during the cruise to Jupiter with remote support from doctors on Earth. The net result would be, if they followed the nominal mission plan, a small echelon of seven- or eight-year-olds on their hands when they got to Earth II. This drastic new ruling, coming out of the blue with only a couple of years left until launch date, had led to wild speculation and sexual jockeying among the Candidates.

The dummy child lay over a hull strut, his back surely broken, and his upper body was pinned by a tangled mass of wreckage. "The sim designers went to town on this poor kid," Kelly said. "They ought to provide a few real-life eight-year-olds in these sims; they won't all be killed on planetfall."

Holle laughed. "Who'd entrust their children to us?" She crouched down by the "boy." His chest was crushed, and his pelvis seemed smashed too. She began the grisly ritual of checking for signs of life.

At length all the bodies had been checked. The corpses were moved out of the wreckage, lined up on the ground a few meters from the main crash site, and covered by a bit of cowling.

This time Mel took the lead. He looked around at a featureless lid of sky. "If the timing here on Earth II matches that on Earth, it's late afternoon and we ought to think about shelter. In the morning we can strip the bodies and dispose of the remains. Anybody volunteer to speak for the dead?"

"I'll do that," Susan Frasier said mildly.

Kelly glanced around. "I'd say we should stay close by the wreck. There's wind shelter here, and we won't have to move our gear—the water, the air recycler, the food boxes. Matt, you got that fire out?"

"Yeah. No toxic leaks, no fuel spill—we're pretty safe here."

Mel nodded. "So we set up the shelters here. I'll lead one party— Venus, will you take the other?"

"Sure."

The rule on the ground, as in space, was always safety through redundancy. So though just one of the big fold-out shelters the shuttle carried would have been more than big enough for the pitiful handful of "survivors" of this simulated crash, they dutifully laid out two, side by side in the faked wreckage, and pulled pins to let their struts inflate, forming roomy, angular domes. The shelters were bright orange, like their pressure suits, and were made of tough Kevlar surrounding an airtight inner hull. The shelters were soon hooked up to power units, air scrubbers and water recyclers, all retrieved from the crash and checked over for damage.

Mel decreed that pitons needed to be driven into the stony ground and guy ropes attached against the threat of wind, but the mocked-up radiation and ultraviolet readings his sensors supplied indicated they didn't need any more in the way of radiation shielding, such as a layer of dirt over the fabric hulls. And he decided that for the sake of morale the shelters would be physically joined, with single-thickness zip-up panels leading to a connecting airlock between them.

With the crash site safed and the shelters secured, the crew clambered inside, crawling in with parcels of food and spare clothing. Don joined them, strictly breaking the rules of the sim. The two couples, Mel and Holle, Don and Kelly, took Alpha, as Mel had called his dome. Meanwhile Zane, Venus, Susan and Matt took Beta. Because of Zane's fake leg break he had to be manhandled through the airlock into the shelter.

Holle and Mel crawled around their shelter gleefully, soon losing track of Kelly and Don. The interior was big, roomy, a masterpiece of fold-out architecture, with inflatable panels dividing the shelter up into wedge-shaped sectors, and a central pillar where they could set up a shower room and galley and do some science, investigating the planetary environment within which they were going to have to spend their lives.

But all that could wait. Almost at random Holle and Mel settled on a wedge sector to serve as their own. The sloping roof was just high enough, at the center, to stand. The light came from thick double-paned windows, and a wall panel that glowed brightly.

They threw their bundles of blankets and clothing on the floor and faced each other. With a rasp of Velcro Mel pushed back his hood, pulled his goggles away from his eyes, leaving red panda rims, and pulled his mask away from his mouth; it came off his skin with a sucking sound. He ran his hand over his close-shaved scalp. "Thank Christ for that."

"You stink."

"And you do a great slow strip out of an envo-suit."

"You pervert." She grabbed his chest panel and pulled; it came away easily, and then she pushed up his vest.

He went to work on her, unzipping zips and opening buckles and clasps and ripping Velcro seals. They were trained to get out of their suits fast, if need be, and were naked in seconds. He was already hard when he reached for her, and she squealed and jumped up at him. It took one lunge for him to be inside her, and then she had her arms around his neck, his strong hands under her thighs, and he walked, flexing his feet, letting gravity draw them together. Then, their lips locked, they fell together to the floor.

As with so many other aspects of their lives, they had practiced their lovemaking assiduously, and they were proficient.

Though she had known Mel since they had both been thirteen, when he and Matt Weiss had been foisted on the Candidate group by Gordo Alonzo, it was only recently, the last few months, that they had hooked up together. Holle still wasn't sure why it was Mel who had emerged as her partner, out of the swirl of brief, intense relationships that had swept through the Candidate group like a firestorm when they were fifteen, sixteen, seventeen. Their relationship had never been obvious, the way Thomas and Elle had been obvious since they were kids, or Mike Wetherbee and Miriam Brownlee, thrown together through their work. And Holle wasn't a voracious sampler like Cora Robles who, starting with poor, hapless, loyal Joe Antoniadi, had worked her way through most of the unattached men in the cadre. Holle had even had a brief experimental fling with Kelly Kenzie, when they found themselves isolated together on one desert-training exercise on the Uncompahgre Plateau—they'd both enjoyed it, but decided once was enough. Maybe it was because Mel had come from outside, having spent his first dozen years with his air force family in an environment quite unlike the one in which Holle had grown up since the age of six. Maybe something in her longed to be grounded— ironic for a woman who was likely to spend most of her life drifting among the stars.

They lay together under a heap of blankets, and drank a little fruit juice.

And then they began again. This time Holle worked her way on top. She'd discovered a variant of the on-all-fours back-flexing yoga exercise called "cat" that drove him crazy.

Then they pulled on fresh AxysCorp coveralls, grabbed some food packets, and went to find the others.

As Holle had expected Kelly and Don were waiting for them at the transparent airlock, the narrow neck that connected the two shelters. Zane and Venus were there in Beta on the far side, easily visible through the lock's faintly misty transparent panels. Zane was on a low fold-out chair with his "injured" leg thrust out before him; he was sharing a pack of hot food with Venus. There was no sign of Matt or Susan.

It was obvious that Kelly and Don had been making good of their opportunity just as had Holle and Mel. They sat huddled together, wrapped in blankets, sharing sips from a plastic flask. Kelly raised the flask to Holle. "Malt whiskey. Smuggled it in inside my suit." Her blond hair was loose, and falling down her neck. Her eyes were sleepy, a half-smile on her lips, and the curve of her bare back showed where the blanket had fallen forward.

Holle smiled at her. "That's what I call your just-fucked look."

"Well, you should know."

Zane and Venus worked doggedly at their food, their eyes lowered, and Holle regretted her remark.

Whenever sex came up among the Candidates, Zane and Venus and Matt always held back, or got out of the way altogether. None of them had been known to have a relationship with anybody in the Academy. Holle had had a whispered conversation about this with Kelly one night. Zane and Venus were both close to Harry Smith. Maybe Matt too. Kelly said bluntly that she thought Harry was running some kind of harem, of both men and women. Holle suspected she might be right. But none of the "harem" were talking. It was up to them to fight their own battles.

Mel asked, "So where's Matt and Susan?"

"Matt's off by himself," Venus said. "Working, I think."

Kelly frowned. "He spends too much time alone. He'll be marked down for that." On the crowded Ark, it mightn't be possible to go off in isolation; you were supposed to socialize.

"And Susan's gone out," Zane said bluntly, around a mouthful of food.

"Out where? Oh, shit," Don said. "Not to meet Pablo?" Pablo was a kid, a bit younger than Susan, from one of the big IDP camps near Denver. "She should keep away from eye-dees like him."

Kelly reached out of her blanket and slapped his beefy arm. "Stop using that disgusting word."

"Well, President Peery uses it," said Venus, her eyes on Don, provocative. "All your DPD buddies use it—don't they, Don?"

"What if they do? Just a word."

"You still hanging around with those Covenanters?"

Don snapped, "That's my business."

The Covenanters were a quasi-religious network with a philosophy that justified personal survival. This had come out of the circles of the superrich, safe in their fortress-like gated communities and their vast oceangoing craft. In contrast to his predecessor President Peery endorsed their creed, and was plugging it in his speeches, as a justification for his regime's treatment of refugees. Holle's father said that he believed people were reaching for theological justifications for the cruelty they were forced to inflict by circumstance, and that was what Peery was providing. It might be a comfort for somebody like Don.

But Venus said, "Everything the Covenanters say disgusts me."

Don took a slug of the liquor, unperturbed. "Everything *you've* heard, maybe. You want to come along on a patrol some time?"

"Can it," Zane said sharply. "We're going to be too busy to squabble. We just got sent an exercise for tomorrow." He had a laptop at his feet. "I'll send the details to your machines."

Mel groaned. "What exercise?"

"They're making us go through a root-and-branch review of the

launch system, the Orion stage. The engineering decisions made so far.
We have to come back with a retrospective report on everything: the
use of polyethylene versus aluminum to line the pusher plate, the two-
stage shock absorber system, the nonlinear instabilities you get when the
plasma flow from one nuclear blast mixes with the turbulent ablation
products left over from the previous blast, how we can cut down the AI
systems to fit the capacity of the mil-spec radiation-hardened chips we'll
have to use . . ."

Kelly frowned. "What's that got to do with the sim? The Orion will
have been discarded light-years back by the time we get to Earth II."

"Yes. But there will be science to be done on Earth II, from the moment we land. The science of how to stay alive, to begin with. I think
they wanted to set us some useful academic work to do in these conditions—hard thinking, in surface suits. Oh, and they gave us a swing. An
hour per day for each of us, mandatory, in our envo-suits."

More groans. But a swing, no more elaborate than a child's garden toy,
had been found to be a good sim of the crew's experience of the Orion
in flight, with a surge in acceleration of a few gravities coming every few
seconds as each bomb went off under the pusher plate—surge, float, surge,
float, just like riding through the bottom of a swing's arc.

Kelly quickly brought the conversation around to the topic that had
been dominating their small world since the social engineers had dropped
it on them: the issue of newly pregnant women being allowed into the
crew. In her competitive, logical way Kelly had done more hard thinking
on the topic than anybody else.

"You see how it affects us? Think of this. You go for it, you see the
launch day coming, so two, three months ahead you find some stud at
random and get yourself knocked up. You're increasing your chances, you
think. You'll be just ripe when the launch day comes, so you plan. *But
then there's a postponement.* Six months, say, nothing drastic. But that's the
end of you because when the Ark flies you will have a belly like a balloon,
or, worse yet, a kid in your arms. Wave bye bye, and book your swimming
lessons."

Venus said, "You're talking about giving birth. About the bond between mother and child. The most primal aspects of our humanity. How can you be so calculating?"

"Because that's the position the social engineers have put us in," Kelly said fiercely. "You have to take this seriously, because if you don't some hardheaded bitch out there is going to play the game better than you and steal your seat."

"Whatever the soc-eng people say, we don't have to dance to their tune—"

There was a scream.

Venus shut up immediately. It had been like a bird's call, muffled by the shelter's thick layers of fabric.

"Human," Don said.

"Susan," said Holle.

Don jumped to his feet, exposing his legs and backside. "Let's go."

Zane struggled with the inflated splint that encased his leg. "Wait—the sim protocols—"

Don had a gun in his hand. It must have been under the blanket. "Screw that." He ran to the wall and pulled a quick-release tag; the panel peeled away. Against a background of mountains and dull early evening sky, Holle saw people, and drifting smoke. Don rushed out, blanket clutched around his waist, gun held out before him.

26

The Candidates emerged from the shelters' linked orange bubbles, their blankets wrapped around them. None of them were armed, save Don.

Holle tried to take in the scene. Ragged people, a line of them, marched warily toward the shelters. They were armed, but as far as Holle could see only with torches, knives, what looked like machetes. They were all adults, but Holle couldn't tell their ages in the dim light. She wasn't even sure if they were men or women. She wondered how they had got past the Academy security cordon. It was obvious what they wanted. The Candidates had good-quality shelter, warm clothing and blankets, food, clean water—a mess of matériel that could transform the lives of these people.

At the center of the line was Susan. She had her jumpsuit pulled down to the waist, revealing her underwear, her white bra; they must have caught her with Pablo. She had her hands tied behind her back, and her head yanked back by a woman who had her hand wrapped in her hair. Susan seemed calm enough, uninjured.

Don stood with his gun held before him in both hands. His blanket had dropped, leaving him naked, his body pale. He said nothing. The others gathered behind him.

"I'm sorry," Susan called. "They followed me, and when I met Pablo they grabbed us both. I think he's OK—they hit him—"

"He's alive," said the woman holding her. She had a Californian accent. She sounded young, maybe no older than Susan herself. "We're not killers. We're just hungry."

"That's close enough," said Don.

They stopped. The woman stepped out from behind Susan, just a single pace. "We just want—"

Don fired.

The woman's head exploded, a crimson flower. She twitched, dropped. Her hand stayed clamped on Susan's hair, and Susan was dragged down on top of her, screaming. The other bandits stood in shock, for a heartbeat, two. In that time Don plugged his way along the line, one shot, two, three, a single round for each victim. They fell in the dirt, their blood bright. Before he got to the fourth the others had broken and were running. Don shot off a fourth round, a fifth, but they were soon out of range. Don started speaking to his bare wrist; he must have had an implant radio.

Holle was the first to break out of the shock. She ran to Susan. She was crying, and her right shoulder and breast were covered by streaked blood, and a paler fleshy material, and what looked like shards of bone. She was plucking ineffectually at her coverall. Holle helped her get her arms into the sleeves.

Kelly stood before Don, her blanket wrapped tightly around her body. "You killed them," she said. "Without hesitation."

"Fucking eye-dees," he said flatly. He was breathing hard, but was otherwise calm. Holle was astonished to see he had an erection.

Kelly stared at him, then, abruptly, she clutched her stomach and cried out. She doubled up, the blanket exposing her shoulders, her blond hair drifting over her face.

Venus hurried to her. "Kelly? Kelly, honey? What's wrong?"

Kelly shuddered and threw up, a thin bile spewing from her mouth in loopy strings. She looked up at Venus, and at Holle, and at Don, with his gun, naked. "Shit." She wiped her mouth with the back of her hand. "I think I'm pregnant."

27

When the Academy's final evacuation was called, the Candidates were told to assemble in the hollowed-out shell of the old museum's IMAX theater.

When she got to the theater Holle looked around frantically. The theater was in chaos, mobbed by cops and air force troopers and Homeland drones. The theater's terracing of seats was covered with people and their gear, hastily packed up. Mixed in with the drab military colors, the Candidates stood out, colorful as exotic birds.

She spotted Kelly standing close to the theater exit, bundles piled at her feet. Don Meisel was at her side in police body armor with a heavy automatic weapon cradled in his arms. Like Holle, Kelly wore a label on her chest numbered "B-6," the number of the armored bus they were supposed to take out of Denver. Kelly had her baby, Dexter, just two months old, in a bright red papoose on her chest. Kelly bounced the little boy, murmuring to him, while his father glared around, tense, nervous. Parenthood had made the two of them seem older than their age, just twenty-one.

Holle shoved her way through the crowd, her own pack on her back and with the last of Kelly's gear, baby clothes and diapers, in big canvas holdalls in her hands. When she got through she dropped the bags at Kelly's feet. Everybody seemed to be yelling, and she had to shout to make herself heard. "I think I got everything this time."

"Thanks, Holle, you're a true friend."

"It was hell getting through to here. Why did they switch the egress point to the IMAX?"

"No choice," Don said. "There's trouble at the main entrance. Too many people want a piece of you Candidates today. We couldn't guarantee your security. So it had to be this way."

That was not reassuring. The Academy was being cleared in the midst of the chaos of a city-wide evacuation. Mel was already gone, sent on ahead to the Candidates' new facility at Gunnison. She wished he was here, so they could support each other like Kelly and Don. "The sooner we're on that bus heading down the 285 the better."

"Rog that," said Don.

Kelly asked, "Have you heard any news about the warp test?"

"Not yet." Amid the chaos of the abandonment of Denver, Project Nimrod continued its own dogged course. Today was the scheduled date of an unmanned test of the warp bubble technology. A speck of antimatter had been tucked into the nose of an Ares stick, the intention being to create a bubble in Earth orbit. The bubble would fly off at superluminal speeds, but not before being sighted by observers on the ground and by spaceborne instruments. A corner of Holle's mind fretted over that crucial milestone, even if it was just a distraction from more immediate problems.

Edward Kenzie and Patrick Groundwater came bustling up. They both wore AxysCorp coveralls emblazoned with bus numbers, "B-6," the same number as Kelly and Holle. "Thank God." Patrick grabbed Holle's arms and kissed her. She thought he looked more strained, more tired, grayer every time they got together. "Are you OK?"

"I'm fine. It's just, it's a workday and you're not in a suit." She forced a laugh. "It makes everything seem real."

"Oh, it's real, all right," Edward Kenzie growled. "And getting more real every damn second." He was plump, determined, and angry, Holle thought, angry at the encroaching flood, or angry at the swarming crowds who were causing such peril to his daughter and grandson, and his project. He was listening to an earpiece. "They're loading our bus. The National Guard have kept this doorway clear. But they lost control of the main entrance and there's some kind of pitched battle going on around the old school group entrance. You wouldn't believe it, that it's come to this."

"That's the flood for you," Patrick said. "It reaches us all, in the end."

The exit door was opening at last. It was a big heavy security gate that had replaced the old theater entrance. They picked up their gear and formed a shuffling line. Holle saw a glimmer of daylight for the first time that morning, and heard shouting.

She turned for one last glance back at the theater. A forest of cables and pulleys hung from the ceiling, from which the Candidates had been suspended during zero-gravity sims, assembling spacecraft components and squirting themselves this way and that with reaction pistols. She remembered how they had swooped like birds, laughing, while their tutors had watched, smiling, earthbound. Now she was leaving this haven, and would never play such games again. She turned away and walked out into the daylight.

28

Out in the open air the sky was clear, blue as a bird's egg; it was a beautiful Colorado fall morning of the kind the old-timers said you rarely saw any more. To the west the Rockies rose, serene as always, grand above the human fray. But Holle was shocked at the barrage of noise, and an overpowering stink of burning.

There were people everywhere, confronting lines of cops and National Guard troopers. The crowd was surging around the main entrance on Colorado Boulevard. The intention was to take the Candidates south down Colorado, and she could see that the roadway was being kept clear, a corridor of fencing and barbed wire manned by troopers stationed every few meters. The buses were lined up waiting for them, fat with armor, their windows sealed up with bulletproof plate, weapons bristling from gun ports. There was her own bus with B-6 clumsily marked on its unpainted flank.

The Candidates were smuggled through a wire tunnel toward the junction of Colorado with 17th Avenue, and the buses. And suddenly, beyond the fence, just a meter from Holle's face, were hostiles, as Don called them, mostly young men, but older folk and women and children too. Some, crushed by the great weight of the people behind them, were pressed up against the wire so hard the diamond mesh pushed into the flesh of their hands and faces. When the Candidates were recognized there was a kind of howl. The mob pressed harder, and the fence actually swayed. Troopers fired warning shots in the air.

Kelly flinched. "Jesus."

"Just keep moving," Don murmured, his automatic rifle ready in his hands.

Edward Kenzie grunted. "Strategic errors. You're too close to the City Park and its eye-dee camps. And we should have got you guys out of here long before evacuation day."

"But they're not all eye-dees," Holle said. "Look, that guy is in a cop uniform."

"It's all breaking down," Don said bleakly. "There just isn't room for everybody in the big new fortified camps in the Rockies. Even if you were a federal worker or a cop or a doctor or a lawyer yesterday, if you lost out in the block ballots you're on that side of the fence now, suddenly you're an eye-dee, just as worthless as the rest."

Holle knew the basic plan, the city's response to the final crisis. Although the experts said it might be another year yet before the waters actually lapped over the steps of the Capitol and the famous "mile-high" engraving, Holle had heard that from downtown skyscrapers you could already look out over the city, and see the bare peaks of the Rockies Front Range to the west, and to the east a shimmer of blue-gray, the ocean that had drowned America. And as the eastern states collapsed, Denver, the largest city for a thousand kilometers and the home of the federal government for nearly twenty years, had become a sinkhole for refugees. Holle had seen satellite images of the great transportation routes turned to muddy brown threads by the unending columns, each pixel a human being, adults laden with children and old folk and pulling carts and barrows.

President Peery and his administration had fled already, nobody was sure where to—perhaps to the great Cold War bunker buried deep inside Cheyenne Mountain. The bulk of the urban citizens, those selected by the lotteries and who had chosen to go, were being shepherded west to new fastnesses in the Rockies, cities of tents and plastic panels thrown up on the remaining high ground. The main official evacuation route ran from the south of here, along Sixth Avenue which then became US 6, and from there along the 470 beltway to the I-70 and west. Holle and the rest of the Project Nimrod people, however, were being sent south of here, down Colorado Boulevard through Glendale to Englewood, and then they would take the I-285 toward the southwest, where some would be siphoned off to the Mission Control complex at Alma or the launch center at Gunnison. Both of these centers had been well provisioned and fortified.

This was the best the government could do in this final emergency, as its very capital was overrun, and its control over the people and their resources began to dissolve. This was the plan.

But right now Holle still hadn't got on the bus.

"See that pillar of smoke over there?" Kenzie said harshly. "The State Capitol building burning to the ground. These people make me sick. They should be building fucking rafts. Not taking it out on the cops or smashing stuff up or screaming at a bunch of kids."

Kelly's baby started crying.

And the fence collapsed.

Holle saw the glint of wire-cutters. The great press of people did the rest. Hundreds of ragged bodies spilled forward onto the ground. The troopers, reacting to bellowed commands, stepped back, firing into the swarming mass. Blood splashed and there were more screams. But the danger came not from the initial heaping of fallen people but from those who followed, who stayed on their feet and stepped over the bodies, armed with knives, clubs and machetes.

Holle saw all this in a few blurred seconds. She stood in shock, still clutching her pack.

Then there was a crush from behind as the bus passengers closed up, driven by Don and the other military. "Get on the buses! On the buses!

Drop all your shit, just get on the buses!" Holle fought to stay on her feet, to move forward. Her pack was ripped off her back in the crush. She didn't know where her father was.

The eye-dees closed in. Now Candidates were fighting, using fists and feet. She saw Wilson Argent in his bright costume driving his fist into the face of an eye-dee who was trying to haul him out of the line.

But she was close to the buses now. The first bus was actually moving off, its doors and windows sealed up, driving purposefully with people clinging to its doors and its armored roof. She was only a couple of meters away from B-6, but a mass of people were still in her way.

"Holle! Here!" It was her father. Over the heads of the struggling crowd she saw that he had got to the bus. He was clinging to a rail with one hand, and was reaching out to her with the other. "Holle! Grab my hand! Come on—"

Holle launched herself through the crowd, struggling and pushing. If she could just get to her father she could yet be safe. She reached out. His hand was half a meter away.

Kelly screamed, somewhere to her left. "Get off me!" A couple of eye-dees had hold of her. She swung her fist, but, clutching her baby in his papoose, there was little she could do.

Holle didn't even think about it. She hurled herself into the struggling mob. Sheer momentum carried her past Kelly, who broke free. Holle landed one satisfying fist in the face of an eye-dee—a middle-aged man, she saw, his face bloodied, dirt-streaked yet neatly shaven, a bewildering detail.

But he didn't fall. He grabbed her by her shoulders and hauled her bodily out of the melee. Now more hands grabbed her arms, legs, somebody even got a handful of her short hair, and she was hauled away into a crush of squirming bodies and legs. She was being carried away from the bus, from her father. Panicking, she struggled. She was kicked and punched. Nobody reacted when she screamed, because everybody else in the world was screaming.

Then she was dumped on the ground, still surrounded by the mob. A face loomed over her, a man's face, neatly shaven. The man she had first attacked. "I'm sorry!" he yelled down at her. "Sorry! It's for my daughter. Try to understand . . ."

She felt hands at her neck, her waist, her clothes being pulled from her. A blinding pain erupted in her head.

29

"You might want to put those on."

A breeze on her face. Something hard, lumpy under her back. Fragmentary impressions. She felt water trickling into her lips, stale, sour. Was somebody fooling around, Wilson or Kelly maybe?

But she wasn't in the dorm. She shook her head, trying to get away from the trickle of water, and moaned. Her head *hurt*.

She opened her eyes. She saw a slab of blue sky, between the walls of two tall buildings. The water hitting her face came from some overflow pipe, high on the wall above her.

Disgusted, she rolled over. Every movement set blinding lights flashing in her eyes. She was sitting in the dirt, on flagstones. And she was stripped to her underwear. "Shit." She closed her arms over her chest and crotch.

"I said, you might want to put those on."

She turned around. Somebody sat in the shade, leaning against one wall. He had bare feet, ragged jeans, a jacket with a logo faded almost to invisibility. His hair was a black mop, and he had a wisp of beard. He couldn't have been more than seventeen, eighteen. He was staring at her chest.

"Quit looking at me."

"Well, you're the one with her boobies out. I say again, you ought to put those on." He was a Latino, she thought, his voice lightly accented.

She looked, and found a heap of filthy clothes beside her, a kind of coverall, an undershirt. They stank. "These aren't mine."

"I know. The guy dumped you here, he left them. Said they were his daughter's. Said you'd understand."

She stared at him. "Where are my clothes?"

"He took 'em. Guy with the daughter. Fancy red and blue gear, right? I thought I knew your face. You're a Candidate. What's it like to be famous?"

She heard shouting, whistles blowing, a crackle of radios somewhere nearby. Dogs barked. She stared at the garbage clothes, uncomprehending. "This guy—this man. What was he trying to do, make out his daughter is a Candidate? Who did he think that was going to fool? We know each other. Our families, our tutors—*you* know us."

"That's true, but it's a kind of mixed-up day, don't you think? Lot of people going to end up in the wrong place today. Can't blame a man for trying. And he didn't do you much harm. Left you your boots."

So he had, she saw; her blue plastic boots were still on her feet, below bare legs.

"Course," said the Latino kid, "I left you your boots too. Mind, blue ain't my color." He cackled another laugh, and she saw his teeth had great gaps. "You put your clothes on now."

"These aren't mine."

"Well, you can tell that to the sweep when it comes, can't you? They come block by block." He got to his feet stiffly, wiping his nose on the back of his hand.

"What sweep? Where am I?"

"Corner of Garfield and East Colfax."

Only a couple of blocks from the City Park, where the museum was. She got to her feet, ignoring the banging in her head. She could hear the whistles, the dogs coming closer. If she could talk to the cops maybe she could get some kind of escort back to her people, and this nightmare would be over.

The kid was staring at her again. She couldn't stand here in her bra and pants. She grabbed the filthy, ragged clothes and pulled them on. She snapped, "I'm going to star in some kind of porn movie in your head tonight, aren't I?"

He shrugged. "Could have taken your boots. You were out cold. Could have hurt you. You could have done a lot worse than have me find you." The whistles and barking grew louder. He turned to face the north end of the street. "Coming that way, I reckon. Listen. Tell them you know how to mix concrete."

"Tell them *what?*"

"Just remember. Woah, here's the man."

A squad of military types, National Guard maybe, came marching around the corner from the north end of the block. They wore body armor and helmets that hid their faces. To Holle's disbelief they carried a net, like a fishing net, stretched out on two poles, extended across the width of the block. Engines growled behind her, and when she turned she saw a lorry, a big farm wagon, pulled up at the south end of the block. More troopers jumped down and lined up in front of the truck. They carried nightsticks and wielded handguns, and they had dogs that barked and snapped.

Now the units from the north end began to work their way down the block. Only Holle and the kid stood here in the street, but troopers broke down the doors of the properties to either side, yelling orders that any-one inside had to come out. Holle heard shouted protests, the yap of dogs, the crack of weapons—even a dull crump that must be a grenade.

People came trickling out of the houses, some ragged eye-dee types who must be squatters, but others who looked like regular residents, old folk, a young couple with a kid of about ten. Some had belongings, oth-ers came out empty-handed, bewildered. There weren't many, maybe twenty. Holle guessed that most had gone already, trying to join the of-ficial exodus west.

A family had to be dragged out of one house. A girl, just a teenager, was hanging onto her dog, a ragged mongrel. Pets weren't allowed on the evacuation marches. Maybe that was why this family had refused to leave. Eventually a trooper got hold of the dog and threw it against the wall. The girl's father held the girl back as she raged and wept.

And that net swept on down the street, step by step, inexorable as the flood itself, driving them all forward toward the waiting truck.

Holle pushed through the sullen civilians toward the net. None of the troopers looked like an officer. She couldn't see their faces, their eyes behind their faceplates. "Hey! Can you help me? I shouldn't be here."

There was a rumble of laughter. The troopers didn't break their step, and she had to back up.

"None of us should be here, lady. What you gonna do?"

"I'm a Candidate."

"Yeah, you look like it."

"I should be on the buses to Gunnison. Maybe there's still time. I'm Holle Groundwater. My father's Patrick Groundwater, who—"

"Yeah, and I'm Kelly Kenzie's left tit. Just get in the damn truck with everybody else."

Holle glanced around. She saw that the people driven out of their homes were clambering meekly onto the bed of the waiting truck. This couldn't be happening. To these other people, yes. Not to *her*. "I'm a Candidate! Oh, listen to me, you fools—"

A nightstick came out of nowhere, wielded in a gloved hand, and slapped across Holle's face. She was thrown to the ground. Maybe for a second she lost consciousness again. The line closed on her, the heavy net dragging across the ground. She tried to move, couldn't. She got a kick in the chest that knocked her back out of the way, rolling like a rotten log.

Somebody was pulling at her. "Come on. Up you get. That's it . . ."

Leaning on the stranger's arm, she got to her feet, and managed to stagger away from the advancing line, one meter, two. But now she was nearly at the truck.

"Are you all right, dear?" The person who had helped her up was a woman, maybe sixty, solid, her hair a mass of gray. She was wrapped in a heavy coat and had a backpack on her back and sturdy shoes on her feet. She, at least, had been prepared for the day.

Holle said, "All right? I—"

"I know. None of us are all right today, are we? And now it's come to this." The woman climbed up a short stepladder onto the truck bed. She reached down and helped Holle up in turn. "I lived here with my husband, even before the flood, you know. It was our first home but we never thought we'd stay here. A nicer place in the suburbs, when we could afford it. That was the plan. Well, that never came about, did it? But I don't complain, and nor did Herb before the consumption carried him off in '35. We've had it better than many in this suffering world, haven't we?"

More civilians clambered aboard, and the troopers closed up the truck. Holle looked around for the Latino boy. He was still in the street, surrounded by troopers. She called, "What are you doing?"

He shrugged and took a step. His leg was withered and he limped heavily. "Can't walk, can't work. Never could. Special Processing for me. Just remember what I told you."

The truck's engine coughed to life, and it rolled away with a jerk. Looking back, Holle saw the troops were preparing to repeat the sweep operation in the next block, with their net and their dogs and another empty truck. And the Latino boy was being led away, into the shadows.

Standing with the others in the back of the swaying truck, the weak stink of biofuel exhaust filling her head, Holle was driven, not south and west to the I-285 and Gunnison, but the other way, east along East Colfax and then north along Quebec Street, toward the I-70, the main route from the east. After a few blocks they merged into a larger convoy, trucks mostly carrying civilians but a few laden with troops and other gear.

Everywhere Holle saw troops in action, National Guard and army and Homeland and police, shepherding orderly streams of civilians west, or rounding up more discards like her own companions, and engaging pockets of resistance in firefights. In one place she saw snowplows, brought down from mountain roads where snow no longer fell, driving people along urban streets. And in abandoned districts she saw fires being set, mines laid. In Sandown, near the rail track, she saw the blunt profile of a tank.

Mary Green, the older woman who'd helped her, thought she knew what the government planned. "They've abandoned Denver now, and everybody's gone west, and the city's only remaining use is to block those refugee streams from the east, who will otherwise chase after us and overwhelm everything, like locusts."

"So they're setting mines? Killing people?"

"Well, they shouldn't be here, should they?" Mrs. Green said reasonably. "This isn't their place, wherever they came from; it never was. We wouldn't have to move, not for months yet, if not for all this. No, they should have stayed home and built rafts."

"Where are we going?"

"I think we'll soon find out, dear."

The truck reached a slip road for the I-70 and turned, heading east. There was some military traffic on the one lane kept open. On the other lanes more flows of walkers headed steadily west, supervised by troops and cops in cars and trucks.

They reached the intersection of the I-70 with the 470, Denver's patchwork beltway. But the intersection had been dynamited, the flyovers collapsed, the roadways blocked with rubble. A wire fence with gun towers was strung north and south along the length of the 470, along which no traffic moved. Beyond the fence Holle saw more strings of barbed wire, and moving figures silhouetted against the eastern sky, and she heard distant shouting.

The trucks stopped, and they were made to climb down.

"Help me, dear, I'm stiff after standing all that way."

The people from the trucks were formed up into a line, and were shepherded toward a kind of stockade, constructed of girders and concrete panels, thrown across the highway. It was almost like a toll gate.

Holle saw that after a quick assessment they were being sorted into four lines. The people walked forward meekly, submitting to the verdict passed on them.

Holle and Mary Green lined up with the rest. "Why didn't you go west with the others, Mrs. Green?"

"We all have our part to play. Didn't you hear the President's last speech? You have to walk, you know, walk all the way to the Rockies. Then you have to help build new cities and so forth. There's no way I can do that, not at my age. But I couldn't sit at home either, could I? So here I am, doing what I can to protect the others. The President has promised to help us once the crisis has passed."

"Protect others? How?"

"There's more than one way to fight a war." Mary Green eyed her, the dust from the road clinging to a face coated with anti-sun cream, and her voice became stern. "You don't know anything about this, do you? Maybe you really are a Candidate. I've always thought they weren't teaching those Candidates anything worthwhile. I don't know what they have planned for you, nobody does. But what's the point of surviving if you don't know anything about what matters?"

They neared the desks. Listening in to the brief interviews Holle got a sense of what was happening. Each person was grilled by a police officer, and what sounded like a doctor. Your name was taken, your skills assessed, your basic health checked over quickly. There was no screening for bio, retinal or other idents. If you had papers of any kind you showed them. The very old, the very young, the disabled were taken off down one stream, to a set of huts by the roadside. Special Processing, maybe. The relatively young and healthy were sorted into two groups. One set were taken away to a kind of compound, where Holle could see they were being handed weapons—just clubs, pikes and knives, no guns—and put through rudimentary fight training. The others were led away down the blocked highway, toward the improvised fortifications. A construction crew?

Mrs. Green went ahead of Holle, and was judged to be too old for

building or fighting. So she was assigned to the fourth stream—the
"Honor Corps," the police officer called it. She was given a badge to wear.
She smiled back at Holle. "Look at that, my own little badge. It's even got
a Stars and Stripes on it."

"Be careful, Mrs. Green."

"I think it's too late for that, dear. Good luck."

Holle stepped up to the desk. The police officer eyed her. Aged maybe
forty, he had a livid scar on one cheek. He wore a uniform but had no
badge, no identification. "Name?"

"Holle Groundwater."

He just laughed. "Fourth today. You have papers?"

"No."

"Step over for your medical."

She considered resisting, demanding her rights. She was surrounded
by people with guns and nightsticks. She stepped a meter to the left,
where the woman who looked like a doctor, no older than thirty, smiled
at her. She rolled back Holle's sleeve, took her pulse and blood pressure
and a pinprick blood sample, and made her blow into a bag.

The cop kept talking. "I guess you're going to tell me you got left
behind while all your buddies flew off in Air Force One, right?"

Holle thought it over. "No."

"Then what do you do?"

"I mix concrete."

"Really?" He laughed, then looked at her more soberly. "Where did
you work?"

"Last, on the ramparts around the Academy. I mean, the Museum of
Nature and Science. In the park, you know?" She forced a grin. "I saw
the Candidates every day. Stuck-up assholes. Can't blame me for trying."

"OK." He made a tentative tick in a box on his list. "You going to tell
me your real name now?"

"Maybe not. There are people I'd rather didn't know I was here."

He made another tick. "OK, Jane Doe, that's up to you. Line three,
behind me."

She saw with relief that that was the line she'd tentatively pegged as the construction workers. Most of those here were young men. Some even carried hard hats and sets of tools. She got a few sideways glances, but nobody called her back. She guessed she wasn't the only bogus laborer or bricklayer or electrician in this line.

She shuffled forward with the rest.

30

The construction gang was marched away from the junction and moved down the line of the 470, maybe half a kilometer to the south.

Holle caught glimpses of the tangle of fortifications that lay beyond the perimeter of the road, further east. A swathe of properties had been demolished or bulldozed, leaving a scar a hundred meters wide in the landscape. This open ground was populated by rows of barbed-wire fencing and big concrete blocks, each of them as tall as she was, set out in rough lines like tank traps. There were people everywhere, some in uniform, standing or sitting in silent blocks, or marching purposefully. The most impressive single fortification was a ditch big enough to contain whole digging machines, with a sharp slope on the near side and a shallower slope on the other. Groups of machine-gunners and snipers had been drawn up on the lip of the ditch. She saw the idea; coming from the east you'd tumble in easily enough, and would be exposed to the guns all the way down the slope, but you would have a tough time climbing out up that sharp western slope, into the teeth of the guns. It was like an earthwork out of the Iron Age.

Then they came to a slight rise, and Holle was able to see further to the east, along the line of the old I-70 and beyond the limit of the fortifications. As far as she could see the road was full of people, gray with them, a river of humanity pouring along the highway toward Denver, spilling onto the verges and crowding under the battered road signs. This was the invading army all these defenses were intended to repel. She heard the distant pop of rifles, a crump of grenades.

"So you're the concrete mixer," a man said, behind her. "I was after you in the line."

She turned. He wore a patched AxysCorp coverall; he was aged perhaps fifty, but looked strong, like a farmer, with big, dirt-encrusted hands. She said defiantly, "So what, are you going to turn me in?"

"Not me. I don't know much about construction." He looked at his big hands. "But I used to run a smallholding, on the east bank of Back Squirrel Creek. I can use my hands. I can dig a ditch or lay a fence, I think. Anyhow sooner here than in the combat units, or the Honor Corps."

"What is the Honor Corps?"

"Look." He pointed to blocks of people sitting passively just behind the fortifications on the highway surface. "If they get through the fence our eye-dee friends are going to have to fight their way through that. Could you take a machete to a disabled boy in his wheelchair? It's a human shield, an old tactic perfected by Saddam Hussein—well, I suppose you've never heard of him."

"Never work," somebody said, a burly man in a hard hat. "If those eye-dees have fought their way through the National Guard they'll not stop for that."

"But they aren't monsters," the smallholder said gently. "They are like us. They're Americans."

"Tell you what I'd do. Grab those guys in front, give them a gun, and turn them around the other way. That would work, let them grind each other down. Eye-dee bastards . . ."

"Looks like I found you just in time."

Holle whirled. Kelly was standing right behind her, in a drab olive green coverall, a rifle in her hand and a phone clamped to her ear. Holle felt a peculiar mixture, of intense emotions and yet a kind of disappointment. She was aware of how the smallholder pulled away, watching her. She hugged Kelly. "You came for me."

"Well, you did bring me those bags of diapers," Kelly said. "Come on, Mel is waiting in a jeep back beyond those processing desks. We can catch up to the buses but we'll have to cut across country."

They hurried away, back down the line. Kelly had a pass she kept flashing at the supervising soldiers and cops. Holle glanced back, looking for the smallholder, and for Mrs. Green in the shield units, but she couldn't see them. It was hard to believe how lost she had felt just seconds ago.

"How did you find me?"

"Not easily," Kelly shouted. "You'd be surprised how many Holle Groundwaters passed through here today. But you made the right choice, to bullshit your way into the construction corps. If you'd been sent out to the front, out to the fucking First World War they're mounting out there, I couldn't have got to you. I'd like to have seen you try to mix concrete, though. Hah! Listen, by the way. It worked."

"What did?"

"The warp test. We saw it. Or rather Venus and the planet-finders in Alma did. The optical distortion—the gravitational lensing as it went past the face of the moon—it was unmistakable. They sent a feed to the buses."

"My God." Holle looked up to the sky, trying to imagine the relativistic miracle that had come to pass far above her head, all on the same day as the urban horrors she had gone through. It didn't seem to fit, as if it wasn't possible for both these things to be true. One must be false, or the other.

Automatic fire clattered. Kelly dragged her down. Holle fell heavily, old bruises aching.

And a bomb went off, the detonation massive, overwhelming. The ground shook and hot air washed over them. Holle found herself covered in dust, with her ears full of a close ringing noise.

Kelly stirred, and helped Holle get to her feet.

Not everybody had reacted as quickly as Kelly. All around them people had been thrown to the ground. Their mouths moved, but Holle couldn't hear their voices.

She was distracted by a metallic glinting, off to her right, out along the line of the highway to the east. The attack on the junction seemed to have been the signal for the eye-dee army to mount an advance. They cut their way through the lines of the city's conscript army, a gray swarm washing through the brown lines, marked by a sparkle of knives and machetes rising and falling in the morning sun, and rising puffs of smoke from the guns.

Kelly was tugging her sleeve, shouting in her face to get her attention. Kelly's face was dust-coated, blood trickled from her mouth, and her hair was a tangle. Holle couldn't hear a word she said.

A wall of dust was scouring along the 470, away from the intersection where the bomb had exploded, driving people like cattle.

They turned and ran.

31

nside, the office block in Alma was corridors and offices and computer rooms, suffused by a hum of air-conditioning. It reminded Grace Gray of facilities aboard Lammockson's Ark Three, the bridge, the engine room, the ship she'd left only that morning, and would now never return to.

She and Holle Groundwater didn't meet anybody else until the corridor opened out into a glass-fronted room with banks of chairs, microphones, screens. Through the glass Grace saw a larger chamber, dug some way into the ground so that she was looking down on rows of people before consoles, where screens glowed brightly, text and images flowing. Before them the front wall was covered by two huge screens. One showed a map of the world—continents outlined in blue, surviving high ground glowing bright green—with pathways traced over it. On the second screen concentric circles surrounded a glowing pinpoint, each circle labeled with a disc. Gary's amateur education program had always heavily favored science. Grace understood that she was looking at a map of the solar system.

Holle was watching her curiously. Grace felt utterly out of place in this technological cave, still in the clothes she had put on that morning on Ark Three, with her pitiful collection of belongings lost forever.

"This is at the heart of what we do," Holle said.

"What is this place?"

"Mission Control. We're running a simulation right now—"

"And this?" Grace held up the key-ring globe Gordo had given her.

"Our spaceship." Holle smiled, a basic humanity shining through the competitiveness. "Come on. You look like you need a coffee. We'll talk about how Harry Smith got killed. And I'll tell you how we got started here."

The restaurant was square, basic, reminiscent of one of Ark Three's feeding stations. Holle went to fetch coffees, and Grace sat at a plastic-topped table and looked around. You helped yourself to food from big pots and trays, and drinks from dispensers. The food was piled high. The staple seemed to be some kind of chili, made of what looked like real meat, not the processed fish or seaweed Grace had been eating the last few years aboard Ark Three. The smell made her feel hungry, she hadn't eaten since being taken off Ark Three hours ago, hours that felt like days. And she had her old walker instinct that you should eat what you could, when you could. But her stomach was a knot, and she wondered if the food might be too rich for her.

The walls were bare, unpainted. Everything was functional, nothing decorative. One wall was dominated by a huge clock, counting down:

124 DAYS 6 HOURS 12 MINUTES 14 SECONDS
124 DAYS 6 HOURS 12 MINUTES 13 SECONDS
124 DAYS 6 HOURS 12 MINUTES 12 SECONDS

And there was that slogan again, that she'd seen over the external door:

Now nothing will be restrained from them, which they have imagined to do. Genesis 11:6.

Under the clock and slogan was a big animated map, showing the

North American archipelago. Grace had seen the same sort of display aboard Ark Three, though the ship's elderly processors had not been able to project an image of this quality. Sitting here in Colorado, she was in fact on the largest surviving contiguous island, dominated by the Rockies, with peninsulas extending into the old high ground of the neighboring states, Idaho and Wyoming to the north, Nevada, Arizona and New Mexico to the south and west.

On the ocean to the east, deceptively featureless on the restaurant map, the ship on which she had lived for six years of her life might be burning, sinking, the people she had lived with fighting and dying right now. She wasn't sure how she felt about that. It hadn't been her choice to be on the ship in the first place, any more than she'd chosen to leave it to come here today.

It was all irrelevant. Here was the flood, gathering around this last remnant of America. And here she was, with her baby growing inside her. It was as Gordo Alonzo had said. No matter how she had got here she had to consider her own survival, and her baby's.

Holle brought her coffee in a chipped mug. When Grace sipped the coffee it tasted richer than any she could remember.

"So I'm investigating a murder. Tell me who died," she said bluntly.

Holle leaned her elbows on the table, clasped her hands, and faced her frankly. "A man called Harry Smith. He was one of our tutors."

"What did he teach?"

"He had a general role. Personal development. He was a kind of overall guide."

"How did he die?"

"There was an accident at Gunnison. The launch center. A pulse unit test went wrong. There was an explosion."

Grace was going to have to find out what a "pulse unit" was. "So this Smith got killed in the blast? Why is it thought to be murder?"

"Because the unit was tampered with. The test was with conventional explosives, not nuclear. But the detonation products were supposed to be shaped as in a full-scale Orion pulse unit." She mimed a cylindrical form with her hands. "You get a concentration of vaporization products axially, which facilitates momentum transfer to the pusher plate—"

"Who figured out that this unit was tampered with?"

"Zane Glemp. He's one of us, one of the Candidates. He has special areas of study—well, we all do. We learn about aspects of the project's development, and monitor their progress. Zane's includes the pulse units."

"OK. So Smith was murdered. Who do you think might have killed him?"

Holle looked shocked. "Why would you ask me a question like that? A cop wouldn't."

"Well, I'm not a cop." Grace studied Holle. If she was going to survive here she was going to have to work with exotic, alien creatures like this child-woman, this Holle Groundwater. "Look, Holle. You've grown up living in a functioning nation, the United States, with a continuity of institutions and laws reaching back to the pre-flood days. For me it's been different. From the ages of five to twenty I lived in a migrant refugee community. Any law we had we worked out and applied ourselves. I'm not a cop, or a government worker. Gordo Alonzo wants me to solve this crime. Fine. But I don't have any procedures, or rules. I'll just get to the truth as fast as I can—or if I fail, I'll pass it back."

Holle nodded, interested. "I guess it makes sense in a way. On the Ark, we'll be a self-governing community. We'll have to work out our own ways to resolve issues like this. Maybe Gordo is using you as an example of how that might be done."

Grace felt faintly disgusted. "Somebody died. You're talking as if it is some kind of training exercise?"

Holle looked embarrassed, but then her natural defiance reasserted itself. "We've been training for this our whole lives, since I was six. How else do you expect me to react? Besides, you might find that some of us have got wider experience than you seem to think. And didn't Gordo set this up as a kind of selection exercise for *you*?"

"Maybe. But I haven't decided if I'm going to play his game. So can I ask my question again? Who do you think killed Harry Smith?"

"One of three people, all of them Candidates. Zane Glemp. Venus Jenning. Matt Weiss."

"I need something to make notes."

"I'll get you a handheld."

"You said this Zane discovered the pulse unit had been tampered with. But of course he could have been bluffing, he could have done it himself. What about the others?"

"They were all close to Harry. Closer than the rest of us."

"Close?" There was something odd in the way Holle said that, a subtext. "You mean sex?"

"I think so. I don't *know*."

"And all three are still up for crew selection?"

Holle shook her head. "Not Zane. He was scrubbed a month ago. You understand we're only a few months away from the launch target now. That's our latest revised target—we had a lot of slips—originally we should have flown last year. Anyhow things are getting hectic." Holle eyed Grace, sideways. "Suddenly lots of people are being nominated for the crew, some we've never heard of. Like you. But there are only eighty places. Every time somebody comes on board, somebody else has to go. Even us, the core group who have been training for this since we were children."

"That's tough."

"Of course it is. Even Kelly Kenzie washed out because she had a baby, even though she's kept up the training program for the sake of the rest of us . . . You'll meet her. The point is they're constantly reviewing us, looking for ways to wash us out. Zane went through a psych test and was told he wasn't emotionally stable enough. It was Harry's recommendation that did it, actually. Zane took it hard. His father was the main initiator of the whole program. But we had a disaster back in '36. Jerzy was injured; he was removed from the program and died a couple of years later. So you can see why this was tough for Zane, to be excluded from the final selection pool. He wanted to be part of his father's legacy."

"So this Zane could have had a motive. And the means, he worked on these pulse units."

"Yes, but so did Matt Weiss. Zane's more a specialist on the warp generator, actually. I'm sure Venus could have messed with the pulse unit trial if she'd wanted to, maybe with help. Any of us could; we're all familiar with the ship's systems. But we all have specialisms."

"So what's your specialism?"

"The ship's internal systems. Life support, the power supply. Plumbing," she said, with a self-deprecating grin. "Right now I'm working on the installation of HeadSpace booths. Virtual reality systems, donated by the corporation that manufactured them. The social engineers think they'll be a benefit in terms of morale, but they're demanding in terms of computer resources."

"And—what was the third name—Venus?"

"She's a planet-finder. Looking for our destination. But as I said, we all multitask. Any one of the three could have set the charge, I think."

"I'll need to speak to these three."

"Venus and Zane are here at Alma. Matt is over at Gunnison."

"I thought Zane was off the project."

"He's still working as part of the ground support team. That's what we do, how we are. Look, if you wait here, you can get more coffee or some food, I'll send Zane or Venus down. Then I'll organize a drive for you down to Gunnison, if you like."

"I appreciate your help."

Holle grinned. "If Gordo Alonzo is setting some kind of test for *me*, I'm determined to pass it." And she walked away, her colorful uniform bright, striding confidently.

32

lone, Grace got herself a fresh mug of coffee, and watched the oppressive wall clock.

124 DAYS 5 HOURS 55 MINUTES 1 SECOND
124 DAYS 5 HOURS 55 MINUTES 0 SECONDS
124 DAYS 5 HOURS 54 MINUTES 59 SECONDS

She was repelled by all she had seen so far of Project Nimrod. The huge engineering, the arrogant old men like Gordo Alonzo who appeared to run it, the spoiled children like Holle Groundwater who had grown up cosseted by it, while Grace and so many others had walked and worked, starved and drowned. Her instinct was still to walk away. But Ark One appeared to be the only show in town.

A girl walked into the restaurant, black, about the same age as Holle. Another Candidate, judging by her bright uniform. She walked up to Grace and dropped a handheld computer and a pen and pad of paper on the tabletop. "These are for you. I'm Venus Jenning. Holle said you wanted to see me. Is this about Harry?"

"I'm afraid so."

"You want another coffee?"

Grace shook her head. The girl walked over to the dispenser to help herself.

Grace inspected the handheld and the paper. The handheld was an antique, scuffed from years of use, and heavy, milspec maybe. The paper had a peculiar smooth sheen, and was stamped with the AxysCorp cradled-Earth logo. She knew this stuff; it had been manufactured from seashells on Ark Three.

She took the pen, and wrote down four names. *Harry Smith. Zane Glemp. Venus Jenning. Matt Weiss.*

Venus sat down. "I didn't kill him," she said bluntly. She faced Grace, making frank eye contact. She struck Grace as tough, clever, motivated, but reserved. "You got my name from Holle, did you?"

"I needed some kind of steer, to get started on this. You're all strangers to me, you Candidates and your teachers, this weird little family of yours. Don't blame Holle if she got it wrong."

"I don't blame Holle. You had to ask the question, she had to give you an answer. But she doesn't *know.* She only knows what she saw from the outside. I never spoke about it to her, or anybody else." She grimaced. "I was hoping the whole thing would die with Harry. Then when I found out it was murder, I realized it was all going to get opened up. So go ahead, ask me your questions."

"Did you have sex with him?"

"Yes, I had sex with him. Look, he was my tutor, he tutored all of us from when we joined the program. I joined at eleven, myself. I wasn't happy. I missed my family in Utah, my home. Everybody else had been in the program for years—Holle, Kelly Kenzie, people like that. I was an outsider."

"Harry comforted you."

"He counseled me. That was his job. That was all it was at first. I liked him and I trusted him. But it started to change, after a couple of years."

"Change how?"

"He started talking to me about how the final selection would be made. You know there are only eighty places available on the Ark. There have been far more than eighty of *us*. Every so often there would be a policy change, and a whole swathe of us would go.

"Harry talked to me about my color, my race. He said that the social engineers were concerned about ethnic divisions. He said they were considering restricting the crew to all-white. Harry said this policy was being pushed by some kind of white-supremacist cabal within the project organization, but it had logic behind it in terms of crew stability, and might carry the day. All this was confidential—he said. I had to keep it quiet. Well, you can see how that would affect my chances. But Harry said he would protect me."

"In return for sex."

"It wasn't as simple as that." Her face showed anger, irritation. "He was smart. I guess he'd played fish like me before. All he wanted in return, it seemed to me then, was respect. Loyalty. Affection. Love, if you want. Look, a good teacher can win all those things."

"So when did the sex start?"

"We were on a field trip at the Monarch Pass. I was fifteen then. It had been a bad day. Back then Utah and the Denver federal government were still fighting, sporadically. Utah had just mounted a raid in the north, and the talk was all of retaliating. Look, I was frightened for my family in Salt Lake City, they weren't Mormon but some of them were still in the war zone. And I was frightened for myself. It wasn't just a case of getting thrown off the program. I thought I might end up in internment, or a labor camp."

"So Harry came to you."

"I had a two-person tent. I shared with Cora Robles, but she was away on a night exercise. I was asleep. He unzipped my sleeping bag and got in behind me. You want the details?"

"I—"

"He made me masturbate him. I had to reach behind my back to do it." She shrugged. "That was it. I cleaned up after he left. I always thought Cora suspected something. Maybe she could smell him, I wouldn't be surprised. I couldn't wait to get to the shower the next day. I was shocked by the whole thing. Not so much by the sex itself, I was no virgin. Everything he had done for me was compromised."

"And it went on from there."

"I didn't see a choice. He did have real power over me. Frankly, I thought I was fighting for my life. And I didn't care about the sex. He just disgusted me. We never had full sex by the way, he never penetrated me. He liked to touch, and for me to use my hands or my mouth. I thought he preferred boys, if you want the truth. He was using me the way he might a boy. Maybe it was the power he got off on."

"So this went on until he died?"

"Hell, no. I guess it lasted a couple of years. Then I found out the truth about the social engineers' ethnic selection policy."

"Which is?"

"There isn't one. Their mantra is genetic diversity, in the first generation and afterward. They're more likely to select a rainbow-colored crew than a white one. I found out in fact that there was a lobby, not for a white crew, but for an entirely African-American crew, because diversity among Africans is greater than anywhere else; humanity came from Africa. So Harry lied all the way through.

"When I discovered that I kicked him in the balls, if you want to know." Her eyes were hard at the memory. "I was old enough by then to know that I had as much power over him as he did over me. To work on the project is a prized berth, even if you aren't a Candidate, and Harry didn't want to become an eye-dee. He liked his comforts, did Harry. But he was going to get no more comfort from me. In the end, you know, he cried, and not just from the ball-kicking. He asked me why I'd stopped loving him. Maybe he really believed I loved him. Or maybe he was lying to himself. I don't actually care what was going on in his head."

"Did you kill Harry Smith?"

"No," she said bluntly. "Why should I?"

"He abused you. He lied to you. He misused his power over you."

"Look, there are a lot of people with too much power in this world.

You must have seen that. Harry with his grubby, pathetic fumblings was no worse than many. I took control in the end. I didn't need to kill him. He was out of my life long before he died." She said this flatly, quite composed. "You can believe that or not. I couldn't prove any of it. Is there anything else you want to ask me?"

33

olle came to fetch Grace from the restaurant, and took her out of the building to where a small convoy of armored vehicles was waiting. "We do several runs a day between here and Gunnison. This is the next to go."

Here too was Zane Glemp, a little younger than Holle and Venus, thin, pale, intense under his shock of black hair. He wasn't in a Candidate uniform, and looked as if he wouldn't have been right in it anyhow. He was carrying a laptop computer. Holle had suggested he ride with Grace to Gunnison, where he had work to pursue, and talk to her on the way.

So Grace found herself sitting alone with Zane in a self-drive vehicle, with thick glass windows and a closed aircon system, sandwiched between two heavy-duty trucks, each of which bristled with weapons. The vehicles set off at a brisk speed, fast enough to push Grace back in her seat, and she grabbed at a rail.

Zane had been unfolding his laptop. "Are you OK?"

"I'm just not much used to speed. I spent most of my life walking, and the last six years on a cruise ship. A motor launch is about as much acceleration as I ever got used to."

He brought up a map on his laptop screen. "This is the way we're going." It was a drive of maybe a hundred and fifty kilometers through mountain country, south from the Hoosier Pass through Buena Vista and Poncha Springs, and then west through Monarch to Gunnison. "They're mountain roads but the military have strengthened them and put in barriers and they're pretty good. It's safer to get through the open country fast, but you do get thrown around. Here . . ." He showed her how to tighten her restraints.

"Why is it safer to go fast?"

For answer he pointed out of the window. Beyond the thick wire fence that lined the road, the country was littered with people, looking out of tents and shacks as the convoy went by. In some places they seemed to be trying to farm, with furrows scratched in the thin dirt, plots jealously guarded. Elsewhere they just sat silently by the road. Children watched blank-eyed as the vehicles passed.

"Sometimes they take potshots," Zane said. "Or they try to block the road. There's a system of watchtowers between Gunnison and Alma. If there's trouble, you get heavier units coming from either terminus, or from Twin Lakes or Monarch."

"It looks like it's been raining people."

"Well, Colorado's a big country, but we ran out of room a long time ago. The sea's not far from Gunnison itself, actually. When the wind is right you can smell it. The engineers worry about salt corrosion of the spacecraft and the gantries. But they had the same problem at Canaveral." Zane's face was oddly expressionless, as if he was not quite engaged with the world, with her. "You're here to ask me about Harry Smith."

"Yes." Zane was evidently a more complex personality than Holle or Venus. Grace tried to work out a way in. "He was killed by a pulse unit."

"A mock-up, yes."

"I'm new to all this. I don't know what a pulse unit is."

On his screen he produced a cutaway diagram of an object like a vase, with a round body and a flared throat, sitting in a cylindrical casing. The top was sealed by a plate. "You understand that the Orion launch stage is propelled by a series of nuclear explosions."

She stiffened. She hadn't known that. What the hell was she getting into here? "Go on."

"The idea is to shape each explosion so that it doesn't just blast out its energy in all directions, but channels its energy and momentum transfer to the spacecraft's pusher plate." He mimed with his hands. "Which is like a big cymbal sitting over the throat of the pulse unit, up here. So when the bomb goes off the energy is confined by the radiation case around the charge, which is a shell of uranium, then it is passed up through this channel filler of beryllium oxide in the throat, and thus it's focused onto the propellant slab—this lid of tungsten at the top. You understand this all happens in an instant, it's all blown to atoms, but the setup lasts just long enough to direct the bomb energy. The tungsten slab vaporizes, and it's that product that flies up and hits the pusher plate.

"The early nuclear engineers found out some interesting stuff about how objects vaporize when hit by a nuclear charge. If you have a pancake-shaped object, like this tungsten slab, you get a cigar-shaped plasma cloud. That's because the center vaporizes first and kind of leads the way. Conversely, if you have a cigar-shaped object it turns into a pancake-shaped cloud, as the energy works its way up the length of the thing. The cigar cloud is better for us, because you get your momentum transfer focused on a small area. You can demonstrate all this with bomb design software, we dug up some of the old code from the 1950s and implemented the algorithms with modern methods. And that's why this design—"

"It's something like this that killed Harry Smith."

Zane hesitated. Evidently he was happier with the technical stuff. "Harry was supervising a few of the Candidates involved in the test. There was meant to be a controlled detonation with conventional explosives to demonstrate some of the principles. Somebody loaded in ten times the nominal charge strength. The way the explosion was shaped—it smashed the containing bunker wide open. It killed Harry, and one other man."

"You think it was deliberate, then?"

"Oh, yes. Somebody engineered this to kill Harry; I'm sure the other guy was only caught by accident."

"Except it wasn't an accident."

"No."

"How many people on the project could have set that up?"

Zane shrugged. "A handful of ground engineers. But none of them knew Harry well, which is the point, isn't it? Of the Candidates, Matt Weiss or myself, without independent help. Many of the others could have done it with support, they'd know the principles."

"Venus Jenning, perhaps."

"She'd have needed help with the details."

"So that leaves you and Matt."

"I guess."

"Venus told me about her relationship with Harry."

Zane's face went blank. "And you want to hear the same from me?"

"I know it's difficult. Just tell me how it started."

It had been the day of the 2036 accident that had almost killed Zane's own father. "That was the lowest point. That was the opportunity to exploit." He told her something about that first sexual encounter, which was similar to what Harry had done to Venus, her first time. It sounded like a practiced technique. But Zane told this oddly, describing the incidents and actions with passive verbs, entirely impersonally.

"Did he tell you he loved you?"

"That remark was made."

"Did he ask you if you loved him?"

"The question was asked."

"*Did* you love him?"

"There was a problem to be solved."

Grace stared at him. She had met many bruised people in the course of her life; it was a bruising world. But Zane was exceptional. "Do you think any of the others loved him?"

"Matt loved him, I think, Matt Weiss. Matt told me so, once. He was drunk."

"Did you ask anybody for help? Did you tell anybody what was going on?"

"He asked the father," he said oddly. Then, a double-take: "I asked my father."

"And?"

"He said a Candidate for the Ark crew should sort out such issues himself. He said such a victim was dirty and unworthy."

She pressed him for more details, and he replied in the same abstracted, impersonalized way.

For Zane there had been no sudden fracture of his relationship with Harry, no revealed lies, no blowup, no rejection, as there had been for Venus. Zane had never taken control. The relationship had gone on and on, the sex. Yet there had been an ultimate crisis.

"Harry said he'd protect you. But in the end he failed, didn't he? You were deselected."

"There was a psych test. Zane Glemp is technically capable but emotionally unintelligent. That was what the doctors said."

"So in the end Harry didn't fulfill the bargain. All that sex, all the creeping around, your father's anger—the shame you must have felt. Despite all that he didn't deliver the one thing you wanted, a place on the crew."

"Perhaps that was never possible. His influence was always more negative than positive, the ability to stop people with a bad report rather than confirm a place."

"It was all a lie, then. You hated him for it," she said, pushing. "You hated him for blackmailing you, for not delivering you a place on the Ark. You had means and motive to kill him."

"There was no hate. There was nothing. Murder was not necessary."

And instinctively she believed him. Zane was a victim, not an perpetrator; he could never have taken control, as Venus had, and as the killer evidently had.

"Then if you didn't kill him, who? It sounds as if it must have been Matt."

"I don't know."

"But logic suggests—"

"Logic?" For the first time he turned to look at her directly; his eyes were surprisingly soft, full of character. "To see the logic, ask yourself what Matt wanted. And, indeed, what Harry wanted. We're here. Gunnison."

The car was slowing. Grace peered out of the windows, curious. The sky had cleared to reveal a deep blue, and the old town was a pretty place of clapboard buildings, surrounded by pine trees and with the Rockies floating on the horizon. But it was overwhelmed by Project Nimrod, crowded with fresh-looking prefabricated buildings and industrial facilities, gantries, rails, pipelines that bridged the road, immense storage tanks that were plastered with frost even in the August heat. She thought she recognized a rocket gantry, slim and upright, with propellant hoses dangling.

The car pulled up at the foot of a massive building, like a factory, a rectangular block maybe thirty meters wide and three times as tall. A tangle of cylindrical tanks and immense coiled springs were contained within a framework of scaffolding.

"So where's your spacecraft?" She had been expecting something like the moth-shaped space shuttle orbiters in the photos Gary Boyle used to show her.

He smiled and pointed at the large industrial building. "That's it."

34

Where Venus Jenning and Zane Glemp had seemed indifferent to Harry Smith's death, Matt Weiss was heartbroken.

Grace spoke to him in a small conference room in the basement of one of the launch-center buildings. It was a bare, bleak room, with unpainted plaster walls and a concrete floor. The room was hot, stuffy, stale, despite the noisy aircon. There was evidently no luxury in any of these new project installations.

Grace gulped more coffee. She had had one hell of a long day. She didn't even know where she'd be sleeping that night. She tried to focus on the young man in front of her.

Around the same age as the others—Zane was twenty-one, Holle and Venus twenty-two—Matt Weiss was stocky, strong-looking, with a broad face with a wide nose and heavy lips. He wore his hair severely crew cut, military style. He wasn't in the usual red-and-blue Candidate suit; he had been working on some heavy engineering project and he wore jeans and a vest. His bare arms, heavily muscled, were streaked with oil, though his face and hands were clean, and his boots left dirt marks on the floor. He looked down at his hands, which were folded on his lap. He seemed to be on the brink of crying.

"I knew the sex was wrong, sort of," he said. "I was never like that. I had girlfriends, before I joined the Academy. I was a cadet with the Denver PD. Once I got in here, when I found out how competitive it was and how easy you could get washed out, I got scared." He had a broad Texan accent.

"Scared of being sent back."

He looked up. "I don't know what you've seen. My parents died in a food riot in Dallas when I was a kid. Then with the cops I was on the front line, even as a cadet. There's never enough cops. I was still just a kid. Once, in Nebraska, these rafters tried to crash the barriers. We had riot shields and we linked arms, and we just shoved our way down that old roadway and threw them back into the water. There were mothers holding their babies up to us. Everybody was screaming."

"I understand—"

"Every second from age twelve, I was afraid that I'd screw up somehow and end up on the other side. With the eye-dees. I mean, what's the difference between me and them? We're all just Americans, just people."

"And Harry Smith said he'd save you from being sent back."

The pattern, as it had begun, was familiar to Grace by now. Harry homed in on his students at their most vulnerable, seduced them with promises of loyalty and safety, and then subjected them to the strange choreography of his first nighttime visit. And then, just as before, he told Matt he loved him.

"And I loved him back," Matt said defiantly now, and he wiped a running nose on the back of one massive hand. "Why shouldn't I? He was protecting me, like a father, or a brother. You love the people who protect you. That's what love *is*. So he made me suck his dick. Probably half the fucking Candidates are sucking dick to stay in the program, who cares?"

He talked a while longer about his relationship with Harry, how it had continued right up until the time he had been killed. And he talked about the accident. He spoke of the technical details of how the test bomb had been tampered with, the additional charge loaded in. After Zane initially discovered the tampering, Matt had helped the forensic team piece together what had happened. Yes, he could have been the one who did it. No, he hadn't done it. "Ask Zane," he said coldly. "I loved him, Harry. I really did. Zane didn't."

"Setting the charge," she said. "The bomb that killed Harry. How much planning would it take? I mean, could it be done on impulse, quickly, as soon as you had the idea? Or would it have taken some planning?"

He hesitated. "You could do it fast. If you knew what you were doing, and you were in the right place with the access to the stuff you needed. Wouldn't take no planning. Ask Zane."

When she was done, she had Matt escort her out into the open air. Gordo Alonzo had come down from Alma and was waiting for her. He nodded to her, eyes hidden behind huge black sunglasses.

They walked the few hundred meters to the Orion spaceship, in its vast, gleaming, uncompleted frame. The stack was topped by a pyramid shape of black, gleaming tiles. She could hear a hiss coming from deep within the structure, and saw showers of sparks—welding torches, perhaps. It looked so massive it might sink into the Earth, rather than rise up from it. The ship was closely guarded, with armed troopers patroling a wire-fence perimeter, and others walking along gantries in the guts of the thing itself.

Standing at the building-ship's huge base, Gordo Alonzo pulled a cigar from a slim metal case. As an afterthought he offered one to Grace.

"Thanks, no. I guess my generation never had a chance to get the habit. They must be precious."

"Nah. Got a whole heap in cold storage in the bunker in Cheyenne. Cold War vintage, 1960." He stuck it in his mouth unlit. "So," he said briskly. "You got our killer?"

"Matt Weiss," she said.

He flinched, his eyebrows raising. He took off his cap, and wiped a sweating scalp. "You surprise me. I had Zane Glemp pegged. That little weasel got kicked off the crew, after all."

"Zane's a victim, not a killer. He couldn't have done it. And Venus didn't need to. She'd beaten Harry already, in her way. That leaves Matt."

"OK. But of the three of them Matt Weiss obviously did care for Harry, in his screwed-up way. And Matt got to stay on the crew, so Harry kept his promise. So where's the motive to kill him?"

"Jealousy. Matt thought he loved Harry, and so he must have been jealous of the others, Zane, Venus, maybe others—I don't know if Harry had any more victims."

Gordo shook his head. "If he did, nobody's talking."

"Look at it from the point of view of a jealous lover. Harry was sending Matt off into space. But he kept Zane on the ground, close to him."

"Shit. So Matt read his own crew selection as a kind of *rejection* by Harry?"

"I think so. He kept it bottled up. These kids of yours seem to have learned to hide their emotions. But when Harry happened to come out to see this bomb test—"

"Matt saw a chance to take revenge."

"Yeah. He said himself it was easy to have set up the lethal charge, if you knew what you were doing."

"Well, I'll be." Gordo took his cigar from his mouth, cut it and lit it. "Of course you don't have a shred of proof for this."

"No. But I think Matt will confess if you push him. I didn't want to do that—"

"We'll handle it."

"What about Matt's place in the crew?"

"Well, he's scrubbed." Gordo grinned. "Ironically he opens the door again for Zane. The best replacement. Matt Weiss has screwed himself every which way. Miss Gray, you've had a hell of a day. But I guess you passed the test I set you." He eyed her. "We'll have to let out one of those fancy jumpsuits."

"I don't know if I want to become one of your Candidates."

"OK. I understand that. And there's no guarantee you'll make it even if you want to; I guess you can see how tough the selection process is." He waved his cigar at the Orion. "And there's no guarantee this ramshackle thing is even going to fly. But look, Miss Gray. I was assigned to this damn project against my will too. I thought I had better things to do with my remaining years than this bullshit, a pack of kids and a dumbass plan. But look where we are now. The flood has washed away every hope of recovery, every other thing we planned. Suddenly Project Nimrod is the *only* positive hope we have left, the only chance we have to send the memory of what we were into the future.

"That's why I've busted my balls trying to make it work. Banging the eggheads' big skulls together to make them come up with a feasible design, a ship that we can build and we can test, and will *fly*. And working my damnedest to turn this bunch of kids into a crew. But that's all they are—kids. They don't even know what it is they're being saved from. I think they need you, and people like you. I remember when I first saw you in that okie city of yours, and you were sixteen years old, and you'd stitched up some old guy's stomach wound with thread."

"That was Michael Thurley. And it was fishing line."

He smiled at her over his cigar, and she saw herself reflected in the twin lenses of his sunglasses, her hands on her belly, her lank hair, her drawn, tired face. "So what do you say? Will you ride to the stars with us?"

35

November 2041

Holle woke in an empty bed. She could feel it, feel the cold of a pushed-back duvet, even before she began to move.

Seven days. That was her first thought. Just seven days to launch, after a lifetime of training, of friendship and rivalry, triumphs and breakdowns, wonder and tragedy. But first she had to get through today.

She opened her eyes slowly. The room was filled with gray light, the light of another murky November morning; the weather had been lousy, depressing for weeks. She rolled on her back, feeling the aches in her stiff muscles, her body's memory of the hours she'd spent on the centrifuge yesterday. She'd been too exhausted even to make love with Mel. When they'd rolled into the room they shared here in the crew hostel at Gunnison they'd spent an hour on massage, working out the knots of pain in each other's body, before succumbing to sleep.

Now Mel stood before the window, naked save for a pair of boxer shorts. His body was silhouetted against the sky, and she could see the hard outline of his waist, his muscled arms. After these final intensive months of training, they were all super-fit.

"Mel? Come back to bed."

He didn't stir.

She clambered out of bed, wrapped a blanket over her shoulders, and shuffled to the window. They were on the tenth story of this residential facility, a concrete block hastily thrown up to house the Candidates, and the engineers, managers, trainers and other ground-support staff who out-numbered the potential crew many times over. Glancing down she made out the triple fence, ditches, gun towers and patroling dogs that walled her off in this particular haven from the rest of a crumbling world.

And looking out, as the eastern sky brightened over to her right, she had a grand view of the Gunnison valley, cradled by the bulk of the Rockies. Her eye was drawn to the Orion launch stack itself, a complex block bathed in spotlights. She was ten kilometers away from the ship, and she made out the cluster of support facilities around it, ugly, functional concrete buildings with the gleam of gravel roads snaking between them. That was the Zone, as they had come to call it, the two-kilometer-wide launch center with the monstrous spacecraft at its heart. The old town of Gunnison itself was to the east, off to the right of the launch facility. All this was contained by a wider secured perimeter within which lay what the military planners called the Hinterland, a concentration of industrial facilities sixteen kilometers across. Traffic crawled everywhere, the lights of the convoys like strings of jewels, and if she pressed her ear to the glass she could hear the rumble of vast machines. The work went on twenty-four seven, and it had been that way for months.

Mel only had eyes for the Ark itself. "Look at that bird."

Holle wrapped her arms around his waist. "And it's all ours."

"Or will be, in a week."

It wasn't like Mel to be up like this. He generally slept like a log; he'd been in the military long enough to learn the trick of grabbing sleep whenever he could. She asked, "You OK this morning?"

"I guess so. Just the tension closing in, I guess."

"Those damn clocks ticking down everywhere."

"And something else. Don't you feel it?"

"What?"

"Euphoria," he said. "I guess that's the word. It feels like we're the center of the whole world. We're young, fit, ready to go and do what we've trained all our lives for. I can't imagine ever feeling better than this.

Gordo Alonzo talks about how it was for a shuttle crew before a space-flight. Some things don't change, I guess."

He was right. Everything was heightened, as if it was all more real—even now, the warmth of Mel's flesh against her cheek, the prickle of the rough carpet under her feet, the twinkling lights of the sleepless industrial landscape before her. "Yeah. We're running on adrenaline. I'll probably sleep for a week once we're on the damn ship."

He turned and took her in his arms, his face shadowed as he looked down at her. "Do you have any regrets?"

"Like what?"

"You aren't sorry we didn't try for a pregnancy?"

Many of the female Candidates had done so, getting themselves knocked up in the final weeks. Some had succeeded, including Susan Frasier, who was bearing the child of her long-term boyfriend Pablo Mason, an eye-dee who had turned out to be a math whiz and, through Susan's persuasion of Gordo, got himself a place on the project ground crew. But there were others who had ended up getting too sick to complete the training program, and had washed themselves out.

"It might have boosted your chances."

"No," Holle said firmly. "We've been through this." If she had got pregnant with Mel's kid, his genes would have become redundant. "I wasn't about to leave you behind. We can have kids on Earth II."

"Not for eight years."

She shrugged. "I can wait."

A wall panel flashed, bleeping softly.

They broke their hug. Holle called, "On."

The screen lit up with Alonzo's craggy, deeply tanned face. "—is a loop recording. The final crew selection commences at 0800." An hour from now. "If you believe yourself to be eligible for selection, get yourself to the crew center on time. If you ain't there, even if your name is Neil Armstrong, you wash out. I hope that's clear. Bring only what you need." He glanced down at a note. "That's all." There was a flicker, as the recording restarted. "This is a loop recording. The final crew selection process commences at 0800 . . ."

Mel and Holle looked at each other for one second. There had been no warning of this. "Move," he said.

"Yeah."

Mel ran for the shower.

Holle grabbed their underwear from the closets, and their red and blue Candidates' uniforms. "What do you think he meant, 'Bring only what you need'?"

"That we're not coming back," Mel called from the shower.

"Shit." But she should have expected something like this. So the end game begins, she thought. She grabbed backpacks and started ransacking the room, seeking what was most precious to her—books, diaries, data sticks, hardcopy images, letters from her father, her Angel. What could she not bear to leave behind?

She heard a growl of heavy engines, carrying even through the thick window glass. Looking down she saw armored buses pulling up, ready to take them to the launch facility. She glanced at a clock. Five past seven. She threw stuff arbitrarily into the backpacks. "Will you hurry up in that damn shower?"

36

There was a corridor of photographers, held back by lines of military, waiting to greet the Candidates as they came out of the building in pairs or threes, clutching their bags, their gaudy uniforms bright against the drab military shades. Flashes and spots glared in their faces. There was even a ripple of applause. Kelly, ever the showman, threw a handful of Ark key rings from her gloved hand. People jumped to catch them. Holle, dazzled by the flashes, was aware of a sullen watching crowd beyond the well-wishers.

The bus moved off from the foot of the building at seven thirty precisely, a tank-like vehicle with caterpillar treads and minuscule windows. It joined a convoy that rolled briskly out of the compound's security fence, then along a short stretch of road lined with troops, shadowy in the uncertain morning light, heading for Gunnison.

They slowed at a checkpoint at the Hinterland's outer perimeter, a great circle of fences, ditches and watchtowers some eight kilometers in radius drawn around Gunnison. More spectators were waiting here, some applauding, mostly just staring. The security was heavy-handed, ferocious.

Even once they were inside the Hinterland they bowled along a road lined with wire fencing and more armed troops. Beyond the roadside fence civilian workers were laboring, scraping holes and ditches in the open spaces and planting ugly metal eggs in the ground. They were laying mines, Holle saw, seeding death into the ground, presumably all across the Hinterland. Maybe even the road she traveled on would be mined once she had passed. Nobody else was to come in after them. That was the meaning of these preparations. She had the sense of great doors slamming closed behind her one by one.

A kilometer from the Ark they were halted at another security fence around the Zone, the inner ground zero that contained the launch facility itself and the infrastructure that supported it. This time the buses were boarded, the occupants' cards and biometric ID signatures checked over, and the buses moved on with armed troops aboard.

It was five to eight by the time the buses rolled to a halt outside the big doors of the Candidate Hilton. Holle had spent so much time in this big training center the last couple of years that it had come to feel like home. And here, in a few days, they would undergo their final preparations for launch. Now, as the Candidates spilled from their buses, chattering and nervous in their bright costumes, she longed only to get inside, to meet Gordo's deadline. But even here the security clamped down hard, and they had to line up for yet another ID check before being allowed in.

The light was brightening now. As Holle waited to be processed she looked around. It was remarkable to remember that within the last few years this whole launch facility had been set out from scratch, including manufacturing plants, propellant stores, test, assembly and integration facilities, this crew training and preparation building, the control centers. And all of it was focused on the ship itself, picked out by its spotlights and looming over the blocky buildings that surrounded it.

This morning there was much activity around ramps that led up from the ground to the gaping doors of the twin hulls' holds. Holle knew that the Svalbard vault was being loaded. This was a seed vault, containing around two billion seeds, established around forty years earlier deep inside a mountain on some Norwegian island—the seed that would help build a new world, on Earth II, once it was selected and reached. It was rumored that the seed vault had been the price paid by Grace Gray's sponsor, Nathan Lammockson, to get her aboard the Ark. There were already banks of zygotes stored deep in the Ark's hold—the frozen embryos of animals, of dogs, cats, horses, cows, sheep, pigs, a variety of fish, and of a whole range of critters drawn from across the rich living tapestry of Earth, all loaded in not quite two by two. And Holle knew that equally precious but less tangible treasures were also being loaded aboard the ship today, via fiber-optic connections and tight beams: millions of books going back to the first Sumerian scratchings, music in sheet form and recordings, Library of Congress records, even the big genetic libraries the Mormons had built up—digital vaults containing the wisdom and collective memory of mankind, flowing into the Ark's radiation-hardened memory stores.

Even as the loading went on, cranes pecked at the huge structure like birds, spotlights glinted, welding torches sparked, and vapor hissed from valves, flaring bright white in the spotlights. It was said that the engineers wouldn't stop building the ship until the moment it took off. It was impossible to believe that such a thing could fly at all.

And it was also impossible to believe that of everything in her field of view, only the Ark itself would survive a microsecond after the very first of the thermonuclear detonations that would lift her into space.

She and Mel got through the final security checks at two minutes to eight, and, following a sign, hurried to the Hilton's big assembly hall.

Gordo Alonzo stood on the stage, before a contraption of glass and plastic that looked like a lottery machine. Edward Kenzie was up there with him, and Liu Zheng, Magnus Howe and other instructors. Holle couldn't see her father.

The floor before the stage, cleared of the usual clutter of chairs and desks, was crowded with Candidates, swarming in their bright uniforms. She and Mel worked into the crowd, looking for their friends. There were plenty of strangers here too, young people of around Holle's age, some in the uniforms of military, Homeland, police or National Guard, and some in civilian clothes, in AxysCorp coveralls or even just plain jeans.

She spotted Grace Gray standing alone, looking detached from the rest; she must be one of the oldest here, and her pregnancy was clearly visible through the loose coveralls she wore.

They soon found Kelly, who as ever was at the center of others from their cadre: Susan with Pablo, and Venus Jenning and Wilson Argent, Thomas and Elle together, and Mike and Miriam, and Cora Robles who, heavily pregnant, had found time to put makeup on, and Zane Glemp, who looked the least agitated of any of them. Don Meisel was here in his DPD uniform and armor, standing with Kelly, the mother of his child. Holle's heart went out to Kelly, who had given up her chance of a place on the Ark when she had chosen to bear her kid to term, little Dexter, now two years old. She had stayed with the program, training with the rest to lend her expertise and experience, and here she was now with her old colleagues, right to the end.

Holle pulled Kelly's sleeve. "Come to say goodbye? Where's Dexter today?"

Kelly just raised her fingers to her lips, and smiled.

Holle glanced around. "For sure there are a lot more than eighty people here. I guess the recruitment program was always wider than we knew about."

"Yeah. And I happen to know that there have been a lot of last-minute switchovers. Kids of military and politicians being forced on us. Just as well President Peery is a childless widower or we'd have a dozen of his brats on board."

Holle frowned. "So how many of us made the cut?"

The big doors at the back of the room slammed. There was a squeal of feedback, and on the stage Gordo Alonzo thumped a microphone with his finger.

Kelly whispered, "I guess we're about to find out."

Gordo Alonzo cleared his throat.

"OK. Welcome to the final crew selection process for Ark One, the culmination of Project Nimrod. This is going to be damn melodramatic, but it's the best way we can figure to do it.

"Now listen up. I know my best crew. I have the final eighty stored in my head, up here." He tapped his forehead. "That takes account of skill sets and diversity and all of that shit, *and* of the horse market that's been going on the last few days. But we can't just read out a list. Not everybody qualified even made it to this room. And some who made it here might not want to go, now we're at the crunch. After all, this is a one-way trip.

"So, we're going to go through a decision process. We have a smart piece of software that at each stage is going to maintain a list of the optimal crew from the eligible candidates, small 'c,' remaining. It's that expert system that will make the final individual decisions. Understood?

"OK, first stage. I want any of you who's not a flier to step back, go to the rear of the hall. That includes mom and pop and the sweetheart you're leaving behind." He glared around. "And that includes *you,* if after all you don't want to go, even if you think you're eligible, no matter how long you trained, or who paid for a seat for you on this scow. It's your choice. Step back now."

The crowd began to shuffle, sorting itself out. Venus, Wilson, Mel, Zane and the rest all moved forward, toward Alonzo. Susan Frasier kissed Pablo—and, to Holle's shock, stepped back with him, holding onto his arm.

Holle grabbed her hands. "Susan, what are you doing? This is what you trained for, your whole life. You even got yourself pregnant to boost your chances."

Susan just smiled a wide oceanic smile, and looked at Holle with brimming eyes. "It just isn't what I want, Holle. I don't think I ever did. It got harder and harder for me to imagine leaving Pablo, for one thing. And I won't want that kind of future for my baby either, not a whole lifetime in a tin can." She took a breath, and blood flushed her cheeks. "I mean, even if he grows up on a raft at least he'll have the sun and the sky and the sea . . . He'd have none of that on the Ark. *You* won't. I think I'd die without it."

Holle was horrified at the thought that this sane, grounded woman would not be one of the eighty. "We need you. *I* need you. Please, Susan."

Susan shook her head, her tears spilling over. "I can't. I'm sorry."

Pablo smiled at Holle, and drew Susan away.

Holle, bewildered, turned back to Kelly and Don. Suddenly she realized she was facing more goodbyes, because Kelly couldn't go any further.

But Don was kissing Kelly, hard on the lips. When he pulled away his eyes were wet, though Kelly's were dry, bright. Don said gruffly, "So this is it."

Kelly cupped his cheek with her hand. "It was so unfair how you were washed out, just a stunt by Gordo that first day. But you were never bitter. What incredible strength. I'll remember that about you."

"Christ, Kelly—"

"I'll see you before the launch," Kelly said. "Both of you, and Dexter. There's time yet." She glanced around at the line that was forming on the stage, beside Alonzo and his lottery machine. "Look, I need to go."

Don nodded. "Go, go." He seemed on the verge of saying more. Instead he turned on his heel and marched away to the back of the hall, stiff, upright in his police uniform.

Kelly was left standing with Holle. She took Holle's hand. "Come on—let's see if we won the game."

But Holle, stunned, drew her hand back. "Kelly, what are you doing?"

Kelly stiffened. "I need to explain? Look—a few months back, Alonzo asked me if I wanted my name to be restored to the active roster. I had time to think it over. I spoke to Don about it. I said yes."

Holle simply couldn't understand. "You said yes? But that means you'll have to leave Dexter."

"He has his father. My dad will take care of them both. He'll live."

"You're his mother," Holle blurted.

"I won't be the first mother in this drowning world to have left a kid behind," Kelly said harshly. "I would have thought you would understand, you of all people. Christ, we grew up together, we got through that fucking Academy. But you really are a mouse, aren't you? It's not even a question of survival. *It's the mission.* Holle, they offered me the role of commander of the trans-Jupiter phase! That's a mission in itself. Then I'll be in prime position to become captain of the interstellar phase. Come on, Holle, how could I turn that down? I'm meant to fly the Ark. I was born to it. I spent my life training up for it. There's nothing else for me."

"Not even your little boy?"

Kelly just repeated, "I thought you'd understand. Come on." She turned and led the way through the thinning crowd toward the stage, and Alonzo's lottery machine.

37

People were called up in groups of eight or ten, and briefed by Gordo on the process. Holle watched Grace Gray going through. She touched her hand to a pad on the machine, which turned and produced a disc, like a coin, that Gordo handed to her with a smile. Grace took it incuriously, and moved on.

Holle and Kelly caught up with Mel, Venus, Wilson, Zane, in the slowly moving line. In among them was a boy in an ill-fitting military uniform, who Holle hadn't seen before. He looked uncertain, out of place, avoiding eye contact. It seemed to Holle that the regular Candidates in their uniforms made up no more than half the number lining up, half of this crowd of people all of whom thought they were entitled to a berth on the Ark.

Mel came back for Holle. She grabbed his hand and squeezed hard.

He glanced at her. "You OK?"

She shook her head, compressing her lips.

Kelly murmured to Wilson, "Who the hell's the kid in the army colors? I'll swear he never wore that uniform before today."

Wilson whispered, "Rumor has it he's the son of General Morell. You know, the guy in charge of Zone perimeter security. He briefed us once—"

"Well, he's no chance of making it onto our ship, whoever spawned him." Kelly's face was hard, her eyes alive, every fiber of her being focused on the selection process. She didn't glance once after Don.

Zane paid no attention to any of this. His slight body clumsy in the bright Lycra uniform, he looked disconnected, as if barely conscious of what was going on around him—barely aware of the gravity of this moment, which could shape his entire life.

They neared the selection machine, and the line ahead cleared. They were all in the next group of ten to be called forward and lined up before Gordo Alonzo. Holle noticed an armed man behind Gordo, and another by the machine, watching silently. Behind them senior figures like Edward Kenzie and Liu Zheng stood waiting. Holle glanced over her shoulder. There was still no sign of her father.

Gordo faced them, uniform sharply creased, hands folded. "OK, you people, time for the game show. By standing here you're stating your willingness to serve on the Ark. Yes? Now we'll see if you're selected.

"You'll each step up, in turn. You'll place your right hand on this pad." He showed them how. "If the machine's uncertain of your identity you'll feel a prick of your thumb, a blood sample. OK? And if you're on the list you'll be given a token." He held up a gold-colored coin. "Like this. Numbered one to eighty. Don't lose it. Seems kind of crude I know, but once the tokens are issued you have your pass to the Ark come what may, even if we get hacked, even if the systems crash, whatever. Now, if you don't get a token, you haven't been selected, and we ask you to move on." The armed soldier beside him stiffened, cradling his rifle. "Who's first?"

Zane stepped forward. He placed his palm where they had been shown, the machine rotated, and coughed out a token. Gordo handed it to Zane, who closed his hand over it without looking at it, and moved on.

With no further trouble, Wilson and Venus both passed through. Venus was trembling; she looked hugely relieved to have made it and clutched her token to her chest.

Kelly went next, striding confidently. When Gordo handed over her token she held it aloft and whooped, as if she'd won an Olympic medal.

Her father, Edward, clapped his liver-spotted hands. Holle couldn't believe Kelly could behave this way.

The army boy, Morell, went forward next. He was shaking visibly. Gordo had to show him where to place his palm; the kid wiped his hand on his trouser leg and reached out nervously. But the machine produced a coin for him; he grabbed it and hurried on.

"I don't fucking believe it," said Mel. He patted Holle's shoulder. "You next, hon. See you on the other side."

Holle stepped forward, alone. Suddenly she was nervous, her heart hammering, a feeling of lightness in her head. She was aware of Gordo watching her, the guard at his side, Kelly and the other successful Candidates waiting for her, Mel behind her. It was as Kelly had said. All her life she had been preparing for this mission. She would never know how much she had sacrificed for it, what kind of a childhood she might have had otherwise. And it all came down to this one moment, to a decision made by some intangible expert system cooked up by Gordo and the social engineers.

There was no point hesitating. She slapped her palm on the pad. It was greasy with other people's sweat. The machine turned. A token dropped into the slot with a rattle. She just looked at it for a long second, barely believing it. Then Gordo handed it to her, and she clutched it tightly as she marched over to join Kelly and the others. Nobody slapped her back, nobody hugged her—nobody grinned, save Kelly. It didn't feel like that kind of moment. The Morell kid just stood there shaking, maybe more afraid that he'd made it than if he hadn't.

Mel approached the machine. He placed his hand on the pad. The machine turned, but no token emerged. Mel frowned, staring at the machine. He went to put his hand down again, but the guard stepped forward.

Gordo put his hand on his shoulder. "I'm sorry, son."

Mel stood straight for a long second. Then he nodded, turned on his heel, and marched away, without glancing back at Holle.

Holle couldn't believe it. "There's been a mistake."

Kelly said, "Somebody had to make room for daddy's little soldier. Tough break."

"No!" Holle lunged forward. Kelly grabbed her arms and held her back.

38

The successful crew, the final eighty, were led by Gordo and his staff out of the hall into a smaller lecture theater. Gordo climbed up to the stage, where a podium with a blue seal on the front had been set up. A glass-walled compartment at the back held spectators. The candidates—no, the *crew,* Holle thought—sat in their rows, filling barely a quarter of the theater. There were so terribly few of them. And she estimated that no more than sixty percent wore the uniforms of the official Candidates.

Kelly and Wilson escorted Holle to a seat and sat to either side, making sure she stayed put. Kelly couldn't conceal her exhilaration. Wilson was grim-faced, massive in his determination.

Holle couldn't believe Mel wasn't here, beside her. She felt as if she was on autopilot, unable to make decisions for herself, unable to imagine a future without Mel. She didn't even know if she'd be allowed to see him again, unless she somehow busted out of this crew assignment.

Everybody around her shuffled to their feet. Glancing at the stage, she saw that President Peery was walking up to the podium.

Pat Peery was a short, stocky man, with a bald pate and a wide face; he wore a dark blue suit and lapel pins, a US flag to the left and his own patent whole-Earth pin to the right. He was followed onstage by a phalanx of dark-suited men and women, some of them surely security peo-ple, others maybe aides. Holle had never seen Peery in person before. He looked more like a comedian than a president, she thought, one of the stand-up comics whose improvised black humor about food shortages and eye-dees and epidemics was pumped out on the news channels in the small hours to distract insomniacs.

Peery spread his hands. "Please, sit down. I can imagine how you're all feeling after the lottery business out there." He patted his own belly. "But-terflies, right? I don't want anyone fainting on me."

His audience sat, and there was a tangible sense of relaxation, Holle thought, even a ripple of laughter.

Peery said, "Now, just nine years after my predecessor spoke to this project, we got our eighty, we got our crew. And before you prepare for your ascension I thought I should address you, and remind you of where you've come from, and where you're going, and why." He spread his hands. "These are extraordinarily difficult times for all of us. Well, you know that. You wouldn't be riding an atom bomb to the stars otherwise. And it has been an extraordinarily difficult time to be President of this great country. You may not agree with every decision I've made while in office, every measure I've ordered. But I can assure you that every step I took was intended to ensure the survival of something of our nation beyond this dreadful historical terminus—survival of its heart and soul. And every step I took, I took in the eyes of God.

"That is as it should be. In a sense the whole trajectory of our nation's history has been a kind of mission—I use the word in the best and brav-est sense. I reversed President Vasquez's policies regarding the seculariza-tion of the state. I may say I never tried to tamper with the Ark crew selection in that regard; things had gone too far. But you will know, if you have listened to my words at all over the last five years, that I have brought God back to the heart of our nation's destiny.

"And in doing so, I believe, I have preserved your great project. I have argued in these final days that *you,* your Ark, are a pure and noble expression of the mission brought to this continent by our founders, an expression in an age of an ultimate crisis they could never have foreseen. That is how I have rallied the nation to support you. And I have also ordered the continuation of a second mission, a second Ark, a project to build a sanctuary on the Earth itself. No, I know you never heard of that before—*they* never heard of *you*. Such are the times we live in.

"And to ensure these great projects were protected and adequately supported, I have had to take measures that many of you would find unpalatable. Which *I* find unpalatable. I'll pick out one example that has affected you directly, right here today in Gunnison.

"We brought you in here to the Zone early, without warning, so as not to allow the eye-dees and saboteurs and other crazies any chance to blow up the Ark or throw their babies over the fence, or otherwise disrupt the mission. We got you locked down before they knew what was happening.

"But here's the blunt truth. In order to secure the loyalty of my generals, my senior military people, I had to grant their children places on the Ark. This wasn't done arbitrarily; the kids had to satisfy basic standards of health, genetic diversity, competence and the rest. But now those men, those senior people, will be protecting their own children. They'll do a job, believe me. But the process to which some of you have devoted your whole lives has been subverted at the very last minute. Maybe you hate me for this. I don't blame you if you do. But if I had not, I don't believe I could have guaranteed your security for the seven days left before you launch. I hope you understand, and will forgive me.

"Look, that's enough from me. You have an enormous amount of work to do, and not very many hours left to do it in. Just remember that I, and all of your parents' generation, have given you all we can to ensure your remarkable journey is successful. Some of us have blackened our very souls. Remember us, on Earth II." He glanced at his watch, and at his aides. "I guess that's it." He walked away from the podium.

Everybody stood up.

———

As the President's party left the stage, Edward Kenzie and Patrick Ground-water walked in from a side door. They hurried to the stage to join Gordo Alonzo, who was earnestly talking to Liu Zheng. Patrick looked around, scanning the audience anxiously, until he saw Holle, and he beckoned her urgently.

Holle ignored Kelly and the rest. She grabbed her bag and hurried down the steps, rushing to the stage. "Dad, oh, Dad—"

"Sweets." Patrick grabbed her, hugging her close. He was hot, sweating, unshaven, as if he had been working through the night.

"I thought I wasn't going to get to see you again."

"Don't be silly." Patrick stepped back, smiling tiredly. "I just had to wait for the President. Quite a speech."

Gordo grunted. "Same old horseshit from Pat Peery. It wasn't about the project, he's angling for the statues you'll build to him on Earth II." He shook his head. "Well, he's a brutal operator. Including wrapping the whole thing up in a holy mission. What the times need, I guess."

Holle didn't care about Peery. "Dad. You know what happened—you know about Mel?"

"I'm sorry, sweets. You know there's nothing I could do about that. You load in twenty outsiders at the last minute, you're going to have to make space by dumping twenty insiders."

"I won't fly without Mel."

Patrick cupped her cheek, as he had when she was very small. "Your whole life has led to this. You have to fly. Do it for me."

"And besides," Edward Kenzie murmured spitefully, "here you are. I don't see you handing your token back to Gordo."

Patrick turned on him. "You arsehole, Edward—"

Gordo said, "Can this wait until later? Holle, we got a kind of urgent situation on our hands we need your help with."

Holle glared at him. "You'll get no help from me."

Gordo sighed and rubbed his face. "Jesus Christ—kids! Look, can you just pretend you're still part of the fucking crew for another hour?"

Liu Zheng said, "Of all the Candidates, he will only speak to you."

"Who?"

"Matt Weiss. He is waiting."

Bewildered, she let herself be led away, while Kelly and the others stared after her.

39

Matt's cell was basic, a cave in a concrete block of a building, the walls rough and unfinished. He had a chemical toilet, a sink, a cupboard with books, a bunk, a TV. But there were no windows, no natural light.

Matt was sitting on his bed when Gordo opened the door. Liu and Gordo followed Holle in; Patrick stayed outside.

Matt stood up, looking away as if embarrassed. He wore a coverall of some rough recycled material. "Wasn't expecting you," he said to Holle. "I know I said that I'd speak to you if you came, but—"

She forced a smile. "Wasn't expecting to be here." She still didn't know what they wanted of her. She sat down on the bunk, and he sat beside her. Liu Zheng sat on the room's only chair, a hard plastic upright, and Gordo leaned against the wall, arms folded.

"Sorry it stinks in here," Matt said. "I shower every three days. But it's poky, you know."

"In a couple of weeks the whole Ark will probably stink just as bad."

"Maybe. I'll never know, will I? I bet you didn't know they had a prison on the launch site."

She shrugged. "I'm not surprised. The whole place is like a prison now, crawling with cops and soldiers and National Guard. They've kept you here since—"

"Since I confessed to killing Harry, yeah."

"What about a trial?" She glanced up at Gordo.

Gordo said, "We're kind of busy. Mounting trials isn't a priority."

"I don't want a trial," Matt said firmly. "What would be the point? It would make no difference to the outcome."

Holle shrugged. "OK. But what now? I guess they're going to move you away from here." In this cell they were no more than four hundred meters from the base of the Orion stack.

Liu Zheng leaned forward. "That's what we need to speak to you about, Matt. We need volunteers."

"Volunteers?"

"Look—" Liu pointed up and out, in the vague direction of the Ark. "You understand that when the bird flies, everything within several hundred meters of the launchpad will be destroyed. The Zone will be smashed to the ground, and much of the wider Hinterland—"

"I know, I know. Nothing close in to the Orion will survive. So what?"

Gordo said, "But somebody needs to stay 'close in.' Right to the end, right to the moment when those cannon start spitting their thermonuclear shells down through the pusher plate."

Liu Zheng sighed. "Matt, the Ark is an experimental machine. It is a sick joke that we will still be building it at the moment it flies. Well, it is true. Even now a slew of design modifications afflicts us. We will have no time to implement most of them, let alone test them. You know that launch control will be run out of a bunker at Pikes Peak. But remote command and support will not be enough. In the final hours, as we run down the countdown clock, we are expecting many failure modes to occur—some we can anticipate, surely many that we cannot.

"There will be a team," Liu said. "A team who will stay right until the final minute, until it is too late to escape the blast zone—you must understand—a team who may find themselves crawling through the Orion fixing leaks even as the atomic bombs begin to fire."

"A suicide squad," Matt said slowly. "And you want me to be on it."

Holle felt she could barely breathe. After a day of shocks, this was one development she had not foreseen.

Gordo said, "According to your aptitude tests, you were pretty good at math and physics and nuclear engineering, but you were one of the best hands-on mechanics in the Candidate corps. So here's a chance, kid. A chance to do something for the project you devoted your life to."

Liu Zheng reached out and grabbed his shoulder. "And I," he said, "will be with you. I will lead. This is my project, after all." He smiled. "It will be glorious. Think of the honor. Think of the spectacle as the bird flies, seared on your retinas—"

"Before my brain fries."

Gordo said, "You get a full pardon. In writing from the President, if you want. We need you, kid. Holle needs you."

Holle snapped, "That's so manipulative. It's a death sentence!"

Matt looked at her. "You're flying?"

Both Gordo and Liu looked at Holle. Now she understood why they had brought her here. Miserably, she said, "Yes, Matt. Yes, I'm flying."

Matt nodded. He reached out and shook Liu's hand. "Give me a monkey wrench and I'm your man, boss."

Holle could bear no more. She ran to the door, which opened to release her, and fell into the arms of her father.

When they took her out to the car she smelled burning. From all around the horizon, smoke was rising, black and ugly. It turned out that President Peery had ordered the firing of a trench, more than six kilometers long and filled with precious oil, that ringed the whole of the core Zone. The trench would be kept burning until the engines of the rising Ark obliterated it.

40

December 2041

The siren echoed in the corridors. Its pulse came every one and one-tenth seconds, Holle thought sleepily, to match the rhythm with which the thermonuclear charges would detonate beneath the pusher plate to shove the Ark, and herself, into space.

The siren.

She sat bolt upright. The duvet fell away from her bare upper body. A panel flashed brilliant red on her bedroom wall. The wall clock showed her it was a shade after 1800. She'd been asleep since noon, after pulling another thirty-six-hour shift in the sims. "On!"

The screen cleared to reveal Gordo's face. "—is Pikes Peak control. Get your asses to the Ark, now. Launch has been pegged for 2000." Flicker. "This is Pikes Peak control. Get your asses—"

She rolled out of bed and ran across the room to slap the panel. "Gordo! It's Holle."

The recording broke up to reveal a live feed of Gordo Alonzo with his tie loosened, and frantic scenes in launch control in the background. Gordo kept his face rigid, his gaze unequivocally not straying over her bare body. "Good evening, Ms. Groundwater."

"Gordo, what's happening? The launch was set for 0800 tomorrow."

"Not any more," he said gruffly. "Morell says he can't hold the line for more than another few hours."

She was bewildered. "We're not ready."

"You'll have to be."

"There are still civilians here, in the Hilton. Mel's here somewhere. My father—"

"They'll have to get out of there." He pressed a pad, out of her sight. "No, Argent, it's not a fucking drill. Get your skinny ass to that pad now." Another touch to the pad, and his hand hovered near his loosened tie. "Mr. President. Yes, sir, this is launch control at Pikes Peak. After the message from General Morell we accelerated the schedule. I'm confident we—yes, sir, I understand. If you'll excuse me one second." He glared, as if straight at Holle. "Any of you assholes on the crew listening to me talk to the President rather than getting your butts over to the ship are going to have a long time to regret it. Yes, sir, go ahead . . ."

"Off." The screen blanked.

Stunned, she looked around. Half-anticipating something like this, she'd got her stuff ready. Her launch suit lay sprawled over a chair, a loose undergarment with sewn-in medical sensors and comms links, and a tough AxysCorp-fabric bright blue coverall, bulky with built-in anti-impact air bags and cooling system and snap-on interface for the waste system. And she'd half-packed the small pouch that would contain the only personal stuff she'd be allowed to take aboard the Ark, data sticks, Angels, hardcopy photographs—a lock of Mel's hair.

She moved. She ran around picking up the last items from the bedroom and bathroom, her toothbrush, her case of sanitary towels.

She could hear shouts, revving vehicles, running footsteps, the continual blaring of the siren, and a pop that sounded like small-arms fire. Her hands were trembling as she pulled on the layers of the flight suit. She couldn't believe this was happening, that the time had come, this final sundering. She longed to pee. She could pee on the Ark.

She hunted for her boots. Outside the window, red lights flared with that ominous atomic rhythm.

The exit chamber on the ground floor was a swarm of crew members, ground staff, military with weapons at the ready, ushering crew members to the armored buses waiting to take them to the Ark itself.

A glass wall had been erected down the center of the hall. For days nonessentials had been excluded from the crew areas in an attempt to keep the crew clear of bugs. Mel wasn't here. But, among the handful of lovers, children and parents standing bereft on the far side of the barrier, Holle saw her father.

She ran to him. She dropped her bag and pressed her hands against the glass; he matched hers with his. "Dad—oh, Dad. I want to smash this glass."

He forced a smile. "That wouldn't be a good idea."

"I tried to get them to pass you through for the last night. I was going to cook you paella."

"I'll cook it myself in your honor, don't you worry. Anyhow I'll be speaking to you on the comms links; you won't get rid of me that easily."

"Mel isn't here. He said he'd be here."

"It's hard for him, sweets. I'll talk to him. I'll make sure he's fine."

Somebody was blowing a whistle, the last boarding call for the buses.

"Dad—"

"I'll tell you one last thing, love, I never told you before. Your mother and I listened to Thandie Jones telling the IPCC in New York how the world was going to end. You were conceived after that. Conceived in hope. But I never told you why we called you Holle. On Orkney my grandmother told me old Norse stories . . . You're named for the old Norse goddess of the afterlife—Holle, Hel, Hulda. Holle is the goddess of transformation." He was crying now. "I always hoped you would fulfill that promise somehow. And now here you are, a part of the afterlife of the whole world."

This was more than she could bear. "These are the days of miracle and wonder, aren't they, Dad?"

He stepped back deliberately. "Don't cry, baby." His voice was muffled.

Kelly Kenzie ran up and grabbed her arm. "You still here? Come *on,* damn it, that fucking bus is going *now.*"

Holle let herself be pulled away. When she looked back, Patrick had deliberately lost himself in the crowd.

They crowded onto the armored bus. It rolled away before Holle had a chance to sit down, before the door was properly closed. Everybody was stumbling around, dragging their bags, their suits half zipped up; this was nothing like the orderly embarkation they had rehearsed.

Holle got to a seat, but it was too small for her, padded up as she was in her layered suit. Bad design, she thought. Make a note for the integration oversight committee. But this bus would be vaporized in a couple of hours, poorly designed seats and all. She felt a hysterical giggle bubble up. She looked out of the window. Brown, greasy smoke from the oil fire in the moat rose into the air, as it had for six days now.

A dull roar reached a crescendo that crashed down, making them all duck. Two fighter jets screamed across the sky, their lights bright, burning up a bit more of the nation's dwindling store of aviation fuel. She wondered what threat they had been sent aloft to face.

The bus lurched to a stop. The driver opened the doors, and stood up and waved her arms. "Out! Out! Move it!" She was a middle-aged woman in an NBC coverall, for nuclear-biological-chemical protection. Holle understood her urgency; if the driver didn't get her bus turned around and out of the blast zone, she wouldn't survive the launch, NBC suit or not.

Holle got off the bus, clutching her bag. The Ark towered above her, gleaming in a bath of light cast by the powerful floods at its feet. Tanker trucks were pulled up at the ship's base, their hoses snaking into the superstructure, while far above her head valves vented white vapor.

There was no time for reflection. Kelly hurried ahead, and Holle followed, clutching her bag.

They got to the foot of the boarding ramp, where ground crew and military, all in NBC suits, checked their boarding tokens and rushed them through retinal checks. One last security check, the last of all. Kelly and Holle got through and joined the line leading up the sloping ramp into the maw of the ship.

And then it struck Holle. "Hey," she said, panting. "I just took my foot off the Earth for the last time."

Kelly was striding hard, working the big, deep stairs like an athlete in training. "You need to focus, Groundwater."

Holle hurried after her. "These moments are unique. I don't believe this is happening this way."

"You've got years to believe it. Come *on.*"

The line slowed as they neared the hatch, some twenty meters above ground level. People jostled as they tried to board. From this vantage Holle could see further out, across the Zone with its frantic activity to the rising curtain of ugly oil smoke, and the terrain beyond. The lights of Gunnison were bright in the dark of a December evening, and plumes of smoke and dust rose up across the wider Hinterland. Over the hiss of the Ark's giant valves she heard the popping of small-arms fire, the crump of heavier munitions, and, she thought, distant screams. The Ark was the center of a war zone. It was impossible to believe that everything she saw from up here was going to be destroyed as soon as the Ark's extraordinary engine fired up. But beyond the human sprawl the Rockies rose up, huge and impassive, dark against the sky. They would withstand even the launch of an Orion. She wondered if Earth II would have mountains.

She was approaching the hatch. She took one last deep breath of the air of Earth, but it tasted of gasoline, and the ammonium of the piston coolant, and the harsh metal tang of the Ark's multiple hulls.

And now she heard shouting from down below. She glanced back. The security barrier at the base of the ramp was failing. Some of the military seemed to have mutinied, and were fighting with cops and ground crew, trying to get on board the ship themselves. Everything was dissolving, she thought.

More planes roared over, impossibly low. She ducked, and hurried inside the ship.

41

"The leak is here." Liu Zheng unfolded a big paper schematic, and with a pointing finger showed Matt a feed leading from a secondary coolant reservoir. His hand was gloved; they both wore lightweight NBC suits. He had to shout to make himself heard over the hiss of vapor, the roar of engines as buses and trucks raced around the base of the Ark, the urgent yelling of voices, and an ominous clatter of gunfire. "See? Just above this O-ring."

"Why can't the automated systems handle it?"

"They froze," Liu said. "A multiple failure. Shit happens. Well, that's why we're here. The leak has to be fixed; without coolant, if one of those suspension pistons overheats and seizes in flight, the Ark will fall out of the sky. You have your tools?"

Matt hitched a pack on his back.

"OK. Take elevator three." Liu grinned. "This is your moment, Mr. Weiss." He stuffed the schematics into Matt's pack. "Go, go!"

Matt ran to the elevator cage, one of a dozen that allowed access to the Ark for maintenance. He slammed shut the gate and grabbed the dead man's handle that sent the cage rising up into the shadowed innards of the ship. He rose past the curving flank of one of the crew hulls. A wall of white insulation blanket rushed past his face, pocked with maintenance hatches, safety warnings, valve sockets—and handhelds, labeled with up-side-down stencils, for use by spacewalking astronauts in the extraordinary future when this ship would be taken apart at the orbit of Jupiter, and reassembled for interstellar flight. He felt light-headed, unreal. He hadn't slept much in the last week. Since his liberation from jail a week ago he had dedicated all his time to memorizing every aspect of the systems to which he was going to be assigned. He figured he could catch up on his sleep when he was dead. And with the Ark launch being brought back, he had, of course, suddenly lost twelve hours of his life. Quite a big percentage when you only had a day left anyhow.

He looked up, trying to spot the problematic feed. The Ark's interior was as brightly lit as the exterior, a mass of gleaming metal, pipes, vast tanks connected by ducts and cabling, all contained within the mighty struts of the frame. He saw cameras swiveling, and, clambering over the wall of one of the big crew hulls, a maintenance robot, a thing like a spider armed with a camera for a head, sucker feet so it could climb vertical walls, and a waldo arm with a Swiss Army knife selection of tools.

Still rising, he looked down the flank of the crew hull, and saw, down below, through gaps in the cluster of tanks and pipes, the impassive bulk of the pusher plate itself. An inverted dish of hardened steel, it was itself a beautiful piece of engineering, forty meters across and just ten centimeters thick. The bombs would be detonated below the plate, a weapon five times the strength of the Hiroshima bomb detonating one every one and one tenth of a second. The bombs would be fired into place by the simplest method imaginable, by shooting them down out of a cannon set square in the middle of the pusher plate. The propellant produced by each pulse unit would bounce off the pusher plate, transferring momentum but evaporating too quickly to damage the plate, which would be further protected by a screen of anti-ablation oil, constantly renewed. The resulting thrust would be soaked up by the shock absorber system, immense pistons that rose up above his head, each with a stroke of eleven meters and with a complex dual action that protected the vulnerable parts of the ship from rebound in case a pulse unit failed.

After studying the technical issues from scratch themselves, the Ark's designers had reverted to something close to what had become the stan-

dard design for much of the duration of the original Cold War Project
Orion: a four-thousand-ton brute with that mass split evenly between the
pusher plate, the ship's structure, the bombs, and a full thousand tons of
payload. By comparison the Saturn V, the booster that had launched
Apollo to the moon driven by chemical energies alone, had weighed in
at three thousand tons, of which only forty tonnes was payload. It was
hard to grasp the reality, even now. When the ship was in flight this whole
space would be the scene of huge engineering activity, with splashes of
blinding atomic glare coming from all around the rim of the pusher plate,
and those pistons shuddering with each mighty stroke.

Looking up now, Matt could see he was approaching the huge tanks
of coolant fluid and ablation oil suspended in their frame, and the complex
network of pipes that connected one to the other. That was where his leak
was. In flight, an ammonia compound was used to cool the pistons after
each stroke. The resulting high-temperature compressed gas was then used
to power the pumps that squirted a sheet of anti-ablation oil out over the
pusher plate before the next detonation, and to thrust the next pulse unit
from the charge magazine. Using the products of one stroke to prepare for
the next was pleasing for an engineer, a process that reeked of thermody-
namic efficiency. But that complexity led to many failure modes.

The light in his elevator cage died, and the cage jolted to a halt.

"Shit." Matt squeezed his dead man's switch, and rattled at the cage
door. All power to the cage and the pulleys that had been hauling it had
been lost. Matt flicked a microphone at his throat. "Liu, it's Matt."

As the link came active, Matt heard Liu Zheng break off another
conversation. "Go ahead."

"I lost power, in number three elevator."

"Wait . . . I can see. We lost power all down that side, a generator
broke down. Damn." Liu sounded desperately tense. What they feared
above all was multiple failure, one problem compounding another. "You
still on that coolant leak? You fixed it yet?"

"Negative." Matt resisted the urge to snap; of course he hadn't, in the
couple of minutes since he'd left Liu's side. Liu was juggling a hundred

tasks simultaneously, all as urgent as Matt's; time must be stretching for Liu, in this last hour of his life. "I'm still on my way up."

"We can't get power back until—I don't know. Matt, can you improvise? Yes, Mary, what is it? . . ."

Matt snapped off the comms link. *Improvise.* Well, there was no choice, and there were access ladders fixed all over the ship.

He fixed his tool pack on his back, grabbed the manual handle, and hauled the gate open. The nearest ladder was just outside the cage, and there was a rail to which he clipped a safety attachment to his belt. He got hold of the rail, swung out one foot, and reached the nearest rung. He tugged the safety harness to test it. Then he looked up into the cathedral of gleaming metal forms above him, and began to climb.

As he passed, monitor cameras swiveled to track him.

42

From the ramp, Holle followed Kelly across a mesh floor and through a brightly lit chamber, before they joined yet another line for access to the higher decks.

Holle looked up through layers of flooring. This crew hull was an upright cylinder. In fact the hull was a remodeling of one of the big propellant tanks of the Ares V booster, and a relic of the project's dysfunctional design process; when the decision was made to scrap the use of Ares boosters and fly with Orion, the engineers had scrambled to make use of the components of the abandoned Ares technology. The hull was divided into decks by mesh panels that could be disassembled to open up the interior space. For now the decks were set out with the crew's fold-out acceleration couches. Down through the center of the mesh flooring came a pole, like a fireman's pole. One by one the crew were climbing metal rungs bolted to the pole's side.

They reached that central ladder. Kelly went up first, Holle following, climbing up through the hull.

The hull's interior architecture was modeled on what had been proven to work on the space station, with color schemes and lighting strips designed to help you orient yourself in zero gravity, and a variety of fold-out stores, workstations and consoles. There were Velcro pads and handholds everywhere, in readiness for free fall. For now the only important functionality was on the twin bridges, situated in the nose of each crew hull, and the workstation screens all showed the impassive, reassuring face of Gordo Alonzo, with a blurred view of the Pikes Peak launch control center behind him, and a countdown clock.

But Gordo's voice was drowned out. On each deck there was chaos. People were in the couches, tightening their harnesses and plugging in comms and waste systems. But Holle saw others arguing over seats, waving tokens in each other's faces. While most people were in standard-issue flight suits as she was, a significant number weren't. She didn't even recognize a good number of the people on board.

She called up to Kelly, "Where's security? How the hell did these people get aboard?"

"Doesn't matter," Kelly called down, climbing the ladder as determinedly as she'd climbed the ramp. "There is no security any more, Holle, not in here. It's up to us now. We'll sort it out in space. This is your deck, right?"

"Yes." Kelly had to go on to the bridge. "Have a good trip, Kel."

Kelly grinned, exhilarated, fearless. "This is what I waited all my life for. You bet it will be a good one. See you beyond the moon." She clambered on, heading up out of sight, while Holle stepped off the ladder.

She found her own couch easily enough, one of an empty pair. Your couch was numbered to match your boarding token. The couch was a simple foldaway affair of plastic and foam, but it had been molded to the shape of her body, and she'd got used to it in training; she settled into it now with relief, and tucked her pack into the space underneath.

She saw Theo Morell, the general's son, trying to climb down the fireman's pole, moving in a different direction from everybody else, in a coverall too big for him. Holle called over, "Theo. Hey, Theo!"

He looked around, confused by the noise. Then he saw her and came over hesitantly. "Holle?"

"You look lost."

"Somebody's in my couch," he said miserably. "Up on Deck Nine. I showed her my token, the number on it, but she just said—"

"Never mind." She looked at his anguished face. She ought to hate him; he had taken Mel's place. "Here. Take this one, beside me."

"But it doesn't match my number." He dug in his pocket. "I have the token—"

"Things have got a bit chaotic. Just sit down, strap in, and if whoever has the number for that seat comes along—well, we can deal with that when it happens. Look, put your pack under the couch. You have your pack, don't you?"

"I lost it," he said. "I got knocked off the pole."

"God, Theo, you're a clown. Well, you've got years to find it before we get to Earth II. Just pray it doesn't hit somebody on the head when we launch. Come on, sit down and strap in."

Hesitantly at first, but then with relief, he obeyed her and clicked home his harness. They were lying on their backs, as if in dentists' chairs, staring at the deck above. Somewhere above their heads, the noise of an argument over a couch grew louder.

43

Don Meisel took Mel's arm and pulled him out of the line for the passenger buses that would have taken him out of the blast zone. Don was in combat gear, wearing a heavy bulletproof vest and carrying an automatic weapon. Under his helmet his face was smeared with dark cream, but it was streaked by sweat on his forehead and under his eyes. "You up for a little action?"

"Are you serious? I haven't fired a gun in years."

"We need everybody we can get. Although you fly boys never could shoot straight anyhow. Come on." He set off jogging toward a big, blunt-nosed military truck in bottle green.

Mel had to wait as a bus roared past him, heading down the heavily reinforced corridor away from the Candidate Hilton and out of the blast zone. Then he followed helplessly.

"So," Don asked as he jogged, "you see Holle off?"

"I chickened out," Mel admitted. "Seeing her through a wall of glass—what difference would it have made?"

"Fair enough," Don said, jogging. "Best to keep busy."

"So what's going on?"

"Action all around the perimeter. Here." There was a heap of armor and weaponry by the truck; Don handed Mel police body armor, helmet and gun. "They're coming in worse from the west just now. We think it's an abider faction. But it's hard to tell, everything's mixed up to hell with eye-dees and rogue elements of cops and military and National Guard running around everywhere. You strapped up? All aboard." He helped Mel climb up onto the bed of the truck.

There were maybe twenty troopers jammed in here, cops and National Guard and regular army troops. An officer tied up the tailboard, and they rolled off, heading west, with an engine roar and a plume of dust rising up into the evening dark. The truck followed a trail of white rags tied to sticks, evidently leading it through a minefield.

Don stared straight ahead. Mel couldn't judge his mood. "So—you OK with everything? The launch and stuff."

Don forced a smile, and adjusted his chinstrap. "As much as you'd expect. We'd both rather have sent Dexter, but they ain't taking two-year-olds. Kelly's gone on our behalf, to live on a new world as we'll never be able to. As for me, what the future holds God only knows. At one time I had a career path, you know. Worked in the city, in a CAPs squad under an officer called Bundy. Good man."

"CAPs?"

"Crimes Against Persons. Homicides and assault. It was regular police work. And I was smart. I was thinking of going into Special Investigations. It was compensation, you know, for being thrown out of the Academy. But we kept being pulled out to go man some barricade or other, or break up another food riot at another eye-dee camp. Now it's all kind of liquefying, and so much for my career plans." He looked at Mel. "But there's still work to be done. If you like I'll put in a word, and—hey, we're there."

The truck growled to a stop. The officer let down the tailgate, and the troopers clambered down. There was a sound of gunfire, a stink of burning, a pall of smoke.

Don beckoned to Mel. *Stick with me.* They made their way across broken ground, the smashed foundations of some building. The gunfire, the shouting and the screams, got louder. I should be on the Ark right now, Mel thought. Not here.

They came to a trench system, and at the officer's signal dropped down into it and made their way along in a file, Mel sticking close to Don's back. This trench had been dug out carefully. It was walled with sheets of plastic, and it twisted this way and that, a snakelike layout to reduce the damage from a grenade blast that would clean out a straight-line ditch. The defense of the Ark launch site, on this ultimate day, had been planned over months and years.

There was a deep, double-barreled thrumming noise. Mel looked to the west, and he saw the unmistakable profile of a Chinook helicopter rise up, huge and ugly, its double rotors turning, silhouetted against the darkling sky. It swept low over the ground, and guns in its nose spat visible fire at the trenches.

"Not one of ours," Don shouted.

With a thunderous crash two more aircraft roared in, passing north to south and screaming over the Chinook. Mel, an air force brat, was pretty sure they were F-35s, Lightnings. Everybody cowered; the aircraft noise, vast and oppressive, was terrifying. But there was no firing; maybe the Lightnings were short of munitions. He yelled, "Where the hell did they get a Chinook?"

"Some rogue faction in the army or air force. Or maybe it's the Mormons. I told you it's a mess—"

There was a muffled boom.

"Mortar!"

"Down!"

The shell looped over them. Mel felt Don's hand on the back of his neck, pushing him facedown onto a torn plastic sheet. The shell passed over them and detonated, and the ground shook.

Mel got up gingerly. "Somebody got a mortar."

"Yeah," Don breathed. "And now they got their range."

The officer leading them pointed. "You, you, and you two, take out that damn mortar. The rest of you follow me."

"That's us," Don said. The other two picked out by the officer had already scrambled over the trench wall, and were making their way west, the way the mortar had come from. Don squirmed up and out after them.

Mel followed without thinking. He lunged over the perimeter and got down into the dirt, crawling after the other three, trying to keep up, squirming through the mud toward a mortar nest. It's for you, Holle, he thought. All of it's for you.

The others got to the mortar pit before Mel could catch up, and rushed it. Mel heard the slam of a grenade, screams, and then a bloody gurgle.

By the time he reached the pit Don was already clambering down into it. The mortar itself, looking antiquated, was ruined, but there was a pile of shells that looked salvageable. Don and the others were pawing through them. There was a butcher-shop stink of blood and burned flesh. There had been two people in the pit, Mel saw. One, a man, had been blown in half by the grenade that had destroyed the mortar, his legs reduced to shreds. But he had a pistol in his hand, and blood ran down his chest. He had evidently resisted his attackers.

The other in the pit was a woman. Bloodied, she wore the ragged remains of a dress. She was holding a baby, Mel saw, astonished. The kid, no more than a few months old, was wrapped in a filthy blanket. He was awake, but seemed too stunned to cry. When the mother saw Mel, she held the baby up to him and stumbled forward. "Please—"

A single shot from one of the soldiers felled her, leaving her sprawled on the broken ground, her back a bloody ruin where the bullet had exited.

An engine roar crashed down from above.

"Down!" Don yelled.

Mel threw himself flat on the ground. He pulled the baby from its mother's arms, tried to cradle it under his body armor, and tucked his helmet down over his face. The roar overhead grew louder, and light splashed around him. He risked a glance up. That Chinook was directly overhead, barely visible behind the glare of its spotlight. Mel thought he saw figures in an open hatch, aiming some kind of weapon at the ground, like a bazooka.

A plane came screaming in, an F-35, no more than fifty meters off the ground. The Chinook gave up on the trenches. It rose up, dipped its nose and headed east, straight toward the center of the Zone, and the Ark, surely its ultimate target. The F-35 continued its run. Mel waited for it to open up its cannon, or fire an air-to-air missile, or evade. It did none of these. No ammunition, he remembered.

The plane rammed the chopper.

The explosion hammered at the ground, and filled the sky with light. Mel cowered in the broken mud, clutching the baby, and waited for the wreckage to rain down.

The baby started crying.

44

Wilson lay beside Kelly and Venus in their acceleration couches on the bridge of the Ark's crew hull B, called Seba.

"One minute," Venus said.

Wilson couldn't keep from talking. "Jesus. We must be insane. A fucking atom bomb is about to go off, right under my ass."

Kelly grinned at him. "Too late to bale now."

Venus said, "And this is going to be Gunnison's worst day since the Alien fought the Predator."

"What?"

"Never mind. Everything's nominal." Businesslike as ever, she checked the displays before them.

The Ark was very heavy engineering, but it was also very simple, and there were few instruments. Aside from housekeeping displays showing the condition of the air inside the pressurized hulls and the acceleration to which the crew would be exposed, gauges showed the pulse-detonation timing rate, and the levels in the tanks of anti-ablation oil and coolant fluid, and the pressures in the steam lines. The controls were simple too, a manual control of the pulse unit drop rate, a T-handle and stick to adjust the bird's attitude. These were a last-ditch resort if the automatics failed. However, Wilson knew, nobody had survived a sim in which some faked disaster had made it necessary to use the controls.

And now, in these last seconds, Wilson could feel the beast stir, as the nuclear pulse units in their charge magazines were lined up in the throats of their delivery mechanisms, and the coolant liquids began to pump around the great pistons. He glanced over the monitors that showed the crew in their rows of seats, deep in the bowels of the hull. The bright amber launch-imminent lamps were flashing, and a voice message resounded at every level. But people were still fighting over the couches.

"Twenty seconds," Kelly said, matter-of-fact.

Wilson felt his anus clench. "Shit, shit."

"Fixed, damn it," Matt yelled, and his voice echoed from the metal walls around him.

"Fifteen seconds," called up Liu Zheng, from the ground.

"I know. I can hear the coolants flowing." Matt glanced around at the mighty metal walls surrounding his own mote of a body. "Can't believe I'm here, listening to this."

"Ten . . . Nine . . . I suppose we don't need a countdown."

"No. I finished the job, didn't I?"

"That you did, Matt. Good work."

"Where are you?"

"Right under the pusher plate. Where else would I be?"

"If it goes wrong you'll be the first to know, Liu."

There was a rush of steam, a clang. That must be the first pulse unit rushing down its launch chute. In this last instant Matt felt a stab of fear. "Liu, I think—"

He saw the detonation, lapping around the rim of the pusher plate. He *saw* it. And then—

An immense fist slammed into the back of her couch. Holle heard gasps all around her, and a groaning, as if the ship itself were being torn apart.

And yet I'm not dead, she thought. She was only thirty meters above the plasma cloud from a five-kilotonne nuke, and a pusher plate that had been hurled upwards at a thousand gravities. But the suspension system had to be working, the great pistons absorbing the shock. If not she'd be dead by now, the ship destroyed as the thousand-ton plate, forced up by that first explosion, rose and smashed through the Ark's gargantuan structure.

The gravity dipped, sickeningly. The end of the first pulse. Was that only a second?

And then the next came, another shove, smoother this time, that pushed her back into her couch. The pressure yielded once more. And then the push came again. And again. It was working. She heard people whooping, applauding.

She lay back and closed her eyes, and tried to imagine she was on a kid's swing in the training facilities at Gunnison, harmlessly rocking back and forth. It wasn't too bad, a G or so of eyeballs-in acceleration, an easy training session. Not so bad to be riding an atomic booster into space.

But the launch facility, any ground crew who hadn't got away from the Zone, were already gone, the hapless town of Gunnison flattened like Hiroshima. The journey hadn't even begun.

Now she felt the ship judder, shift violently from one side to another, shaking her in her cozy couch. The Ark was mounted with beefy auxiliary rockets, attitude thrusters meant to tweak its trajectory against the brute pushing of the nukes. Swing, swing, swing—

She was thrown forward against her straps, as if the ship had hit a brick wall. The applause turned to screams.

Unit failed. They had simulated this.

She glanced around. Morell looked terrified. "A pulse unit failed, Theo!" she yelled. "Just one unit, out of hundreds. That's all . . ." It was always a chancy business to throw a device as complex as a thermonuclear bomb *into* the expanding plasma cloud left by another only a second earlier and expect it to detonate. But if the *next* unit failed, and the next, they would fall back into their own radioactive mess . . .

Another surge. God, had that only been a second, once again? Time was elastic.

And another surge. And another. Now there was some pogoing, longitudinal juddering as the bulk of the Ark soaked up that missed stroke. Then the acceleration dips settled down to that steady swinging once more.

She felt Theo's hand flapping, grasping for hers. She took it and held on firmly, wishing that Mel was here, and her father. Swing, swing, swing, the pulsing a little slower than her resting heartbeat, swing, swing, and the carcass of the Ark groaned as it rose like a dark angel from the ashes of its launchpad.

Something splashed on her face. It was urine, dripping down from the deck above.

Swing, swing.

45

Thandie Jones stood in the control room at Pikes Peak, surrounded by a scene she'd thought she'd never see again, a scene she'd thought lost with so much else of the pre-flood world: a launch control, rows of earnest technicians murmuring into comms links as they monitored the progress of a spacecraft rising from the Earth.

But what a spacecraft.

Gordo touched her shoulder. "Look. We got some image capture from before the first detonation." The images had been taken from a camera directly beneath the pusher plate. "See that?" Gordo pointed, intent. "That puff of steam is the injection of the charge. There's the pulse unit it-self . . ." A vase-shaped object falling down into the air, from a hole in the great metal roof above it. "The anti-ablation oil sprays over the pusher. And—*bang*—the detonation of the bomb itself." The sequence ended as the camera was fried.

Thandie had first worked with Gordo Alonzo twenty-four years ago, when they had gone diving together in a museum-piece submarine, seeking evidence of subterranean seas. Now, having forced her way back to his attention over the issue of Grace Gray, he'd invited her to come here to watch the climax of the project. She would never have dreamed that after all these years she and Gordo would be standing side by side in a situation like this. She'd never even liked the man.

There were gasps as images from an aircraft just outside the blast zone were fed to the screens. Thandie turned to see.

A crater, kilometers wide, had been burned into the Earth. Above it rose the familiar sight of a nuclear fireball, a mushroom cloud. But a spacecraft contrail punched astonishingly up and out of that cloud, powered by more detonations, more fireballs, a string of them. Soon the plasma glare from the rising craft outshone the atomic glow on the ground, and cast light across the remnant of the land and the encroaching sea, a lethal sun rising.

"What did I start, Gordo? Maybe I should have kept my mouth shut."

He grunted. "You always did take all the credit, you ballsy dyke."

Three

2042–2044

46

t was a relief for Wilson Argent to drift out of the airlock and into the blackness beyond the hull. A relief to get out of the small chamber where for hours he had been pre-breathing the low pressure pure oxygen that filled his suit. A relief, forty days after launch, to get out of the cramped, noisy environs of Seba and Halivah, the twin hulls of the Ark, that competitive, fractious hothouse. Yet he was still deep within the bowels of the ship, deep within the factory-sized Orion launch stage, and his view of free space was obstructed by struts and tanks and shadows. He could hear nothing but the whirr of the pumps in his backpack, the hiss of static from the comms units in his Snoopy-hat headset, and the rasp of his own breathing.

The latching end of the manipulator arm—formally the Mobile Servicing System—was waiting for him, just as according to the EVA plan, right outside the hatchway. The arm was like an ungainly robot hand, sprouting latches and tool stubs and cameras, swathed in white insulating cloth, bright where it caught the spotlights.

Wilson turned around, grabbed the edge of the hatch with his gloved hands, and launched himself feet first toward the arm's latching end. His Kevlar tether unrolled behind him. The bulky gloves were a smart design that enabled his fingers to bend easily, but his legs were stiff, stuck inside what felt like an inflated inner tube. His Extravehicular Mobility Unit, his suit, insulated and cooled him and kept him under pressure and even offered some protection from micrometeorites and radiation, but it made him as rigid as a plastic doll. But then he wasn't planning on walking on the moon today; he was to make an eyeball inspection of the pusher plate, and most of the movements he would be making would be controlled by the arm.

His aim was true, and his booted feet settled gently against the arm's end. He heard a distant scrape as latches closed around his boot soles. A rail swiveled up to meet him, and he grasped a double handle, so that it was as if he was riding a scooter. He clipped a harness around the stem of the handle. More security: if the arm failed altogether, he could conceivably work his way back to its base hand over hand. He was ready.

"Cupola, Argent," he said, his voice muffled in his own ears from the enclosure of the helmet. "I've interfaced with the arm. I'm good to go. Preparing to release the hull tether."

"Copy that, Wilson," Venus called from the cupola. "Your medical signs are a little off. You're breathing too hard, your heart rate's above nominal. Take a few seconds."

He supposed she was right, but she didn't need to say it out loud. He knew that many of the crew would be following his progress on the internal comms, and he no doubt had an audience Earthside via the continual live feed. "Venus, I know what I'm doing. We practiced this very maneuver for hours back in the Hilton. I could do it in my sleep."

"That's what's worrying me. Take a breath, have a drink, and blip your SAFER again."

"Damn it." But as capcom today she was the boss, sort of. He sipped a little water from his in-helmet bag.

And he pressed the button at his waist. His SAFER gave him a subtle kick in the back, and he could feel how the arm assembly rocked and quivered as it absorbed the impulse. His Simplified Aid For EVA Rescue was a cut-down compressed-nitrogen jet that would allow him to steer himself back to the Ark if the worse came to worst and he was cut loose from the hull altogether. Like the arm and his suit, the SAFER was a design relic of the International Space Station. He waited for the arm's vibrations to damp down.

Sort of the boss. After years of pursuing his specialism in the ship's external systems he was damn sure he knew a lot better than Venus how to run this routine inspection EVA, which had been scheduled in principle since the Ark had been nothing more than a paper design on a desk in Denver. But there was no point railing at Venus. She was just one link in a chain of command which ran up through the Ark's nominal onboard commander Kelly Kenzie to Gordo Alonzo, ensconced in Mission Control in Alma, to where the running of the mission had been transferred from Pikes Peak after the Orion engine was shut down. That chain of command would be in place for the next two years, until they had fulfilled their mission at Jupiter and shot off to the stars in a warp bubble. After that the superluminal Ark would not be contactable, and Alma itself, submitting to the flood, would cease to transmit anyhow, and the Ark would be on its own.

But remoteness was already a problem. Earth was five light minutes away, making it impossible for Gordo to manage the EVA hands-on. It wasn't Venus's fault. If not for lightspeed Gordo would be chewing him out just the same way. And anyhow, he admitted, he did feel a little better for having rested a few seconds.

"Cupola, Argent. OK, Venus, I'm set."

"Keep your hands inside the car at all times."

"Roger that." That phrase had been the mantra of the sim runners in Gunnison, many of them aging veterans of the pre-flood space program. As every theme park on Earth had shut down before Wilson or Venus had been born, none of the Candidates was clear what it meant. But it felt like good luck to repeat it now.

The arm juddered, Wilson felt a thrum of hydraulics, and then he was swung smoothly away from the hull.

He rose up through a tangle of struts, spars, pipes and cabling. It felt as if he were moving fast, and he passed alarmingly close to some of the heavy struts and tank walls. The arm, too, wobbled and vibrated more than he had expected from the sims, but then he was a heavy mass on the end of a long jointed structure. He concentrated on his breathing, and kept his face expressionless. He didn't want loops of his face with some bug-eyed scared expression showing on the in-hull screens, and back on Earth.

After only a few seconds he was clear of the Orion superstructure, and the arm lifted him out of shadow. The sun rose, a lantern hanging beyond the ship's prow, and his visor immediately tinted, blocking out much of the glare. Somewhere out there were stars, the Earth and moon, the planets, but he could see nothing but the sun.

As he rose further he got a good view of the full length of the Ark—the first human to do so with his naked eye since launch, he reminded himself with some pride, although drone robots had been sent out for inspections since the Orion had been shut down. The twin hulls of the ship were still bound up within the components of the Orion launch stage—hulls now called Seba and Halivah, named for the brothers of the biblical Nimrod, all great-grandsons of Noah. He could see the shuttles that would some day take them down to the surface of Earth II, four brilliant white moths clinging to the hulls' flanks. A constellation of artificial lights was scattered through the Ark's tangled structure, and the sunlight splashed highlights from polished metal. It looked extraordinarily beautiful, he thought, drifting in interplanetary space like this, and yet odd, not so much a spacecraft as an industrial plant somehow uprooted and flung into the light. All this would be taken apart and rebuilt at Jupiter, as the Orion was discarded and the Ark was readied for its interstellar cruise. But before then the Orion would have to fire up one more time to slow the Ark into Jovian orbit. And as a result Wilson needed to make this inspection of the pusher plate. There had been two misfires of pulse units during the launch sequence, the first only a few seconds after liftoff. The longitudinal jarring delivered to the ship by the missing pulses, and possible damage caused to the pusher plate by any misplaced bombs, needed to be checked for.

When he looked down, beyond his feet, he could make out the dim red lights of the cupola where Venus sat, following his progress. Another space station relic, it was a hexagonal glass blister, the window hatches folded back, stuck to the side of Seba. The cupola was Venus's domain, and during most of the mission she would be using it to run her astronomy experiments, and the guidance, navigation and control functions of which she was leader. On impulse he waved a hand, and he saw motion inside the cupola, a shadow in the low-level eye-saving illumination.

"We see you, Wilson."

"Cupola, I see you too, you're looking good."

"How's the ship looking?"

"I can see no obvious damage, from this vantage. No sign of leaks from the wall tanks." Much of the Ark's onboard water was stored in fine curving tanks just under the outer skin of each hull; the water, wrapped around the living volume, provided some protection from cosmic radiation. "Scorching around the attitude rockets' nozzles. Perhaps some scarring of the heat insulation tiles on the nose fairing."

"The Geiger readings show no relics of the Orion bombs at your position, Wilson. Cosmic background only."

"That's reassuring," he said dryly. The arm swung him away again, bending at its multiple joints. He passed the great limbs of the shock-absorber pistons and approached the base of the ship. The circular rim of the pusher plate was now clearly visible, gleaming in the steady sunlight. "I can see the plate. Will be entering its shadow soon."

"Roger, Wilson. Don't take any chances."

"I won't." As the plate's sharp rim neared he gripped the scooter handles hard, and tried to keep his face still, his breathing regular. "Here I go . . ." Damn, his voice was a squeak.

The arm dipped down, and the rim of the plate slid up over the glare of the sun and plunged him in shadow. For a few seconds his visor failed to react to the change in light level, stranding him in darkness. The arm stopped, slow vibrations washing along its length. He felt very remote, very fragile, here on the end of this unlikely cherry-picker.

Then the visor cleared, and lamps on the arm lit up, splashing light over the steel gong before him. "I'm there," he said. "I see the plate." He reached out with one arm. "Almost close enough to touch."

"Roger that, Wilson. Take it easy now. Have another break, let your eyes adjust. All your systems are go, your consumables are fine. You could stay out there another twelve hours if you had to. You've plenty of time."

"Copy."

He deliberately steadied his breathing. He turned, looking back the way he had come. And there were Earth and moon, hanging in space, visible now that the pusher plate eclipsed the sun. Both showed half-discs, separated only by about as much as the moon's diameter as seen from the surface of the Earth. He held up his thumb, and was able to cover both of the twin worlds. In the first few days, as they had looked back at the receding home planet, they had all been shocked by how little land remained. Even Colorado, which had seemed so extensive when they were down there living on it, was only a scatter of muddy islands, threatened by the huge curdled semipermanent storms that stalked the ocean world. But from here he could see no detail.

They had already come so far. The brief, explosive Orion launch had hurled them directly away from the Earth, without pausing in orbit, and they would cruise with only minor course adjustments all the way to Jupiter, slowing as they climbed out of the sun's gravity well. But right now they were traveling at an astounding speed: eighty-five thousand feet per second in Gordo's astronaut units, or twenty-six kilometers a second, or fifty-eight thousand miles per hour. This was more than twice as fast as any human had traveled before; the record had been held by an Apollo crew.

Even at such speeds the whole journey was expected to take them a year. But in their forty days so far they had already traveled around ninety million kilometers—more than two hundred times the distance from Earth to moon, around a tenth of the distance to Jupiter, orders of magnitude further from Earth than any human before them. Even light took a nontrivial time to span such distances. It was astounding to think that the image he saw of Earth was already five minutes old.

Slowly, as he watched, the silent stars came out, filling the sunless sky beyond the bright Earth.

"Argent, cupola. You OK out there, big guy?"

"Yeah. Just taking in the view."

"You ready to proceed?"

"Roger that."

"The arm will move you to plate sector one-A . . ."

The arm juddered into motion again, swinging him closer to the pusher plate. He sighed, and turned away from the Earth.

47

Grace Gray found Kelly Kenzie at her station on Seba's fourth deck, a few minutes before the crew council meeting was due to start. Grace hauled herself up from Deck Five along one of the cables that had been strung between the decks to help with mobility during this weightless cruise, and swiveled around to arrive legs first. She carried a handheld, and now sent it spinning through the air.

Kelly caught it easily and began to inspect it. Kelly, alongside Holle Groundwater and Zane Glemp, sat with her legs wrapped around her T-stool's restraint bar. She had handhelds and scratch pads scattered on the tabletop in front of her, held in place with Velcro pads, though a couple of styluses floated in the air. Kelly looked stressed, sleepless. Grace knew that she had found the first couple of months of her command of this trans–Jupiter mission tougher than she'd expected. But then, she faced problems none of them had planned for.

Holle smiled at Grace, and poured her a coffee. This involved injecting the liquid from a flask into a mug with a nozzle like a baby's first cup.

"Thanks." Grace sipped the coffee cautiously. It was pretty foul, and was likely to get fouler once they started running low on the compressed, freeze-dried ingredients in a few years' time. She settled in place, with her back against a wall.

Kelly thumbed the handheld, scrolling through Grace's report, occasionally muttering expletives under her breath. "This is the complete census?"

"I spoke to everybody, in both hulls," Grace said. "I checked their boarding tokens, if they had them, and biometric ID. I even got their names independently verified, and checked their claims about their skill sets and genetic background with Gordo on the ground."

Holle asked, "You didn't have any trouble getting the data?"

Grace shrugged. "It was fine. I guess the fact that I don't belong to any one faction was an advantage. Everybody distrusts me equally."

Holle eyed Grace's belly. "You're nine months gone, but you've taken to weightlessness better than some of us Candidates. Life in space is a pain in the arse, isn't it? All the little things. You can't wash or shower like you can on the ground. You can't even use toothpaste without it floating into your eye . . ."

Grace smiled carefully. Holle was about the most open of the Candidates, and she'd always been friendly since Gordo had foisted gatecrasher Grace on her last year. But even Holle struck Grace as spoiled. The Candidates constantly carped about their lot, and rarely empathized with the plight of those millions, maybe even still billons, suffering on the drowning Earth. She patted her belly. "This doesn't seem so bad to me. The spacesickness was no worse than morning sickness. And zero G helps me carry this lump around, I guess." Though there were other side-effects. Sometimes her body emitted alarming gurgling noises, as it tried to compensate for the lack of the gravity field that every other baby since Cain and Abel had been born into. But at least she would not be the first to give birth, out here in space; two of the Candidates, pregnant on boarding, had already delivered successfully in the expert if overworked hands of Doc Wetherbee, and the crew's genetic diversity had therefore increased.

"Here they come," Kelly said. "Time to get your body armor on, gang."

Grace glanced around. People were converging on Kelly's station,

coming down the fireman's pole through the decks, or swimming through
the connecting tunnel from the second hull.

Kelly had her closest allies with her already, Zane and Holle, Venus
reporting in via a screen from the cupola where she was supervising Wilson Argent's spacewalk. Other Candidates showed up, Joe Antoniadi looking wide-eyed as ever, as if the world was a continual surprise, and Thomas
Windrup and Elle Strekalov clinging to each other, and Cora Robles
looking petulant and bored, a party girl five light minutes from the nearest club. Doc Wetherbee arrived too, bringing a handheld of his own, and
with a thunderous expression on his face.

Now here came a few of the "gatecrashers," as the Candidates dismis-
sively called those like Grace herself who had been foisted onto the crew
by special interest groups late in the selection process. Theo Morell looked
even more nervous than usual. And, even more insultingly labeled, some
of the "illegals" arrived—rogue elements from the security forces, supposedly charged with guarding the ship, who had stormed their way on board
themselves during the last moments. Grace knew their names by now,
such as the Shaughnessy brothers, and Jeb Holden and Dan Xavi, two
tough-looking former eye-dees. The illegals were led, informally, by
Masayo Saito, a young Japanese-American lieutenant and the most senior
of the military people. Masayo claimed he wasn't here by choice, but had
just got swept along with the rest. Grace actually believed him; she
had seen pictures of the wife and baby he had left behind on the ground,
and would now presumably never see again.

After the Orion engines died and they had started to move freely
around the ship and through the transfer tunnel between the two hulls,
Grace had been amazed at the sight of the illegals, in their dirtied, blood-
stained remnants of military uniforms. She didn't even recognize half the
gatecrashers. So many people had made it onto the ship who she'd never
laid eyes on before. But everybody was young, almost all of them younger
than Grace at twenty-six. Well, most front-line military personnel were
young, so maybe that was no surprise.

The space began to fill up. The crew members crowded around Kelly's table, or they found struts on the wall or ceiling, hanging like bats, and they messed about, passing coffees to each other. There was a constant hubbub of noise coming from the decks above and below, easily visible through the mesh partitions. The hull was only eight meters across from wall to curving wall. The available volume was reduced further by the curved-back racks that were crammed against every wall, repositories for the equipment and stores that contained everything needed to run a starship for a nominal ten years. Grace had seen enough of the hull's design to accept it was a miracle of packing, of space and storage efficiency. There just wasn't enough damn room. She sometimes thought it was like living on a vast, crowded staircase, or maybe in a prison.

As booted feet waved around in front of her face, Grace huddled in on herself, dreaming of walking over empty plains.

At last they were convened, and Kelly rapped a stylus on the tabletop to call them to order.

"OK, this is the ship's council, held today, fourteenth February 2042, Kelly Kenzie presiding."

"Happy Valentine's, sweet cheeks," called one of Masayo's boys, and there was a ripple of laughter.

Kelly ignored this, stony-faced. "The discussion is being beamed back to Alma for comments and guidance later. We'll start with section reports. Zane, you want to go first?"

Zane nominally led a team that covered the more exotic engineering. He reported that the Orion drive had been shut down and safed for now, with no major defects reported, and pending completion of inspections like Wilson's there seemed no reason the drive shouldn't serve them just as well when they arrived at Jupiter. "We're likely to finish with a cargo of spare nukes," he said.

Meanwhile the Prometheus reactors should soon come online. These were advanced engines based on designs for a canceled unmanned spacecraft called the Jupiter Icy Moons Orbiter. When brought into operation the pressure would be taken off the fuel cells. And the warp-bubble equipment, stowed for now in the hulls' lower sections and to be assembled in Jovian orbit, showed no signs of damage from the launch events.

Venus, calling in from the cupola, reported that her planet-finding project was under way on a trial basis. The idea was to make observations that would supplement those made from Earth-orbit telescopes like the Hubble and the surviving ground-based instruments such as in Chile. The most useful work would be achieved in the months they would spend in Jovian orbit, at a stable distance from Earth, and the work of selecting the Ark's destination would begin in earnest. Meanwhile Venus also had responsibility for GN&C, a NASA-type acronym for guidance, navigation and control. She gave the results of her most recent course-correction vernier burn, in terms of the accuracy of their trajectory on three axes: "Minus one, plus one, plus one. You don't get much better than that."

"OK. Holle?"

Holle Groundwater ran a team responsible for more prosaic aspects of the ship's systems, but she gabbled out acronyms with the best of them. "Comms" Grace grasped easily enough. "EPS" was the electrical power system. "ECLSS" was the environmental control and life-support system, complicated mechanisms devoted to the air scrubbing and water cycling on which all their lives depended. The target was ambitious. There would always be leaks and wastage, but they were aiming to keep the loops of air and water and other essentials closed tight enough to last for years. Right now Holle was leading her team through a complex series of configurations and tests, bedding down her systems for flight. These tasks included establishing a hydroponic garden on Seba's lower deck. So far, she reported, things were going well.

The gatecrashers and illegals listened silently to all this. All the section heads were, of course, Candidates, and had been trained for the job. That alone made a point about the divisions in the crew.

Doc Wetherbee was the last to report. Only twenty-four years old he was a Candidate too. As well as his formal education he had served in general practice in Denver, in hospital emergency rooms, and on triage teams in eye-dee camps and processing centers. With one eye on his handheld he ran through a brief survey of the general health of the crew, of whom only three were still suffering from spacesickness, another two had fluid balance problems, and the woman who broke her leg when her couch collapsed during the launch was recovering—as was an illegal who had cracked a knuckle while beating up a Candidate. Depletion of his various medical stores was actually less than had been expected.

"Our two new mothers and their babies are doing fine," he finished up. "Which leaves me with one question. Is there a doctor in the house? Aside from this one."

There was a general stir; the crux of the meeting approached. Wetherbee was understandably furious about the outcome of the launch, because among those who hadn't made it on board had been Miriam Brownlee, qualified psychiatrist and surgeon, and Wetherbee's lover.

Kelly said, "Grace, you ran your census." She flipped back the handheld. "You want to field that one?"

Grace caught the handheld. "OK. You all know the boarding process on launch day was a mess. At Kelly's request I've been running a simple check of who's actually on board this boat—who you are, what skills you have, what sicknesses or inherited disorders, all the rest. I asked you all for data, and also asked you to confirm what your buddies told me.

"Here's the summary results. I'll download the detail to the ship archive if the council approves. The nominal crew was eighty adults. There are actually seventy-eight adults on board. Well, the head count we did on the first day told us that."

Kelly said, "So the mutiny actually caused us to leave Earth with two wasted berths. Go on."

"Of the seventy-eight, forty-nine are ex-Candidates. Of the remainder, twenty-one are late additions to the crew, but formally approved by the command team under Gordo Alonzo on the ground. That includes myself. And that leaves eight, who got on board in those last moments before the ramp came up."

Masayo Saito said, "Just use the word. We've all heard what you call us. Illegals."

"As for medical staff," Grace said, unperturbed, "the original crew plan was to have three doctors on board, with specialisms in surgery, psychiatry, child care, other fields."

Wetherbee asked, "And after your careful survey, the number of trained doctors who actually made it on board is—"

"One. You, Mike. It's just bad luck, I guess. I'm sorry."

He laughed bitterly. "Well, it's not your fault."

"What a screw-up," Kelly said. "What else, Grace? How about first-aid skills?"

"There we're better off. All the Candidates have decent first-aid or first-response training. So do Masayo and some of his boys."

"Well, there you go," Masayo said. "You need us after all."

"But," Kelly said, "we're heavily dependent on Doc Wetherbee here. Gordo Alonzo will come down hard on us to find some way to back him up. Look, Mike, I don't mean to put you under any extra pressure. But maybe you could work with Grace and pick out the most promising paramedic-type candidates we have. Figure out some kind of training program. For now we have remote support from the ground; for anything less than surgery or trauma cases I guess that's going to be a help."

"But we will lose the ground once we go to warp," Zane said coldly. "And when the waves close over Alma."

"I know that, Zane," Kelly snapped. "We've got time to come up with solutions before then. Grace, what about genetic diversity? The social engineers tried to stick to their selection parameters even with the gatecrashers."

Grace said, "We'll have to run a DNA analysis for a full answer. But only one of the military people is female. And two are actually brothers, the Shaughnessys."

"Brothers." Mike Wetherbee barked a laugh. "Christ! We even fouled that up."

Masayo said heavily, "Is this how it's going to be all the way to fucking Jupiter?"

Kelly folded her arms. "I don't like you, or the way you got yourself aboard. But we're all stuck in this tub together, for the rest of our lives. And we don't have room for passengers, Masayo."

"Fine," Masayo said. "We want to work."

"Good. Holle?"

Holle smiled around at the group, looking as if she was actually enjoying the meeting. The tension palpably lessened. Grace admired her unobtrusive skill. "We urgently need to establish a maintenance routine. There are seventy-eight of us, crammed into a small space."

"Yes, and it seems a damn small space to me," Masayo said. "How much room do we actually have?"

Holle tapped her own handheld, searching for figures. "You know that the two hulls are based on Ares propellant tanks—in turn derived from the old space shuttle external tank. Each is a cylinder about eight meters in diameter, and fifty meters long. We lose some of that diameter to the water tanks under the hull, the equipment racks, and so on. We're left with about forty-seven hundred cubic meters of living space, in the habitable hulls. That's around three times the pressurized volume in a Boeing 747. About five times the pressurized volume available in the ISS—"

"But thirteen times the crew size," Kelly said.

"And actually the space available to us right now is less than the maximum, because we've had to stow the warp-generator components in the lower third of each hull.

"We're going to have to work hard to keep such a small volume habitable. Masayo, we'll run some education on spaceflight basics for you guys. For example, all the stuff that falls to the ground under gravity, the dust that settles, well, it won't in microgravity, and so the air we breathe is full of garbage—including bits of us. We're going to have to scrub down the walls every day, if we're not to pick up algal growth and mold.

Also we have fuel cells to purge, batteries to charge, waste water to collect, carbon dioxide scrubber canisters to change, drinking water to be chlorinated, and so on. We need to draw up rotas. I'll post drafts to the ship's archive when we're done."

Masayo folded his arms. "You want us to be cleaners. That's what you're saying."

Kelly leaned forward. "If you've got skills more appropriate to this interstellar spacecraft right now, let me know. In the longer term, with help from the ground, we can work out how to make the most of the skills and experience that each of us brings. But for now, yes, you're going to be cleaning. And so am I, so are we all. Holle, when you draw up your rotas, put me and Lieutenant Saito at the head of the wall-scrubbing detail for the first period."

Holle nodded.

Kelly looked around at them all, at the table, suspended at various angles in the air around her. "OK, I guess this meeting has been productive. But it's only a start. We're just going to have to learn to get along with each other. And *work* for each other, and for the good of the ship. Whatever else we differ on, I hope we can agree on that much. AOB? No? Then we're done here."

But as the meeting broke up, Kelly motioned Holle and Grace to stay behind.

Once Masayo and his boys were out of earshot, she murmured, "What about weapons? That gang of soldier boys must have come aboard armed. Grace, you got any hint of where they stashed their guns?"

Grace shook her head. "Didn't occur to me to ask. You need to talk to Masayo."

Kelly looked absent. "No," she said. "I can't afford a confrontation over this. Holle, I want you to round up some people. Make it two, at least, for every one of the illegals. Mount a raid. Pin them down and get their

damn guns off them. Use some muscle you can trust. Wilson, for instance."

Holle looked doubtful. "That will cause problems long term."

"Let Masayo squawk. Better that than arms inside the pressurized
hulls. Get it done." She checked a clock. It was set to Alma time, as were
all the clocks on the ship. "I need to go check how Wilson is progressing
with his EVA."

48

race Gray's favorite part of each day on the Ark was the end
of it.

Mission Control back at Alma had imposed a three-shift system on the crew in their twin hulls, so that Seba slept one shift, then
Halivah, then both were awake. That way at least half the crew was awake
and functioning at any given moment, increasing the chances of the Ark
as a whole surviving any sudden calamity.

But there was no real privacy in either hull, aside from doors on the
lavatories, though some kind of partitioning-off of the big volumes had
been promised for the long interstellar cruise phase. That meant that you
had to learn to sleep as if in a huge dormitory, with others above and
below you—their groans and snores all too audible, their couches visible
through the mesh of the deck—and you would see ghostly figures swimming back and forth, silent and weightless as bubbles.

But still Grace had learned to relish the moments when she strapped
herself loosely in her couch, inside a cocoon of sleeping bag and blanket.
This was the best of microgravity, away from the petty irritations of the
day when you would find yourself drifting through other people's garbage, or clouds of loose stuff, screws and plastic scraps and bits of sealant,
all evidence of the hasty construction of the ship. In your couch you
floated, as if you were in the most comfortable bed on Earth.

And just as the sleep period began the ubiquitous cameras, mounted on wall stanchions, turned themselves away. Earth didn't need to watch you sleep, either Mission Control or the wider public who, Gordo assured them, otherwise watched their every move, as if the ship was a reality show designed to distract them from the awful truth of the flood. The ratings were high, Gordo said. Grace believed the surveillance was inhibiting conflict aboard the ship, so she didn't object to it, but it was pleasant when the electronic eyes turned away.

And then Kelly Kenzie would make her final round, a visual inspection that all was well. This was a good instinct by Kelly, Grace thought, a way for her to bond with her crew. Maybe it would make up for rash actions like her planned gun raid. As she passed, Kelly had the ship's systems dip the hull lights down to their emergency settings, one by one. Thus the hull grew dark in sections as she floated by.

Once, when Grace was with Walker City, she had been no older than twelve or thirteen, the okies had stayed for six months working on a construction project near Abilene, Texas. One of her companions, an Englishman called Michael Thurley, had grown up a Catholic, and when he had discovered a small, pretty Catholic church in the city he had taken to attending Mass there. A few times Grace had sat with him. She particularly liked the end of the service, when an altar boy would go around the church snuffing out candles. That was what Kelly's quiet daily procession was like, as if they were children sleeping in a vast church where the lights were snuffed out one by one. Grace drifted off to sleep thinking of those days, of Michael and Gary Boyle, and their tents and their portable gadgets and all the walking, and the church in Texas where the lights went out one by one.

She was woken by a stab of pain in her belly, and a surge of dampness between her legs. Her waters had broken. It was three a.m., Alma time.

49

June 2043

Gordo Alonzo, his words limping across the forty-five-light-minute gulf to Jupiter, announced that he would deliver the verdict of the interservice tribunal on Jack Shaughnessy's misdemeanor to the senior crew on the control deck of Halivah.

Masayo Saito hadn't been out of Seba since they had reached Jupiter and the hulls had been separated and the connecting tunnel broken. But now, to attend Gordo's session in Halivah, Masayo was going to have to cross in a spacesuit, the astronaut's way. You always crossed in pairs, and Holle volunteered to accompany him. She saw a chance to build some metaphorical bridges with Masayo, as they crossed the real bridge between the hulls.

Masayo was ahead of her when she got to the pre-breathing chamber, a domed room in the tip of Seba's nose. You had to pre-breathe for hours to prepare yourself for the lower-pressure pure-oxygen air of a pressure suit; otherwise you risked the bends. Masayo didn't have much to say as she entered. Already in his suit save for helmet and gloves, he sat with his legs locked around a T-stool while he worked through crew assignment rotas on his handheld. She guessed he was fighting his nervousness.

And also the whole Windrup-Shaughnessy affair had inflamed tensions between illegals and Candidates. You couldn't keep a secret aboard the Ark, that was one lesson they had all learned in the early days in the always combustible atmosphere of a crowded ship. Even if what you said didn't get passed on in crew gossip, there was a good chance that the Earthbound fan of some star crewperson such as Kelly or Cora, glued to the live feed, would upload your comments back to her heroine in a piece of fan mail. Holle hoped to be able to talk to Masayo in the privacy of space, and was prepared to wait.

She had brought along some work to fill these hours too, and it was more interesting than Masayo's wall-scrubbing rotas. After seven months in orbit around Jupiter, the first results of Venus Jenning's planet-finding survey had been published.

Venus's survey derived from data from over forty years of work by Earth-based instruments and planet-finder space telescopes, supplemented by observations made by telescopes deployed from the Ark. A greater precision had been possible because to some extent two telescopes at Earth and Jupiter could serve as components of a single instrument nearly a billion kilometers wide.

Because it had been anticipated that better data about nearby exoplanets was going to be acquired after the Ark reached Jupiter, no firm decision about the Ark's target had been made before launch. But, according to the nominal mission plan, the current phase in Jupiter orbit should come to an end in another nine months—provided they completed the reconfiguring of the Ark, the construction of the warp generator, and the collection of antimatter from Io. They were going to need a decision before they left Jupiter because a warp journey, uncontrolled from within the spacecraft, was point and shoot; once they launched, they would be committed. So they had nine months to decide.

Hundreds of exoplanets had been cataloged. The difficulty was, which to choose?

The sun was a G-class star, compact, yellow, with a stable lifespan of billions of years. But G-class stars were comparatively rare, making up only one in thirty of the Galaxy's population. Of the hundreds of billions of stars in the Galaxy, the most common, two-thirds of the total, were red dwarfs, small, cool, so parsimonious with their hydrogen fuel that they were very long-lived, lasting hundreds of times as long as a G-class like the sun. The astronomers labeled these M-class stars.

The interstellar cruise was planned for a nominal duration of seven years. Inside its warp bubble the Ark would be able to reach velocities of around three times light speed, so that put a limit on the journey of some twenty light-years. There were around seventy star systems within that radius, most of them systems of multiple stars. But among those seventy targets there were only five G-class stars, excluding the sun.

The nearest was in fact Alpha Centauri A, ten percent more massive than the sun, the senior partner of the triple system that was the closest to Sol, just four light-years away. It had long been concluded that there were no worlds remotely Earthlike to be found in that system: only re-motely orbiting gas giants, labeled "cold Jupiters," and swarms of asteroids that might be the relic of failed planetary formations. The next closest G-class was a star called Tau Ceti, in the constellation of the whale, nearly twelve light-years from Sol. But no suitable candidates had been found there either. The nearest analogies to Earth—worlds of about the right mass, in stable orbits, and orbiting at just the right distance from the par-ent star, so neither too hot nor too cold—had in fact been found orbiting the "wrong" stars, either dimmer or brighter than Sol, even some of the many M-class candidate planets.

Fueled by all this data, arguments raged both on the Ark and down at Alma. A strong faction led by Gordo Alonzo insisted that the G-class stars had to be the priority, with a risk taken over the planet's precise analogy to Earth conditions. A different lobby, led vocally by Venus herself, argued for world first, star second. It was a passionate debate; after all, what was under discussion was the selection of Earth II, of a new home for man-kind. But it seemed to Holle to be devolving into an almost theological argument, a question of whether you would want your descendants to grow up under a wrong-colored sun.

To complicate this discussion further had been Venus's accidental dis-covery of an immense comet nucleus, swimming out of the trans-Jupiter dark and heading on what had looked like a collision course with the Earth. The sudden threat, piled on top of the ongoing calamity of the flood, had felt unbearable, the coincidence monstrous. "Proof that the devil exists," Gordo Alonzo had growled, "if not God." According to Venus's report, more data and analysis had now shown that the comet would pass close to the Earth but would not impact; it would provide a dramatic spectacle when it reached the inner solar system in a few years' time, but no more. Holle thought the strange incident had brought the fractious planet-spotters on Earth and Ark closer together for a while. But they had soon resumed their arguments.

Masayo's timer chimed. Holle closed down the report.

Masayo, already suited up, helped Holle put on the layers of her suit, the tight-fitting liquid-cooled undersuit, her pressure garment, and then the bright white micrometeorite outer cover. To do this Masayo had to get up close and personal to Holle in her underwear. Contact between the sexes could be awkward on a ship where there was an imbalance of men over women, a legacy of the chaotic final boarding process. And, in the open hulls, it was too easy to watch your neighbor all day and all night, and work up fantasies. This, in fact, had led to the assault that had got Jack Shaughnessy into so much trouble. But Masayo was brisk, professional, showing no particular interest in Holle beyond getting the work done.

She strapped her personal identification band around her leg, a color code with a crew number, so she could be recognized on visuals once outside the ship. For good measure she slapped an "EVA One" disc on her chest, and a number two on Masayo's. Then they pulled on their Snoopy-hat comms gear, helped each other with helmet and gloves, and checked over the display consoles on their chests.

When they were done, Holle raised a thumb to a watching camera, and called up to Zane, the duty officer today. "OK, Zane, this is EVA One, both EVA One and Two are good to go."

Zane's voice crackled in her ear. "Copy, Holle. Let me run through my checks of the lock."

They stood and waited. Zane sounded absent, as always. Maybe he was absorbed on some project of his own—the warp assembly was demanding enough. But it seemed to Holle that he increasingly disappeared into the dark places inside his own head. He would lie in his couch, or just float, hanging from some bracket like an empty suit. She'd tried to persuade Mike Wetherbee to take a look at him, but the doctor had protested he was no psychiatrist, and anyhow he was in a tremendous sulk about Miriam's stranding and wouldn't consider psychiatric cases. Holle, still smarting herself over her separation from Mel, could sympathize with that. Mike had tried to get Zane to talk to specialists on Earth by the downlink, but the time delay had destroyed any chance of empathy.

However, Zane was on the ball today, it seemed. After a couple of minutes an indicator over the airlock door flashed from red to green. Holle turned to Masayo. "You want to lead?"

"What, a jarhead like me? You go ahead."

"This is your first EVA of any kind, right?"

"Thanks for reminding me."

"Just don't throw up inside that suit, there are only five that fit me and that's one of them. Let's go."

She pulled down a handle and the door slid open, revealing the gleaming airlock chamber, and a small window showing the blackness of space beyond.

50

They emerged from the airlock into sharp, dim sunlight.

Holle and Masayo, weightless, stood on the nose of Seba, an insulation-blanketed tower fifty meters high. The tether between the hulls was a triple steel cable that ran vertically up from the nose of the hull, gleaming in the flat sunlight. Holle showed Masayo how to fix the attachment at his waist to the tether cables. Leaning back she followed the tether's line up through the incomplete circle of the warp generator, hanging directly above her head. Beyond that the second hull, Halivah, was suspended in the sky, nose down, two hundred meters away. It was an extraordinary metal sculpture, hanging in the pale light.

She looked at Masayo. He stood awkwardly in the stiff suit, his face hidden by a gold sun visor. She asked, "Ready?"

"Let's get it over."

Holle threw a switch. The suit winches cut in and they rose up, smooth and silent, their legs dangling, climbing the cables effortlessly, with Holle just ahead of Masayo. "The crossing will take a few minutes."

"Kind of slow," he muttered.

"Well, that's for safety. You in a hurry? I could always override the regulator—"

"Hell, no."

"Oh, come on, enjoy it. Look around. Get your bearings. There's the sun, over there." She pointed. The sun, five times more remote than from Earth, cast an oddly dim light and sharp, strange shadows. It was no longer bright enough to banish the stars that filled the sky all around them, more crowded than seen from any mountaintop on Earth. "Look, you can see the launch stage . . ."

The Orion launch frame drifted alongside the tethered hulls, its thermal-resistant pyramidal cap still in place, the pusher plate still gleaming. Without the bulk of the hulls the interior looked gutted, and that mighty thermonuclear engine was stilled for good. The hulk was now serving its final purpose as a construction platform as spacewalking astronauts, all of them Candidates trained for the job, put together the warp assembly at the hull tether midpoint. Aside from that Holle could see the freeflying platforms that supported Venus's planet-hunting telescopes, both of them sailing far from the vibration and bright lights of the hulls. There was no point looking for the antimatter miner; that was fifteen million kilometers away, plying its hazardous trade between Io and Jupiter. All these components were scattered in the blackness, but they twinkled with lights, with humanness, like a little town in the orbit of Jupiter.

Masayo was looking around uneasily, his hands clamped to the restraint at his waist.

"And there," she said, "is Jupiter." She pointed the other way from the sun.

Jupiter was a disc, golden-brown, visibly flattened, the only object in the whole universe away from the Ark cluster itself large enough to show as anything other than a point.

"Kind of disappointing," Masayo said.

It was a common reaction among the crew. "Oh, you think so?"

"It looks no larger than the moon, from Earth." He held out a thumb, waggling it, occluding the planet from his sight. "King of the worlds! Somebody told me it masses as much as all the other planets combined. Is that right?"

"Yeah. More than three hundred Earths."

"But it's just a ball of gas. I can see those big cloud bands, but so what? Even the Great Red Spot is just kind of mud-colored."

"You should talk to Joe Antionadi."

Joe had specialized in climatology, among other disciplines, and he spent long hours in the cupola studying Jupiter, a super-laboratory of climate. The Great Red Spot was actually a permanent storm system, centuries old, that prowled endlessly around Jupiter's cloud bands. There were disturbing parallels between it and some of the huge new hypercanes roaming Earth's equator.

But they weren't here for Jupiter itself, but for the products of its magnetosphere.

"You need perspective, Lieutenant. Why are we so far out? Why don't we orbit close in, skimming a hundred kilometers over the clouds like they used to orbit Earth?"

"Radiation, right?"

"That's it. Jupiter is a high-radiation environment. A human worker down there would pick up over three thousand rem a day—a lethal dose is around five hundred." She leaned back, trusting the tether, and waved her suited arms. "And believe me, if you could see the planet's magnetic field you wouldn't think Jupiter is so small. It has ten times the strength of Earth's, it stores twenty *thousand* times as much energy, and it stretches far out, even beyond our radius here, twice as far. And it traps charged particles from the sun."

"That's what makes the radiation environment so lethal."

"Right. But it's the interaction between Io and Jupiter's magnetic field that's important for us." Through Venus's telescopes Holle had seen the mighty aurorae that played over Jupiter's nightside, and heard the crackle of radio waves emanating from the tortured gases. Io's flux tube, a system of high-energy plasma, was a natural antimatter factory.

"Hell of a way to go about your business," Masayo said.

They had reached the tether's center point now, and Holle slowed them to a stop. Looking around from here she could see the great band of the warp generator, essentially a compact collider ring, wrapped around the tether. Spokes like a bicycle wheel's attached the ring to a hub at the midpoint of the tether. On the ring she saw a welding spark, and two suited workers moved patiently around a freshly installed panel.

Masayo asked uneasily, "Is there some reason why we stopped?"

"Point to the sun. Just do it."

"It's over there." He pointed again, his finger fat in the heavy glove. "Oh. No, it ain't." The sun had shifted visibly around their sky, as had Jupiter, the stars. "We're *turning*." He grabbed onto the tether.

"Take it easy. That's Seba down below, where we came from." She pointed. "That way is down. The other way's up. OK?"

He forced himself to relax, muttering. "Up, down, up, down."

"Good. We'll make an astronaut of you yet. It's just a slow rotation for now. Takes an hour to complete. Not enough so you'd notice the centripetal force inside the hulls, but it's enough to keep the tether under tension. Later we'll spin up faster."

When the warp assembly was completed vernier rockets would be used to spin the whole assembly, the twin hulls rotating around the tether midpoint like two handholding skaters whirling around on the ice. The rotation, completed once every thirty seconds, would induce an apparent gravity of about forty-four percent of a G in the nose airlocks—and because the centripetal forces increased the further you got from the center, the gravity would rise too, to around sixty-six percent of a G at the base of each hull.

Then a warp bubble would be thrown up around the whole unlikely jury-rigged assembly, snipping it out of the universe and sending it flying across the Galaxy at multiples of the speed of light.

Masayo said tightly, "So are we going on now?"

"In a minute." This was her chance. She dug a lead out of her pocket; she plugged one jack into her own chest console, the other into Masayo's.

He looked down. "What's this?"

"Direct suit-to-suit comms. Overrides the radio signal."

"Oh. Nobody can hear us, right?"

"That's the idea."

"So what do you want to talk about?"

She thought it over. "It just seems a good idea for us to communicate. I mean, we've been on this Ark over five hundred days now."

"Five hundred and forty-eight. Paul Shaughnessy crosses it off on the wall by his couch, like he's in prison. In fact he was once in prison."

"There you go, I never knew that."

"And does it do you good to know that the guy responsible for beating up Thomas Windrup has a brother who's an ex-con?"

"Look, I'm not probing. You're very defensive."

"Do you blame me? You know we're all up on a variety of charges, us illegals, from insubordination to trespassing on federal property to mutiny. The parents of some of the stranded Candidates are suing us in the civil courts. Just as well we can't turn this Ark around and go home; I'd be in jail myself."

She said carefully, "I always heard that you never wanted to be here in the first place. That you just got sort of swept up."

He hesitated. "Well, it was true. I was the lieutenant, remember. The guys pulled a gun on me and frog-marched me up that damn ramp. I thought I'd have time to talk them round, or disarm them, and get us off the Ark again. And then, once we launched, I figured I should stick with them. At least I had a chance of keeping them in order. Not that I did a good job with Jack, I admit. But you got to see their point of view, Holle. Look, on Earth we were on the front line. We were armed responders. Here, we're scrubbing gunk off the walls."

"I get the same complaints from the gatecrashers, if you want to know," she admitted. "Maybe it's our fault, the Candidates. I know we can be dismissive."

"Well, hallelujah. A self-aware Candidate. It would also have helped if you hadn't taken away our weapons." When the men discovered their weapons had gone there was a near-mutiny, a riot. "My guys all came from tough backgrounds, mostly eye-dee camps or bandit communities.

Their weapons are their identity. When Kelly did that it was like an emasculation."

"Kelly thought it was necessary. That the risk of having weapons on the ship was greater than the risk of any psychological harm of that kind."

"And you agreed with her?"

Holle thought it over. Kelly was still only twenty-five, only a year older than Holle herself. She had been very young to have to make such decisions. Yet she had made them. "Yes, I agree, looking back. It wouldn't have occurred to me at the time. I guess I'm not as farsighted as Kelly, or as decisive. But I agree, yeah. And, given what happened between Shaughnessy and Windrup, maybe it's as well neither of them had access to a gun."

They rested for a moment, as sun, Jupiter, Ark wheeled grandly around them.

She said at length, "I feel like we just lanced a few boils rather than talked. We need to do this again."

"Yeah. But not out here, OK?"

"Sure." She unplugged the lead between them and stowed it away. She reached for the tether attachment at his waist. "You ready?"

"For what?"

"This." She touched a control, and his attachment swiveled him around the fixed point on his waist, so that his "down" was now toward Halivah, his destination, rather than Seba.

"Oh, shit."

"The suit! Mind the suit!"

51

By the time they got through the Halivah airlock, Gordo Alonzo's broadcast from Alma had already begun. Kelly, Venus, Wilson and others sat on T-stools before a big wall screen, along with a handful of other crew, Candidates, gatecrashers and illegals, gathered at all angles around the central group.

Jack Shaughnessy was handcuffed to his brother Paul. Jack had a busted nose and a thickening bruise around his right eye. Rumor had it that he had got those, not from Thomas Windrup, but from Elle Strekalov, Windrup's partner and the girl on whom Jack had made the move that sparked the whole thing off. Thomas himself was still in Mike Wetherbee's minuscule infirmary, recovering from a punctured lung.

Alonzo, insulated from interruption by the forty-five-minute each-way time delay, was pontificating on one of his favorite subjects: crew morale. "You guys need to cook up more celebrations. Your Polyakov Day back in February was a good idea." On the four hundred and thirty-eighth day of the mission, the crew of the Ark had simultaneously beaten the space endurance record, previously held since 1995 by a Russian called Valeri Polyakov. "Trouble is I can't think of anything much significant in the near future until day eight oh four, when you'll beat old Sergei Krikalev for most time spent in space total by any human . . ."

Holle peered at the screen. Gordo himself, seated at a desk, was brightly lit, but other figures were in the shadows behind him. She was

fairly sure she saw Thandie Jones there, and Edward Kenzie. If her father
was there, she couldn't make him out. She gazed at the screen, drinking
in every pixel, frustrated.

Something landed softly on her neck. She reached back and found a
screw, come loose from somewhere. She looked up, and saw a rain of dust
gently drifting down over the people, the handcuffed brothers. The slow
spin was making all the garbage they had accumulated since engine shut-
down drift out of the air. And through the layers of the mesh deck she
saw the activity of the hull going on, as always. People were playing zero-
gravity Frisbee in the big open space, and an infant gurgled as her mother
set her spinning in the air. Good pictures for the live feed, Holle thought.
All the Ark's babies were a year or so old now. How strange that there
were already human beings who knew nothing of the universe except the
inside of this hull—but for that child's generation, that wouldn't seem
strange at all. The baby laughed in the air, rotating slowly, its chubby limbs
waving.

"For sure, improved morale is the way to stop you turning on each
other, as in this Windrup-Shaughnessy case . . ."

Gordo, in his heavy-handed way, was getting to the substance of the
address, and Holle focused her attention.

Gordo put on reading glasses, and looked down at a page of notes.
"Now, we've carefully considered the evidence you sent down. We being
the senior project management. Also we consulted General Joe Morell,
who commanded the army group of which Jack Shaughnessy was a part
before he absconded. So I hope he and all of you will accept our verdict
as being properly considered and having full military authority."

He took off his glasses and peered out of the screen. "Listen now. I'm
not a lawyer, and I won't talk like one. This is a sorry case, very sorry
indeed. Locked up as you are, all young people together in those tin cans,
you're going to get jealousies, tensions. Human nature. But you have got
to learn restraint—to respect each other. Shaughnessy, that young woman
owed you nothing for your uninvited advances but a polite 'no.' Which is

what you got, but you had to take it further, you had to take it out on
Windrup. Think of the harm you did to the mission as a whole, as well
as to Thomas Windrup—incapacitating a member of a crew that's already
under the numbers.

"Now, if you were back on Earth you'd be serving time for what you
did. But there's no jail on a spaceship. Commander Kenzie can't afford to
lose your labor—and she certainly can't afford the effort and resources it
would take to keep you locked up in some damn cupboard doing nothing
but jerk off all day. So we tried to come up with a suitable alternative, and
this is what we instruct.

"Shaughnessy, you just doubled your workload. From now until
Dr. Wetherbee signs off Thomas Windrup as fit to work again, you are
going to do his job for him. You'll cover for Windrup to the best of your
technical abilities, and where that breaks down I expect an officer dele-
gated by the commander to find you some suitable alternative. This is in
addition to your own chores. And if that leaves you no time to take a shit,
I ain't weeping for you. Is that clear? Finally you'll wear a tag so the whole
damn crew knows who you are and what you've done." He glared into
the screen. "That's how it's going to be. There's going to be a rigorous
rule of law applied aboard that damn ship, just as on Earth. The only difference is the punishment has to fit the crime *and* the environment you're
stuck in. I'll give you a minute to think about that, and see if you got any
questions." He turned away, picking up a tumbler of water.

There was silence in the group. Kelly floated up into the air and
turned around, facing them all, before her, above, below. "Well, that's the
verdict. Do you all accept it? You, Elle?" She glared at Masayo and the
Shaughnessys. "And you? Will you serve your term? And keep your fists
to yourself in the future?"

Jack Shaughnessy looked beaten.

His brother was more defiant. "He ain't wearing no tag."

"Yes, he is," Masayo said firmly. "You heard the man, Paul. Let him
serve out his punishment."

Paul shook his head, but subsided.

It seemed to Holle that the tension was seeping away. She drifted down to join Kelly, before the screen where Gordo was talking to somebody out of shot. "Maybe that's worked. They seem to accept it."

"Yeah," Kelly muttered. "But what are we going to do when something like this comes up when we're in warp, and we don't have a panel of old men and generals to tell us how to handle it?"

From the screen Gordo Alonzo coughed theatrically.

"One more thing. About the comet you observed as you were testing your planet-finder gear. Dinosaur Killer Mark II, or not as it turned out. I have some more information about that. As it turns out, it's no coincidence that thing came wandering in from the dark just as we're reeling from the flood." He peered at the camera. "I wonder if Zane Glemp is there. If not, show him this recording later. This relates to testimony from one of your tutors, Magnus Howe—something he remembered Jerzy Glemp said to him before he died . . ."

In the early years of the flood, Glemp had worked for the Russian government. Russia was hit hard and fast by the flood, losing swathes of territory. As massive refugee populations headed south and east, and war seemed inevitable with China and India over the high land of central Asia, the civilian government struggled to hold the line against hard-line generals.

"Some of the military urged using their surviving nuclear stockpile in an all-out attack against China and the west, while they had the chance. The desperate theory was that Russians might survive in an empty if radioactive world." Gordo grunted, looking at his notes. "I have a feeling that what they actually did with all those nukes in the end was cooked up by some smart guy in an effort to prevent the generals from making a bad situation even worse.

"In 2024—this was the year Moscow flooded—a significant element of the Russian intercontinental nuclear capability, mostly inherited from the old Soviet regime, was launched, aimed not at any point on the ground but sent off into space. President Peery kindly allowed me to confirm Glemp's reports about this from old CIA surveillance records. It caused a lot of alarm, you can imagine, but it was immediately clear the birds were not targeted on US territory, possessions or allies. Of course not all of their inventory could be retargeted in this way.

"Then we come to 2036, over a decade later. And we have an anomalous sighting by a telescope in Chile, which by then was dedicated to deep-space planet-finding. This big eye spots a flash, out in deep space. Some time later our surviving interplanetary probes report a trace of anomalous radiation." He looked into the camera. "You see where I'm coming from. This was the Russian nukes, or those that made it out there, all going off at once. A hell of a bang.

"And we move on to 2043—this year. And you characters detect a comet rushing in toward the sun, all but damn it on a collision course with Earth.

"I think you see that we are drawing a line to connect these three events. We think that the Russians tried to deflect a giant comet nucleus toward the Earth. They actually tried to create an impact.

"There is some logic. In the Earth's early days, deep global oceans were repeatedly outgassed from the planet's molten interior, where water had been captured during the world's formation. But in those days the sky was still full of big rocks. Earth got slammed, and the whole damn ocean was blasted off. This happened time and again, and each time the ocean was refilled by outgassing, or maybe from lesser cometary impacts.

"You see the idea. It's possible these Russian crazies believed that they could beat the flood by bringing down a comet on all our heads and blasting away the whole global ocean, just like in the good old days of the late bombardment. Maybe they actually thought they were saving the world. The fact that they would have left the Earth a desolate wasteland, devoid of air and water and inhabited only by crusty Russian Strangelove types in deep bunkers, was an unwelcome detail.

"My scientists tell me deflecting a comet is a chancy thing to do. It's remarkable they managed it at all. Thank God they didn't get it right.

"So that's the end of that. What's next?" He glanced over his shoulder at his team of advisers.

52

March 2044

Not long after dawn Mel's National Guard detachment was rousted out of its barrack, an abandoned, rat-infested liquor store in Alma's small town center.

To brisk orders from the sergeants they formed up in the dim morning light, a few dozen men and women in rough but orderly ranks. Then they began their march along Main Street, heading out of the Buckskin Street compound gate and north through the picked-over ruins of the town toward the outer perimeter. The tarmac surface of the highway was rutted and cracked by the passage of tanks and other heavy armored vehicles. It wasn't so bad to walk on, but you had to watch you didn't turn your ankle in some pothole. Weeds flourished, green and vigorous, grabbing their opportunity in this short interval between the ending of the dominance of humankind and the coming of the flood.

The air was full of the stink of the night's smoke. The eye-dees burned shit these days, human excrement dried and compressed, the hillsides long having been stripped of their lumber. And, under all that, there was a faint tang of salt in the air, of ozone, the smell of the global ocean reaching even here to the heights of the Rockies.

The troopers were laden with their packs. This assignment was going to last several days, how long was unspecified. As they walked they checked over their elderly weapons—mostly Kalashnikov AK-47s, probably manufactured before the flood, and many of them liberated from survivalist types during a raid into the higher ground a couple of years back. The troopers were a mixture, everything from veterans with genuine combat experience to healthy-looking rookies plucked out of the eye-dee streams, to relics with a more complex past, like Mel, who had been a USAF cadet before being diverted into the Ark Candidate corps, and then left abandoned on the ground at the last minute. For all their raggedness they were probably as disciplined a military unit as existed anywhere on the planet. But they grumbled as they marched, their voices rising in the still air. Everybody grumbled all the time, about the lousy food and the broken toilets in their billets and the state of their hand-me-down combat gear.

Mel Belbruno felt as uncomfortable as everybody else. His boots were a major problem, misshapen from a dunking in salt water when in the care of some previous unfortunate owner; he had padded them with layers of filthy socks. But this morning he was distracted by the unpleasant possibilities of the new assignment.

Alma was surrounded by a system of concentric fortifications. The best place to serve was inside the Buckskin Street compound itself, at the heart of the old town, a fortress improvised from a triangle of land where three roads intersected, South Main Street, South Pine, and Buckskin Street running down from the gulch to the west. The Ark's Mission Control had been relocated into the center of this fortified area. Outside the compound there was little left of the quaint old mining town, with its embattled claim to be the highest in America. It had been pretty much dismantled by labor crews, first to provide raw materials for the fortifications, and then to build rafts, big buoyant structures of oil tanks and plastic sheeting and tarpaulin that for now sat ominously on the open ground, ready for the final evacuation.

Failing an assignment inside the compound itself, you were best off running patrols into the hinterland, as the commanders called it, a broad area a few kilometers across centered on Alma, a patchwork of high ground and flooded-out valleys. Here, high ground once colonized by pine trees was stripped of lumber and was being turned into farmland, a thousand tiny, scratched-out farms on the poor soil. They were farming

even all the way to the summit of Mount Bross, the highest point here-
abouts, breaking the poor land with human muscle, for there was no oil
left to run tractors and pull plows, not even any horses left. Mel had once
heard Patrick Groundwater say that Americans were having to revive
methods of subsistence farming once used in medieval Europe.

Today was the first time Mel had been sent further out still, beyond
the hinterland to one of the eye-dee processing camps that blocked the
valleys and gulches that led into Alma. He didn't know what to expect at
the camp, up Highway 9. He tried not to listen to the shit from the veterans, of the things they'd seen and had to do, but their words wormed
their way into your head, as they were meant to.

He wished he didn't have to face this distraction, this upheaval, today
of all days.

He looked up at a murky, cloud-scattered sky, wondering where Jupiter was—Jupiter, where the Ark crew had almost completed their fifteen-
month-long stay. It was now less than twenty-four hours before the next
phase of the Ark's mission was due to begin, when the ship would cloak
itself in a warp bubble and hurl itself at the stars. These last few hours,
after which Holle wouldn't even be inside the same solar system as Mel,
were not a time he wanted to be away from Mission Control, and news
of the stupendous events unfolding in the sky. But he didn't have a
choice.

In March 2044, with the global flood nearing three kilometers above
the old sea-level datum, not many people got choices.

At the processing camp the unit was siphoned off to a tent city, their bil-
let for the next few nights. Another unit of battered-looking, weary young
people was forming up to be marched south in turn. They were silent,
sullen.

Don Meisel was waiting at the side of the road, a lieutenant now in a
relatively crisp and clean Denver PD uniform. When he spotted Mel he
called him over. His right cheek bore a deep scar, a wound badly cleaned

out and amateurishly stitched, and thick sunglasses hid his eyes. His red hair was speckled gray. At twenty-six, Don was a year older than Mel. Mel thought he looked a lot older than that.

Mel forced a grin. "I wish I could say I was glad to see you."

"Yeah. Not in these circumstances. The Ark—"

"Everything's on track, last I heard." Which had been last night, when Patrick Groundwater had called him at the barracks.

"Nothing we can do about that now." Don glanced around. "Your unit will be working with mine today. Listen, the first day's the worst. I got through it—just remember that. If a sap like me can make it, you sure can too. Go take your boots off for a few minutes. I think there's some hot food." Don touched an earpiece, and nodded absently. "Catch you later." He strode away.

Mel followed his buddies into the tent city, where the men had already begun arguing over bunks that were still warm from the bodies of their last occupants. The respite was half an hour, long enough for them to grab some food and drink, to take a dump, to massage feet that were already sore from the hike out of Alma in their ill-fitting boots. Despite the complaints, the food wasn't so bad, a kind of rabbit stew. Cops and troopers got to eat better than almost anybody else—better, even, than the engineers and scientists in Mission Control, which was why it was the ambition of most able-bodied eye-dees to join a military detachment.

Then they were formed up again and marched the last few hundred meters north along the highway, to the processing camp.

53

As they neared the security perimeter Mel tried to take in what he saw.

He was approaching a fence, a complex of barbed wire and watch towers and earthworks that spanned the old highway. He could see the fence reaching high up into the hills to either side, cutting across the brown, exposed ground, passing through the rough rectangles of the scrubby new farms. The highway itself was straddled by a massive steel and concrete gateway, bristling with watchtowers and spotlights. The fence was manned by soldiers or National Guard or Homeland or cops, who could be seen walking the wire or sitting in their towers.

This was the boundary of the territory, centered on Alma, that was still under the protection of the federal government, with Colonel Gordo Alonzo, the most senior surviving commander of Project Nimrod, named by the President himself as military governor. The boundary between order and governance within, and the chaos without. There were rumors that this was about the only significant enclave left under federal government control, outside seaborne assets like the surviving Navy ships and submarines. But few people were in a position to know if that was true.

The refugee-processing center had been set up where the fence crossed the highway. A couple of buildings, rough concrete blocks, were set back behind the line itself, connected to the gate by a kind of corridor of barbed wire, the walls at last three meters tall and patroled inside and out by armed soldiers. There was a small industrial facility set up here, like a chemical factory with tanks and drums and gleaming pipework. A sign over the door read:

ALMA, CO.
RESPITE CENTER
US FEDERAL GOVERNMENT PROPERTY

To his amazement Mel saw that flowers bloomed at the doorway of this unit, in pots hanging from metal brackets.

At the gate itself Mel saw a row of desks, manned by soldiers and civilians, with laptops and electronic notepads. These were interviewing eye-dees, one at a time. A queuing system, a line beyond the gate itself, stretched back, rows of ragged, dirty, scrawny people working their way through a zigzag of metal barriers. Further out, soldiers in pairs were roughly gathering people into preliminary lines.

And beyond that, Mel saw more people, a crowd of them sitting or standing in the dust. Just in that first glimpse there must have been thousands of them.

"Shit," he murmured to Don, who stood at his side. "If that crowd lost patience—"

"Don't think like that," Don murmured. "It's our job to see that they don't." He stepped before the unit he commanded today, his veterans and Mel's rookies from Alma. "OK, listen up. We'll break you up into squads, two, three or four at a time, veterans paired with rookies. For today you'll be rotated through the various elements of what we do here, so you see the bigger picture. Training on the job, you follow? After that, beginning tomorrow, we'll fix you up with permanent assignments." He grinned, fiercely. "I'll say to you what I said to my buddy here. The first day's the worst. But if I got through it, you can. And just remember how important the work is. *This* is where we hold the line—not back in the Buckskin Street compound, not in those scrubby farms in the hinterland. Everything depends on how well you do your jobs, right here. OK, fall out and buddy up; B Company have been given the names of the inductees they're to supervise."

The company broke up, the troopers milling around, the new arrivals looking for the veterans who would shepherd them through this first day.

Don again beckoned Mel over. "It's you and me for today, buddy." He glanced over the new troopers mildly. "There's generally a couple who crack, even on the first day. Maybe not with this bunch, they look solid enough. Come on. I need to troubleshoot."

Don led Mel up the stub of highway toward the gate. Waving a pass at a guard, he pushed out past the row of desks and toward a kind of access alley that ran alongside the queuing system. Armed troopers patroled the alley. Glancing up, Mel saw watchtowers looming, more troopers with binoculars scanning the lined-up crowd.

Mel got a chance to see the processing clerks in action. Some of them were doctors or nurses, or anyhow they wore prominent red cross armbands over the sleeves of their uniforms. They took down basic details from the eye-dees standing before them.

"It's a screening," Mel said. "I didn't think Alma was still taking in eye-dees."

"It looks like a screening," Don murmured. "Don't jump to conclusions. Just watch, listen, learn. And keep your weapon to hand."

The two of them walked out, beyond the big perimeter fence, and along a broken highway surface kept reasonably clear but crowded to either side with eye-dees waiting to join the lines for the processing system. They weren't the only troopers out here, but, outside the fence, Mel felt exposed, unreasonably nervous.

Beyond the queuing crowd they reached a kind of shantytown, which was set out in rough squares, each about the area of an old city block. Each zone had drains cut into the ground, trenches leading to sewers that ran down the sides of the highway. There were few tents, but here and there stood the remnants of buildings, and the eye-dees had constructed shacks and lean-tos of sods and whatever debris they could get hold of. It was still only mid-morning. Fires burned and smoke rose up, and pots had been set out to catch rainwater from an increasingly cloudy sky. Babies cried, a multitude of tiny voices. There were even children playing, with battered toys or deflated soccer balls, but none of them ran about, and in faded rags they were stick-thin, the skulls prominent under their faces. Some had the swollen bellies of malnutrition.

Mel saw agents from the Alma protectorate, identifiable in relatively bright AxysCorp durable coveralls and accompanied by armed troops, working through the camp. Some wore medics' armbands. They spoke patiently to the eye-dees and handed out leaflets.

The leaflets surprised Mel the most. "Where do they get the paper from?"

Don dug into his pocket, produced a folded scrap, and handed it to Mel. It was densely printed on both sides, and the only color was a tiny red, white, and blue Stars and Stripes in one corner. It turned out to be a kind of primer on how to construct a plow, meant to be drawn by humans. Don said, "Feel the paper, that glossy sheen? It's made from seashells."

"I didn't know the government was still supporting eye-dee camps so far out."

"It's not. Supervising, maybe. Advising. But not supporting. Look around. The drainage ditches, the shanties—all constructed by the eye-dees themselves, using whatever tools and resources they could find, their bare hands if they have to. These leaflets we give them—hints on farming, on hunting—all to be achieved without material support from the center. Even the doctors give out more advice than medicine. We just don't have the resources for any more." He glanced around, making sure they weren't overheard by any eye-dees. "We don't even police out here. We encourage them to set up their own security structure, under the nominal authority of Alma. We give out paper badges—that doesn't cost much. Usually it devolves pretty fast into the dominance of some warlord, but we don't care about that so long as there's order. Oh, and we always shut down the brothels. Gordo says we're fighting against human nature with that one, but the commanders have made it a priority, and we try."

"It's all a kind of illusion," Mel blurted. "They think they're under the government's protection. In fact—"

"It keeps people quiet. Sedated. It works because people want to believe they're safe, that *somebody* is thinking about their welfare, just as it has been all their lives, at least for the older folk who remember how it was before the/flood. Things are relatively stable here." He pointed further out, to the north, where the highway arced away through stripped hillsides. "There are more out there, thousands. We mount punitive raids, we mine the roads, trying to keep them out. But they would have to get through this zone of settlement first, before they can get to us. There are camps like this all around Alma, in a ring."

Mel saw it. "You're using all these people as a screen. A human shield."

Don eyed him. "Look—the flood just keeps on coming, the water pushes on up the valleys, the Platte and the Blue river and the rest, warm, frothy, salty water all poisoned with the mess from the drowned towns, and the corpses floating like corks. I've seen it. We're losing places like Leadville and Hartsel and Grant now. And it drives people on ahead, like cattle.

"Everybody knows there's an enclave at Alma. So they come in search of sanctuary, wave after wave. We don't know how many there are out there, in the hills around Alma. Some think it might be as many as a million. We just can't cater for them all, not for one percent of that number. And we can't run away, like when we evacuated Denver. All we can do is keep them at bay, until the job at Mission Control is done. To do that we've had to figure out how to use every resource we have left against the eye-dee flow. And the most significant of those resources is the eye-dees themselves."

Mel glanced at Don's face, expressionless behind the mask of his scar, the sunglasses, the layer of stubble over his dirty face. Mel thought he saw nothing left of the boy he had met in the Academy. "We're going to win, aren't we?"

"If you want the truth, I ain't sure," Don said bleakly. He glanced at the cloudy sky. "This stunt of timing the warp launch to coincide with the lunar eclipse—I don't know whose dumb idea that was. My guess is that when the moon goes red all the crazies out here will start howling, even if they haven't heard any specific rumors about the Ark. Well, we only need to hold the line for twenty-four more hours. So do you think it's worth it—all that you've seen today—worth it if it gives the Ark the best chance of getting away to the stars?"

"Holle and Kelly are aboard. Relying on us. Yes, it's worth it."

"OK, kid. I think you're ready to see the rest of it."

"What 'rest'?"

For answer, Don led him back through the shantytown to the security gate, and the patient line of applicants.

54

With Don, Mel shadowed an old couple, maybe late sixties, as they were interviewed by a sympathetic woman at the processing terminal.

They were called Phyllis and Joe Couperstein. They had children, and they believed there was a grandchild, but they'd heard nothing from their kids for years. They both had bloodied, swollen feet. They had started walking in Omaha, years ago. They weren't sure, in fact, where they were now; they had just followed the crowds from one scrap of high ground to the next, working wherever they could, at whatever they could. The woman had once been a civil engineer, the man a chef, highly qualified, but there wasn't much call for either now. Even up to a couple of years ago they had been able to work in the fields, but now arthritis, and a mild heart attack for the man, had put paid to that.

The Alma official was sympathetic. Alma had all the cooks and engineers it needed. Besides, she said gently, their skills were most likely out of date. But they might be reconsidered if they'd like to wait a while—meaning days, a few weeks—in a holding area?

Don murmured, "Which is just another corner of the shantytown. They never get called back, but they wait patiently."

The Coupersteins didn't even seem disappointed. But they were very tired, just from standing in this line for hours. They didn't ask for anything specific. They lingered a moment before the smiling woman.

The official seemed to relent. She handed them a slip of paper. They looked as if they were in need of respite, she said. A break, somewhere to sit, a place to bathe and clean your clothes and get a good meal, a quiet place to sleep for a night. The city had the resources to offer that, on a strictly discretionary basis. How did that sound?

The Coupersteins looked at the ticket, and at each other, and at the long line behind them. They smiled. It sounded wonderful.

"That's our cue," Don murmured. He stepped forward. "Mr. and Mrs. Couperstein, was it? Come this way." Don escorted them through the security barrier. "Yes, you need to give me the paper." He handed it to Mel. It was grubby, well fingered, much used. "No, you don't need to show me any more ID . . . This way. Come on, Mel."

Mel passed the paper slip back to the woman at the desk, who glanced at him cursorily, and stuffed the slip in a drawer. She was already busy with the next applicant.

Mel hurried after Don and the old couple. They were heading up the lane of barbed wire that led to the Respite Center. From this vantage the building's ugly concrete bulk and that industrial plant were hidden, and the doorway looked attractive, welcoming, with some kind of plastic veneer over the door, and the sign and the flowers. Even the path under their feet had gravel laid down, Mel saw. It was like walking in a park, the Coupersteins said to each other, and they walked slowly as they approached the doorway, hand in hand, as if relishing these few seconds.

At the door Don entered a security code into a keypad and submitted to a retinal exam. Heavy locks opened with a clatter, and the door swung back. Mel glimpsed a corridor within, softly lit. Music played, a wash of some gentle, almost melody-free ambient sound. Over that there was a distant murmur of voices—soft, as if sleepy. He was expecting some staff member to come forward, a nurse in a crisp white uniform, but nobody came.

Don, apologetically, ordered Mel to search the couple before they went any further. He found no weapons, not so much as a kitchen knife.

"Mr. and Mrs. Couperstein, you can just go ahead," Don said. "You'll find a bathroom, a coffee machine, a reading room with books . . . Others are waiting there. Somebody will be with you shortly."

Mr. Couperstein hesitated for one second, a complex expression crossing his dirty, gnarled face, and he shook the dust from his roughly cut gray hair. But Mrs. Couperstein sighed. This would be fine. This was just like a hotel, like the one they stayed in once at Aspen where they had gone skiing, and now you'd scarcely believe they had ever been young enough to do that. She kicked off her battered shoes and stepped through the door. Her feet left blood on the floor. The door slid softly shut behind them.

Don stepped back, and checked his watch. "It's only half an hour to the next cleanup. We'll stick around here. Come on." He led the way back to the processing barrier.

In the next thirty minutes two more offers were made of a stay in the Respite Center. One was to a man who pushed an elderly lady in an impossibly battered wheelchair; he must have been fifty, she eighty, and suffering from dementia. A foul stink of ordure came from beneath her dirty blanket. The other went to a young father with a child aged about three, a collection of skin and bones with a head that lolled, too heavy for her body. The mother had run away that morning, taking their packs and the last of their food with her. Yes, the man longed for a break. Mel and Don escorted the son with his mother, the young father and his daughter, to the Respite Center, which they entered with as much relief as the Coupersteins had shown.

Don checked his watch again. "One p.m. Almost time."

There was a whistle from a Homeland officer. Soldiers and cops came trotting up, and Don led Mel to join a rough perimeter around the center. An engineer approached, and showed his credentials to the senior officer. He checked the door to the center was sealed, and worked a handheld.

"Have your weapon ready," Don murmured to Mel, hefting his own AK-47.

The engineer pressed one last key on his handheld, and stood back. Mel heard a whir of pumps, a hiss of some gas. And he smelled a strange, elusive smell, something like almonds.

The sun was breaking through the cloud. None of this seemed real.

Mel said, "I guess the gas pipelines run underground."

"Be a bit obvious if they didn't."

"Why the perimeter?"

"Sometimes the respite patients change their minds at the last minute. Try to break out."

"And we shoot them."

"If we don't contain them we get a hell of a security mess, and a health hazard." Don glanced at Mel. "I know what you're thinking. They taught us about the Nazis in the Academy, didn't they? We aren't Nazis, Mel. Hang on to that. This is an American government doing all it can for its people. We've got nothing else left to offer them."

"They think they're going in there for a break. Not to die—"

"No. They *know*, on some level, even if they wouldn't admit it to themselves. It's OK. I know how this feels. It's only a few more minutes."

Mel saw it all now. This was the very essence of the engine that had protected him, and the Ark, for years, an engine that ran on flesh and blood and false hope.

It seemed a long time before the hiss of gas stopped. A man in a pale blue NBC suit approached now, and a trooper came along the line of the soldiers, handing out more suits.

Mel took his numbly. "What now?" he asked Don.

"Cleanup," Don said. He put his weapon on the ground and began pushing his legs into the suit trousers. "Just a precaution. The gas has been pumped away."

"I can't."

"You must. It's your duty. One job we can't delegate to the eye-dees. Come on, man, help me zip up this damn thing."

That was how it went for the rest of the day for Mel, until his watch ended at around eight p.m.

Don walked him back to the tent city, and helped him find his bunk, his stuff. Mel's mind seemed to have shut down. The other bunks around his were full of sleeping troopers, men and women, most still clothed, their boots on the ground under their bunks. Officers moved silently between the rows, offering quiet words when a soldier stirred.

Mel drank some water, but found he didn't want to eat.

"That's fine," Don said. "Just sleep. That's what you need above all. Sleep." He had a flask, a plastic cup. He poured a golden fluid out of the flask. "Drink this."

Mel took a sip. It was strong, flavorful, and as he swallowed a mouthful he felt a kick at the back of his head. "Wow."

"Alma's finest." Don grinned. "And there's something in it, a powder from the medics. It will help you sleep."

"I don't want to sleep. It's too early. Eight o'clock—"

"It's an order," Don said gently. "Go ahead, finish this, lie down. Go right to sleep now and the memories won't get a chance to form, and it won't feel so bad in the morning. You know, the guilt."

Mel hesitated. But he was too exhausted to argue. He sat on his bunk and pulled off his heavy boots. His feet stank, after sweating all day inside the layers of socks. He rolled onto his bunk and pulled his blanket over him. "Where did we learn these procedures? Maybe this is how the Nazis enabled their death squads to function."

"I wouldn't know," Don said grimly. "If not, I guess we had to figure it out for ourselves."

"Holle—the Ark. I don't want to miss seeing that."

"I'll wake you." Don glanced at the roof of the tent. "Holle and

Kelly will never know how lucky they are, to have ascended from all this."

"Don't forget to wake me," Mel whispered.

"I promise. Sleep now."

When Don did wake Mel, in the small hours, it was to the sounds of shouting, and a stink of burning.

55

Even inside the Buckskin Street compound there was chaos, with troops and civilians running everywhere.

Patrick Groundwater checked his watch as he ran, his coat flapping around him. He'd meant to be at Mission Control by now. The warp bubble fire up was only minutes away—or rather, off in the orbit of far Jupiter, it had or had not already happened, his only daughter was on her way to the stars, or not. And the news of that terrific event was limping its way at mere light speed across the solar system, with no regard for the anxious beating of a human heart. He looked up, but the sky was full of broken cloud, and pillars of smoke rose up to obscure it even more. If the eclipsed moon was risen, he couldn't see it.

He was fifty-nine years old. He couldn't run any faster. Damn, damn.

By the time he reached Mission Control the smell of burning was looming close, the crackle of gunfire closing in. He found troops ringing the building. Even in the urgency of the moment he had to show an ID and submit his retina to a laser-flash test. As he fumbled for his papers a great beating, as of huge wings, descended on him from above. He ducked, and some of the soldiers around him flinched and raised their weapons. It was a Chinook, maybe the last one flying anywhere in the world, its dual rotors roaring over the battered township, and playing its lights down in dusty beams to assist the ground operations.

When at last Patrick got inside the Mission Control building, Gordo

Alonzo was making a speech. He was standing on a table at the front of the room, before the rows of consoles with their glowing screens. At his back a map of the solar system glimmered, the dark swoop of the Ark's orbit like a loose signature. Thandie Jones stood beside him, enigmatic.

Alonzo was saying, "In the generations to come, in the long centuries that will unfold on Earth II, what we have achieved together in this place, and in Gunnison and Denver, will always be remembered. *You* will be remembered. You know, Alma, the town, was named for the daughter of the guy who ran the grocery store when the town was incorporated in 1873. But I'm told that 'alma' is also the word for 'soul.' in Spanish. And that's what you have been here—the soul of the grandest mission in human history . . ."

Patrick scanned the room. The technicians still manned their stations, and data chattered in scrolls of numbers and in graphic forms across the screens. But, short of a catastrophic failure, there was nothing more these people could do to influence the Ark's fate, its stupendous flight across twenty-one light-years to the planet of a star in the constellation of the river. The ship had either gone, or it had not. He checked his watch again. There was still no confirmation.

Edward Kenzie came bustling up to him. Even now he wore a suit and tie, though his shirt hung out of his pants and his hair was mussed. "Patrick. Thank God you're here."

"You can't stop Gordo Alonzo making speeches."

"At least he's keeping these people calm. After all, if there has been some disaster up there, we need to keep the technicians in their seats as long as we can."

"And how long is that?"

"Take a look," Kenzie said grimly. He offered Patrick a handheld.

The screen showed a map of the area, of the military assets in green, the deployment of hostiles in angry red. The outer cordon had been broken to the north and south along Highway 9, and to the west from up Buckskin Gulch. Elements of the mob coming in from all three directions were already closing on the bright green triangle that marked the Buckskin Street compound, and the glowing yellow jewel of Mission Control itself.

"Shit," Patrick said. "This looks organized."

"Precisely. Abider agitators, that's what I'm told. Weapons caches and radios. I heard the military saying it was a mistake to time the launch to that lunar eclipse. They were right."

Gordo had finished his speech. Seventy-three years old, he jumped down off his table with an almost arrogant athleticism, and the controllers applauded. But a rattle of gunfire, clearly audible through the walls of the building, drowned them out. Tailed by Thandie Jones, Gordo came striding up to Patrick and Edward. "You guys see a Chinook hovering outside? That's our ride out of here."

Patrick felt oddly betrayed. "But the project isn't over—we don't even know about the warp bubble—"

Kenzie said, "You know, Gordo, I always thought you'd be the last man to leave the bridge."

"That's the fucking Navy," Gordo said. "And anyhow we did all we could. We kept the lamps burning in Alma, Colorado, we didn't let those kids go off into the dark alone. But our job's done now."

"And he really does have his orders," Thandie Jones said. Here she was at the end of it all, Patrick thought, as she had been at the very beginning, when she had spoken to the IPCC as another, earlier disaster unfolded around New York, back in the days when Holle the interstellar astronaut hadn't even been conceived. "President Peery has ordered that the continuity of the nation should be preserved. According to the Presidential Succession Act the line runs through the Vice President to the Speaker of the House of Representatives, the President Pro Tem of the Senate, and then selected members of the Cabinet—"

"And at last me," Gordo said, "as governor of this fucking fortified mountaintop. Peery wants us out, dispersed, safe."

"Safe?" Kenzie asked wildly. "Where?"

"Into whatever assets are available."

"In our case the USN *New Jersey,*" Thandie said. "Of which I'm an informal crew member, and I have orders to make sure Gordo here gets his ass on the sub."

Kenzie said, "And then, maybe, Ark Two, which—"

There was a boom, like a huge door slamming. The building shook, and the screens fritzed, flickering on and off, while plaster rained down from the ceiling. Smoke started pouring in through the aircon.

Troopers formed up around Gordo. "Time to go," he said. "Get behind me." Thandie Jones stayed with him, and Edward Kenzie.

Patrick longed to stay in Mission Control, to wait for news of the Ark, but the screens were failing anyhow, and he submitted when Edward grabbed his arm.

The troopers formed a flying wedge and pushed through the crowd. The main doors were forced open, and smoke billowed out around them as they staggered into the open air. Patrick was briefly overwhelmed by the screams, the gunfire, the smoke-filled air, and another immense crash that seemed to shake the very ground. He saw a line of troops not fifty meters from where he stood, trying to hold their position against a mob of eye-dees, who bayed, throwing bits of rubble and waving glinting machetes.

Over their heads, hovering in the air, the Chinook waited. An airman dangled a rope ladder from an open hatch. Two troopers ran up, clutching the base of the rope ladder. Patrick's heart thumped when he recognized Don Meisel and Mel Belbruno, his daughter's lover. But Mel's face was hard, pinched, his eyes hollow.

They shoved forward, to the ladder.

"This isn't going to be glamorous," Thandie shouted.

Gordo growled, "I just hope none of those ragged assholes have got a surface-to-air."

A woman broke out of the melee and hurled herself at the ladder. She was young, no more than twenty, twenty-one. She was dressed in rags, and she had a baby in a kind of improvised papoose on her chest. Don and Mel fielded her. She started struggling. "Let me on that thing!" The baby was wriggling, screaming. Don and Mel were reluctant to deal with the woman, Patrick saw, for fear of harming the baby.

Gordo stepped forward, a knife in his hand. Briskly he cut the papoose harness, plucked the baby off its mother, and hurled it away into the crowd. The woman instantly gave up her struggle and followed it. Gordo said, "And I will see that woman's face on my deathbed." He tucked his knife into a sheath in his sleeve.

Don was all business. He handed the ladder to Gordo. "Sir, there are four places on the chopper. We can't take everybody."

Thandie pushed Gordo forward. "Up you go, Colonel. Orders, remember."

"And you," Gordo snapped, and grabbed her hand.

Edward Kenzie dragged Patrick forward by the arm. "Come on, Patrick, we've been in on this from the beginning. Without our money the Ark wouldn't have got built—and that's our kids flying the bird. We're owed."

But Patrick pulled his arm away.

The chopper dipped and bucked; some sniper was getting his range, and a round pinged off the hull.

Don said, "Sir, this bird is lifting in one second."

Edward Kenzie was on the ladder. He yelled down, "Groundwater, what the fuck?"

"Not me, Edward. We had our time." And just as the chopper lifted Patrick lunged forward and shoved Mel against the ladder.

Mel grabbed on to keep from falling, and was immediately borne away, raised up from the ground like an angel. Patrick could see Mel's open mouth, his shocked expression.

Patrick said grimly, "That's for Holle."

Don Meisel just laughed. "Nice timing, Mr. Groundwater."

A trooper faced Don, a woman, her face hard, a frizz of gray hair loose under her helmet. "Sir. The position is lost. Some of us are going to try to break out to higher ground."

Don nodded. "Stay close to me, sir," he said to Patrick.

"I'm no soldier, son."

Don thrust an AK-47 into Patrick's arms. "You are now."

The Chinook had gone, its roar receding into the sky, its lights a dying constellation. And over Patrick's head the sky was clearing, to reveal a bloody eclipse light.

56

When the moon had gone into totality, when the Earth's shadow crossed its face entirely and that compelling bloodred color bloomed, Lily Brooke had heard the gasp that went up across the community of rafts, a crowd's murmur of awe, children saying, "Look at that!" in a variety of languages. As the sky was stripped of moonlight the other stars emerged, dominated by Jupiter, king of the planets.

Lily tried to imagine how it would be to look back from the moon itself, to see the breast of Earth's ocean glimmering in the tainted moonlight, unbounded from pole to pole save for the last scattering of mountaintop islands with its speckling of rafts and boats and islands of garbage, and the people turning up their faces to see the show in the sky.

She sat with Nathan Lammockson on her scrap of plastic tarp, salvaged from Ark Three, spread out over the sticky seaweed-algin floor of the raft. She'd tried to make Nathan comfortable with a heap of blankets. In the last few years he had become plagued with arthritis, blaming the damp of the sea.

Nathan, rocking gently, kept talking, the way he used to, as always setting out his vision of the future.

"The Earth birthed us, and then shaped us with tough love. This new watery age, the Hydrocene, is just another rough molding, and we'll come through it, smarter and stronger then ever. We are the children of the Hydrocene. Yes, I like that . . ." He looked around, as if seeking somebody to write the phrase down for him. "Damn chimps, I mean kids, they just swim . . ." His eyes were closing, as if he were falling asleep even while he was talking, and he rocked stiffly, seventy-three years old.

"Nathan, maybe you should go to bed."

"They just swim . . ."

A light flared in the sky. Lily glanced up, thinking it must be the end of totality, the bright sunlight splashing unimpeded once more on the moon's face. But the moon, still wholly eclipsed, was as round and brown as it had been before.

It was Jupiter: Jupiter was flaring, still a pinpoint of light, but much brighter, bright enough to cast sharp point-source shadows on the glistening weed of the raft substrate. But the light diminished, as if receding with distance. And soon Jupiter shone alone as it had before.

That was the Ark, she thought immediately. That was Grace. What else could it be?

Then a sliver of white appeared at the very rim of the moon, lunar mountains exploding into the sunlight. She was quickly dazzled, and Jupiter was lost. She was never going to know.

"I got you here, didn't I? I kept you alive."

"Yes, Nathan." She pulled a blanket around his shoulders as he rocked and mumbled about evolution and destiny and children, an old man bent over his arthritic pain. "Yes, you did that."

But if it had been the Ark, she thought, maybe the crew *planned* the timing of that strange departure, knowing that over much of the dark side of the Earth eyes would be drawn to the eclipse, the spectacle in the sky. It would be quite a stunt, one hell of a way to say goodbye.

"I kept you alive. We've got to adapt. The chimps, I mean the kids, they've got to learn . . ."

Four

2044–2052

57

September 2044

An hour before Kelly's parliament, Holle, on a whim, tried to get inside the cupola. She felt like talking over with Venus the encounter with Zane she was building up to.

But Thomas Windrup, sitting in the airlock working through some kind of data-reduction exercise on a laptop, was acting as a gatekeeper. Slim, dark, his bookish looks spoiled now by Jack Shaughnessy's gift of a broken nose, he checked over an admission schedule.

"Oh, for God's sake, just let me in," Holle said. "I only want a few minutes."

"We got work to do in here," Thomas said, with the pronounced Omaha accent that he'd maintained all through their years in the Academy. "And then there's the dark adaptation."

"What do you think I'm going to do, shine a light in your eyes? Let me in or I'll turn off the water supply to your coffee machine."

Venus turned at that, her eyes bright in the dark. Over her shoulder, in the cloistered darkness of the cupola, Holle could see Elle Strekalov, and beyond them both a star-littered sky. "That is seriously not funny," Venus said. "Power like that is real in this dump, Holle. Even if Kelly Kenzie wants to believe we're all one big happy family. Oh, let her in, Thomas."

Thomas stood aside with a grudging grin.

Holle entered the cupola and sat on a lightweight swivel chair beside Venus. Now that the hulls were spun up, gravity was less than half Earth normal here, up near the nose of Seba. Every chair you sat on felt soft as feathers, and this transparent blister attached to the flank of Seba had become a dome fixed sideways-on to a vertical wall, separated into horizontal levels by mesh decking. Venus and her team worked at stations equipped with dimly lit screens and red lamps, to protect their dark-adapted eyes. Venus's wide pupils gave her an eerie, doped-out look.

Holle peered beyond the curved window into the deeper dark, at the sharp, intense star fields. There was little apparent distortion from the passage of the light through the wall of the warp bubble, at least if you looked away from the axis of the bubble's motion, and the stars looked much as they had always done in the skies over Colorado. But as her own eyes adapted it was as if more stars were emerging from the velvet blackness, layer upon layer of them beneath the scattered sprawl of the constellations she'd been familiar with from Earth. This grand panorama turned over, all the stars in the universe orbiting the Ark, once every thirty seconds.

Venus didn't offer her coffee. Venus was always mean with coffee. Or maybe it was punishment for that crack about the water supply.

"So," Venus said at length, "what's new with the plumbing?"

"On schedule and under budget."

"And how are your illegal brothers getting along?"

"The Shaughnessys are doing fine. With the simpler stuff anyhow—the big junk you can see and fiddle with, like the oxygen generation system and the water recovery racks. They find it hard to grasp the overall systems flows, or even to see why they need to."

Venus was dismissive. "That's jarheads for you."

"They're more than that. At least we better hope they are."

Venus nodded, watching Holle with those strange, large eyes. "I'll tell you something. There's nobody I'd trust more to run such essential subsystems than you, Holle. That might be important, when things get tougher later on."

Holle didn't like this kind of apocalyptic talk, that she heard from Venus and Wilson and a few of the others. "Then let's make sure things don't get tough in the first place."

"Yeah. So are you up for a little star-spotting? Can you tell me which way we're headed?"

That wasn't a trivial question. Holle turned in her chair. She looked out through the window and up along the flank of the hull, a vertical curving wall covered with insulation blanket and pocked with hand-holds, instrument mounts and micrometeorite scars. She could see the big particle-accelerator ring of the warp generator suspended above, and beyond that she glimpsed Halivah, a cylinder poised nose-down in the sky, with the tether a gleaming thread between the twin hulls. All this was picked out by starlight and the ship's own lights. The hulls were turning around the tether's midpoint, and their orientation at any moment had nothing to do with the Ark's overall direction of motion. However, Holle knew how to find her bearings. "Look for Orion . . ." She scanned around the sky, and it wasn't long before she found the proud frame of the hunter, with his distinctive belt of stars. "And Eridanus is that sprawl to his right." It was in the constellation of the river that their destination G-class star lay, still more than nineteen light-years away.

"Well done," Venus said. "I guess our naked-eye astronomy training is paying off—all those observing trips up in the mountains. Remember how Magnus Howe used to yell at us when we got bored waiting for breaks in the clouds? But Magnus was lucky. There was a window after the air cleared of human pollution, and before the global-ocean weather cut in with all those clouds and storms, when you had the best seeing since the Stone Age. The result was a generation of natural naked-eye astronomers. Grace Gray remembers it. But we were born that bit too late."

Holle, who had never been too strong on warp physics, had always been faintly surprised that the outside universe was visible from inside the bubble at all. It was, but the view was distorted. A warp bubble was a patchwork of universes, stitched together by a thin, dynamic, highly deformed layer of spacetime. That deformity meant a strong gravity field, and the path of a light ray could be bent by gravity—which was how Einstein's relativity had first been validated, when starlight was observed to be bent by the sun's gravity during a solar eclipse. So the warp bubble acted as a lens wrapped around the ship, a lens of gravity that deflected the starlight that washed over the Ark.

The distortions were strongest ahead of and directly behind the ship's motion. Ahead, space appeared crumpled up around the destination point, like a blanket being gathered in. Behind, though, in the direction of the sun and Earth, it was a different story, and a stranger one. The sun lay in the constellation of Opiuchus, the serpent-bearer, directly opposite Orion and Eridanus in the sky. But in that direction there was only darkness, a murky, muddy disc surrounded by faint stars. The ship was simply outrunning the photons coming from the sun and its planets.

Holle said, "If we could see the solar system—"

"Imagine a disc the size of the moon, as seen from Earth. That angle in your field of view. From here, that tiny disc would cover a volume of space ten times wider then the orbit of Neptune. After six months we've traveled around one and a half light-years—that's a third of the way to Alpha Centauri, if we happened to be going that way. But even now we're still within the solar system, just, approaching the outer limit of the Oort Cloud." A vaguely spherical shell of ice worldlets and inert comet nuclei, following million-year orbits yet bound by the sun's gravity, just like Earth.

When the warp bubble had first wrapped itself around the spinning ship, they had swept past one tremendous milestone after another at an astonishing rate. Even after the mighty push of the Orion drive it had taken them a whole year to coast to Jupiter. Under warp, within the first few *hours* they had sailed past the orbits of the outermost planets, and had soon overtaken the decades-long slog of Voyager One, the most distant spacecraft before the Ark.

And it was impossible to imagine that seen from outside, the ship and its crew and all their dreams and ambitions and conflicts would be almost entirely invisible, the warp bubble just a speck, smaller than microscopic, fleeing the solar system like a bullet.

"So," Venus said, "you spoken to Zane yet?"

"I've been waiting for the right time. Maybe after the parliament. At least that will take him away from his work for a while."

Venus pulled a face. "If I were you I'd wait a bit longer before you make your choice of life partner. Losing Mel is still an open wound, it's obvious. See if there's somebody else aboard you could fall for."

"I've looked," Holle said earnestly. "Believe me."

Venus shrugged. "Your choice. Your risk."

Holle often wished she could speak to her father about this. Or even Mel. But nobody on Earth could speak to the Ark, not since the instant they had gone to superluminal speed. Maybe, Holle thought, it was just as well that that disc of warped space hid the sun and Earth. It was as if all that had gone before warp had never existed anyhow, as if the twin worlds of the hulls contained all of reality.

Venus pushed out of her chair. "Time for Kelly's talking shop. Come on, let's get it over so we can get back to some real work."

58

olle and Venus passed back through the small airlock between the cupola and Seba. They emerged onto a gantry fixed to Seba's curving, green-painted inner wall. They were up near the nose here, and Holle looked down through a mesh of decks and partitions and equipment. The light was bright, coming from an array of arc lamps that, during a ship's "day" still slaved to Alma time, shed something like sunlight. It was like being inside some big open-plan building, Holle thought, a little like the science museum back in Denver. This was Holle's world, or half of it. The furthest point she could see, the curving base of the pressure shell below all the decks, was only about forty meters away, and when she looked across the hull to the opposite wall she was spanning a distance of only eight or ten modest paces.

People swarmed everywhere today. There was a steady hubbub of voices, and the occasional squeal of a child. Most of the crew had come across to Seba for the parliament, though some would have stayed behind in Halivah according to ship's rules. This parliament was a special one, being held to mark the end of the first six months in which, having unpacked the warp generator from its twin holds in the hulls, the crew had completed the reconfiguring of the hulls' interior.

Kelly was holding her parliament on the eighth of the hull's fifteen decks, counting down from the top, so Holle and Venus clambered down a spiderweb of lightweight catwalks and ladders. The hulls had served as zero-gravity space habitats during the cruise to Jupiter and the years of their stay there; everything possible had been packed out of the way, and the hulls' roomy interiors left open for the crew's weightless maneuverings, and their games of Frisbee and microgravity sumo. Now the interior had been remodeled for a long voyage under steady gravity. Decks had been strung across to provide floor space, and partitions had been set up, places for work, sleep and privacy. The design was ingenious, with equipment no longer necessary after one mission phase being reused in the next; thus the catwalks and ladders on the walls had been constructed from the frames of acceleration couches. The social engineers in their offices in Denver and Gunnison had based their interior design on the dynamics of hunter-gatherer groups, the most ancient human social form, with a "village" on every deck and a "clan" uniting each hull. The social engineers, of course, didn't have to live here.

The green shades deepened as they descended further. The hulls had been planned to maximize the visual stimuli given to the crew, and on Seba the design conceit was that each deck represented a different kind of terrain on Earth. The lowest levels, where the effective gravity was the highest, were meant to be rainforest, and the green paint was darkest there, the mid-levels temperate forest or grassland, and the highest montane, painted with the pale colors of mosses and lichen. There were real-life plants nestling among the paintwork, living things from Earth growing in metal tubs welded to the walls, plants and grasses and even dwarf trees. In a morale-boosting gimmick the crew had to tend to the plants themselves. It had worked; even when a clogged filtration unit had shut down the reclamation systems for twenty-four hours and the crew had had to ration their available drinking water, they hadn't let the little plants die.

By the time they reached the eighth deck Kelly was ready to start her parliament.

Kelly sat at the table she regularly used as a command position. She was flanked by those Candidates Gordo Alonzo had always referred to as the senior officers, such as Wilson Argent and Mike Wetherbee, the doctor.

Holle and Venus took their places, and Holle looked around at her crewmates. Zane stood near Kelly's desk, an absent look on his face. Masayo Saito sat slightly away from the rest, more wary. Wilson had changed a lot since they'd left Jupiter, Holle thought. He was bulking up for one thing; they were all supposed to exercise, to ensure the low gravity didn't cause their physiologies any long-term harm, but Wilson spent long hours pounding at the treadmills and weights machines down in the lowest deck of Seba, the heaviest gravity. There was a rumor that he was screwing Kelly Kenzie, though Holle had no proof of that, and there was no sign of it in their body language now.

The rest of the crew stood around the table or sat on the deck or on chairs, jostling to see. There wasn't much room; the partitions crowded close. Holle spotted Grace Gray cradling a sleeping Helen, now two and a half, the kid's mop of blond curls bright in the fake sunlight. Joe Antoniadi stood by Sue Turco, the only female illegal and already pregnant with Joe's baby. And there were Jack and Paul Shaughnessy, illegal brothers side by side. Holle saw Jack wore his tool belt with a kind of pride. She felt obscurely pleased at the sight; maybe he wasn't missing his gun quite so much now.

With everybody gathered together like this, it struck Holle once again how young they all were—nobody much older than Grace at twenty-nine, nobody much younger than Theo Morell at nineteen, aside from the handful of kids born in flight. Even the irruption of the illegals and the gatecrashers hadn't made much of a difference to that basic balance. Holle had the feeling that if an authentic grown-up walked in here even now, someone like Gordo Alonzo, they would all defer in a second. But Gordo was not going to do that ever again; they were on their own.

Kelly hopped up onto her table so everybody could see her. In half a G it was an easy jump. "Welcome," she began. "You know why I called this parliament. This is a special day. Today we mark the end of the opening phase of our cruise to 82 Eridani, and hopefully to Earth II. We finally got the ship up and running, and the warp bubble is stable and whisking us to the stars, and now we can put everything that happened so far behind us, and look ahead.

"And we need to think about the command structure within the ship.

"Even while we were at Jupiter we still had Gordo Alonzo and the Nimrod project executive as a chain of command above us. But now there's *no* higher chain of command, outside of the Ark. And we need to find a new way of running things.

"This isn't a warship; it's our home. And so I don't think a military-style hierarchy of command is appropriate. That's why I liked Grace's suggestion of the name 'parliament' for these bull sessions with the council, which you based, Grace, on how Nathan Lammockson ran Ark Three?" Grace nodded. "A parliament is a place where you talk.

"As for leadership—well, we need a leader, a focus for decisions and disputes. Before we went to warp Gordo appointed me captain for the interstellar cruise, and it was an honor, I'm proud of that. But I don't need, and shouldn't have, the absolute authority of a captain of a ship at sea. I propose that I should be referred to as the 'speaker'—that is, my only real privilege is that I'm the first to speak at these sessions, and each of you, when you speak, should address me. OK?"

Without giving anybody a chance to respond she pressed on.

"Furthermore, when it comes to the laws by which we order our lives, we have a manual, a law book drawn up by the social engineers back at Denver. But they aren't here—and neither are half the Candidates it was meant to apply to. We can use that as guidance, but I propose that instead we should develop what we already refer to as 'Ship's Law.' Iron rules regarding safety and the maintenance of the ship and its systems, rules that we all accept can be the basis of a set of laws which will emerge as we need them, by precedent, on a case by case basis. A law we don't need is a bad law, in my book. Let's work it out ourselves. I might say that I am making these recommendations having consulted with my senior colleagues here; these are collegiate proposals.

"Furthermore . . ."

Holle detected a slight shift in the crowd at that second "furthermore," the first signs of strained patience.

"Furthermore, I don't want myself or anybody else to be imposing decisions on the crew, on you. The ship's too small for that. I want to govern by consensus. Not even by majority vote, which always leaves a rejected minority. I want to work by unanimity, if we can achieve it. If there's a dispute, we'll just talk it out as long as it takes. God knows we've got the time to do that, between here and 82 . . ."

Theo Morell murmured, "Oh good. We can talk, talk, talk all the way to the stars. I can imagine what my dad would have said about *that*."

Holle dared not so much as grin in a forum like this.

She did wonder how long these fine ideas would last. As Kelly spoke, Venus sat behind her at the table, her face expressionless, and Wilson was staring around at the crew, challenging, ape-like. Holle believed Venus and Wilson and maybe others were playing a long game in the increasingly intricate political arena of the Ark. Having grown up with these highly competitive and gifted individuals in the Academy, Holle knew that was inevitable. These were games Holle herself shied away from. But she had a feeling that whatever structure of power and command emerged in the months and years to come would have little to do with Kelly's Utopian visions.

She tried to focus on what Kelly was saying now.

Some of it seemed to be well thought out. Kelly had given some consideration to the nature of liberty in the environment of the Ark. The need to maintain essential common systems would lead to a natural tendency to the centralization of power. But in such a confined space you couldn't hide from any tyranny, you couldn't flee—and, so fragile was the Ark, no rebellion could be tolerated. So the usual mechanisms by which tyrannies might be challenged on Earth were not available here.

"And that might still be true after we reach Earth II," Kelly went on. "Even there we'll be living in sealed shelters, at least at first; we will be reliant on shared systems even for the air we breathe. What we need to find is a way to ensure compliance with the basic, life-preserving rules that will always dominate our lives, without succumbing to tyranny. It's a whole new experiment in human affairs—*our* experiment. And the way we conduct our affairs now, if we get it right, might serve as a model for the generations to come." She said this with a smile and an open-armed gesture, to which people didn't quite respond.

That was it with Kelly. She was able, intelligent, articulate, forceful, and in that sense a natural leader. But in all the years they had grown up together Holle had always been aware of Kelly's intense, overriding ambition, above all else—an ambition that, as many people knew, had led her to leave a kid behind on Earth. People didn't quite get Kelly Kenzie. Now, rather than be inspired by her visionary talk, they tended to look away.

The arguments started now, questions about shared ownership and the collective raising of children. Somebody suggested they model their new society on the old kibbutzes of Israel. Kelly responded forcefully. The atmosphere became like the Academy in the old days when a tutor would throw them some hot topic to gnaw over.

Kelly's senior colleagues sat patiently at the table, Venus glancing discreetly at her wristwatch. But others on the fringe of the crowd started slipping away.

When Zane turned on his heel and left, having said nothing, Holle gave Kelly an apologetic wave and cut away to follow him. For her the day's real business was about to start. Her heart beat faster.

59

She followed Zane to his small, solitary cabin. It wasn't exactly far.

He seemed surprised to see her, and wouldn't meet her eyes. But he didn't object when she asked if she could come in and talk. Her nervousness increased as she followed him inside, and she wondered how she was going to broach the subject she wanted to discuss.

But she was distracted by his cabin. It was nothing but a box of partitions. Everybody else had personalized their cabins one way or another. Holle's small room had her personal stuff, her bits of clothing, her images of her father and mother, her Angel. And if you had a kid, like Grace Gray, you had a spontaneous homemaker on your hands. There was none of this about Zane's space. The furniture was functional, just a bed, a couple of chairs, a cupboard. There was work stuff here, an elaborate workstation and some precious hardcopy manuals on relativity and warp drive and space engineering. But, aside from heaps of clothes on the floor, that was it. This was just somewhere Zane existed, rather than lived.

She sat on a chair; she had to clear off a heap of socks first. Zane sat on the edge of the bed, his hands folded on his knees. Uncertain of his mood, uneasy about the space he lived in, she became even more unsure about the wisdom of what she was planning to do. But, overwhelmed by her own nervousness and self-consciousness, she went ahead anyway.

"It's this way, Zane," she said.

His head turned toward her.

"I've been thinking. Look, you know the nature of the mission—the social design. The crew was chosen to be as genetically diverse as possible, so that when we have kids they have the best chance of avoiding inbreeding. This was drummed into us at the Academy. But that means we all have a duty. We need to become parents. It's our responsibility to ensure that all our genes join the pool of the colonists on Earth II."

"So why are you telling me this?"

She bit her lip. Did she really have to spell it out? She began to suspect that something was wrong here, something beyond her own nervousness. But she pressed on. "Zane, you've seen people pairing up, especially since Jupiter. The rumor is Kelly and Wilson are a couple now."

He frowned again. "Wilson. The external systems engineer."

"Yeah," she said, confused by his response. "That Wilson, Wilson Argent who you grew up with . . . The truth is, Zane, I left Mel behind on Earth. Well, you know that. And I can't see myself falling in love with anybody else on this rust-bucket. And, frankly, I can't see you pairing up with anybody either."

He looked baffled.

She felt concern, and a spasm of affection. She crossed to him, kneeled on the floor, and took his hands. "Zane, we may not be soul mates. But we've known each other most of our lives. We've worked together for the same goal. And we always supported each other. I remember how you waited for me on my first day at the Academy, and got yourself in trouble as a result. I wondered if—I mean, it doesn't apply now, not until we get to Earth II. But maybe we should think about having kids together. You and me. There. So what do you say?"

He raised his head and for the first time looked straight at her. "Do you believe in the warp bubble?"

She settled back on her ankles. "What did you say?"

"Do you *believe* in it?" He glanced at his workstation, and laughed, and spoke rapidly. "I mean, I've studied the theory. But it's impossible! Basic physical principles would have to be violated for it to work. Aside from obvious issues of causality and the breaking of the weak, strong and dominant energy conditions, the vacuum stress-energy tensor of a quantized scalar field in an Alcubierre spacetime *diverges* if the ship exceeds the speed of light. Diverges! That would lead to the formation of a horizon, which, which . . ." His voice cracked, and he stopped speaking, as if he had run down. "I can show you the mathematics."

"Zane? I don't understand what you're saying. The warp *works*—we're in flight. You worked on the design solutions, with Liu Zheng and the others, which got us to this point . . ." As she had been holding his hands, his coverall sleeves had ridden up his arms, and she saw a pattern of marks on the skin of each forearm, small cross-shapes. She touched them cautiously. Some were healed-over scabs, other were more livid. It looked as if he had been jabbing the point of a Phillips screwdriver into his flesh.

"I can't have kids with you." He laughed, but it was a ghastly, hollow sound.

She looked up. "Why not?"

"I'm dirty. You must know that."

"Dirty?"

"It's all in the journal." He pulled away his hands and tapped at his workstation. A kind of diary came up, text and short video clips, Zane's own talking head. "He tells it all there."

"Who does?"

"Zane. He says he's going to kill himself, in some of these clips. Like suicide notes."

"He . . . Zane, that's *you*. Is that why you're harming yourself now?"

"What do you mean?"

She took his right arm, turned it over firmly and pointed at the screwdriver marks. "Here, and here."

He shrugged. "I don't remember doing that. I guess I wasn't here."

"Then where were you?"

"I'm faking it, you know," he said abruptly. He laughed again. "That's the truth." He stared at her. *"I don't know who you are.* None of you. I listen to you speaking, and I make notes of what you call each other, and I check for surnames and so forth on the system. I make notes, and try to remember. It's been that way since Jupiter."

She stared at him. "Then what do you remember?"

"I woke up," he said.

"Woke up?"

The words came tumbling out now. Evidently he hadn't spoken of this with anybody else. "I was in a pressure suit. I was floating in space. I was surrounded by the warp generator, the collider. He was with me."

"Who?"

"The external systems engineer."

"Wilson?"

"Yes. There was a shimmering around me, a visual effect, the stars. Wilson grabbed me and started slapping me on the back. Big gloved hands. He said we'd done it, that I'd done it."

Holle remembered. She had been in Seba watching this very scene on 13th March 2044, the day the warp generator had first been activated.

"I didn't know what I'd done," Zane whispered.

"Zane—you'd initiated warp. It was everything you'd been working for."

"Wilson took me on an inspection tour of the collider torus. I just followed his lead. When I got back inside, everybody was smiling and nodding and shaking my hand, and I just smiled and nodded back. I didn't even know their names. When I got to a workstation I looked up the relativity. I understood *that,* it's so elementary. And I studied the warp generator, so called. It can't work!"

"You don't remember anything before warp day?"

"And I have blanks."

"Blanks?"

"Other times since then that I don't remember. It's like I just wake up again." He rubbed his face. "But I'm not getting much sleep."

She smiled, and backed off. She needed to get to Mike Wetherbee, she realized. She needed to tell him that their only warp engineer might be schizoid. And so much for having his babies.

"Just wait here, Zane. Will you promise me that? We need to talk some more." Leaving him sitting on the bed, she turned and fled.

60

December 2046

Holle was woken by a soft whisper from her Snoopy cap, on the low cupboard beside her bed. The in-suit systems had been adapted by the senior crew as a clandestine communications channel for times of crisis. In the dark, she grabbed the set and pulled it over the pillow. "Groundwater."

"Holle? Wilson. Could do with some help over here."

"Over in Halivah?" She was half asleep; her thinking was fuzzy. "Light." A soft glow filled the room, and she checked her watch. Four a.m., not yet dawn here in Seba or in Halivah, in either of the Ark's twin hulls. She propped herself up on her elbow. "Go ahead, Wilson. What's up?"

"We lost a kid."

"A kid?"

"Meg Robles."

Now four years old, going on five, Meg was one of the first cadre of babies born on the Ark. Her mother, Cora Robles, had been pregnant on embarkation.

"Wilson, how do you lose a kid? . . . Never mind."

"We're searching. But the kid's only half my problem."

My problem, Holle noted. He might be Kelly's partner, but Wilson did have a way of treating the whole of Halivah as a personal fiefdom. "The mother?"

"Theo can't get her out of HeadSpace, and he's worried how she'll react if he pulls the plug."

"And you're calling me because—"

"I need your feminine intuition on this one, Holle."

"Oh, piss off, Wilson." But he knew she wasn't about to refuse a request for help; she never did. "OK. Give me a few minutes."

"Out."

In her sleep suit, she stumbled out of her cabin into the cool dim green of nighttime Seba, heading for the deck's communal bath block. Nobody was around, nobody moving on the decks above or below. She made a mental note to check that whoever was supposed to be on watch tonight wasn't goofing off asleep or in a HeadSpace booth. When the hull was empty like this it seemed bigger, grander, somehow, almost church-like. You were more aware of the sounds, the smells, the tang of electricity and metal that never let you forget you were in the guts of a big machine—and the lingering staleness, a sewer smell that was the signature of thirty-some people having lived in this tank for nearly five years already, since the launch from Gunnison.

The toilet block was part of a pillar structure that spanned the hull longitudinally from one end to the other; the sinks and showers and toilets on each level connected to a common water and drain system. She used the toilet and washed her face. She derived some satisfaction from the smooth running of her systems, the freshness of the cold water on her face, and the even hum of pumps and fans and filters. This was what she did, she and her apprentices, and she didn't really care that amid all the politicking and bickering and daily crises nobody ever seemed to notice.

Back in her cabin she pulled on underwear, coverall and boots.

Then she clambered up the series of steel ladders that led to the nose of the hull, and the airlock for the tether transit to Halivah. Wall-mounted cameras swiveled, following her passage incuriously. The paintwork hadn't been modified from the natural green scheme that had been bequeathed them from the ground, although after five years the paint was chipped, flaking. And there were no particular signs of the upcoming thousand-day festival. Kelly, following a lead from Gordo Alonzo, was keen to promote celebrations whenever there was an excuse, a mission anniversary, a birthday. Given how short they were of such basic materials as paper and fabric, the crew's artistic leanings were expressed in more ephemeral forms: oral poetry, music, dance. When the festival day came, the thousandth since the warp launch from Jupiter, the hull would briefly be filled with a carnival. But for now the crew's artistic endeavors slept in their heads with them.

At the nose of the hull she slipped off her boots, pulled her Snoopy comms hat on her head, and clambered into one of the three transit suits stored here, hanging like pupae from the wall. It closed up easily, the joints and seals well lubricated, but it smelled of stale farts. She ran through basic integrity checks. Then she climbed up into the nose airlock and waited for the pumps to drain the precious air from the small chamber.

These cut-down pressure suits were an innovation of Wilson's, who had grown impatient with the time it took for crew to complete a spacewalk transfer from one hull to another. The most important change was to the suit's air content, which was an oxygen-nitrogen mix of about the same pressure as within the hulls. The higher pressure made the suit rigid and all but impossible to move around in, but that didn't matter if all you had to achieve was this simple transfer. Most importantly the higher pressure cut out the need for the hours of prebreathing you had to endure before a full EVA.

The hatch opened. She pushed her way out into space, and found herself standing on the nose of the hull. The insulation blanket was soft under her booted feet, worn by years in space, pocked by micro-meteorite scars, crisped by solar radiation, and stained a faint yellow by the sulfurous compounds emitted by Io. But the Stars and Stripes were still bright in the ship's lights, and from here she could see the bold black U and N and I of the words UNITED STATES painted down the hull's flank, the identity of a drowned nation displayed to the stars.

She clipped herself to the winch unit and began her ascent, up through the lessening gravity toward the accelerator ring. Unlike some of the crew she wasn't troubled by the transit itself, or the peculiar sensations as gravity faded away to zero and then flipped over past the midpoint as she began her descent to Halivah. But she was always disconcerted by the unnatural sight of huge masses of engineering hanging in the sky; some animal part of her was always convinced the whole lot was going to come crashing down.

Only minutes after leaving Seba her booted feet descended toward Halivah's nose.

"Welcome aboard," Wilson murmured through the comms. "I'm down on sixth."

"Copy that. I'll find you."

61

Halivah was stirring, ending another ship's night, but the lights were as low as aboard Seba. The ground-mandated routine of having the two hulls on different day-night cycles, so there was always half the crew awake and functional, had soon been abandoned for the tensions it caused between two sets of crewmates in different states of wakefulness. There had even been a petty dispute about which hull should have the honor of being slaved to Alma time, and which should be eight hours out of sync. Now both hulls followed the same clock cycle, both mirroring Alma time, with a rota for a small night watch in each hull.

The feel of this hull was strikingly different, however. The social engineers' paintwork, urban design in contrast to Seba's natural colors, had been meticulously scrubbed away, to reveal the raw textures of the artificial surfaces beneath, the plastic, the metal, the glass. Even the mesh decking plates were bare. The Halivah inhabitants as a group had decided on this as a kind of artistic gesture of their own—they chose to live with the cool mechanical reality of their environment, rather than try to mask it with the colors of a planet none of them would ever see again. Holle was enough of an engineer to appreciate the stripped-down beauty of the result.

But some surfaces had been filled in with artwork, rendered with precious smears of paint, crayon and pencil. On the fifth deck Holle paused by one painting of a kind of house filled with light, surrounded by a dark, threatening sky—and a knock on the door represented by arcs of yellow paint. The painting was signed: HALIV. DREAM CIRCLE 4.

"Psst."

The whisper came from under her feet. She glanced through the mesh floor to see Wilson on the next deck down, in pants and a vest that showed off his muscular torso. "You like the artwork?"

"Not much. It's well enough done. But the subject's obvious, isn't it?" This was one of the most common dreams, or nightmares, endured by the crew. Here were the last humans alive (possibly), fleeing through space in these metal hulls: what if there were a knock on the wall?

Wilson grunted. "I don't like these damn dream circles. All they do is recycle morbid rubbish like this. Feeding off each other's mental garbage."

"Maybe. But some days there's nothing to do but scrub down the walls, Wilson. People need some kind of stimulus from outside their own heads."

Wilson wasn't impressed. "It's just another fucking fad. The circles only caught on when we started rationing access to the HeadSpace booths. And speaking of HeadSpace—"

"Let's go see Theo."

"Yes."

Holle followed Wilson down a few more decks. They passed through cabin villages that were subtly different from those aboard Seba, the crew fiddling with the partitions and gradually modifying the place to suit their own tastes.

Holle said, "I take it you haven't found little Meg."

"No. I got the night watch searching, and when everybody else has woken up we'll start a top-to-bottom inspection. Probably have to take the damn ship apart to do it."

"These kids are growing up here. I guess they're going to know these hulls better than we ever will."

"Yeah. Poor little bastards. Morning, Theo."

Theo Morell was waiting for them outside a small cabin, the eleventh deck's HeadSpace booth. He was leaning against a wall, arms folded, a handheld dangling from his waist. "I see you brought backup."

"Thought it was safest to have a woman here, in case Cora kicks off again."

"Oh, she will," Theo said airily. "She always does."

Wilson glanced at the booth, where a red light glowed over the door. "She's in there now?"

"Yeah. Been in all night. She's alone. Doesn't even take her kid. You want to see?" Theo hefted his handheld and pressed a button.

A screen on the wall lit up to show a little girl playing on a sunlit patio. She was outside an apartment that overlooked a sparkling sea. Dimly realized avatars shared the space with her. The patio was wide, the sea a gleaming plain that stretched to a sharp horizon with a blue sky.

The basic premise of the scene was obvious: it was about space, room to run and play, alone and free of the pressure of people all around, free of adult responsibility. A copyright stamp, dated 2018, said that the scenario, based loosely on Sorrento, Italy, had been devised as a personal space by Maria Sullivan, a HeadSpace user in Manchester, Britain, and donated to the Nimrod project by the corporation. Holle wondered what had become of Maria Sullivan.

"So Cora is the little girl?"

"You got it. Look, I tried to get her out of there. I tried all the tactics you recommended, Wilson. Like doing deals, another half-hour and then you come out. Nothing works, not with her. Believe me, calling you was the last resort."

"I don't want to hear your justifications," Wilson said. "Just shut it down."

Theo raised his handheld, and poised his thumb over a key. "You ready for this?"

"Just do it."

Theo stabbed down his thumb and stood back. The light over the door turned from red to green.

Almost immediately the booth door slammed open. Cora Robles came staggering out, pushing a sensor mask from her face. She wore a black all-body suit, gloves with thick touch-stimulating finger pads, and she trailed a fat cable back into the booth. She glared at Theo. "You shut it off? I wasn't done!"

He backed off. "Cora, look, I asked you enough times—"

"Give me that console."

"No, Cora."

"Start me up again, you little prick!" She launched herself at Theo, her gloved fists raised.

Holle lunged forward and put herself between Cora and Theo. She took a couple of blows on the chest, and then she got her arms wrapped around Cora's torso. Cora flailed, trying to get at Theo, but for all her anger she was weak and not difficult to contain. The suit was tight enough for Holle to feel how thin she was, her bones prominent, her shoulder blades, her hips. Either she had been skipping meals or she had been swapping food for HeadSpace credits. Wilson hauled at the data cable connecting Cora to the booth, pulling her away from Holle. Cora slipped and fell backward to the mesh floor. She lay there, panting hard, her face twisted.

Holle was shocked at the state Cora was in, and felt guilty she hadn't noticed. Holle had grown up with this woman. Cora had always been beautiful, bright, flirtatious, a live-wire party girl. Maybe all that energy had been turned in on herself, in the confines of the Ark.

Holle kneeled down beside her. "Look, I'm sorry that had to happen, Cora. You needed to come out of there. Your little girl's lost." As Cora had left Meg's father back on Earth, she was the child's prime carer.

Wilson snapped, "She knows. We fed it into the booth. Didn't make any difference. She cares more about her HeadSpace fantasy than about her own kid."

"And she's out of credits," Theo said, grinning down at her.

Wilson wasn't impressed by his attitude. "What are you laughing at? You run this fucking system, gatecrasher. You should take responsibility for dealing with hassles like this."

Theo held his hands up. "Last time I tried to get Cora out of there she accused me of assault. Not risking that again. She's a Candidate, after all, she's one of you. At least I want witnesses."

Once it became clear it would be necessary to ration access to the HeadSpace booths, it had been Holle's idea to give Theo the responsibility of running the rationing system. He did it competently enough, with a system of credits maintained in the public areas of the Ark archive. But Theo was too damn cocky. Maybe there was truth in the rumors that he had been bartering HeadSpace credits for other stuff, that he was turning into a kind of pusher for addicts like Cora. Holle hadn't wanted to believe it. Theo had grown up a lot since the launch, she thought, though he was still only twenty-one. And not all that growing up had been in a good way.

She turned away and put an arm around Cora. "Come on. Let's get you on your feet and out of this stupid suit. You look like you need a drink, food and sleep, not necessarily in that order. And then you're going to have to help us figure out where Meg might be . . ." She led her away.

Wilson stormed off, with a final glare at Theo.

62

Back in Seba, Kelly had started her day at her table on Deck Eight with her usual series of rolling meetings. Holle showed up to report on what was going on over in Halivah regarding Meg. She settled at the table with a coffee, knowing that she'd have to wait her turn to speak.

Kelly looked tired, sleepless. The thousand-day festival, because it was forcing all the Arks' factions and rivals to come together to cooperate on a single event, was causing Kelly and her senior people even more grief than usual. But right now Kelly and Masayo Saito were listening to Elle Strekalov complaining about Kelly's proposed new procreation rules.

A mother went by with a little kid, not yet two years old. Kelly pointed grandly. "Look at that! Sue Turco with her brat by Joe Antoniadi—what did they call her, Steel?—and the rumor has it she's got another one on the way already. You know the basic rule: we aren't supposed to be pupping until we reach Earth II. It's only another four, five years to wait. The only kids on this ship should be the ones that came aboard in utero, like little Helen Gray. But there's been a steady trickle of pregnancies. People are having babies because they *want* them."

Masayo said, "Doc Wetherbee says procreation is a natural reaction after a trauma, like how the birth rate rises after a war. The flood, the whole launch process, the severing from everything we knew—that was traumatic enough, surely."

"Or maybe they're just bored," Holle suggested.

"Why ever they're doing it? That's not the policy. That's not what the social engineers' maximal genetic diversity rules say. That's not what Ship's Law says." Kelly emphasized her words by thumping the tabletop with her open hand.

Elle Strekalov broke in, impatient. "But that's got nothing to do with my issue. It's the talk of a ballot for second children that's caused the problem for me."

Holle, new to the conversation, asked, "What's wrong, Elle?"

Elle smiled at her, looking tired. "It's Jack Shaughnessy. This new policy of Kelly's has got Jack 'sniffing around' me again. But that's how Thomas puts it. I won't have anything to do with Jack, any more than I would before. Thomas doesn't believe it. He thinks Kelly's policy will open the door for Jack."

Kelly shook her head. "It's not *my* policy. Right now it's just the recommendation of the task group I asked to consider the problem. Look, we have a conflict between two obligations. We have to try to ensure maximal genetic diversity in the next generation. But at the same time, thanks to the presence of the gatecrashers and illegals, we have a gender imbalance on the Ark . . ."

There were more men than women. Three gay couples, two male and one female, eased the burden slightly, although there was another issue in that the gays would also be expected to contribute to the gene pool of the next generation; the social engineers had at least bequeathed guidelines as to how *that* should be handled. But the guidelines were no help with the basic issue of imbalance.

Elle said hotly, "I have the right to choose who my life partner is going to be."

"Yes, you do," Kelly said patiently. "But the excess men have rights too. And we as a group have an obligation to ensure we preserve as wide a gene pool for the future as we can."

"So I have to spread my legs for some illegal?"

Holle laughed. "Nicely put."

"Artificial insemination is possible," Kelly said to Elle. "You wouldn't have to sleep with anybody."

Masayo said mildly, "Sometimes I can't believe we have these conversations."

Elle said, "But I would still have some illegal's brat in my womb. That's how Thomas will see it for sure."

Kelly said with a kind of brittle patience, "We get this kind of issue all the time, Elle, you know that. Your right to control your own body conflicts with the rights and responsibilities of the group as a whole. The proposal is that each of us women should choose a second partner from among the men involved, that we each have children by more than one man. If you can't choose, there will be a ballot—"

Elle snorted. "Rigged like every ballot on this tub since the day we launched."

"There'll be no rigging. We're all going to have to face this, Elle. All the women, all the men come to that. We'll have to separate partnerships for companionship from partnerships for procreation. The former is entirely your choice, and the mission has no need to interfere with that, but the second has to have some direction from the crew as a whole, to fulfill our wider obligation. It's the only way a crew this small can maintain genetic diversity. We're in a unique situation which—"

"Oh, I've had enough of this." Elle stood, knocking back her chair; it fell languidly in the half-gravity. "You always come out with this super-ethical bullshit. Kelly. You never focus on the human being in front of you. Well, I'm going to talk to Venus in the cupola. *She* won't let you go ahead with this. And maybe she'll do something to keep Thomas and Jack apart before they kill each other." She stalked off.

Kelly sighed, and sipped water from a covered tumbler. "Christ, Christ."

"I'll have a word with Jack Shaughnessy," Holle said. "Just quietly. Try to make sure he keeps his distance from Elle."

"I've seen no signs he's still after her. That fight with Thomas seems to have convinced Jack that Elle wants to stay where she is. This whole thing is probably just Thomas's paranoia. Be careful, Holle, say the wrong thing and you might make things worse."

"We're going to get this kind of conflict over and over," Masayo said.

"I know," Kelly said. "All the way to Earth II. But what else can we do? This is the nature of the mission. It wouldn't be half so difficult if we were crewed by the full complement of Candidates as we should have been, with a proper sex balance and training in the issues."

Masayo rolled his eyes.

Kelly asked Holle, "So what about the missing kid over in Halivah?"

"Wilson said he'd call if there was any news."

"Damn kids," Kelly said. "They're so weird. You know, I've seen them catch spiders and flies and make pets of them. You wouldn't believe it. You'd think they'd go crazy, growing up in a bottle like this. But I suppose they've never known any different. What about Cora?"

Holle summarized what had happened, how she and Wilson had had to help get Cora out of the booth. "I asked Doc Wetherbee to take a look at her. I don't think she's even been eating properly."

"It's not food that's her problem," Kelly said. "It's her addiction to the HeadSpaces. You know, we excluded alcohol and every drug we could think of, and yet still we're raising addicts. There's always some damn thing." She looked at Holle sharply. "What's your opinion about Theo? Do you think he is dealing in HeadSpace credits like Wilson says?"

"I think it's possible," Holle said carefully. "But Theo's naïve. Or he was when he came on board the ship. It may be he doesn't understand what he's doing, the moral implications, the effect on other people."

Masayo laughed. "So he's inventing a drug-dealing trade from first principles. God bless human nature."

Kelly shook her head. "You know, I've been doing some research in the archive on prisons. There you have people marking their territory, picking fights over food, swapping stories about dreams for lack of stimulation, pushing drugs. Just like us. Is that all we managed to build here, a prison between the stars?"

Masayo Saito said, "Grace Gray's mother was held hostage in Barcelona for years. Chained to radiators in cellars. Grace herself was the result of a rape by one of the guards, and was born in captivity. An unbelievable story. And yet, are we all hostages on this Ark, hostage to the ambitions of the mission designers?"

Holle said, "I'd say they were our ambitions too."

"God only knows," Masayo said.

"Sometimes I think that's the problem," Kelly said. "God, I mean. The social engineers always tried to keep God out of our lives. The Ark is a mission of a state that was deliberately secular, a state that was trying to be a reverse image of the Mormon state in Utah it was at war with. And despite the gatecrashers and illegals, they succeeded in that goal, didn't they? Many people on the Ark are religious, but we aren't a religious community. Sometimes I wish we were, that we had a common mission ordained by one god or another. A monastery would surely be a better social model than a prison."

Masayo shook his head. "Too late for that, Kelly. I think we left God behind back on Earth."

Holle stood. "I need to go. Doc Wetherbee says he wants to review Zane's therapy."

"Well, that's also a priority. And keep me informed about the progress on the kid. OK, Masayo, what's next?"

63

M ike Wetherbee invited Holle, Venus and Grace into the small cabin that he called his surgery, with its bunk beds and persistent antiseptic smell, and cabinets of medical gear to treat everything from eye conditions to bad teeth. On a monitor he showed a recording of himself and Zane at their last therapy session, the latest of a program which had now been going on for over two years. On the monitor, Zane and Wetherbee spoke quietly, over a game of infinite chess.

"This is the bullshit part," Wetherbee murmured. "How's your day been, and so forth. Takes him an age to warm up. I do most of the talking. And I hate that damn game."

"Let's just watch," murmured Grace. She was perched on the edge of one of the patients' beds.

Infinite chess was in fact an invention of Zane's. It was played with regular pieces on a regular board, save that the players had to imagine the board wrapped around itself, so that the right edge was glued to the left, and the upper edge glued to the lower. So, given normal restrictions on movement, a given piece could move right, off the edge of its world, and reappear to the left. It gave the illusion of infinity on a finite board. Zane said, and he liked to produce computer graphics showing how the wrapped-around board was topologically equivalent to a torus, a dough-nut. A queen became particularly powerful; faced by an empty diagonal, row or column, she could leap, theoretically, an infinite number of squares in a single move. Zane and other keen players were busy working out variants to standard rules, and to standard sequences of game play. For instance, white had an immediate advantage with the first move. Your queen could step backward and wrap around the world to take your opponent's queen, though she would then fall to the opposing king. Your rooks, stepping back into your opponent's back rank, could do a lot of damage before being quelled. End-game analysis was less affected, as the board was so open anyhow.

The game was an obvious psychological metaphor for the freedom they all sought in an enclosed world, but it was ferociously difficult to play. "Bastard beats me every time," Mike Wetherbee murmured.

"You're very patient," Grace said.

"Yeah, right," Wetherbee said sourly. "When he's in this phase he's so depressive, so passive, he just sits there soaking in misery. He sucks the life out of you."

Holle knew that Wetherbee was uncomfortable with the therapy program, although he had finally accepted the responsibility given how essential Zane was to the mission. That was why he had got others involved in the treatment: Holle who had referred Zane in the first place, Venus who had also suffered abuse at the hands of Harry Smith, a likely trigger for Zane's condition, and Grace Gray, who had spoken to Zane on the ground after Harry's murder. Grace was turning out to be one of the more competent of Wetherbee's backup paramedics, having picked up a lot of field experience in her years with the okie city on the Great Plains. They made a good team, Holle thought, emotionally strong even if they had no experience with this kind of case.

But really, Wetherbee was just sharing the burden around. He had the mentality Holle had seen in a lot of medical students and doctors on the ground. Brisk, good-looking and competent, he didn't have a steady partner, but he had had a string of relationships with women among the crew—a lot of people would want to tie the ship's only doctor to them, and their children. But he'd never show a trace of survivor guilt, or any interest in the fate of his drowned homeland. And he maintained a kind of distance from his patients that sometimes made you wonder why he had ever gone into medicine in the first place.

Now Mike leaned forward and touched the screen to up the volume. "We'd been talking about the chess. Then suddenly he started talking about his father. Look, see the switch there?"

Holle saw how Zane sat up straight and looked around, almost as if he'd just arrived in the room. "Dr. Wetherbee?"

"Zane, I'm right here."

"We're in the surgery. We're playing chess." He glanced at the board. "I'm two moves away from getting you in check." He smiled. Everything about Zane seemed brighter, Holle thought, as if he was another person.

"Two moves? I can't see it, but that doesn't surprise me."

"I play chess with my father."

"Note the present tense," Wetherbee murmured to the women.

"I never beat my father. He'd hate that, if I ever did."

"Did you, I mean *do* you let him win?"

"Oh, no. He'd hate to think of himself as weak. And he'd hate to see me being sentimental. The game is everything, winning . . ."

"You see the conflict," Wetherbee commented. "I think he did let the father win, and then blocked it out. The old man kept setting up barriers the kid couldn't break through. Listen to what he initiates now."

"I tried to tell Dad about Harry Smith," Zane said, on the screen.

"About what we talked about? The touching—all of that."

"Yes. I tried more than once. The first time Dad just wouldn't listen. The next time he hit me. He said I was lying about Harry Smith, who was a good man, a man he knew well. And he said I was dirty, soiled. He said I should shut up. He said if I told anybody these lies it would make trouble for no one but me, and get me thrown off the Ark, and then the eye-dees would rape me and kill me, and if they didn't the flood would drown me."

"But now that's all over. You're on the Ark. You're safe."

Zane smiled, looking quizzical. "Well, I'm still a Candidate, Dr. Wetherbee. That's not the same thing at all."

"Like he's stuck in the past," Venus said. "He doesn't know he's on the Ark."

"Something like that, some of the time . . . Listen."

On the screen, Wetherbee asked, "If you do make it onto the Ark, how do you think all this will affect you? The business with Harry Smith and your father."

Zane frowned. "I don't think much about that. Launch is years away."

"You'll have a duty," Wetherbee said, pushing. "You won't be there just as a person, but as a repository of genes. A contributor to genetic diversity."

"I'm interested in the engines, the theory of the warp field—"

"Yes, but this is a key part of the mission, the human side of it. You will have to have children, on the Ark, or on Earth II. That's the whole point. How do you feel about that?"

"Dirty."

"That's what your father said. But it isn't necessarily true."

"Dirty, dirty!" Zane swept his arm, scattering the pieces from the chessboard. Then he slumped.

Wetherbee paused the recording.

"You pushed him pretty hard," Grace said.

"I know, I know." Wetherbee sighed, and massaged a pale, stubbly face. "But when he gave me the opening about the father, I thought it was an opportunity I shouldn't miss. I think the relationship to the father is the key to the whole mess.

"Look at the contradiction he's trying to resolve. His father loaded onto him all the pain and the blame of the sexual abuse, and the father's own drive and ambition, and maybe his own shame at what became of his son. So Zane's dirty because of the Harry Smith thing, and isn't fit to have kids. But on the other hand if he can't contribute to the gene pool he shouldn't be on the Ark. He should have been left back on Earth in the hands of the monsters his father depicted. But that's a primal choice, of life and death. He could hardly be put under more pressure. Maybe deep inside he's always just evaded the whole issue, buried the contradiction. It was showing up in the memory lapses, the self-harm. And then—"

"And then I triggered the crisis," Holle said. "That day I suggested he and I could have a kid."

Grace said, "That's one of the kindest gestures you could ever have made to a man like Zane. You weren't to know what was going on inside his head. He didn't know himself."

"Even I still don't," Wetherbee said, "after years of my ham-fisted therapy. But, look, I think he has some kind of dissociative disorder. He has splits in his identity, caused by the contradictions he can't resolve, the pain he has to bury. That explains the memory lapses, the apparent shifts in identity—the way he seems to 'wake up,' uncertain of where he is, or even when."

Venus said, "You're saying our only warp engineer is Jekyll and Hyde?"

"So what do we do?" Holle asked.

He shrugged. "I have limited facilities for MRI scans. I tried that but can see nothing physically abnormal in his brain functions, whichever aspect of himself is apparent. I think the only answer is therapy—to understand him fully, and the damage that's been done. And then to find some way to start the healing. Hypnosis is often used in these cases. I never hypnotized anybody in my life, but there are routines in the archive I might be able to adapt." He grimaced. "This is going to take years more, if it works at all."

"I guess we don't have much choice," Holle said. "Thanks, Mike. I know you didn't sign up for this."

"No, I didn't." Wetherbee looked resentful, then grinned. "But then, neither did Zane." As they got up to leave, he cleared the screen and turned to a computer program.

It snagged Venus's attention. "What's this?"

"I'm trying to teach the ship's AI to play infinite chess. With some prompting in my ear at least I might be able to put up a fight against Zane . . ."

In the small hours of the next morning, Holle was woken by two more calls. The first was from Wilson Argent in Halivah. They had found the little girl, Meg Robles.

"She zipped herself up in a pressure suit. You wouldn't think a four-year-old could do that. Then she got stuck, and couldn't get out."

She listened to his tone. "She's dead."

"I'm afraid so. First death since launch. And the first dead child."

"I'll be right there."

"No, we'll handle it. We're looking after Cora. Just let Kelly know."

"Sure."

And later, she had a call from Mike Wetherbee.

"I got an e-mail from Zane's user ID. It was in kind of broken English, and it asked for a meeting, asked for my help."

"So?"

"The sender signed himself Jerry. Holle, there's no Jerry on the ship. And when I checked the surveillance monitors, when he sent it Zane was alone in his room."

64

May 2048

The siren's guttural blaring almost drowned out the voice alarm: FIRE, SEBA DECK TEN. FIRE, SEBA DECK TEN. FIRE . . .

Holle had been working on a replacement for a failed component in the Primary Oxygen Circuit, figuring out a simplified design that the Ark's limited machine shop would be capable of turning out. She was listening to Paul Simon's "Darling Lorraine" on repeat on her Angel, a favorite of her father's because, he said, it reminded him of his relationship with her mother. And she was daydreaming of seasons on Earth, of autumn. It took her a second to clear her head.

She shut off the Angel and grabbed her Snoopy cap. "Groundwater. Watch, what's going on?"

Masayo Saito's voice came on the line. "Holle, get down here, we got a problem."

She smelled smoke. Maybe that had triggered her dying-leaf dream. She could *see* smoke seeping under the door of her cabin. She pulled the Snoopy cap on her head and rummaged in a cupboard for a face mask.

Kelly Kenzie's voice blared over the PA. "This is Kelly. We have a major incident. Seba crew, to your fire stations, we've rehearsed this often enough and you know the drill. Halivah, seal up and prep for support operations. Anybody in transit to Seba, go back to Halivah. Let's move it, people."

Holle rushed out of her cabin and emerged into chaos.

———

The fire was a few decks down. A brilliant glow shone up through the mesh flooring, as if she was standing over a furnace. Hot air and smoke billowed up through the length of the hull, gathering in the upper decks and beneath the domed roof. People were running, some shouting. Holle could hear the rush of extinguishers and sprinklers, precious volatiles being expended to fight the fire. Over all this was the clamor of the siren, and Kelly Kenzie's voice booming out instructions echoing from the metal walls.

Holle saw Grace Gray on the far side of the hull. She was awkwardly climbing the ladders between the decks with little Helen, now six years old, clinging to her back, and with three-year-old Steel Antoniadi in one arm. Grace was evidently fleeing the fire below. But smoke was gathering above, and some of the crew were already climbing back *down* from the dome, choking. The hull was becoming a closing trap. Grace made a quick decision, ducking into a cabin and slamming shut the door. If she blocked the door with wet towels, she and Helen might be safe.

But Holle was responsible for more than just Grace and her daughter.

For heartbeats she just stood there, outside her door, uncertain what to do. Four years after leaving Jupiter, this tiny, fragile hull and its twin Halivah were the only refuge to be had in twelve long light-years. An out-of-control fire was their worst nightmare. Holle was senior, as well trained to handle the situation as anybody else aboard. She sensed she needed to make a quick decision—but to do what?

"Holle!" Paul Shaughnessy came clambering down a ladder. He was wearing the outer layer of one pressure suit and he carried another, like a flayed skin draped over his back. He was following the training she'd given him; the suits were fireproof to an extent, and their oxygen supply would enable their wearers to keep functioning even as the air turned toxic. He looked tense, distracted, distressed.

He handed her the spare suit. She pulled it over her legs. "Paul, are you OK? Do you know how this started?"

"It was Jack. I was up in the nose. My brother was down on Ten, in the maintenance area. He was fixing a rip in his own suit. The suit just exploded! I saw it on a feed. It became a fireball, and then it spread."

She shook her head. "That doesn't make any sense." The suits had a pure oxygen air supply, so there was always a risk of fire, but the safety features should have ensured no such accident ever happened.

"It's what I saw. I have to go down to Jack. Masayo's down there."

"Go, go. I need to talk to Kelly and Venus."

He nodded, snapped closed his faceplate, and carried on down into the furnace.

Holle closed up her own helmet. "Venus, are you there?"

"Groundwater, Jenning. We're in the cupola."

"Well, stay put. And start working on contingencies to detach the cupola and fly it over to Halivah."

"We're on it, that's the regular drill."

Holle imagined the calm twilight of the cupola, the silent, wheeling stars beyond, the screens full of images of devastation within the hull. "Can you see what's happening in here?"

"Most of the cameras are still functioning, though they're going down all the time, and the comms lines are fritzing too. Decks Nine through Eleven are gutted. The mesh decking is melting, and dripping down into the hydroponic beds on Fourteen. Countermeasures aren't working too well. The fire has got in behind the equipment racks. *That* wasn't supposed to happen. Casualties unknown, we just can't see."

Kelly's amplified voice suddenly cut out, leaving the hull filled with a cacophony of screams, the roaring of the fire.

"What about the hull temperature?"

"Rising, Holle. I can't trust these readings, but—"

"Understood." The greatest danger of all was that the fire would melt its way through the hull altogether, and breach the pressurized compartment. There was a last-resort procedure to avert that final catastrophe, a drastic step. Holle was starting to think there was no choice. She tagged her microphone. "Kelly, are you receiving?"

"We lost her feed, Holle," Venus reported.

"Venus, I'm thinking of cutting the tether."

"Kelly's out of touch. I endorse your decision. Do it."

Holle started climbing up a ladder away from the fire, into the gathering smoke. "Can you handle the follow-up from in there? Warn Halivah. Run the internal warnings, prepare for microgravity. Take over attitude control—"

"Already on it, Holle. It'll be fine, it will work, we rehearsed for this."

Holle said nothing more and pressed on with her climb. Her suit felt heavy and stiff, and her hands tired quickly as she fought the gloves' stiffness to grasp at the metal rungs. Venus was right. Yes, they had rehearsed on the ground and since launch, simulating situations almost as drastic as this. But all their years of training hadn't prevented the fire, or stopped the situation from degenerating to this lethal point.

She reached the domed roof of the hull. With an awkward twist she flipped over onto the upside of one of the catwalks that ran beneath the dome, and fixed a safety harness buckle to a rail. She paused, breathing hard. The smoke was dense here, making it almost impossible to see, and she wiped soot away from her faceplate with a suit glove.

She found the panel that covered the tether severance handle. She punched in a security code, and flipped open the panel. The handle itself was surrounded by warnings in huge lettering. She wrapped her gloved fingers easily around the handle.

"The situation's deteriorating, Holle," Venus called. "Do it."

Holle snapped the handle down.

At a junction on the tether between the hulls, close to its central point, a small explosive charge popped, silent in the vacuum. A tiny cloud of debris dispersed quickly. Since Jupiter the two hulls had been rotating about the warp generator at their common central point, completing an orbit once every thirty seconds. Now the cable that connected them was cut, and the hulls drifted apart, the severed tether coiling languidly as hundreds of tonnes of tension was released. When the particles of debris reached the wall of the warp bubble they sparkled briefly, their substance shredded by ferocious tides.

It was as if the whole hull dropped like a falling elevator car. Holle drifted up from the catwalk, and with a stab of panic she grabbed at the rail, even though she was safely anchored.

She peered down through the catwalk at the inferno below. The decks, shocked into zero gravity, were full of clouds of junk lifting into the air, furniture, handhelds, bits of clothing, food fragments, tools, even loose bolts and screws, anything not held down suddenly mobile. But the fire was the crux. She thought she saw an immediate difference in the way the smoke was billowing, and maybe the flames licked a bit less eagerly at the decking and equipment racks.

That was the idea. By cutting the tether Holle had eliminated the artificial gravity from the hull's interior. Without gravity there was no convection; hot air could not rise, and the processes that had been sustaining the fire, the updraft that drew in fresh oxygen to feed the flames, had been eliminated. The fire still had to be doused, and there were other dangers deriving from zero-gravity fires, which could smolder unseen for days or weeks. But at least with the fire choking on its own products there was a better chance that the hull as a whole would survive.

The alarm tone changed, and now Venus's voice rang out, relayed from the cupola. "Prepare for vernier fire. All hands prepare for vernier fire . . ."

This was the next step. Right now both hulls, released from the tether's grip, had been flung away from the center. They could not afford to fall too far; an encounter with the warp bubble wall would destroy them. So auxiliary rockets would be fired to hold the hulls somewhere close to the bubble's center, and to still any residual rotation. Some time in the future the hulls could be brought back together, the tether reattached, the assembly spun up again.

If the verniers fired in the first place, Holle thought. If they or their control systems hadn't been ruined by the fire. If there was the fuel remaining to rejoin the hulls and restore their mutual rotation. If, if, if. Holle had always held in her head an image of the long chain of events that all had to occur precisely as programmed if she were ever to walk safely on the ground of Earth II. Just now she could feel that chain stretching, its weakest links straining.

A small bundle floated below her, wriggling oddly. It was a baby, Holle saw, drifting in open space. Only a few months old, bundled in a diaper, it waved bare arms and legs. With eyes and mouth opened wide, the baby seemed to be enjoying the experience of swimming in the air. But now the hull banged, as if huge fists were hammering on its exterior wall. That was the verniers, firing in hard bursts. Holle, hanging onto her rail, felt the jolts as each impulse was applied. The baby caromed off a deck plate and bounced back up in the air, limbs flailing. It was frightened now, crying. Holle unclipped herself from the catwalk and descended like an angel, folding the baby in charred spacesuit sleeves.

65

On the morning Thomas Windrup's sentencing was due to be announced Holle woke in an unfamiliar room, with odd metallic colors and strange smells. This was not her cabin, not Seba, not the hull she had come to think of as home. In the weeks since the fire she had been stationed in Halivah, hot-bunking with Paul Shaughnessy in a tiny cabin improvised from one of their own maintenance lockups. She still hadn't got used to it.

It didn't take her long to get dressed.

Paul was outside the cabin with their pressure suits. He waited while she used the bathroom block. Then she led the way to the hull's nose airlock, where they suited up briskly. Holle didn't try to engage Paul in conversation. Today he was going over to Seba to see the sentencing of the man who had tried to kill his brother by sabotaging his suit. Paul's anger had been barely contained since the incident, and it was best to leave him be.

They cycled through the lock and out into the dark, and latched their harnesses to the cable that now linked the hulls. This wasn't a rotation tether, and wasn't held rigid; the cable was just a guide strung between the two hulls along which they pulled themselves hand over hand, across the two hundred meters to Seba. Traveling this way was hard work, but it saved fuel.

The hulls drifted, stationary with respect to each other but not side by side, and not even parallel; Halivah was tipped up compared to Seba, so that the two hulls lay like wrecked ships on the bottom of Earth's ever-deepening ocean. More lengths of cable connected Halivah to the warp generator assembly, so that the components of the Ark were bound up in a kind of spiderweb, lit by externally mounted lights. And beyond the hulls lay the silent, steady stars.

Once aboard Seba, Holle and Paul made their way down to Deck Ten, proceeding by handholds down from the nose of the hull. Kelly had ordered that the sentencing of Thomas Windrup should be held in the very place where his sabotage had started the disastrous fire. Without spin up the hull was without effective gravity, and people swam everywhere, flicking from handhold to handhold. The children, all too young to remember the weightless cruise before Jupiter, loved it, and flying, tumbling, tag-chasing kids had become a minor hazard. But the hull still smelled of smoke and scorched plastic.

At Deck Ten, Kelly was waiting outside a small cabin, its door shut. Despite weeks of cleanup there was no furniture here, not even any intact decking to which furniture could be attached. But ropes had been strung across the deck from wall to blackened wall, and the gathering people hung onto the ropes, or found themselves corners where they could cling to wall fittings.

Holle seemed to be the last of the senior crew to make it here. She saw Wilson, Venus, Mike Wetherbee, Masayo Saito—even Zane, and Holle wondered which of his alternate personalities had shown up for this meeting. Doc Wetherbee was studiously avoiding everybody's eyes. Wilson, still Kelly's lover, bore the marks of recent hard work; he wore vest and shorts, and his muscular limbs were streaked with ash.

Jack Shaughnessy wasn't here. Presumably he was still too feeble from the massive burns he had suffered over his arms and chest to be released by Doc Wetherbee. And Thomas Windrup wasn't here either, to hear the verdict passed on him. Venus looked wary. As one of her colleagues in GN&C and astronomy Thomas Windrup was one of "her" people.

Kelly, subtly isolated from the crowd, checked over notes on her handheld. She was dressed in a grimy coverall. She had shaved her blond hair, and smoke and soot had stained the lines around her mouth and eyes, making her look a lot older than her thirty years. Nearly seven years of leadership had made her tougher, Holle thought, more decisive, more clear-thinking. She had done her job competently enough. But all her hard work and even her relentless search for unanimity, the hours of talking, hadn't made her popular. Holle sometimes thought the strain was pulling her down.

Kelly glanced around at her silent crewmates. "OK," she began. "I guess everybody who wants to be here, is here. I suspended all regular duties save the watches. You can watch the session live via the surveillance system, or the recordings we'll make, and eventually we'll be shipping transcripts back to Earth too.

"Today I want to draw a line under the fire. The recovery of Seba is going to take us years—we'll probably be still working on it when we get to Earth II, in three years' time. But we've already done a great deal. We buried our dead."

Four crew—one Candidate, one gatecrasher, one illegal, and one ship-born baby—had been asphyxiated by the smoke. Four naked bodies had been sent tumbling away from the hull, to be scattered in the ferocious tidal rip of the warp bubble wall—naked because they couldn't spare resources for coffins or flags or even clothes.

Kelly went on, "We've been through the flaws in our practices that led to the seriousness of the incident, once the fire started. The failures in our maintenance routines in particular. The worst contributory factor was a buildup of dust and other flammable junk behind the equipment racks in their frames against the hull walls. Each rack is supposed to be pulled out and its docking bay cleaned once a week, or more in some areas. Some looked as if they hadn't been shifted since Jupiter."

Kelly's ferocious inquiry hadn't attached any blame to Holle and her internal-systems maintenance team. The failure had been in the laxity of the regular crew, getting worse year on year, in keeping up their daily routine of cleaning out the small spaces they all had to inhabit. Doc Wetherbee had long complained about this, and butts had been kicked after an outbreak of food poisoning caused by poor hygiene in Halivah's galley. But the spread of the fire had been a much more severe consequence.

"We're trying to put this right from here on in. But all of us who cut corners in our cleaning routines are going to have to live with some of the responsibility for what happened to Peri and Anne and Nicholas and little Sasha.

"However, only one of us actually started the fire that did so much damage. Only one of us bears the burden of guilt. Thomas Windrup confessed, as soon as the fire was under control, and you're aware that we ran through the surveillance records to establish that guilt independently. There's no doubt the arson was his, just as he claimed. He was trying to kill Jack Shaughnessy. He nearly killed us all."

Holle supposed you could say it was a crime of passion. Here among the crew, stuck on this Ark as the years wore slowly away, obsession and lust and suspicion had a way of putrefying. Thomas had never stopped believing that Jack Shaughnessy still wanted Elle, and that Jack was playing a long game, waiting until they all arrived at Earth II where he would use the new Ship's Law about multiple fathers to claim her. On the Ark you couldn't get away from your enemies, or even your friends. Endless chance encounters with Jack had, in the end, driven Thomas crazy—or at least crazy enough to try to kill Jack.

But Thomas hadn't meant to hurt anybody else, he insisted. He knew Jack was due to overhaul the pressure suit he generally used. Thomas had rigged the suit so that when a test valve on the oxygen inlet was triggered, a spark would ignite a jet of oxygen, and then the materials of the suit; he had poured flammable solvent over the suit's liner. Thomas had done much of the preparation in the dark, to avoid the ubiquitous gaze of the surveillance cameras. He planned that the fire would eliminate all trace of its own cause, his own guilt. Anyhow his plan had failed. The suit had exploded into flame, too violently. Jack hadn't been killed but thrown back, badly burned but alive, and the resulting fire had quickly spread beyond the suit itself.

"But now we have to handle the issue of sentencing. This is the most serious crime we've seen aboard this Ark since we left Earth—far more serious than anything I expected to have to deal with. I've thought long and hard. I've come to a decision." Kelly looked around at them, her face set. "And I've implemented that decision, with the aid of Masayo, here, and Doc Wetherbee. You know I've always tried to work through consensus, through unanimity if we can get it. But I thought that in this case the choice was too hard, the consequences too grave, to be debated in the open. This decision was mine alone. I bear the responsibility.

"Please hear my logic. Thomas attempted murder. On Earth, while the Denver government was still functioning, he'd have been thrown into jail, or sent to some penal work gang, endlessly building seawalls or processing camps for eye-dees. And if he'd succeeded in killing Jack Shaughnessy he might have been put to death for it. So what are we to do with him here? You Candidates will recall that we debated such issues in the Academy, and then while we were en route to Jupiter and under the auspices of Gunnison. We also have as precedent Gordo Alonzo's verdict when Jack Shaughnessy assaulted Thomas himself back in '43. Jack was put back to work." She glanced at Venus. "As Venus hasn't ceased to remind me, Thomas is her best astronomer. We need him back in the cupola, checking out Earth II. We can't even isolate him socially because we need his genes. But this crime, which could have killed us all, is serious, and I don't believe it can go unmarked. So what do we do?

"I did some research in the archive. We're not the only society to face this kind of challenge—resource-stretched, yet having to deal with miscreant individuals. Medieval England, for instance, and western Europe. They evolved punishments the criminal would have to live with the rest of his or her life—and a visible deterrent to others—yet that wouldn't stop him working. And so—" She glanced at Masayo. "You can bring him out now."

Masayo looked highly uncomfortable, Holle thought. He pulled himself over to the door of the cabin behind Kelly, but before he opened it he glanced around, his arms folded, his chest out. "I don't want any trouble over this. We all need to deal with it calmly, however you're feeling. OK?"

Venus looked furious. Wilson was cold-eyed, watchful. Zane looked amused.

Masayo opened the cabin door. The interior was dark. "Come on out." Holding onto the door frame for balance, he extended an arm into the cabin.

Thomas Windrup emerged into the light. He hung onto Masayo's arm, and wouldn't look anybody in the eye. His face was still puffy from the beating he'd received when Paul and a few of his illegal buddies had managed to get hold of him. But Holle thought he looked paler, more sick; he had suffered something worse than a beating.

Kelly said, "Show them."

Clearly shamed, Thomas lifted one leg. The boot dangled, floating free in the air, and the trouser leg twisted, empty.

There were gasps, muttered oaths. Zane Glemp laughed out loud.

"Shit," Venus said. "You took his *foot.*"

Kelly said, "It will make no difference in free fall. Clearly he'll be impeded under gravity, on the Ark and on Earth II. But the doctor is working on a crutch for him, even an artificial foot. Obviously this won't make any difference to the work he does for you, Venus—"

Venus turned on Wetherbee. "You did this? You're a doctor. You mutilated him?"

Holle had never seen Mike Wetherbee more unhappy than right now. "You would say that. Everybody knows Thomas is one of yours. Anyhow it was a direct order. And who would you rather did it? Should I have let Paul Shaughnessy loose with a chain saw?"

"Don't blame him," Kelly said, and she drifted down so she came between Venus and Wetherbee. "The decision, the responsibility, were all mine."

Venus took a deep breath. "I never thought I'd find myself saying this, Kelly. You know I admire you, what you've done for us. You've held us together through some tough years, especially since we lost contact with Earth. But I can't accept your judgment over this grotesque mutilation. You maimed a healthy crewman. You compromised the doctor, and Masayo, who you turned into a strong-arm thug.

"Kelly, you hold your position as speaker through consensus. Well, I withdraw from that consensus."

There was a lethal silence.

Holle was well aware that there had always been heated confrontations behind the scenes as Kelly tried to get decisions made. But this was the first time anybody remotely as senior as Venus had challenged Kelly in public.

Kelly snapped back, "You want the job, Venus?"

"I'm not saying that. I'm saying *you* need to stand down. And when you're gone, we'll deal with the consequences."

"You're just pissed because I meddled with your fiefdom. Well, I don't have to respond to the challenge of a single individual—"

"Venus is right," Wilson said. He had been sitting on a microgravity T-stool, his legs wrapped around its struts. Now he straightened up so he faced Kelly himself.

Kelly stared. "Wilson? What are you doing?"

"Kelly, you've done a great job. But things have been off course for a while. Not keeping to the cleanup rotas—we wouldn't be in this mess if not for that." He gestured at Thomas. "And you sure got *this* wrong. This isn't a road we can go down. You need to let somebody else take this burden off your shoulders."

"Like who? You?" But he didn't back down. Kelly's face worked, her eyes hard yet red-rimmed, as if she might cry. "You bastard, Wilson. You're betraying me. Did you set this up? Cook it up between you behind my back?"

Wilson spread his hands. "We're just two crew members expressing an opinion."

"Fine. If that's what you want. I stand down." She folded her arms and pushed herself back, so she drifted between Masayo and Thomas.

There was another long silence. Nobody moved.

Holle realized that Kelly hadn't just given up her post as speaker, she'd abandoned chairing this meeting too. As an instinctive backroom worker Holle didn't like to be personally exposed in this kind of charged atmosphere. But she was always prodded by duty, duty. If nobody else shoveled the shit, she would. Even literally, sometimes.

She pulled herself into the space Kelly had vacated. "We need to move on. Anybody object if I chair the meeting from here on in?"

There was a rumble of assent. Crucially, Kelly, Venus and Wilson all nodded. But Wilson sneered. "That's typical of you, Groundwater. Why aren't you up here challenging yourself? Pointless little mouse."

Holle ignored him. "Let's wrap this up as quickly as possible. We need a new speaker. Can I have a show of candidates? Raise your hand if you want to put yourself forward."

Kelly's arm snapped up.

Venus raised her hand, grave.

And then, slowly, as if reluctantly, as if his arm was being dragged up, Wilson raised his right hand. Kelly shot him a look of sheer loathing.

Holle proceeded cautiously. "OK. Kelly Kenzie, Venus Jenning, Wilson Argent, all declare their interest. But not all the crew is here." She glanced up at the nearest camera. "Grace, you're in the cupola?"

Grace Gray was on watch today. Her voice boomed from the PA. "Here, Holle. We see you. Helen says hi."

Holle grinned. "I wish I was in there with you," she said ruefully. "Grace, please send a message out through Seba, and over to Halivah. Anybody who wants to declare their candidacy for this post should show themselves now." She looked up into the nearest camera. "Guys, everybody, let's be thorough about this. We don't want any second-guessing. If your neighbor is sleeping wake him up, and don't let him miss his chance. I'll allow fifteen minutes for responses. Everybody comfortable with that?" She glanced around again. There were no objections.

It was the longest fifteen minutes in Holle's life, at least since she'd waited on the pad at Gunnison for a nuclear bomb to go off under her butt. Everybody on Deck Ten stayed where they were, silent as stones.

After the fifteen minutes there were no more candidates, to Holle's relief.

"OK," she said. "Then I guess we proceed to the choice itself. How do you want to do this—a show of hands? Grace, if you can keep track of what's happening in Halivah—"

"No," said Wilson. He spoke strongly and clearly. "This is too important a decision to screw around with. It's not like when we left Jupiter, when we didn't have any serious divisions over policy, any personal splits. Now there's an argument to be had."

"Then what do you propose?"

"That we take our time. Say, a week. What's the rush? In that interval Holle can stand as acting speaker. In that time we will have a chance to debate where we're going as a crew, as a community. And then we can hold a proper election."

Neither Venus nor Kelly looked happy, but neither was objecting out loud.

"OK. So at the end of the week, then what? We gather for a vote by acclamation?"

"Hell, no. We have a secret ballot. We can find some way to manage that. I suggest we have two rounds—eliminate third place, have a runoff between the top two—"

Kelly snorted. "A secret ballot? You'd really condone such a waste of resources?"

Wilson looked back at her steadily, then significantly at Masayo. "There has to be no intimidation. A secret ballot is the way to ensure that."

He carried the day. And when the wider group broke up, chattering with excitement, Holle kept the three of them back, Kelly, Venus and Wilson, with Grace watching remotely as a witness, to thrash out a basic schedule for the coming week. Kelly and Wilson stayed apart, and wouldn't even look at each other.

Then, when it was done, hugely relieved, Holle fled to the calm and silence of her cabin where she began the business of picking up Kelly's workload, and figuring how she was going to juggle it with her own responsibilities.

But Wilson Argent came knocking on the door. "We need to talk. I need your vote—for all our sakes."

66

"Make yourself comfortable on the couch," Wetherbee said.

Zane, restrained by a loosely fastened belt, was in a foldout couch in Wetherbee's surgery on Halivah, the one on Seba still being out of action. He said, "It's hard not to be comfortable in free fall, Doctor."

Wetherbee bit back on his irritation. This was the alter, the partial personality, that he had tentatively labeled Zane 3, the passive, shadowy, depressive relic left behind when the other alters had taken away their various loads of guilt and responsibility. But even Zane 3 was a smartass. He kept his tone moderate. "You know what we're going to do, the hypnotic procedure?"

"It's not a problem. It's worked for us before. You may know I was noted as readily hypnotizable back in the Academy."

"So you were." And in fact a willingness to submit to hypnotic commands was, Wetherbee had learned, a characteristic of people with Zane's peculiar disorder. "So let's begin. Take deep slow breaths. Feel the tension washing out of your arms, your hands, your feet. Let your shoulders relax, your neck. Let your head just float. You're falling gently, falling inside yourself. Deeper and deeper you go, you're more and more relaxed. You find yourself in the Academy, in your cabin, the old museum building in Denver . . ." With his father close by, long before the damaging serial abuse by Harry Smith had started and the flood was still a remote threat,

Zane had felt as safe in the DMNS as he had ever felt in his life. Now Wetherbee returned him there, to that place and time, as a secure place to begin his analysis.

"What can you see?"

"My handheld, my books, my sports stuff. My AxysCorp coveralls. We're supposed to go on a hike tomorrow."

"OK. Now look around, Zane. Can you see that special door we talked about? The extra one, that leads into the other room."

"I see it. It's open."

"Good. Good." The "door" had always been closed before, and sometimes locked. "Can you see through the doorway? What do you see?"

"People."

"How many? Who are they?"

"There is a boy, and kind of a young man, and an older man."

"All right. Do you think any of them would like to speak to me?"

"I think the older man. He's smiling and nodding."

"Can you describe him?"

"He's about my height. He's a little bulky. He has silver hair and glasses."

Wetherbee was pretty certain this was the alter called Jerry. The description closely matched Zane's father, as did the name—"Jerry" for "Jerzy." Zane was a smartass, but not always very inventive in the details of his alters.

"Would you let the man talk to me? You just have to step back a bit."

"We've done that before."

"Yes, we have. You'll still be in your cabin, your safe place. And you know that if you aren't happy at any point you can just come right back, and the man will go back outside and the door will be locked up, just like that."

"OK."

Zane 3 sounded passive rather than convinced. He was so malleable, so lacking in self-motivation, it was extraordinarily hard not to direct him. "Thanks, Zane. I'll speak to you later."

Wetherbee knew he had a few minutes before the alter communicated with him. He murmured to the camera overhead, "Wetherbee medical log, 30th June 2048. With Zane Glemp. I believe I've been communicating with the alter I call Zane 3, the alter that first presented. I expect to be talking in a moment to the alter known as Jerry, the older man. For the record it's three days since I last repeated the appropriate structured clinical interview as recommended by the *Diagnostic and Statistical Manual of Mental Disorders of the American Psychiatric Association,* 2015 edition; I still uphold my diagnosis of dissociative identity disorder—"

"Hi, Dr. Wetherbee." Zane was smiling, his eyes open; he was looking around curiously. Everything about his body posture was changed. He looked alert, inquisitive, confident, not passive. His accent was faintly middle European.

"Hello. Who am I speaking to?"

"Well, this is Jerry, but I think you guessed that. How are you?"

"Very well."

"And how's the fake mission going? Still happy with your Las Vegas hotel?"

Jerry actively mocked Zane 3's suspicions that the whole mission was unreal, a fake mounted on Earth. "Not enough ice with the room service champagne."

Jerry laughed. He liked it if you played along with him, treated him as a peer.

"You've been busy, Jerry." Wetherbee held up his handheld. "You seem to be running Wilson Argent's election campaign for him."

"Well, I guess I am. That's why I exist, you know, to work. Zane spun me off because he needs organizing skills, which is what I contribute, and I come out to take over when things get on top of him and he can't cope.

But Zane's life is pretty small scale. I have time to do other things." He winked at Wetherbee. "Wilson knows I'm just an alter. Oh, he wouldn't put it like that . . . When he asks Zane a question to do with me, and Zane can't remember the previous conversation, Wilson just smiles and backs off and waits until I can come out to talk to him. He doesn't know the medical stuff, but he has an intuitive understanding of people, I think. Even of us!" He laughed.

"Maybe that will make him a good speaker."

"Well, I think so," "Jerry" said. "You decided which way you're going to vote yet, Doc?"

"I'm still considering. I'm impressed that you put out a manifesto." He scrolled through it now on the handheld. "You caught the other candidates on the hop with this."

"Nothing wrong with being professional. We put a lot of thought into the proposals in there, especially the bill of rights."

"I see that." This was a document, still in draft form, that would assure the crew of what Wilson called fundamental human rights. This included the right to the basics of life, to free air and water—a right you wouldn't have to spell out on Earth, but in a ship like this where every cubic centimeter of air had to be supplied by a machine that somebody else maintained, it wasn't a given. "Alongside our rights, you also spell out our responsibilities. Maintaining the ship's systems, not threatening its integrity. I see you're planning to introduce a credit system."

"Hell, yes." He smiled. "That's one of mine. We need basic incentivization. Do more good work and you accumulate wealth, you can buy stuff from other people, and your status goes up. Simple human nature. We have to move away from the vague socialist stuff Kelly spouted. This isn't a kibbutz. We're all Americans, for God's sake."

"I'm not."

"Well, mostly. No offense. Oh, some of the stuff in Ship's Law can stand. We figured most of it out by precedent, after all, and much of it is fit for purpose. But we need clearer thinking about the rest."

"Such as, you specify here, the freedom to marry who you choose, to have babies with who you choose."

"Yeah. We're restoring the right of each woman to control her own body, her womb."

"But this flies against what the social engineers recommended for optimal genetic mixing. That was a basic requirement of the mission."

"The social engineers aren't here," Jerry said firmly. "We are. And no policy is going to fly if it's rejected by the people, no matter how smart those long-drowned guys who thought it up were. My own and Wilson's belief is that we should put our trust in the collective wisdom of the crew—of us."

"You're proposing education reform too."

"Certainly. The curriculum we've developed for the kids so far has been based on wishy-washy stuff from the Academy. Ethics, for God's sake. Philosophy. Comparative theology. Blah, blah, blah. Thank God none of the kids are old enough yet to have been too damaged by this stuff. We should stick to what these kids are going to need to learn in order to survive."

"Such as, don't dismantle the life support? You're even restricting the science they'll be taught. Usually in a school you'd reward curiosity, initiative, an ability to learn."

"This mission is all about balances. Curiosity can come later, when we're safely established on Earth II, and we have the luxury to wonder what's over the next hill."

"Hmm. Interesting experiment."

Zane smiled. "In time basic human nature will reassert itself. But that time isn't now. For now, we have to consider ourselves at war with an environment that will kill us unless we manage to maintain our defenses, without a single waver of concentration. And that's the message we have to hammer home to the kids."

"You assert we have rights concerning a supply of air and water. But that hands a lot of power to the central functions that maintain those resources."

"Sure. Which is why Wilson is courting Holle Groundwater, getting her on his side, as I'm sure you already know. Because that kind of power resides with her and her team."

Wetherbee came to the most controversial piece of proposed legislation. "You're going to stop in-hull surveillance, the routine recording of everything that goes on."

"Unless it's for a specific purpose—yes. Humans have a basic right to privacy, of thought and deed. We need to trust our people, Doctor."

"Thomas Windrup—"

"Was a one-off. And besides the surveillance didn't stop him, it just proved his guilt when he'd already committed his crime, been caught, and confessed." He laughed. "Of course Zane 3 thinks that if we pull the plug on the reality show, the controllers in Las Vegas will come in and shut us down, or punish us."

"You know there's a lot of debate over this. The crew will have no means of surveilling *you*, I mean Wilson and his team."

"Oh, that's just a theoretical quibble."

"Theoretical? Maybe." Wetherbee pressed his fingers to his lips, wondering how far he should take this discussion. His concern was Zane, not Wilson and his manifesto. His long-term goal was the reintegration of all Zane's partial personalities. But to achieve that he was going to have to understand and work with each of them. He said carefully, "Kelly Kenzie is openly calling this a coup."

Zane laughed. "Well, she would." He actually winked at Wetherbee. "Listen, Doc—I think you and I can talk freely. I mean, you're under no threat no matter who wins out on Friday. You can look at this on a number of levels. The social engineers tried to set up our little ship-based society the way the hunter-gatherer bands used to organize. There you have leaders on sufferance, their most important quality being prestige—ability. That's Kelly all over, isn't it? But Wilson looks ahead to tougher times—times like now, times when we came close to being destroyed by our unrelenting enemy the environment. At such times you need a more basic kind of leader."

"Basic how?"

"Well, Wilson was always taller than Kelly. He's been pumping up for years. And he's a man—"

"Being a big strong man qualifies him as leader? Are you kidding?"

Zane smiled again. "You have to consider what reassures people. And then there's the timing. This is the year the flood wins . . ."

They had had no news of Earth, not since going to warp, but they had all followed the likely progress of the flood with simulations based on the best science models available. This year and the next were seeing the succumbing of whole continents. In January, Europe must finally have gone when Mount Elbrus, Russia's highest point, was covered. In May it was Africa's turn, when Kilimanjaro drowned. And the continental US would all be gone too by now, save a couple of mountains in Alaska. Next year South America, even the Andes, would be covered, and there would be nothing left in the western hemisphere at all, no trace of land.

Zane said, "Wilson always thought there would be trouble this particular year, the year the survivor guilt really cuts in. What people want above all else is stability, and that's what Wilson will provide. People will welcome his rule, believe me." His smile flickered. "I think Zane 3 is getting restless. Maybe I should go back now?"

"If you wouldn't mind."

"It's always stimulating talking to you, Dr. Wetherbee."

"For me too. Thanks, Jerry . . . Zane? Are you there?"

Zane slumped in the chair, and his face crumpled, as if he was about to cry. "Dr. Wetherbee?"

"Do you remember anything?"

"I don't think so. I thought I saw you . . . I don't remember."

"It went very well. Close the door and lock up your room now. Have you done that?"

"Yes."

"OK, come back to the surgery with me. Here we go, come back as I count backward from five. Five, four, three . . ."

67

They held the ballot using paper from a sacrificed social engineers' manual on optimal breeding policies. Holle moderated the process, with observers from all the crew's principal factions. She even got little Helen Gray and Steel Antionadi, just six and three, to help gather the ballot slips and count them, as a way of tying in the new shipborn generation to the results.

In the first round Venus came third, and was eliminated. And in the runoff Wilson beat Kelly by two-thirds to one-third. Much to Holle's relief, nobody disputed the result.

68

September 2049

"We might have a problem," was all Venus would say to Holle, very quietly, over the command crew's Snoopy-hat comms link.

So Holle made her way to the cupola, and took a seat, and waited in the humming dark while Venus and Cora Robles completed some complex number-crunching procedure, the data passing back and forth between their screens in columns of numbers, swirling curves and eye-boggling multidimensional displays.

In the cupola, you got used to long silences. That was Venus Jenning's way. The cupola was an island of calm, with its scents of plastic and metal and electronics, even a new-carpet smell of cleanness, and the smooth humming of the air-cycling fans. It was like sitting inside a computer core. And beyond the glass walls there were only the patient stars. Sitting in here you could forget the hulls even existed, with their chaos and shabbiness and endless fractiousness, ruled over by Wilson and his allies with their aloof, faintly menacing power.

The cupola was a refuge for Holle, she freely admitted, and it was obviously a refuge for those who worked here too. All of Venus's people were damaged in one way or another. All of them Candidates, all of them around thirty, roughly the same age as Venus and Holle herself: Cora Robles who had lost a child, Thomas Windrup mutilated in Kelly's last act as speaker, and Elle Strekalov, traumatized by the long-drawn-out dispute between Thomas and Jack Shaughnessy.

Even Venus had become more withdrawn since the bruising events fourteen months ago, what Kelly continued to call Wilson's coup against her. Venus had always suspected that she had been maneuvered, somehow, by Wilson into challenging Kelly first. She felt betrayed. She conceded Wilson had brought a certain stability that had been lacking under Kelly. But she always pointed out that the one part of Wilson's draft constitution that had been quietly struck out after he took office was a limitation clause, restricting any speaker to one term of four years. At least this peculiar relationship, between Venus and Wilson, was stable. Holle hoped it would remain so for the remaining couple of years of the cruise to Earth II.

And it was Earth II, and Venus's latest data on it, that Holle had been summoned to discuss today.

The astronomers reached some break point in their study. They sat back and breathed deep and stretched, as if coming up for air. Cora smiled at Holle, and clambered out through the airlock into Seba. Venus and Holle were left alone. Venus tapped a key on a laptop, and Holle heard a faint rattle of bolts.

"You locked us in," Holle said, surprised.

"You got it." Venus produced a flask from the low shelf unit beside her workstation. "You want some coffee?"

"I'm honored."

Venus poured out two cups.

Holle sipped gratefully. The ability of the processing systems to keep producing a hot, warm liquid that still tasted something like actual coffee nearly eight years after launch from Gunnison was one of the Ark's minor miracles. "You always seem to have the best brew in here, Venus."

Venus smiled, her face dimly illuminated by her glowing screen. "Got to give people some kind of incentive to visit. By the way, when that hatch is locked the data feed to the rest of the ship is cut too. So we have a little privacy."

Holle stared. "You cut yourself off even from Wilson?"

"Oh, our great leader gets a continuous feed." She winked at Holle. "Which isn't to say he's fed the unvarnished truth the whole time."

"You manipulate the data feed?"

"Wilson needs us, he needs what we do. As long as I'm no direct threat to him, I think he lets me keep my little secrets."

And there was an expression of the most basic tactic for survival on this Ark: to grab a bit of power and hold on to it.

"So you have a 'little secret' today?"

Venus nodded. "I'll tell Wilson about it when I'm ready. We need more data to establish the case. But—"

"You said there's a problem."

"With Earth II," Venus said. "I think there's a problem with our destination, Holle. I need you to help me figure out how to handle it."

"Shit."

Venus grinned. "That doesn't begin to cover it." She swiveled a screen so it faced Holle. "We have images of Earth II. Still rudimentary, but—"

Holle was astonished. "Wow. *Images.* And you kept them to yourself?"

"So far."

"Suddenly I feel like Columbus."

"More like the crew of Apollo 8," Venus said. "Remember how Gordo used to claim to have met them all, Borman, Lovell and Anders? The first to leave Earth orbit, the first to see the world whole and complete . . ." Her finger hovered over a key. "Let me show you how we got the data."

Since going to warp, Venus and her team had continued to use the Ark as a mobile telescopic platform for inspecting the nearby stars and their planets, extending the depth and quality of the searches that had been possible from Earth, and from the Ark itself at Jupiter. It seemed remarkable to Holle that it was possible to perform such fine work from within a warp bubble, with the telescopes peering out through a wall of folded spacetime. But the lensing of the light was easy to unravel; you just traced the rays back along the paths they had followed, following solutions through the forest of relativistic equations that described the Alcubierre warp.

Even now that they were out among the stars, the feeble light of a planet, reflecting a scrap of its parent star's radiation output, remained difficult to detect. So Venus had her telescopes look for the subtle dips in a star's light when a planet transited before its face—a technique that would only work if the orbit happened to be edge-on to the Ark. Or she looked for the wobbles in a star's motion characteristic of it being pulled around by the orbiting bulk of planets. What struck Holle as the cleverest technique involved a pair of telescopes observing the same star but from some distance apart. Light acted as a wave, and waves when combined interfered with each other, constructively or destructively. The signals from the two telescopes were combined so that a destructive resonance occurred between the two feeds of the star's own light—and with the star itself made invisible, any planets, each no brighter than a billionth or so of the star's own luminosity, could be made out.

With such techniques a planet could be observed closely, its mass and gravity estimated, the spectrum of its light analyzed for signs of water and for such atmospheric constituents as methane and oxygen. Before the Ark left Jupiter these Earthlike signatures had been recognized of a planet of 82 Eridani, a star not unlike the sun.

"But," Venus said, "we're not just staring at Earth II the whole time. We've been looking further out, as far as we can see, across a sphere a hundred light-years in radius, trying to map everything we can. Why not? Even if we make it to Earth II it's going to be a long time before anybody else gets a chance to do any planet-spotting, and certainly not from a platform like this. There are limits to detectability, a base of astrophysical noise you can't see through. But we're easily sensitive enough to spot an Earthlike planet at an Earthlike distance from a sun-like star, for instance from stellar velocity oscillations of a centimeter a second or so. So we're drawing up a catalog, a legacy for future generations." She grinned, and the Venus that Holle had grown up with peeked out from inside the grave thirty-year-old woman. "Besides, what else have we got to do all day? It's this or scrub the walls."

"I believe you."

"So you ready for Earth II?"

"Hit me."

The screen before Holle lit up with a disc, a world. It was almost full, with only a crescent in shadow, to the left-hand side. And the lit portion, the right hemisphere, bathed in the sunlike light of 82 Eridani, was dominated by a shield of ocean that gleamed gray. Holle saw a dazzling highlight at the right-hand limb cast by the out-of-sight star. There was a swirl of cloud in that daylight hemisphere, a big storm system of some kind. Elsewhere she saw land, a thin gray belt across the waist of the planet, another landmass below it, a kind of archipelago above. The image was blurred, an artifact of the telescopy; no details much smaller than continents were visible.

Venus watched her, grinning. "Even Wilson hasn't seen this yet."

Holle shook her head. "It's like a special effect in a HeadSpace game. And so Earthlike. No polar caps?"

"No, though the surface temperature isn't much different from Earth's. Well, there have been intervals in prehistory when Earth was ice-free."

"Are these true colors? The landmasses are a little darker than on Earth maybe."

Venus nodded. "True. Not so green as Earth. 82 Eridani is a G5 class rather than a G2 like Sol, and the light is subtly different. We suspect there's some different light-gathering chemistry going on down there."

"But there's life."

"Oh, yes, we think so. No chance of that oxygen-nitrogen atmosphere without it."

Holle peered at the scattered landmasses. Would the shapes of these strange continents become as familiar to the Ark's children as Africa and America and Asia had once been to her own parents and grandparents, before the flood covered them over? "Venus, this looks pretty good to me. What's the problem?"

"Watch this sequence. Earth II's day is longer than Earth's, about thirty hours. These images were taken a couple of hours apart."

It was like a crude, blurry animation, showing the world turning on a horizontal axis. That long central landmass moved downwards, and the other continent moved out of sight, under the belly of the world. The belt of shadow didn't shift. The sun was out of sight, somewhere to her right . . .

Suddenly Holle saw it. "Oh. It's a Uranus. The axis is tipped over, pointing at the sun."

"Tipped through almost ninety degrees. Compared to, what, twenty-three and a half degrees for Earth? Actually we think it's more like Mars, where the axis swings back and forth over periods of hundreds of thousands of years. Earth is stabilized by the moon; Mars lacks a big enough moon—and so does Earth II. The tipping seems to be tied into tidal effects from two big Jovians further out."

"That's why there's no ice."

"Yes. Each pole must be blasted by continual sunlight for half the year, while the other is in permanent shadow."

"How could this come about?"

"Planets, and planetary systems, are common, Holle. We've learned that much—the sky is full of them. But the formation processes they go through are chaotic. They coalesce out of clouds of dust and ice, and then endure a hierarchy of impacts, from dust grains banging into each other up to the point where planet-sized masses collide. Not only that, there's migration. Stars are born in crowded nurseries, and the remnant cloud is blown away pretty quickly by the light from neighboring baby stars. But before then tidal friction with the cloud can cause worlds the mass of Jupiter to go drifting inward through the system, scattering smaller worlds like birds. So there's a lot of chance involved in the process. Anyhow this is probably why we have discovered so few 'Earths;' in nice stable circular orbits just the right distance from their star. And if you put constraints on the *kind* of star you want, you're looking at an even smaller selection."

Holle pulled her nose. "I have this feeling you're drawing me into an argument."

Venus sighed. "Well, it's an argument that was dead before we left Jupiter. Holle, we've found Earths orbiting other kinds of star, not like Sol at all. M-class red dwarfs, for instance. If you orbit close in enough, you get reasonable temperatures. Some of those M-Earths are *better candidates than Earth II*—even based on what we knew at Jupiter. But there was a faction at Mission Control who wouldn't countenance going anywhere but a yellow sun."

"I remember," Holle said. "I tried to keep out of it. Gordo Alonzo put his foot down in the end, didn't he?"

"Yeah. 'I'm not sending this crew to the fucking planet Krypton!' Basically we took a bet that this candidate, from the restricted set we were prepared to consider, would pan out for us. Well, we lost. We're doing some modeling of Earth II's surface conditions. There are complex weather systems, quite unlike Earth. Evidently simple life survives there. But—"

"But it might not be a world for humans."

"I don't know. I hope it is. I fear not." Venus sighed, and shut down her image sequence. "There's a lesson here that just one astronomical parameter, in this case the axial tilt, may ruin a world from a human point of view. Which may be why we've seen no signs of intelligent life anywhere."

Holle stared. "You've been looking?"

"Of course we have. Wouldn't you? We've been looking the way we're heading, and into the center of the Galaxy too, where most of the stars are. We've seen nothing, Holle, no signs of off-planet orbital infrastructures—no Dyson spheres, no ringworlds—and no sign that anybody's meddled with the evolution of the stars. And not a bit of organized data in the radio hiss. It's a big, empty Galaxy. Empty save for us. And that's *spooky.*" Her voice was small, the pupils of her dark-adapted eyes huge in the soft light of her screen as she peered out at the stars.

Watching her, Holle wondered what kind of long-term effect the contemplation of a silent universe might be having on Venus and her people. The Ark sure didn't need any more crazies. "Venus, I think we ought to start talking to people about this. Your doubts about Earth II. The sooner we start planning how we handle the issue the better."

Venus grunted. "Sure. Start with Wilson, as he'll be listening in anyhow. But keep it from the crew for now. No point stirring up negative reactions."

"Thanks for the coffee. Umm, could you unlock the hatch?"

69

olle put off going to see Wilson about Venus's issues. She felt she needed time to think it through.

Instead, back in Seba, she went down to Deck Ten where she was due to meet Doc Wetherbee and Grace Gray for an update on the progress of Zane Glemp's therapy. Wetherbee said Zane was participating in a dream circle there today, and Wetherbee wanted to observe.

Coming out of the airlock from the cupola Holle met Grace, and they crossed the deck heading for the downward stair. In the open area at the center of the deck Grace had to pull Holle back, to avoid the hard body of a kid who went plummeting down the length of the fireman's pole.

"Whee!"

"Jeez," Holle said, breathing hard. "Nearly got me that time."

"Yes. They get faster every day. They dare each other to see how far they can fall without grabbing the pole." They reached the ladders, and began their descent. "I persuaded Wilson to put a net across the hole in Deck Fourteen, to keep them from smashing into the hydroponics at least."

"Little bastards go crazy."

Grace, climbing down below Holle, grinned. "It's hard to control them twenty-four seven, Holle. I mean, my Helen's seven years old now."

"I listen to them speak sometimes. Even their language is different from ours. They play complicated games of tag, and they must have fifty words for 'gotcha.'"

"Yes. But no word for 'sky' or 'sea' . . ."

They reached Deck Ten. More than a year after the fire the deck was still pretty much a ruin, with blackened walls and burned-out instrument racks. Even the flooring was a lash-up to replace the melted mesh panels. The whole of this hull had never really recovered, and had an air of shabbiness and age.

The dream circle was just getting started, and a toll collector was having the dreamers press their thumbs to a handheld pad to collect their payments. Wilson had installed a new currency of credits, collected electronically and stored in the ship's memory; you were paid for your work, and in turn you had to pay for everything save for air and water. You even had to pay for sharing your own dreams on a burned-out deck. And a slice of every payment went straight to the common treasury, which Wilson controlled.

Among the dreamers was Zane, who looked shy, subdued. Holle wondered which alter was dominant today.

Grace was still talking about the children. "Kids just adapt to the place they're brought up in, I guess. On Ark Three we used to deal with raft communities. Trading, you know. We encountered kids older than Helen who had spent their whole lives on the sea, who never saw dry land at all . . . They were happy, or could be. Wherever you're born, you think is normal—all the world, all you ever need."

"But they're so different from us."

"As we were different from our parents' generation. They were bound to be. And I guess the next children, the colonists on Earth II, will be different again."

"If we ever get there."

"Sorry?"

"Oh, nothing. Hey, here's Mike."

Mike Wetherbee came clambering down from the upper decks. He looked harassed, as he always did; his hair graying, he looked to be aging quickly. He carried an emergency medical pack at his waist, and a small camera. He was here to film Zane's participation in the dream circle. You never saw a camera nowadays save for such specific purposes.

As Wetherbee took his place beside Holle and Grace, the dreamers began to listen to Theo Morell, who spoke first. "I was trapped in this tunnel. Like being stuck behind an equipment rack, you know? I was all alone, everybody else was dead—no, they never existed in the first place. It was just me, I was shut in but I couldn't breathe. Then somebody started banging on the outside of the hull, and I started shouting and I screamed, but my voice just echoed. Then I wriggled forward and I saw a kind of light . . ."

The rest listened, spellbound. The dozen dreamers were a mix of the Ark's various factions, Candidates and gatecrashers and illegals. Holle noticed that one girl was making notes on a handheld, a record of what was said. Zane just rocked back and forth, and he jabbed at his bare arm with a plastic toy, a kid's screwdriver. Holle thought it was ironic that Theo Morell should be the one to start the sharing. He remained king of Head-Space, but since Wilson had restricted access to the booths by the simple means of imposing a hefty charge on their use, the cheaper dream circles were flourishing.

Mike Wetherbee murmured, "Classic Ark dream. Confinement, claustrophobia, a fear of what's outside, but a longing for release."

Grace whispered, "Sounded to me like a memory of his birth. Like he was struggling to pass through a giant vagina."

Wetherbee grinned. "Oh, yeah, that too. The dreams are always about sex."

"No kids today," Holle murmured. Generally a few children took part in sessions like this. The transcripts showed how the kids recounted the visions that bubbled up inside their heads of Earth, fantasies of the planet for which they were evolved but which they could never see. Holle found them fascinating, but terrifically sad.

"No," Wetherbee said, "but the kids like Zane. You'd think they'd fear him. They think he's funny, or something, the different people that speak out of his mouth. He's a novelty, in an environment that lacks novelties."

Grace murmured, "What are his dreams like?"

"Depends which alter is speaking." Wetherbee pointed. "I think that's Zane 1, the youngest. See he's playing at self-harm with that plastic screwdriver? I gave him that to deflect him from doing it for real. At least he can't break the flesh. Zane I has anxiety dreams, very sexual. Zane 3's are the most disturbing, elaborate fantasies about rivers and serpents and hunters, in which nothing is real but just melts away when you look at it."

Grace shook her head. "Do you think you have all the alters mapped out now?"

Wetherbee looked pained. "After three years I hope so. I continue to believe he has dissociative identity disorder—more than one personality inside the one head. These alters are spun off at times of extreme stress or pain.

"*This* one, Zane 1, was created when Zane was about seventeen, and was subject to sexual abuse by Harry Smith. Zane couldn't stand the distress this caused him, the shame, the lying, the bullying response from his father. So he spun off Zane 1, who serves as a receptacle for all the pain. It's a coping mechanism, you see.

"The next big crisis for Zane came when he was around twenty-four, as we prepared to go to warp at Jupiter. That crisis caused *two* splits, I believe. He was already guilty at being on the Ark because he was too 'dirty' to be able to contribute his genes to the pool. Zane 2 was a receptacle for all that shame and remorse. And now he felt he wasn't coping with his duties at that key time—which, if you think about it, was the crux of his whole life. So he created another entity, called Jerry—an older man, calmer, away from all the adolescent crises. Jerry comes out, often at night when Zane sleeps, to handle Zane's work assignments. Zane just sort of wakes up to find everything done and sorted out, and he has no memory of doing it, no physical trace of the events save maybe lost sleep.

Jerry is the sanest of the alters, if you can use that word. Pain in the ass to deal with, actually. There may have been other splits, other alters created at earlier points of crisis—the launch from Earth, for instance. I'm not sure.

"All these alters took away an awful lot of Zane's functioning. The alter that's left is the one I call Zane 3. He's an empty shell. He has no real memory of his life before Jupiter. It's as if he just woke up after we went to warp, fully formed. And he doesn't have any knowledge of the work he does aboard the ship; that's all Jerry, you see. In some ways Zane 3 is the craziest. I think he genuinely doesn't believe he's on a ship at all."

Grace asked, "So in all this, where is Zane?"

Wetherbee shrugged. "They're all parts of him. I think Zane 3 serves as a kind of central point, but he's not the leader."

"It sounds fantastic."

"I know. A lot of commentators believed DID was always iatrogenic—that is, a product of the diagnosis itself, a kind of fantasy concocted between doctor and patient, maybe unconsciously. I knew doctors who would have loved to have a DID case on their hands. You could write a book about it."

"But not you," Holle said.

"Hell, no. I'm not smart enough to have cooked this up, believe me."

Grace asked, "So what's the prognosis? What can you do about it?"

"There are ways to reintegrate the various personalities into a whole. But we're talking more years of therapy. I think I'm going to hold off until after '51, when we're due to reach Earth II. That will be the last time we will need Zane the warp engineer. He is in fact functioning, in his strange, broken way. I don't think I can risk endangering that. When I get my clinic up and running on Earth II—then maybe I'll have time to fix Zane."

Holle asked, "Of his alters, which one do you like the least?"

"Good question. That one," Wetherbee said, pointing to Zane. "The alters are stuck at the age they were created. Zane 1 will be seventeen years old, forever. And he relives the abuse, the pain he absorbed, over and over. That's his function, to take those memories away from Zane. But it means he's trapped in an eternal present, like a recording stuck on replay. Zane 1 is in hell."

They fell silent, and watched Zane sitting with the dreamers as he jabbed the toy screwdriver into his arm over and over. These were the crew who would have to face the dramatic, unexpected challenges of Earth II, Holle thought. How could they possibly cope?

70

December 2051

Everybody crowded into Halivah for Venus's crew report on Earth II, all save for a watch crew left over in Seba, and Holle knew that they too would be glued to the comms system. For her presentation Venus set up a crystal ball, a three-dimensional display unit that hadn't been unpacked since they left Earth, that hummed and glistened as its panels rotated, too fast for the eye to follow. Holle knew this was a gift to the Ark from Thandie Jones, and was the very same piece of equipment Thandie had once used to brief the LaRei people in Denver, with Holle and Kelly running around on the floor, and she'd used it even before then in New York for the IPCC.

Holle herself found a place on a catwalk beside Kelly Kenzie. Venus had taken out the mesh panels over three decks to open up a kind of auditorium in the heart of the hull, so everybody could see and hear, and more than eighty people, including kids and babies, were jammed in, clinging to catwalks and ladders and waiting for the show. A rumble of excited conversation echoed, and there was a rare sense of crowd. Holle picked out familiar faces all around the chamber, the people with whom she had shared so much, in some cases since they were all children together in Denver. There was Mike Wetherbee standing by Zane Glemp, his most intractable yet his most valuable patient, and Theo Morell, the half-corrupt king of the HeadSpace booths, and the Shaughnessy brothers, solid hard workers both, Jack with a cap pulled down over his burn-scarred face, and Thomas Windrup and Elle Strekalov, still together despite all their tribulations, and Masayo Saito, the army lieutenant who, thrust into an impossible and unexpected position, had proven to be a bridge-builder of wisdom and courage, and poor Cora Robles who had never got over the loss of her little girl, a shadow of her old brilliant self—yet who was now pregnant again. Helen Gray, nine years old now, stood by her mother on a catwalk on the opposite side of the hull. She was playing pat-a-cake with six-year-old Steel Antoniadi. When she glimpsed Holle, Helen waved her hand. She was growing into a pretty kid with her mother's very English coloring. It struck Holle that Helen had *never* seen as many people together as this in one space, not in her whole life. But Helen's eyes were drawn, like the other children's, to Venus's glittering toy.

Holle felt a mood of exhilaration, of belonging. For all their triumphs and their tragedies, their weaknesses and their strengths, they had got here, across ten years since Gunnison and more than twenty light-years. They had reached 82 Eridani. And they had all seen the prize, Earth II, with their naked eyes. Venus had allowed the crew into her precious cupola, a few at a time, to gaze down on the huge world turning a few hundred kilometers beneath the orbiting Ark, with its creased oceans, scattered cloud, rusty landmasses. There was a sense of unity, at last; together they had achieved a mighty triumph.

But Earth II wasn't what they had hoped for. And now, today, six months after the Ark's arrival at 82 Eridani, they had grave decisions to make. Holle wondered how much of that wonderful unity would survive the day.

Wilson Argent came strutting across the deck, and the conversations hushed. Wilson looked around at the crew, on the decks and catwalks and clinging to the ladders. He was a big man, imposing and impressive. Three years after his takeover from Kelly his power over the crew was absolute, and he was regarded with a mixture of admiration, awe and fear. Today he had opened up for discussion the biggest decision they had had to make since leaving Earth, a decision about the whole future of the mission, the Ark; even he couldn't railroad this. But as a result this decision day was a moment of comparative vulnerability for Wilson.

On impulse Holle glanced at Kelly. Her expression was hard, set. Holle recognized Kelly's "ambitious" face, the face she had worn when she'd announced she was leaving her kid behind to keep her place on the Ark. Since he had ousted her, Wilson had always let Kelly alone, but at best they had been like two warring armies under an armed truce. Well, today Kelly looked like she was planning something, and Holle felt a stab of deep unease.

"You all know why we're here." Wilson's voice, subtly amplified, boomed through the whole hull. "We achieved mankind's first star flight, we reached Earth II, and we've all had one hell of a party. But the job's not done yet—not until we're down on the new ground, turning the turf and planting our first crops. Now Venus is going to summarize what we've learned so far about the planet. And then we'll decide, as a group, what we're going to do about it." That was Wilson, blunt and to the point. He nodded to Venus and backed off to stand with the gang of illegals and gatecrashers who had gravitated to his court.

Venus stepped forward, looking around at the expectant faces. She tapped her handheld. The crystal ball flared with light, and an image of Earth II coalesced.

It was a sphere more than a meter across, turning slowly around a horizontal axis. It was bright and detailed, and its glow, blue and gray, brown and white, lit up the faces of the watching people. Venus stayed silent, giving them a few seconds to take it in. The last murmurs hushed.

Holle remembered the first blurred images of the new planet, images taken from light-years out and constructed with extraordinary care by Venus's planet-finder technologies. This new mapping was as detailed as any image of Earth as seen from space she had ever seen. And the planet wasn't simply some abstract entity any more; now, after their months in orbit, it was a world already replete with human names. They had tentatively labeled the rotation pole that was currently pointing at the sun as "north"; the world turned counterclockwise as seen by an observer above that pole. Subject to months of unbroken heat from 82 Eridani the pole was blanketed in cloud, with storms visibly spinning off a massive central swirl.

At lower latitudes Holle made out landmasses that were already familiar to everybody aboard. A big strip of land stretching north to south across the equator was "the Belt," a kind of elderly Norway with deep-cut fjords incising thousands of kilometers of coastline. The northern half of the Belt was currently ice-free, but its southern half, stretching into the realm of shadow, was icebound, and snow patches reached as far north as the equator. Sprawling across a good portion of the eastern hemisphere was the roughly circular continent they called "the Frisbee," a mass of rust red broken by the intense blue of lakes and lined by eroded mountains. Its center was dominated by a huge structure, a mountain with a base hundreds of kilometers across, and a fractured caldera at the top. The mount was so like Olympus Mons on Mars that giving it the same name had been unavoidable, and it so dominated the overall profile of the continent, giving it an immense but shallow bulge, that the nickname "Frisbee" was a good fit. Then, to the west of the Belt, an archipelago sprawled, a widespread group of islands, some as large as Britain or New Zealand, that they called "the Scatter." There was one more continent at the south pole, currently plunged in darkness and buried under hundreds of meters of winter snow, called "the Cap." The world ocean itself had no name yet; the seas could be named when they were ready to go sailing on them, Holle thought.

The most exciting features were the patches of purple at the coasts of the continents and the shores of the lakes: *life,* native life on Earth II, plants of some kind, busily using 82 Eridani's light to turn carbon dioxide into oxygen with their own unique photosynthetic chemistry.

Venus began without preamble.

"You all have access to the full reports in the ship's archive. Today I'm just going to summarize the key findings.

"We've been here in this system for six months. We've surveyed atmosphere, land and oceans spectroscopically at all wavelengths, and have used radar to probe the subsurface and to map the seabeds, and have also dropped a series of penetrating probes for direct ground-truth sampling." These were landers like slim missiles, hardened to withstand violent impacts and to bury themselves a few meters beneath the surface, with ground cameras that gave a close-up view of the final stages of the descent, and equipped with seismometers, chemical sensors, thermal sensors, magnetometers.

"Here's the good news," Venus said. "Obviously we have a world of about the right mass and the right volatile inventory, orbiting in a stable circular orbit at about the right distance from its sun to allow stable water oceans on the surface. 'Right' meaning it's Earthlike.

"And on a basic level it's habitable. If you landed in one of the shuttles and stepped outside, you'd experience a gravity of about eighty percent of a G; Earth II is less massive than Earth, and smaller in radius. Right now the northern summer is somewhere near its midpoint. If you were to stand at the pole you'd see the sun circle close to the zenith, right above your head. At the equator the sun is circling around the horizon, maybe dipping below for a few hours a day, depending on exactly where you are. It's cold, there's snow on the ground, but it's no worse than a winter day in one of Earth's temperate zones.

"Where the sun is up you could walk around with no more protection than a decent coat, some strong boots, a face mask. You could expose your skin, at least from the point of view of the sun's radiation; there's a healthy ozone layer. You would need some protection from cosmic radiation; the planet's magnetic field is a lot weaker than Earth's. You could breathe the air, we believe. It's basically a nitrogen-oxygen mix of about the same proportions as Earth's atmosphere. In the early days you'll be wearing a face mask, in case of trace toxins from geological or maybe biological sources.

"We know there's life down there. Life at the microbial level and, it seems, at some kind of simple multiple-cell level, something like stromatolites maybe. That's what puts the oxygen in the air. It's unlikely it will harm us, unlikely our alien biochemistries will interact significantly, but we'll have to check it out. We believe that once we establish some terrestrial soil down there, Earthlike flora will take a hold: our crops will grow, our animals, when we incubate them, will be able to feed. Our children will be able to run and play." She got a scattering of applause for that: But there was no joy in her face.

"This much we were able to guess from observations from Earth and Jupiter," she said. "But all we could see from the solar system was a blurry dot with some evidence of mass, orbit, atmospheric composition. That's all. On that basis it looked promising. But as it's turned out, Earth II is not that close a sister to Earth I.

"This is a much less active world than Earth, geologically. You can see that from the eroded chains of mountains, the flat landscapes. The penetrators' seismometers have detected few earthquakes. And we see no significant evidence of continental drift, no active plate-forming mid-ocean ridges, no subduction zones at plate boundaries—no colliding plates to trigger volcanism and to throw up mountain chains, as on Earth.

"Tectonic shift has seized up, here. It's not absent, but is clearly operating at a much reduced rate than on Earth. And the result is the geology we see. The Frisbee is not unlike Australia, ancient and stable, so old its mountains are worn down, the rocks shattered to dust and rusted red. The big volcano at the heart of the Frisbee is a shield volcano, like Hawaii on Earth, and just like Olympus Mons on Mars—we named it well. It's been created by a magma plume, an upwelling of hot material from the planet's mantle, like a fountain. Olympus has been stuck over that plume for a long time—hundreds of millions of years, maybe. Over similar periods on Earth, the continents slide all the way from equator to pole.

"Is that important? We think so, for the sake of the long-term habitability of the planet. On Earth, plate tectonics play a key part in the vast geological and biological cycling that maintains Gaia. This world, with tectonic processes much reduced, can't sustain such a significant cargo of life.

"Why has Earth II turned out to be so much less active than Earth? First, Earth II is that much smaller than Earth. Like Mars, it must have shed a greater proportion of its interior heat of formation, and a greater proportion of its inventory of radioactive materials will have decayed away. So the big internal heat engine that drives plate tectonics has run down. And second, we believe Earth II is actually an older world than Earth, by a billion years or more; whatever triggered planet-forming in this system happened much earlier than back home."

Wilson put in, "So a billion years ago this world might have looked that much more like Earth."

"Yes. With a much richer biosphere. I think we can expect to find traces of past complexity, lost as the planet has run down. That may be why we see no traces of extant intelligence."

Kelly seized on that word. "'Extant'? Does that imply you found traces of nonextant cultures?"

Holle felt unreasonably excited.

For answer, Venus tapped a handheld.

The turning world winked out of existence, to be replaced by an image of one of the larger islands of the Scatter, as if seen from a low-flying aircraft. Once it may have been mountainous; now its mountains were worn to stubs. "We call this Little Jamaica." Venus pointed to features on a plain close to the sea. "Can you see?" There were faint circles, hints of straight-line features. "We don't know what this is. You need to remember that this island is covered by the pack ice every local winter; any traces of surface structures, of buildings and cities, would long ago have been destroyed. It could be the trace of a quarry, we think. That might survive as long as a billion years. Maybe it's something else, like a city. There are other indicators of intelligence. We've found no evidence of deep-buried carbon deposits. If there was any oil or coal on this world, or the local equivalent, it's long gone. No evidence of particularly rich seams of mineral ores near the surface. A paucity of asteroids in this system, too."

Wilson folded his arms. "I don't get it. These are indicators of what?"

"That somebody used up the easily available resources—the oil, the easily mined ores, even off-world resources in the asteroids. And then they died out, or went away. We might find direct evidence one way or the other when we start doing some real archaeology down on the surface." She shrugged. "There's a lot of sand to sift."

"My God," Holle whispered.

"I know," Kelly said. "It's not good for us. But isn't it *wonderful?*" And, just for a moment, it was as if they were Candidates again, marveling together over some wondrous bit of scholarship. But they weren't here for scholarship today.

Somebody called, "And what about the obliquity? I thought that was the big problem."

Venus allowed herself a rueful smile. "I was saving the best until last."

She brought up a fresh display. This showed Earth II and its sun, 82 Eridani. The diagram wasn't to scale, planet and star looking like two lightbulbs, and the planet's orbit was a glowing yellow circle around the sun. The planet's rotation axis showed as a glowing splinter pushed through its bulk, a splinter that pointed almost directly at the sun.

Venus said, "As the planet goes around the sun, the axis keeps pointing the same way—just as for Earth. You can see the consequences." She tapped a key and the planet zipped around its star, keeping its axis pointing in the same direction in space. Earth II's year was about the same as Earth's, so after six months the north pole would be plunged into shadow, while its south pole was in the light. "Earth's obliquity, the tilt of its axis, is about twenty-three degrees, compared to Earth II's ninety. Life on Earth evolved to cope with moderate seasonality. Here you have the most severe seasonality you can imagine.

"Every part of the planet except an equatorial strip will suffer months of perpetual darkness, months of perpetual light. Away from the equator you'll suffer extreme heat, aridity, followed by months of Arctic cold—we estimate the surface temperature will drop to a hundred degrees below across much of the space-facing hemisphere, and there'll be one hell of a blanket of snow and ice. Even the equator would be a challenge to inhabit, for even at the height of summer in either hemisphere the sun would be low, the heat budget minimal, the climate wintry."

Venus restored the image of the planet, the tilted-over world with its friendly looking continents. Now she made the image accelerate through a simulation of its seasonal cycles. Ice crusted the continents, only to clear and leave them desiccated, brick red. "We can't survive this," she said. "Oh, maybe we could adapt to one extreme or another. But not to these swings, year on year, from baking aridity to an Antarctic chill. Our plants, our animals, couldn't cope with it either. The only possible habitation would be on the equator, but there's very little equatorial land, a few islands and a slice of the Belt . . . We lucked out. We couldn't see the rotation axis from Earth. We couldn't have predicted these features."

She fell silent. Her audience, in silence save for the wriggles of children, gloomily watched as her toy planet suffered its cycling seasons.

Theo Morell surprised Holle by calling down, "You say this wasn't visible from the Earth. OK. But you must have been aware of some of these problems, particularly the axis thing, from further out. You've spent the last ten years looking out of that cupola of yours."

"Yes, I—"

"When did you know Earth II was going to be a bust?"

Venus glanced at Wilson, who shrugged and looked away. "Around two years ago. The data started hardening then—we'd had some suspicions. Two years ago I was sure enough to take it to Wilson, for instance."

Mentioning Wilson was a way to bring herself into his protection, Holle realized. But the mood in the chamber was switching, through shock and disappointment to a kind of anger. Theo shouted, "And you kept them a secret, these 'suspicions' of yours?"

Wilson stepped in. "That was all we had. Suspicions. We needed to get here to confirm it all. And besides, we couldn't exactly change course. You know that you can't control a warp bubble from the inside. Now is

the right time to deal with this, and here we are doing just that, everything out in the open." He turned to Venus. "You still have the floor.
What do you recommend?"

She looked up, her face set. "That we can't live here, on Earth II. The
journey isn't over. We have to go on. Sorry, but that's it."

There was a moment of shocked silence. Then people started shouting, pointing at Venus as she stood defiantly by her model, surely wishing
she was back in the sanctuary of her cupola.

We have to go on, Venus had said. But, Holle wondered, thrilled and
awed, go on to where?

71

Wilson stepped to the center of the stage and bellowed, "Shut up! I'm speaker, remember, so stop talking." That raised an ironic laugh, and broke the mood a bit. Wilson said, "One at a time. Elle." He pointed to Elle Strekalov, standing by on a catwalk. "You worked with Venus on all this stuff. What have you got to say?"

"That I don't agree," Elle called down. Holle immediately wondered if Wilson had called her first knowing she would dissent from Venus. "Maybe we can make a go of it here. Venus, you said yourself that there's at least some equatorial land we could colonize. Otherwise we could consider strings of rafts—"

Paul Shaughnessy hooted. "Rafts? If we wanted to live on rafts, we could have stayed on fucking Earth."

"You illegals should have," somebody called back, and there was a rumble of anger, the usual tensions barely suppressed.

"One at a time," Wilson growled. "Go on, Elle."

"OK, not rafts. We need to get down there and understand how the native life survives—because survive it does, we can see that. For instance, trees. Because the ice melts off annually the depth of any freezing would be shallow, maybe two or three meters. You could imagine a tree with long roots tapping into water and nutrients deep down beneath the frozen surface. Needle leaves like a conifer that it never sheds. Some kind of transpiration adaptation for the dry months. We could gen-eng trees from

Earth to live that way," Elle insisted. "As for animals, their crucial feature is mobility. We could develop migratory herds from our stock. The Belt especially is a north-south corridor which the herds could use to escape the aridity and the freezing, going wherever the climate was temperate in a given month."

Masayo called, "And what about the people? Will we have to migrate too?"

"No," Elle said defiantly. "We could seek shelters where we could over winter and over summer, ride out the extremes. Caves, maybe."

"Caves?" Paul Shaughnessy called. "Rafts, now caves?"

Elle pressed on, "Look, this planet is *not* uninhabitable. There are places where the growing season is longer than it was on Earth—though you have to wait that much longer for the next season to come around. With time, with a program of genetic modification, of continent-wide seeding, of building or adapting suitable shelters, and maybe ultimately a degree of terraforming—"

Venus said, "We won't have the resources to achieve all that, even assuming it's possible. We'll be fighting for survival from the day we land."

Wilson said, "Anybody else?"

Holle waved her own hand. "Venus—you said we couldn't stay here, we had to go on. So where do we go?"

Venus smiled. "Thank you, Holle. Look—during the interstellar cruise we extended the deep sky survey begun on Earth, searching for habitable planets as far as we can see. We thought it was one of the greatest legacies we could leave for the next generation. And that's how we came up with this—an alternative destination." Flamboyantly, she snapped her fingers.

The big image of Earth II dissolved, to reveal a glum red star, and a planet orbiting it, glistening with oceans, gray-black in the crimson light. The bloody glow of the star filled the improvised auditorium.

"Earth III," Venus announced. "Or at least I think it could be. The best attainable prospect in our survey. And far more habitable than Earth II. I've lodged relevant data in the archive."

"Crap," Wilson said. "That's a Krypton! Gordo always swore he wouldn't send us to a Krypton. You're just digging up those old arguments from ten years ago."

Venus said doggedly, "Yes, that's true. Yes, it's not a clone of Earth. Yes, we had these arguments back in Gunnison. But—look! Most of the stars in the Galaxy aren't like Sol—two-thirds of them are M-class, like this baby. If we can learn to live here, we can live anywhere."

"Bullshit!" somebody cried, and the mass arguments broke out again, the angry shouts, the finger-pointing.

Holle herself was swept along by Venus's rhetoric. But of course there was one crucial fact that Venus hadn't yet offered.

Grace Gray put her hand up. "Venus—what star is this?"

"It's in the constellation of Lepus, the hare, as seen from Earth. Near Orion. Not naked-eye visible; it doesn't have a name, only a catalog number."

"And how far away is it?"

Venus took a breath. "It's further out, further from Earth. Another ninety light-years."

And at three times light speed that translated to another thirty years' journeying.

More outrage. "Thirty more years in this stinking tank?"

Abruptly Kelly stepped forward, to the edge of the catwalk she shared with Holle. The way she moved made Holle's heart sink. This was her moment, and she was seizing it.

Wilson looked reluctant, but he nodded to give Kelly the floor.

"Let's cut through this," she said. "This business of Earth III is a distraction, a chimera. The solution's obvious. If it takes more effort for us to survive here than to have stayed on Earth and live on rafts, we should never have come, it wasn't worthwhile."

Wilson prompted, "And so—"

"And so we should go home." She glared around, as if daring anybody here to shout her down. "We don't travel on and on. *We go home,* to Earth."

Venus said, "That's impossible. Go home to what? Next year Everest drowns."

"We'll cope with whatever we find. The Ark was designed to sustain us for fifteen years, as a margin; I'm sure we can extend that to cover the seven years of superluminal travel it would take to get us back. Zane, we have enough antimatter stock to re-create the warp bubble, don't we? We can go home. We must! We tried our hardest, we came all this way, it didn't work. This is no place for us, for our children. Let's take them home, and see what we can build on Earth."

A riot of angry arguments broke out again. Holle, utterly shocked, tried to look into Kelly's soul, through that hard, ambitious face.

Wilson faced Kelly, his expression thunderous. "That didn't come out of the blue, did it? How long have you been planning this little stroke?"

She smiled back at him, her eyes dead. "And how long did you spend planning to topple me, while we were still sharing a bed? Don't judge me by your standards, Wilson." She turned and walked away from him, and was instantly surrounded by a chattering gaggle of supporters.

Wilson, arms folded, intense frustration creasing his face, had no choice but to let the furious debate continue, the shouts echoing from the stripped-bare hull walls.

72

E ventually Wilson broke up the session. The Ark wouldn't run itself while they argued, and there were children to be fed.

But, thinking on his feet, Wilson carved up the crew into study groups, to look in more detail at the various options. How survivable would Earth II actually be? Could they really make a home on Venus's Earth III, and would the ship and its crew last out the even longer journey to get there? Or if the ship survived seven years back to Earth, what were they to do on arrival at an ocean world? He said he would reconvene the forum at first watch in the morning, and maybe they could come to a more considered decision about the future.

Holle made sure that her own areas of responsibility were covered, that nothing was going to break down or burst into flames during the night watch. Then, grabbing some food, she moved from group to group where they huddled in corners of Halivah, and talked and talked, some arguing over handhelds or drawing down data from the ship's archive. Some went back to Seba, but most stayed here in Halivah. As the hours wore on, as the arc lights were reduced to their nighttime dim glow, the talking continued, a murmuring that filled the hull.

People were responding emotionally, Holle perceived, not to the science, the facts. Some just longed to go home. Masayo Saito, missing his child, was in that group, and Holle suspected the Shaughnessys and others of the illegals and gatecrashers, who had never expected to join the crew of an interstellar spaceship in the first place, felt the same way. It was possible that was in Kelly's heart too, some kind of wish to put things right with the child she'd left behind. But Holle was pretty sure that simple revenge over Wilson was a motivation too.

Others, unable to stand the idea of more years of their lives lost inside these tin cans, wanted only to get out—to finish the journey, to set down here, however hard a shore Earth II might prove to be. People with kids tended to feel that way, not wishing to doom their children to a lifetime in a tank.

Then there were those who were entranced by Venus's visionary rhetoric. Why not go on and grab the whole Galaxy, rather than succumb to the exhausting, perhaps lethal, trap of Earth II? That was the way Holle's own heart was drawn. But she quailed at the thought of thirty more years in these metal hulls. She was thirty-two years old. She tried to grasp the meaning of herself still shipbound at sixty, but could not.

And then there was the brute politics of the Ark, as they had been festering for a decade already, Kelly and Wilson drawing people apart like iron filings to opposing magnetic poles.

Holle didn't sleep that night, and nor did many others. Yet the hours seemed brief, the arguments still unresolved, before Wilson drew them together again in the improvised auditorium on Deck Eight.

Thandie's crystal ball was inert this morning, a lifeless piece of engineering. In the bright lights of the arc lamps people looked tired, worn out, subdued.

Wilson glared around, hands on hips. Holle saw that he had handled this situation about as well as he could have. He had given people time to cool down, and now, in the morning, the universe seemed a colder and more rational place. Wilson's leadership had its flaws, but he did display a brute understanding of human nature.

"I don't want to waste time on this," he began. "Let's try to make a decision, and get behind it and start implementing it. Everybody agree with that? OK. We have three options on the table, as far as I see. One. Stay here, colonize Earth II. Two. Take the Ark back to Earth. Three. Go on to Venus's Earth III, out in Lepus. Do I have that right? So let's choose. We'll start with a show of hands, and I hope to Christ we get an easy majority for one option or the other." He checked a monitor. "Can you guys over in Seba see me? OK then. Show me your hands for Earth II . . . And Earth . . . And Earth III. Shit."

There was a ripple of amusement among the crew, black humor. It was a split with significant support for all three options.

"Plan B," Wilson called now. "Let's separate into groups. Then we'll get an accurate count and see where we go from there. If you want Earth II, come down and gather over here. Earth, to my left. Earth III, to my right . . ."

Alarm bells rang in Holle's head. She had the immediate fear that if Wilson made the division of their opinions into a physical split, the group might never be put back together. But it was too late. She could do nothing but move to represent her own choice.

She stood with those, led by Venus, who wanted to go on, to Earth III. Wilson himself walked this way. Grace Gray joined them, with Helen, and Theo Morell. So did Zane, which wasn't a surprise to Holle, and Doc Wetherbee, which was.

Holle said, "So you're staying with your warp drive, Zane?"

"Not just that." There was a gleam in his eye, a kind of manic calculation. Holle thought this was Zane 3, the amnesiac shell left behind when his other alters had split off.

"What, then?"

"There's nothing outside the ship. Nothing! If these others step out they will cease to exist. I have no choice but to stay aboard."

Wetherbee gave Holle a grim smile. "How could I leave my star patient behind?"

Venus faced Wilson. "Didn't think you'd join us, Wilson, after what you had to say about 'Kryptons.'"

Wilson grinned. "Base selfish calculation. Look around. In here, in this ship, I'm a big man. Down on a planet I'll be nothing. I don't want to be a farmer. And if I go back to Earth I'll probably be prosecuted. No, I'll stick to what I've got."

Holle glanced around to see how the other groups were forming. The Earth faction was unsurprisingly led by Kelly Kenzie, with Masayo Saito at her side, and a number of the other illegals, including the Shaughnessys. The would-be colonists of Earth II included Elle and her partner Thomas Windrup, and Cora Robles, an expectant mother. Counting quickly she guessed the numbers were forty-plus adults with their children in Venus's Earth III group, the largest, around nineteen in Kelly's Earth group, and maybe fifteen in the Earth II camp.

When the sorting-out was done, Wilson stepped forward. "Now what? It seems to me the obvious strategy is to eliminate the third-place choice. Then, depending on the numbers—"

"Like hell," Kelly Kenzie snapped. She stepped forward and faced up to Wilson. "I can see where that would lead. There's no way I'm submitting to you and your manipulation. Not anymore, not over this."

"Oh, yeah? So, on your say-so, we just bin our process? You're full of shit, Kelly. This has nothing to do with Earth. This is all because of me, isn't it? You and me. Gordo Alonzo would call this a mutiny."

"Gordo isn't here. You call it what you fucking like."

They were in each other's faces. Holle saw Wilson's hard-faced young men taking their positions around the chamber. Suddenly the crisis was here.

And Zane walked into the center of the deck. His stride was bold, and he was actually grinning.

"Strewth," Doc Wetherbee murmured to Holle. "I hope this is Jerry."

Wilson glared at Zane. "You got something to say, nut job?"

Zane glanced around, gradually gathering the group's attention to himself. "I always knew this would be the outcome. This indecision.

We're like a bunch of kids. We'll never agree on anything between us. And so while you were all spending the night discussing how to grow trees on Earth II, I worked out the technical aspects of the most obvious option."

"Which is?"

"We split up," Zane said brightly.

"That's insane," Wilson said immediately.

Zane boldly jabbed a finger at his chest. "No. *You* just don't want to see your kingdom split into three. Technically, we can do it. We have massive redundancy. We can separate the Arks, one for Earth, one for the stars. We can use our spares to build a separate warp generator! And we have four space-to-surface shuttle gliders. We can land the colonists of Earth II in one of those, leaving one for the return to Earth, and two for use at Earth III. It will take time and effort, but we can do this . . ."

There were immediate objections, particularly about the compromise to the basic redundancy design strategy this would entail—no more spare parts, if they were used to build another ship. And the social engineers' plans for genetic diversity would be trashed; Holle had no idea whether even forty would be enough for a viable colony without lethal inbreeding. Every instinct in her told her this was wrong, that three smaller groups would be much more vulnerable than one.

But she saw, too, that Zane's proposal had been greeted with immediate approval. If they split up, Kelly would be able to get away from Wilson. Thomas Windrup would be free of Jack Shaughnessy and his scars. Their future, and maybe the future of all mankind, was going to be determined by the fact that after a decade on the Ark they were all sick of each other.

Mike Wetherbee growled, "You realize what's happened. The craziest man on the ship just determined our whole damn future. And he did it by turning us all into a kind of mirror of his own fractured self. Jeez! He should be giving us therapy, not the other way around."

73

November 2052

It took nearly a year to implement the Split.

They broke up the warp generator, under Zane Glemp's uneven leadership, and used spares to rebuild it as two copies of itself. Kelly and Wilson thrashed out which subgroup would take which hull; it was decided that it was fairer for Kelly's crew, with their shorter journey back to Earth, to take Seba, the fire-damaged hulk, while Wilson took Halivah. That decision seemed logical, but Holle wondered to what extent personal politics had again played their part. And they equipped a single shuttle glider to take Elle's crew down to Earth II, with a share of tools and raw materials and seed stock from the store bequeathed to the project long ago by Nathan Lammockson.

They began to say their goodbyes, first to the colonists of Earth II. Wilson arranged a kind of ceremony, in which each of the colonists was given a small stainless-steel globe of their new planet, manufactured in the Ark's machine shop. Holle found it almost impossible to say good-bye to the Candidates, like Cora and Thomas and Elle, with whom she'd grown up, and shared a common mission all her life, and with whom she'd expected to grow old. Now she'd never see them again.

The two hulls were still linked by the tether, still wheeling around their common center of gravity over the steel ocean of Earth II, when the colony shuttle was released. Everybody left aboard the Ark followed the little craft's progress as it cut into the new world's tall, thin atmosphere, and created a shining contrail of incandescent plasma that dipped down toward its landing place on the Belt.

Then came the final sorting-out between the twin hulls, Seba and Halivah, the last transfer of materials, the last handshakes. Holle hated to let go of the Shaughnessys, who she had worked closely with since the launch at Gunnison. But they wanted to go home.

And then, for the second time since Jupiter, the tether was cut by its explosive guillotine, and the hulls drifted apart.

Seba was to be the first of the hulls to create its warp bubble. From Halivah, Holle watched curiously from the cupola, beside Venus. It happened as Seba was crossing the face of Earth II, from Holle's point of view. A whole section of the planet, a rough disc, seemed to crumple as if crushed by an invisible fist, the colors of land and sea running like wet paint. But then it rebounded, and Seba was gone.

It was only then that Wilson discovered that Kelly Kenzie had kidnapped Mike Wetherbee, the only doctor, and taken him away to Earth. Wilson's rage endured for days.

Five

2059

74

I t was Boris Caistor, thirteen-year-old Boris with his sharp young eyes, who first noticed the new light in the sky, a spark sailing through the deeper dark between the banks of cloud.

"Thea saw it too," he told Thandie Jones. "She says she can see a shape. Sort of long and thin, a splinter."

Thandie, sitting on a surging raft in the middle of the ocean, looking up at a cloud-choked sky, frowned. "Surely two splinters, end to end, connected by a thread . . ."

"Nope. Just one. Of course she might be lying. Thea lies all the time, or makes stuff up anyhow. Once she said she saw this whale which—"

"Never mind!"

Thandie was pretty sure Boris didn't understand what he had seen, not really, nor did he grasp its possible significance. And, worse, she was also sure he didn't give a damn about it. Thandie had followed Lily Brooke's lead in trying to maintain some kind of education program for the kids on the raft. But astronomy was about all you could manage, the changing starry sky the only show in town, all that would actually hook these kids' interest in something other than food and swimming games and each other's pretty bodies. Thandie suspected Boris's brain was dissolving like those of the rest of his generation.

But he was a loyal kid, and he was kind to his honorary aunt Thandie, just as when she'd first met him in a cluster of rafts over the drowning relic of Everest and she'd seen him indulge the whims of another elderly lady, his great-great-aunt Lily Brooke. Boris was also bright and observant, and even though the seeing was always so phenomenally bad on this new, stormy ocean world he had been able to recognize the new light in the sky as something special, and maybe it was what Thandie had told him she had been expecting to see, for a year already.

If Boris had seen it so had others. So Thandie took one of her precious handhelds from within its brine-proof layers of plastic sheeting and let the solar cells power up the internal battery. She posted Boris's sighting up to the hearth, and she sent out queries for other observations, especially of the thing's first appearance in Earth orbit.

But she needed to see it for herself, and maybe get some idea of its orbital elements.

After that, for one night, two, then three, hell, as long as it was going to take, she sat on the raft's deck in her old, much-traveled fold-out bucket chair, with a blanket wrapped over her legs, waiting for the clouds to clear. She kept drifting in and out of sleep. At seventy-three, and after a pretty hard life, she was blessed with reasonable health, but she felt the damp, and spent a lot of time asleep.

The raft was a big one, by the standards of those that had survived twenty years or more on an ocean patroled by the Spot and its offspring storms. It was constructed on pontoons of plastic oil drums and barrels, covered by sheets of slippery tarpaulin lashed down with orange cable. Once, this had been reinforced by a base of gen-enged seaweed, an AxysCorp product, a substrate that would feed on sunlight and the produce of the sea and grow and self-repair. This miracle substance, which Nathan Lammockson had hoped would be the saving of a waterlogged mankind, had turned out to have some fatal genetic flaw. After it had blackened and crumbled away, Thandie's raft community had been able to scavenge replacement materials from the wrecks of other, even less fortunate rafts, all of its garbage recycled from the drowned civilization beneath their keels.

On this base sat a kind of floating shantytown, constructed of sheets of plastic and corrugated iron, proofed against the weather and the salty air of the sea. People lived off fish and other sea creatures, and birds' eggs and processed seaweed, and they gathered their drinking water from the rain in upturned buckets. There was a farm, of sorts, in the middle of the raft, a heap of topsoil detached from the Andean hillside where the raft had first been constructed. Spindly crops grew, lovingly tended by old folk. There were even chickens, in a big plastic cage strapped to a wall. For power, a small bank of windmills stood over the farm, and there were panels of bright green AxysCorp solar energy panels, self-cleaning and self-repairing, almost like living things themselves. It was a constant battle to maintain all this, as the salt water forever poisoned the soil and withered the crops, and corroded electrics and any metal parts.

The younger generations helped out reluctantly. They didn't care about farms. They didn't even care about artificial light. They made fish-oil lamps, but rarely used them. If the skies were clear there was moon-light and starlight, and the luminescence of living things in the sea. And besides, who needed light at night? You didn't need light to sleep or screw. So while the last of the land-born veterans struggled to keep all this junk going, the youngsters, Boris and his generation, went diving off the side of the raft into the endless ocean.

Thandie was tolerated. People left her alone with her obsessions, with her science and her gadgets and her theorizing. The raft was full of kids, and of parents caring for them, feeding, playing, stitching together clothes from faded worn-out relics—though, in the perpetually warm, moist air, a lot of kids were taking to nudity, and even some of the younger adults. The currents of their lives washed around Thandie as if she was a monument in a flood, a statue of some long-forgotten hero . . .

Her handheld, in her lap beneath the protection of the blanket, was bleep-ing softly.

She'd been dozing again. This was the fifth night. The sky was a lid of black cloud. She dug out the little computer and, cursing, felt inside her coat for her ancient reading glasses.

It was a message from Elena Artemova, once Thandie's lover, now separated from her by age, ocean, and a kind of weary indifference. Elena was on another big raft, floating over the drowned corpse of Rio de Janeiro. And she, alert to the new light in the sky, had picked up a chance observation made by a raft over Los Angeles. "So the returning ship first appears in the skies over North America," Elena mailed. "Not by chance, I would be sure . . ."

Thandie eagerly studied the observation, a short, poorly resolved video sequence taken through some raft-borne telescope.

Then she waited until Boris emerged from the water, dripping, thirteen years old, his muscles hard and his belly flat, his mouth smeared with fish oil, his penis limp from enthusiastic underwater sex. She made him sit down beside her, and talked him through the sequence of images.

"See—this shows the arrival of the object you saw, the bright new satellite. This was taken by a telescope that happened to be looking into the right corner of the sky, just at the point where it first appeared. I knew there had to be somebody who'd have caught it. Now wait . . . Watch the clock . . . Pow!" A bright flash appeared, off to the right of center of the star field, that was the ship itself, and a shimmer of light washed away from it, heading left in a dead straight line, fading, as if the ship had sent a bright optical message back the way it had come. "You see?" Thandie asked triumphantly, staring at Boris. "You understand what this is, what this observer saw?"

"No," Boris said bluntly. He looked restless, his focus wandering. The kids had virtually no attention span at all.

Thandie suppressed irritation. "This is a ship that traveled faster than light. It's visible as it travels; its warp bubble emits a cascade of exotic radiation energy, some of which folds down into the visible spectrum. But it outruns its own image. So the ship arrives first and the light has to catch up, all the photons it emitted back along its path arriving at mere light speed. The older images arrive last, and you get this effect as if the ship was receding, not arriving . . ." She played the little sequence over and over. "This is the signature of the arrival of a faster-than-light vessel, Boris, an FTL starship. It's the Ark, Ark One. I knew they'd come back."

He frowned, a comical thirteen-year-old's attempt to feign interest. At least he was being polite. "So what do you want to do about it?"

"Break out the radio beacon. See if the batteries have retained any charge. Let's bring them home."

75

Zane floated into Holle's surgery, a compact, burly thirty-nine-year-old man, confident, definite in his movements in micrograv-ity. He pulled himself down onto the couch and fastened a restraint loosely around his waist. "Ah," he said. "After more than a decade of therapy I feel like this old couch is part of me."

Holle had been waiting for him with Theo Morell, who was setting up the cameras on their wall brackets to film the session. Holle settled in her seat, facing the couch, her handheld on her lap. "I take it I'm talking to Jerry."

"I finished the day's duties before coming here. The warp bubble is functioning within all nominal parameters, incidentally. Driving us onwards to Earth III. I thought I should stay out to, umm, pilot Zane 3 here, so to speak. He knows what you're intending today, it's been on his mind. He's nervous about it, I have to tell you. He fears he will lose something of himself in the process of integration. He's aware he's popu-lar with the crew, the younger ones. That gives him a certain validation." He eyed Holle. "Which is one reason you're pressing ahead with the process, isn't it? I know there are reservations about the influence Zane has on the youngsters."

There was no point lying about that. "Wilson has expressed some concerns."

Zane snorted. "Wilson has his own 'concerns' with the youngsters, as we all know."

"But that's not why we've decided to try to begin the process, Jerry. If we didn't think you were ready we wouldn't attempt it. You're very important to us, obviously. Your needs are paramount."

"All right. The question is, are *you* ready? It's only been seven years since you took over from Mike!"

"Give us a break," Holle said. "I had to learn psychiatry from scratch. It's not easy, Jerry. In fact, I don't think we'd have been able to get this far at all without you." That was true. The alter called Jerry had been like a study partner, as Holle and Theo and Grace had gone through the psychiatry journals, books and expert systems stored in the ship's archive, and Mike Wetherbee's incomplete notes on the case. "And you're happy about undergoing the process yourself?"

"Even a partial integration will strengthen us, all of us, I'm sure of that. And besides, *I* am under no threat today; I don't expect to feel any change."

In the program they had drawn up, a sequence of steps without a fixed timescale, Jerry would be the last of the alters to be integrated.

Theo leaned forward. "Jerry, you know there's another reason we decided to start the process today. Because, if all's gone to schedule, Seba should have arrived back at Earth about now. And if they did it's entirely to your credit. You programmed the warp bubble." Theo mimed throwing a basketball. "You picked them up and threw them home."

Zane grinned. "Well, of course I'm aware of that. If it all worked it's a significant triumph—*if.* But we'll never know, will we?"

Holle touched Theo's arm. "I think that's enough. It's been good to talk to you, Jerry."

"Always a pleasure, Holle."

"Is Zane 3 there? Maybe you could let him come forward."

"Momentarily." Zane closed his eyes and lay back on the couch. For a moment it seemed as if he had fallen asleep. Then he stirred, restless.

His face softened, his lips pushed forward into a kind of pout. He opened his eyes and looked around the surgery. "Oh, crap, I'm still here."

"Hi. Am I speaking to Zane?"

"You know who I am."

"And you know why you're here today."

"You're going to try this ridiculous reintegration procedure, so-called."

"Are you happy about that?"

He laughed, a dull, bitter sound. "What difference does it make if I'm happy or not?"

Theo said, "Seba should be arriving at Earth about now. Doesn't that make you feel proud?"

"They went outside the hull," Zane said. "Kelly and those others. They're either dead, or in a cage somewhere. We'll never see them again." He stared directly at Theo, until Theo looked away.

Holle said to Zane, "Shall I take it you consent to the procedure?"

"Yes, yes. Just get it over." He lay back, his eyes screwed shut.

Holle began the patient process of hypnosis. "Just relax. You can feel the tension, the energy, pouring out of your fingers and your toes, like a liquid. You're sinking deeper into yourself . . ." The trigger words Wetherbee had used to put Zane into a hypnotic trance always worked quickly.

Holle, as she had for seven years, felt the strain of just being in the same room as Zane 3. His passiveness, his depression, his all-consuming self-pity were crushing. It was a small consolation to her that Mike Wetherbee, according to the marginalia of his notes, had often felt the same way.

After the Split and Mike Wetherbee's kidnapping, Wilson had had to find volunteers to take over various aspects of Wetherbee's medical role. Grace Gray, grave, apprehensive but responsible, had taken the lead, and was self-educating into the role of ship's doctor as best she could. And Holle had stepped up to take over Zane's complex case. She had already shadowed some of Wetherbee's sessions, knew roughly what the work involved, and she saw that it needed pursuing if Zane was to be salvaged.

And it had been Wilson who had suggested that Theo support her. Wilson, shuffling what was left of his crew after what he called Kelly's mutiny, thought Theo needed another focus, another key duty aside from his gatekeeping of the HeadSpace booths. Theo had done well, after initial reluctance. He had thrown himself into the studying. His experience with virtual systems was a help, in a way—for it was as if Zane was living in some faulty virtual reality of his own.

As she'd got to know him better, Holle started to see how poor Theo's education had been; rightly or wrongly his father, who he always called "the general," had identified a military career as Theo's only option in a drowning world, and had restricted his wider development. In different times, given the opportunity, his personality and talents might have expressed themselves in quite different ways.

But that was probably true of her too. None of them was ever going to know.

Being with Zane 3 made her realize how tired she was herself. As seven years had worn away since the Split the burden of keeping the hull going weighed ever more heavily. She had very few spares, very little in the way of redundancy or backup, and any fault required ingenuity to fix, even the manufacture of replacement parts in the machine shop that were never as good as the original. The thought that the journey might last another twenty-two years was crushing. She was tired, all the time.

But she had to park that feeling outside the door of the surgery, and focus on Zane. Maybe it did her good to have two burdens to distract her, rather than just one.

When Zane was safely under they checked the recording equipment was working, and Holle made a diary note of date and time. "All right, Zane. We're going to try to help you welcome the alter we call Zane 1."

Theo glanced at the notes on his handheld. "He's seventeen years old.

He carries the shame you felt when Harry Smith abused you in the Academy. That was his purpose, that was why he was created. To help you cope with that."

Zane sneered. "So *you* say."

"Are you in your safe place?"

"I'm in the museum. In my room."

"What can you see?"

"The door is open."

Holle said, "What can you see through the door?"

"A boy. He's frightened."

"I know. Well, you can help him, Zane. Can you go get him, and bring him into the room with you?"

"I don't know." Zane twitched on the couch.

"You can send him out again any time you want."

Zane lay silently for a minute, then stirred.

"Is he there?"

"He's standing beside me. He's smaller than me. Skinny. He's sort of shivering."

"Can I speak to him?"

Zane shuddered, and when he spoke again, his voice had a subtly higher pitch. "I can't see. It's dark."

It had always been dark when Harry Smith had come for Zane. "Do you know who I am?"

"Doctor Wetherbee?"

They went through this every time. "No. I'm Holle. Dr. Wetherbee asked me to help. Do you remember we discussed that?"

"Yes."

"And do you remember what we said we'd do today?"

"You said you'd try to make me go into Zane 3."

"How do you feel about doing that?"

"I don't know what it means." He rubbed his arms, which were pitted with the small scars of the self-harm he still managed to achieve, periodically. "I'm dirty. I should wash first. Zane won't want me."

"No. You're clean. Clean inside. Zane knows that, Zane 3. He wants to welcome you, because that way he can help you, he can take away how you're hurting, and you can help him, because he needs to remember what *you* remember. So it's all a good thing, isn't it?"

"I'll be gone, if I go into him."

"No. You'll still be there, everything that makes you unique. It's just that you'll be inside Zane 3, not outside. I won't forget you."

Zane suddenly opened his eyes and stared straight at Holle, his face twisted. "Promise me that."

Holle had never helped Zane, or Venus or Matt, while the abuse was actually going on, though all the Candidates had suspected what Harry Smith was up to. For years she'd turned her back, afraid for her own position. Now, hearing this plea for help as if from the boy Zane had been back then, but expressed in the gruff voice of a thirty-nine-year-old, her heart broke. "I promise. Maybe you could step back and let me talk to Zane 3 again."

After another pause the alter Zane 3 emerged, visibly. "So what now? How do we actually do this? How do I get him inside me?"

Holle glanced at Theo. The texts and case studies were vague on the precise mechanics of this crucial moment.

Theo leaned forward. "Can you see him? What's he doing now?"

"He's crying." Zane sounded faintly disgusted.

"Then just hold him," Theo said. "Put your arms around him. See if you can stop him crying."

"OK." Zane sounded reluctant, but his upper arms twitched, a vestige of movement. "I'm holding him. He's making my shirt wet. He's stopping crying. I . . . Come on. It's OK."

Holle asked, "What's happening?"

"It's like a shadow falling across me, I—oh, I can see him, but he's inside my head now. Inside my eyelids!"

"Don't be afraid," Holle said, soothing. "It's going well. Everything's fine. Can you hear his voice? Can you hear what he's thinking?"

"I can hear, I can see, oh God. I can see his memories. It's like Head-

Space porn. Did this happen to me? I remember now, I remember the first time, Harry was comforting me about the antimatter accident, he put his big heavy arm around me—oh, shit."

"It's OK, Zane, you're doing well."

"And this poor kid has been carrying this garbage around for all these years?"

"He did it for you, Zane. I'll count down from five, and then you'll wake up, you'll be here with me and Theo in the surgery. OK? Five. Four . . ."

On waking, Zane was subtly different. More anguished. Angrier.

Holle asked, "Are you OK? Do you want anything, some water?"

"No water. I'm fine." He sounded anything but fine. He looked dazzled; he shaded his eyes. "Everything's bright. Ow, and *loud*." But the only noise in the room was the unending hum of the ECLSS pumps and fans. "I hear my heartbeat."

Holle spoke softly. "What do you remember?"

"That I didn't remember before? Years of systematic abuse by that prick Smith. And, in retrospect, years of grooming even before that." His eyes snapped open. Suddenly he was mocking, angry. "Or maybe you put this shit in my head. Nothing else about this experience is real. Why should these memories be any more valid?"

Holle felt beaten. "Zane, we're just—"

"Are we done? Can I go?"

76

Five days after Seba arrived in Earth orbit, Masayo called Kelly to the shuttle flight deck.

She swam through the lock from Seba. Mike Wetherbee and Masayo were waiting for her, loosely strapped into the twin pilots' couches at the nose of the shuttle. Kelly briskly kissed Masayo, and she drifted behind the two men, looking over their shoulders. For long minutes they looked out of the flight deck's big windows in silence.

There, looming over them beyond the windows, was the Earth itself. Even after five days it was hard to believe that they were here, that after a seven-year flight from Earth II they had actually made it home again. Yet here was the blunt reality.

The world was a shield of lumpy cloud, so close that its curvature was barely visible. Looking ahead to the horizon Kelly could see the cloud banks in their three-dimensional glory, continent-sized storms crowned by towering thunderheads. Seba was approaching the terminator, the diffuse boundary between night and day, and the sun, somewhere behind the hull, cast shadows from those tremendous thunderheads onto the banks of clouds beneath. Meanwhile on console screens data and imagery about the Earth chattered and flashed, information on climate and oceanography and atmospheric content and the rest compiled by instruments intended to inspect a new world, and whose electronic eyes were now turned on the old.

Masayo asked, "So how's Eddie?"

"Fine. Going crazy. You know how he gets before he crashes for his nap." Eddie, Kelly's second child and fathered by Masayo Saito, four years old now, conceived and born in microgravity, was a spindly explosion of energy. Eddie was one of just four children born during the voyage from Earth II, which had brought the crew roster up to twenty-three. In a hull designed for a nominal crew of forty or more, there was plenty of room for the kids to play. "Jack Shaughnessy's with him. Says he'll put him to bed when he calms down."

"Good." Masayo smiled, his broad face bathed in the light of Earth.

Kelly felt a stab of affection for him. Now forty-one, Masayo had lost his boyish good looks to thinning hair and a fattening neck, and like all of the crew after eighteen years in the Ark he was sallow, too pale, with a darkness about the folds of his eyes. But his enduring good nature showed in his face, and the easy command that had once won him the loyalty of the Shaughnessys and his other ragtag illegals now inspired love from his son with Kelly.

Did Kelly love Masayo? Did he love her? Those questions weren't answerable, she had long ago decided. They would never have come together, never stayed together, if not for the unique situation of the mission. But that was the frame in which they lived, and within which any relationship had to flourish. For sure, she believed he was good for her.

But Mike Wetherbee was watching Kelly in that clinical, mildly judgmental way of his. "Jack's pretty reliable," he said, his tone needling. "You can trust him. I guess."

Mike seemed on the surface to have got over his hijacking from Halivah, seven years earlier, drugged and bound. But whenever he got the chance he put pressure on Kelly, especially over her children, digging into that dull ache, that awful memory of having given up a child. Mike hadn't trained as a psychiatrist; whatever skills he had he'd picked up on treating patients since the launch, notably Zane. He seemed to have learned well, if his slow, subtle torture of Kelly was any sign.

But today Kelly's focus was on the present, not the past, and she ignored him. "So what have we learned?"

Masayo grunted. "Nothing good. If we'd hoped Earth had somehow healed—well, we're disappointed." He paged through images and data summaries on a screen before him. "There's no exposed land, none at all. But according to the radar the flood's not as deep as we might have expected. It's around fifteen kilometers above the old datum, whereas we were expecting nearer twenty-five from the models the oceanographers produced before we left."

Mike Wetherbee grimaced. "*Only* fifteen kilometers?"

Masayo grinned. "Yeah. How shall we break it to the crew? Do you want the good news or the bad news?" Now he produced a schematic map of the planet's climate systems. "The weather's got simpler now there are no continents in the way, no Saharas or Himalayas. Take a look."

In each hemisphere the sun's equatorial heating created three great convection belts parallel to the equator, transporting heat toward the cooler poles. These tremendous cycles created a kind of helix of stable winds that snaked around the rotating planet. It was a pattern that had endured for billions of years, and even now its continued existence still determined much of the world's long-term climate patterns. Meanwhile in the ocean the network of currents was much simpler now that the continents were drowned kilometers deep, and unable to offer any significant obstacle to the currents' circulation. Even the huge gyres, dead spots in the ocean, where humanity's garbage had collected and hapless rafting communities had gone to scavenge, were dispersed now. A crude system of atmospheric circulation, powerful ocean currents following simple patterns, not a trace of land or even polar ice anywhere in the world: this was an Earth reduced to elementals, like a climatological teaching aid, Kelly thought. Nothing but the basic physics of a spinning planet.

And yet it was not uniform; this ocean world had features. Masayo produced an image of a vast storm prowling the lower latitudes of the northern hemisphere, a milky spiral the size of a continent that continually spun off daughter storms, themselves ferocious hurricanes in their own right. "As far as we know this is the same storm they called the Spot, eighteen years ago," he said. "Maybe somebody down there will be able to confirm that for us. It drives winds at around three hundred kilometers an hour. That's about Mach point two five—a quarter the speed of sound. Must do a hell of a lot of damage to those garbage rafts."

"So we splash down away from it," Kelly murmured. "But where?"

"There's nowhere immediately obvious," Masayo said. "No land, clearly. Nothing but a scattering of rafts. Sometimes you see their lights at night. Some don't seem to have lights at all. They tend to cluster over the old continental shelves, and particularly over urban areas, the great cities."

Mike said, "We picked up some radio transmissions, mostly not aimed at us."

"'Mostly'?"

"It's just chatter. People asking after relatives and lost kids, and swapping news about storms and fishing grounds. A few people still making observations of the climate, the ongoing changes. They can talk through the surviving satellite network. I suspect some of them are trying to bounce signals off the moon—"

"Mike, back up. You said, 'mostly.' The signals were 'mostly' not aimed at us."

He grinned. "That's why we called you in here, Kelly. Half an hour ago we picked up this, from a raft over North America." He tapped his screen, and a speaker crackled with a looped message:

". . . knew you'd be back. I've been waiting a year for you to show up, since the earliest theoretical return time. Earth II isn't so hot, huh? Well, if you need a native guide come down here and look me up. You can track this signal . . . This is Thandie Jones, somewhere over Wyoming, on the Panthalassa Sea. Thandie calling Ark One. I see you! I knew you'd be back . . ."

77

n the cupola's twilit, humming calm, with the hull of Halivah and the silent stars arrayed beyond the windows, Grace Gray gazed on beautiful, spectacular images of young star systems, a million years old or less, in the throes of formation from an interstellar cloud, and tried very hard to understand what her daughter was telling her.

Helen, earnest, seventeen years old, said, "It's like we're putting together an album of the birth of a solar system, frame by frame. You see how the young star, having imploded out of the cloud itself, starts to interact with the cloud remnant. A central collapsed disc slices the wider cloud in two . . ." The sundered cloud, lit up from within by the invisible star, reminded Grace of a child's toy, a yo-yo, with the planetary system forming in the gap between the two halves, where the string would wrap. Tremendous jets shot up out of the poles of the star, at right angles to the yo-yo. Helen spoke on, of ice lines and migrating Jovians and photoevaporation, of how starlight could strip away the mantle of a Jupiter to expose a Neptune or a Uranus.

The cupola was empty save for the two of them and Venus, who, intent on her own work, with headphones and virtual glasses wrapped around her head, was effectively absent.

Helen was beautiful, Grace thought, studying her daughter, her profile silhouetted against the star field. Beautiful in a way *she* had never been, even at seventeen, when everybody is beautiful, even though she shared

Helen's coloring. Helen's father, Hammond Lammockson, son of Nathan, had been short, squat, bullish like his father. Grace could see little of Hammond in Helen—some of Nathan's determination, maybe. Or perhaps she was an expression of Saudi royal blood. Or maybe it was something to do with the microgravity they had all endured for the last seven years, since the Split had made rotational artificial gravity impossible. Helen had only been ten. All the kids who had grown up since were slender and graceful—though, against expectation, they weren't tall. Or maybe she looked like Grace's mother, whom she had been named for, who Grace herself couldn't remember.

Whatever, Helen was a winner of the lottery of genetics—"gifted," Venus Jenning had once called her, one of the handful of the next generation deemed bright enough for an intensive education. Grace had always suspected as much, even back in the days when Helen had tried to teach her the rules of Zane's infinite chess. And she never looked more beautiful than when she was intent on her studies.

She realized Helen had stopped talking.

"Am I losing you?"

"Not quite."

"Look, would you like a coffee before I show you some more?"

Venus pushed her glasses up into her graying hair. "Somebody mention coffee?"

"There may be some in the flask."

"I think that's pretty much stewed by now. Why don't you go fill it up for us?"

"Oh." Helen looked from one to the other. "You want to talk without me being around, right?"

Grace smiled, and brushed a floating lock of blond hair back into the knot her daughter wore at the back of her head. "Well, it was Venus I came to see, honey."

"I can take a hint." Helen had her legs crossed around a T-stool; now she unwrapped, floated into the air, and with a fish-like precision arrowed down and grabbed the coffee flask from its holder beside Venus.

"I'll give you ten minutes. Then I get to show you more good stuff, Mum. Deal?"

Grace smiled. "Deal."

When she had sailed out through the airlock, Venus turned to Grace. "You're here to talk about Wilson, I guess."

"Yeah. And Steel Antoniadi. He's gone too far with that girl. The hull's full of talk about it. I'm seeing Holle later. Maybe you could come. If the three of us confront him—"

"OK." Venus yawned and stretched; she wasn't wearing any restraint, and the arching of her back made her drift up out of her chair. "I guess it has to be done. I have to admit it gets harder and harder to care about that kind of crap." She stared out at the stars. "Sometimes I just lose myself in here. And thank God Wilson got to be speaker, not me. Helen really is one of the best we have, you know. Do you resent me taking her away to study?"

"No. In fact she's spending even more time training up as a shuttle pilot than she does in here. I'm grateful she has these opportunities. But there's plenty of griping about your students and their privileges. To be fair to him Wilson defends you, he always points out how we need the planet-spotting and navigation functions."

"Well, so we do. But how does he feel about my programs of basic research? The fundamental physics, the cosmology—"

"I never spoke to him about it."

Venus looked back to the stars again. "I just think we should be doing more than, you know, washing down walls and clearing out blocked latrines. And if you think about it, this is a unique opportunity. Even if all goes well, Helen's kids will be dirt farmers down on Earth III. It's only this generation, Helen's generation, of all the generations since Adam, who have grown up among the stars, away from the overwhelming presence of a planet. Who knows how that's shaping their minds? Call it an experiment, Grace. Besides, these are seriously bright kids, seriously curious, who aren't allowed to explore anything in case they wreck the ship. So I try to direct their curiosity *out there*." She fell silent, as she was wont to do, drifting into the private universe of her own head.

Grace prompted her, mildly mocking, "And are you coming up with anything useful?"

Venus laughed. "Now you sound like Holle, queen of the plumbers. Hell, who knows? Look at Zane's warp generator. We managed to build a unified-physics engine even before we managed to unify the physics in the first place. It's as if we built it by accident. Maybe Helen's generation will come up with something that will make Zane's drive look like a steam engine. Then we'll have some fun."

But, Grace thought, all this planet-hunting and exponentiating scientific theorizing had nothing to do with the complex human reality unfolding within the shabby walls of the Ark.

The lock opened and Helen came bustling in, floating expertly through the air while juggling two flasks and a bunch of mugs. She looked entirely at home in this microgravity observatory, and her face was intent, alive with intelligence. But she had never looked more alien. Grace felt a stab of helpless, hopeless love.

78

The shuttle from the Ark was a spark, falling down the midday sky. Thandie hadn't seen such a sight in years. As it fell the spark became a glider, white and fat. It banked once over the raft. Then it came drifting down to a cautious belly-down landing that threw up a huge plume of water.

This was literally the most exciting thing that had ever happened in the lives of most of the inhabitants of the raft. The children jumped and clapped. Some of the older rafters, like Boris's parents, Manco and Ana, were more fearful, as if this technological irruption would perturb the calm, relatively safe lives they had carefully constructed for themselves.

The shuttle came to rest only a couple of hundred meters from the raft, an impressive bit of positioning after a journey of forty-two light-years. The downed craft looked harmless enough, bobbing in the gentle oceanic swell, with its upper hull covered with a blanket of insulation, blackened by charring in places, and the Stars and Stripes and the words UNITED STATES still visible as the faintest trace of faded paintwork. But Thandie, operating under instructions from a radio link to Kelly Kenzie on the flight deck, made sure that nobody approached the craft for some hours. The black shield that covered the whole of the shuttle's underside was still ferociously hot from atmospheric friction, and the crew were busy venting gases and other toxins from attitude control systems and fuel cells.

It was the end of the day before the shuttle's hatch swung open at last. The raft kids, some as young as four or five, dived into the water and went splashing over, towing plastic cables.

A pale face emerged from the craft's hatch, a spindly figure standing uncertainly in blue coveralls. Bundles were thrown out onto the ocean, packages that popped open to become bright orange lifeboats, to more gasps of delight from the children. The crew began unloading the shuttle, lowering down bits of equipment first, and then their youngest children, four little ones wrapped up in bulky flotation jackets. Then the adults and older children came out, nineteen of them climbing down the shuttle's short flight of steps. These skinny, pale creatures from space had to be helped aboard their own boats by naked brown raft children. It was like a meeting between separate species, Thandie thought. The raft children swarmed aboard the shuttle, hunting for souvenirs.

The lifeboats set off across the water toward the raft. A couple of the occupants leaned over the side and heaved, miserably sick. One little boy from the shuttle was wailing, "Let me go back! Oh, let me go back!"

At the raft, the shuttle crew had to be helped once more across the short distance between the bobbing lifeboats and the more stately raft. They all had trouble standing, especially the children who panted hard, straining miserably at the thick air.

Thandie had arranged for all twenty-three to be housed together in a hastily evacuated shack, where they were laid down on pallets of blankets padded with dried seaweed. She came to see them a few times that first night, as Manco and Ana led the rafters' efforts to make their strange visitors comfortable, bringing them cups of rainwater and bowls of fish soup. It was like a hospital ward; the stink of vomit and excrement was dense. The raft children looked in, fascinated and fearful, but were driven back by the stink. Thandie had yet to learn what had become of the Ark, and why only half of it, and much less than half the crew, had returned home.

The next morning, at Kelly's request, she and two others were brought out and sat in a row of couches scavenged from the shuttle, so they could talk with Thandie.

Thandie sat before her guests on the raft floor in a yoga posture, back erect, legs crossed, hands resting on her knees.

The space travelers sat out in the open in their couches, tipped back, covered in blankets. Their faces were ghostly pale. They all gratefully accepted cups of hot seaweed tea from Manco. The sea was choppy, and they seemed to cower from a sky where thick gray clouds bubbled. A handful of raft kids hung around them, staring wide-eyed. Thandie ignored the kids, confident they would soon go swimming and forget all about the returned astronauts.

Thandie remembered Kelly Kenzie as one of the brightest buttons among the Candidates. She had gone to space as a girl in her early twenties. Now she had returned as a woman of forty-one, too thin, too pale, her blond hair streaked with gray. She was still beautiful, but she had a face that showed the years she had lived, the choices she had made. Thandie gathered that one of the children from the shuttle was Kelly's. The other adults were both men. One was another Candidate who Thandie vaguely remembered; he was called Mike Wetherbee. The second, a bulky forty-some-year-old called Masayo Saito, she didn't recognize at all. Kelly introduced him as her partner, father of her kid, and said he had a military background.

Thandie twisted her head to the right, breathed in to center, turned to the left breathing out, back to center and breathed in. "Forgive my old lady stretching routine. So how's your health this morning?"

Kelly grunted. "Mike here is the doctor."

Mike Wetherbee rubbed his chest, apparently having trouble breathing himself. "I expected problems with the gravity," he said. "Brittle bones, problems with fluid balance, all of that. Why, we've got children in there, including Kelly's little Eddie, who were *born* in free fall. And I was expecting us to be prone to viruses and bugs, and I shot us all full of antibiotics and antihistamines before we cracked the shuttle. What I wasn't expecting was this damn breathlessness." He had a broad, nasal Australian accent, not much diluted by the years.

"I guess I should have warned you. The air is thicker than it used to be—we're under greater pressure than the old sea-level value—but oxygen is depleted."

Kelly nodded, cautiously, as if her very head was too heavy for her neck. "We got some spectrometer readings from orbit. I didn't believe it."

"The world isn't as fecund as it used to be. Not yet anyhow. When the flood came we had extinction events on land, of course, but in the sea too. No more nutrients washing down from the land. The productivity of the biosphere as a whole has gone off a cliff, and as a consequence so has the oxygen content of the atmosphere—down to sixteen percent, according to some of the hearthers, down five points. That's equivalent to three kilometers' altitude before the flood."

"Great," Mike Wetherbee said. "We drowned the world, but I still get to feel like I climbed a mountain."

"Worse than that, the air's warmer than it used to be. You're panting, trying to keep cool, and you miss the oxygen even more."

"Warmer," Masayo Saito said. He seemed to be having even more trouble breathing than the others, and he spoke in short staccato bursts. "Greenhouse gases?"

"Yes. All those drowned, rotting rainforests. We do think the flood is finally tailing off, however, at last. It seems to be heading for an asymptote of about eighteen kilometers above the 2012 datum. Which means Earth will have an ocean of around five times the volume of the pre-flood value, which in turn matches some of my models of subterranean sea release, as I called it. You can see that even now I am obsessed with academic priority."

Kelly smiled. "I worked with guys like Liu Zheng, at the Academy. I can appreciate that."

"Yeah. I survived to deliver history's most almighty 'I told you so.' Some consolation. We might be heading toward a new climatic equilibrium out there somewhere in parameter space. There's a model circulating on the hearth, called the Boyle model, and that old plodder would love to know he's been immortalized." But none of them had heard of Gary Boyle, or of the hearth, a loose interconnected community of aging climatologists and oceanographers, and she got blank looks. "Boyleworld will have very high carbon dioxide content, very low oxygen. Extreme heating will drive even more violent storms, which could mix up the ocean layers and thereby promote life, and in particular plankton photosynthesis—"

"Which would draw down carbon dioxide," Kelly said.

"Yes. You can see there's a feedback loop to close there, and that's how you get stability. At higher temperatures underwater weathering of limestone kicks in also. But it's all very controversial. Nobody has the computer facilities to test such models any more. And even if Boyleworld does come to pass, it might not be survivable by humans. Too damn hot."

Masayo glanced around the raft, and pointed to a rack of fish. "The ocean's evidently not that unproductive. And are those gull eggs?"

"There's a kind of bounce-back going on among some deep-water species, despite the lack of nutrients in the ocean, now we stopped overfishing and are no longer pumping in pollutants. It's as if the Earth is breathing a sigh of relief. The birds have suffered, of course. No land, nowhere to nest. But some gulls seemed to be surviving. We think they're making their nests on floating detritus."

"We didn't see many congregations of rafts," Kelly said. "Over the major cities mostly. Even there, people are pretty spread out."

"We come for the garbage," Thandie said bluntly. "Even after so many years. Toxic leaks drive the fish away, but conversely they're drawn back to the nutrient upwellings." She didn't elaborate on what that nutrient material might be, but Mike Wetherbee looked at the drying fish more suspiciously. "We do keep in touch, we have radio links, we swap information and we trade kids. We fret about inbreeding, just like the social engineers in your Academy." She pointed. "The kid over there, fixing the cabling on that corner of the raft—he's called Boris. Thirteen years old. I joined this raft seven years ago, after I came to visit a woman called Lily Brooke, so we could watch the submergence of Everest together. Lily was related to Boris—his great-great-aunt, I think. Maybe you heard of Lily. She was a friend of Grace Gray. She made sure Grace got on Ark One."

Kelly said, "Grace is on Halivah—the other hull, the hull that didn't come back to Earth."

"She was pregnant when she joined the crew."

"She had the baby before we got to Jupiter. A girl called Helen. She's grown up now, I guess, she must be seventeen years old."

Thandie nodded. "That's good to hear. Lily and Grace went way back. Lily was devoted to saving Grace's life, saving her from the flood. I guess she succeeded."

"Grace never mentioned her," Kelly said.

Lily had died not long after Everest. She had done all she possibly could for Grace. Thandie was glad she had never learned of this slow revenge of Grace's. Some people never forgave you for saving their lives.

"After Everest, Manco and Ana, Lily's great-nephew and his wife, took me in. Just as they will take in all of you now. They're generous people, fundamentally."

Kelly was staring at the kids, most of whom, as Thandie had expected, had got bored and gone off to their eternal playground of the sea. "They seem—alien. But no more than we are to them, I guess."

"They grew up knowing nothing different from this," Thandie said. "Just the raft and the ocean. Some of them barely learn to walk before they go jumping overboard. Some barely talk. It's not that they're preverbal, but they seem to be evolving a language of their own, of words, gestures, body shapes that they can use underwater. In the end some of them just slip away. Literally; they go over the side and you don't see them again. Maybe the sharks get them; that's what the parents fear. I wonder if they're just finding some place of their own to live. Maybe on the big natural rafts where the gulls live, all driftwood and guano. Good luck to them."

Mike Wetherbee said, "It sounds like the mother of all generation gaps."

"Well, so it is. In five hundred years their grandkids will probably have webbed feet. But I hope they will remember their own humanity, remember the history that bore them, the civilization their ancestors built. I try to teach Boris astronomy . . ."

The kids were kind to Thandie, but they rarely listened to anything she had to say. That was fine with her, fine to be disregarded, as it had been for forty years or more, since she had seen London and New York flooded, and then the huge, astonishing marine transgressions as low-lying continental land was covered over in great sudden swathes, and human civilization dissolved in flight. The flood was just too big; to observe was all you could aspire to. In fact it was a privilege to have lived through this moment of transition. And after all none of these children and grandchildren were hers. She had no stake in their future. The present was enough, and the past . . .

They were watching her curiously.

She had drifted away, into the oceanic depths of her own head, fallen asleep sitting there in lotus. "Sorry," she said. "Old lady narcolepsy."

"And I apologize for staring," Mike Wetherbee said. "It's a long time since any of us saw anybody *old*. Forgive me."

"You mentioned something called the Split. Tell me about it."

Kelly glanced at Masayo and Mike. She shrugged, and related a fast version of her story, of the disputes that came to a head when Earth II was reached, and the three-way split that ensued. Kelly looked nervous, as if she feared she was going to have to repeat all this to some kind of tribunal. Thandie wondered what different versions of this saga she might have heard from Wilson Argent or Holle Groundwater.

When she was done, Thandie nodded. "I always thought you might come home. I never agreed with the basic philosophy of Project Nimrod, to go flying off into the sky. Earth has become alien, but not as alien as another planet entirely. I never thought you would split three ways, which must be about the dumbest choice you could have made from an engineering point of view. Gordo Alonzo would hit the roof. But, wow— three roads, three destinies. I wonder how it will turn out."

Masayo said, "Well, Earth II is twenty-one light-years away. We outran any signal they might send. We might hear from them in another fourteen years or so. But we won't hear from Earth III for another century, at least." He frowned. "Strange thought."

Thandie reminded herself he was basically a military man who had had to learn to deal with some very odd concepts. "You chose to come back to Earth, Masayo. Why?"

"I have a kid, from a previous relationship," Masayo said awkwardly. "On Earth, I mean. I never meant to leave him behind. It was an only an accident I was on the Ark in the first place."

"I've a kid too," Kelly said. "I guess that's what brought me home."

"That and your ambition," Mike Wetherbee snapped. "Your damn pride."

Kelly would have replied, but Thandie held up her hand. "These are old arguments. You may as well leave them behind, leave them up in space." She glanced around at the waters of Panthalassa, a world ocean given a name coined by one of the pioneers of the study of continental drift. "I don't know what you were expecting. This is all we have to offer you. This is where you will spend the rest of your lives—"

"There is something else we're looking for," Kelly said. "We listened from orbit. I hoped we'd make contact, but we heard nothing."

Thandie nodded; she'd expected this. "You hoped to hear from Ark Two."

"It was my father's project. He may even be still alive," Kelly said a little wildly. "It's a long shot, he would be in his nineties, but—"

"I never heard that he died. And I never heard that Ark Two failed. Not spoken to them for years, but that doesn't mean they aren't still sitting there. I can arrange for you to talk to them, if you want. Or anyhow I can try."

Kelly's eyes widened. "And to travel there?"

"That's up to the Ark Two crew. We don't have the means to take you." She eyed Kelly and the others, who looked uncertain. "Are you sure you want to go chasing the past?"

Kelly's face hardened. "I'd appreciate it if you'd make the call rather than psychoanalyze me."

Masayo looked concerned at her aggression. Mike Wetherbee just smiled.

Thandie bowed her head, and rested her hands on her folded knees once more.

"Mom?" Little Eddie Saito came stumbling toward Kelly. Only four years old, he walked like a newborn baby deer, thought Thandie, who was probably the only person on the raft who remembered what a baby deer looked like. "I played with the children. Can I go swimming?"

Kelly ignored him. "So where is Ark Two?"

Mike Wetherbee smiled nastily. "All those years, and your precious father never even told you that? Some relationship you had."

"Just tell me, Thandie."

Thandie pointed down. "Yellowstone."

Eddie pulled Kelly's sleeve. "Mom? Can I go swim?"

79

On her way to confront Wilson over his relationship with Steel, Holle met Grace in the upper cone of Halivah, where they waited for Venus to join them.

They looked down the length of the open tank. In the post-Split microgravity most of the deck partitions had been taken out once more to open up the hull's big inner space. The long fireman's pole was still in place down the hull's axis, and cabins clustered along the length of the pole, attached by staples and cables and sticking out at all angles. It was the middle of the working day. People swam everywhere, engaged on their business. There was a clamor of noise, of voices; the removal of the decks had turned the whole hull into an echo chamber. Down about Deck Five Holle saw a dream circle gathered, mostly youngsters. One of them was Zane Glemp, talking, holding them spellbound. Around Deck Eight half the flooring had been left in place to serve as a base for Wilson's cabin, a grand affair of partitions and blankets, a palace of trash. The whole volume was bathed in the fake sunlight of the big wall-mounted arc lamps, the light diffused in the dust-laden air.

You could easily differentiate the various generations. Like Holle and Grace themselves, most people on board still belonged to the generation that had boarded the ship on Earth eighteen long years ago. Aging now, mostly in their late thirties or early forties, they moved around efficiently but without elegance.

Then came the teenagers, like Helen Gray born after the launch from
Gunnison, who had spent the years of their adolescence in microgravity
and moved with unconscious skill. Most of them weren't much like
Helen, however. They wore basic wraps that left their arms and legs bare,
their flesh adorned with tattoos that matched graffiti on the walls, markings incomprehensible to any adult that badged their allegiance to one
tribe or another. They moved in swarms like exotic fish in a tank, ignoring the adults and eyeing each other with suspicion. Holle knew that few
of these kids ever attended formal classes. It worried her that they were
so disconnected from the ship and its mission; this was the next generation
of crew after all. Wilson claimed not to care. If he ever had to confront
them he sent in his illegal buddies, a bigger, tougher gang than the rest.
But then Wilson had his own take on these youngsters, which was the
reason Holle and Grace were going to see him now.

And then came the youngest of all, the kids of seven and under who
had actually been born and grown up in free fall. Having known nothing
else they rocketed through the air, fearless. One group of kids was working its way up a wall, cleaning it; they had pads in their hands and canisters of water on their little backs. Through the general clamor Holle could
hear the piping of the nonsense song the children sang as they worked:
"I laugh you more my fun / you're my enjee / you're my tee-fee / I laugh
you more my fun . . ." They sang it as a round, overlapping the fragmentary lines, shoving their sponges over the wall to the rhythms of their
music. They were a spindly breed, Holle always thought, surprisingly small
in height, and pale too, pale like the sightless worms that had once swum
in Earth's deep lightless oceans.

And, in a moment of comparative quiet, Zane's thin voice carried up
from the dream circle.

"The doctors, but they're not *really* doctors and even they admit that,
say *I* don't exist. *I* am only a construct of the relationship between
these partial people who live inside my head, who don't exist either.
Maybe that's true of all of us. Maybe none of us exist, except in how we
relate to each other. Maybe if we went out of this hull one by one we

would each cease to be, alone in the dark. And then when the last of us was left, one person left in the hull—maybe he or she would go too, just popping out of existence . . ."

This was clearly Zane 3; Holle recognized the content of what he said, the mannerisms. But it was a more forceful Zane 3, angrier, stronger, somehow more determined. Fueled by the reintegrated pain of Zane 1, maybe.

Grace murmured, "You know Wilson's concerned about the stuff Zane's saying. Zane denies that anything exists outside the hull, and says he doesn't remember anything that occurred before the warp launch from Jupiter. Well, most of these kids have never been outside the hull either, and they remember nothing but the voyage. He's saying what they want to hear on some deep level, I think."

"It's just entertainment. The HeadSpace booths are too pricey, so they swap dreams. Zane is just a storyteller. A spooky one, but that's all."

"Are you sure? He's been developing justifications for his theories for years. For instance he says that warp drive is impossible; he can prove it from first principles."

"But any of these kids can go to the cupola and look out at the stars. How does he explain that away?"

"It's a simulation, with obvious flaws. Such as the warp field lensing, which is just a scrambling of a star field projection."

"What other 'obvious flaws'?"

"Odd matches. We're supposedly fleeing from a flood, but Earth II was in a constellation called the River. Flood, river? To find our destination in the starscape you look for Orion—and yet we claim that we were launched from Earth by a drive also called Orion. Zane argues that these name matches are symptoms of a lazy design regime. Or maybe they are clues smuggled in by some dissident sim designer to help us figure out the truth of our situation."

"It's just coincidence!"

"No such thing as coincidence in Zane's world. Only conspiracies. There's more. To find where we've come from you look back at Opiuchus, the serpent-bearer. That part of the sky is blanked out, so you can't see Sol, the home of man. But why the serpent-bearer? Zane has been into the archive and he found an account of Ouroboros, a myth of ancient Egypt, a serpent endlessly devouring its own tail. So, Zane says, what we see behind us isn't any kind of warp cone but the mouth of Ouroboros, continually devouring our fake reality, just as a fresh reality is continually constructed ahead of us to give us the illusion of movement."

"My God. I had no idea this had got so elaborate."

Grace shrugged. "Sometimes I believe him myself. After eighteen years in this tank Earth does seem a remote memory, unreal. If it wasn't for the way my feet still ache from all those years of walking on the Plains—"

Holle shook her head. "Whether we're buried in some cage in the Nevada desert or not, the plumbing still needs fixing. That's what I cling to. Here comes Venus. Let's go see Wilson, and get this business about him and Steel over."

In his cabin, Wilson wore only grimy shorts, vest and socks, and he lounged, loosely tethered to a heap of blankets. He was putting on weight, and his skin was greasy.

A couple of his buddies were here with him, illegals called Jeb Holden and Dan Xavi. They were both former eye-dees who had switched to the security services, and forced their way onto the Ark at launch. Now, overweight forty-year-old men, they hung in the corners of the cabin, saying and doing nothing, just watching the women with a faintly intimidating air.

There was no sign of Steel, the point of contention.

Wilson knew why they were here. Holle began to speak, self-conscious and nervous, working her way around the issue.

Since the Split, as far as Holle knew, Wilson had never replaced Kelly with any other long-term partner. But he had been taking lovers from throughout the crew. He had fathered a number of kids too. All this was with the consent of the women involved, and the social engineers back in Colorado would have approved of him spreading his genes around. But then Steel Antoniadi had caught Wilson's eye, during a dance festival.

Named for the color of the walls in this stripped-bare hull, she had grown up dark, willowy, unconsciously graceful in microgravity, exotic in her tunic and tattoos, and just fourteen. Her mother, an illegal called Sue Turco, had been too intimidated by Wilson to do anything about it. But her father, Joe Antoniadi, a former Candidate, had protested to the other elders about it, especially Holle, his boss.

Wilson cut Holle short. "The hell with this, Holle. I'm not forcing the kid."

"That's not the point, Wilson—"

"Look at me. I'm the most powerful man on the ship. Have been for ten years. And rich, too! A credit millionaire. But there's nothing I can buy. So what's in it for me? I'll tell you. Only the sweetest commodity on the ship. I'm talking about young flesh, Holle. Young, just coming ripe, and as limber as all fuck after a lifetime swimming around in zero G. That's what's in it for me—or so I decided, when I saw Steel doing that whirling dance in the air."

"The mission is *about* the kids, Wilson," Venus said hotly. "They aren't just some 'commodity' for you to indulge in. What's next, are you going to start raiding the school groups for bait for your henchmen? I can't believe the boy I grew up with has turned out like this."

Wilson just laughed. One of his buddies farted, a liquid sound.

Holle said, "Well, you're asking for trouble, Wilson. This isn't some feudal village. In the end you govern by consent. And you're pushing your luck."

Wilson glanced at Jeb and Dan, who grinned back at him. "I'll take that on advisement. Is there anything else I can do for you ladies?"

80

August 2059

There was great excitement on the morning of the arrival of the submarine from Ark Two.

Kelly watched her fellow space travelers crowding to the raft's edge, waiting for the sub to surface. Compared to the raft's healthy, robust crew, with skins tanned brown and swimming muscles taut, the Seba people looked like ghosts, spectral, their limbs too long, their heads too large. Their eagerness faintly worried Kelly. They had spent most or all of their lives inside an engineered environment, and were too easily distracted from the shabby garbage raft they were going to have to live on for the rest of their lives. But then it had been Kelly herself who had interrogated Thandie Jones about Ark Two, in their very first proper conversation together.

As they waited it started to rain, just gently, the drops hissing on the ocean. The sky held the remnants of a red dawn, with a faint stink of sulfur in the air. Thandie sniffed. "Volcano weather. Rain precipitating out around ash particles . . ."

There was a ragged cheer as the sub broke the surface. Naked brown-skinned kids swam out to it. Kelly made out a boat-shaped streamlined hull, a conning tower with periscope and radio masts, and a bold Stars and Stripes painted on its flank. The sub drew close enough that ladders could be thrown across from raft to sub, and you could simply walk across without getting your feet wet. The raft kids scampered back and forth over the ladders carelessly, playing in the water that streamed off the sub's hull.

A couple of the sub crew emerged, a man and a woman. They were young, maybe early twenties. They wore reasonably clean-looking blue coveralls and boots, and they had their hair cropped short, military style. Sturdy-looking but pale, they had more in common with the Seba people than the rafters, Kelly thought. They crossed the ladders to the raft easily enough. Little kids swarmed around them, plucking at their hands and trouser legs.

Thandie Jones walked up to the two of them stiffly, and Kelly followed.

The young man was about Kelly's height, his hair blond, his eyes pale blue. He wore patches on his coverall, a US flag and a mission badge, like the astronauts' patches Gordo Alonzo used to show the Candidates. The patch was an inverted triangle containing a pie-slice of the Earth's cross-section, with a strip of bubbling ocean and the bold words ARK TWO plastered over a schematic sky. Kelly stared. This patch was the first piece of physical evidence she had ever seen that Ark Two, hidden from her by her father's lies and evasions, actually existed.

"Ms. Kenzie," the young man said.

She was staring. Disconcerted, she said, "Call me Kelly."

"Welcome home. I can't imagine what you've done, what you've seen." His accent was odd to Kelly's ears, stilted, not quite American. He seemed to be having trouble making eye contact with her. "I wish I could see your ship."

Mike snorted. "No, you don't. After eighteen years it's a flying toilet; best to let it burn up." He stuck out his hand. "Mike Wetherbee."

"I know who you are, Dr. Wetherbee. We all read the log you transmitted down to the Ark. You're heroes to us, all of you. It's an honor." She shook Mike's hand, and Masayo's, and then bent down to inspect Eddie, who grinned back. "And I know who you are too."

"This is the party for the Ark," Thandie said. "Me, Kelly, Mike, Masayo, little Eddie here. You got room for us in that tub of yours?"

"It's not the *Trieste,* but we do our best." He faced Kelly, glancing at her, looking away. "You've come so far, across forty light-years. But it's another twelve kilometers to Ark Two—straight down. Are you ready?"

"Help me across that ladder and I'm all yours," Kelly said. "You're being very generous to us—I don't even know your name."

He stared at her with an odd intensity. "You don't recognize me."

"I'm sorry."

His face turned red. "I'm your son. Dexter. Your first son."

This was completely unexpected. Kelly felt as if she had been punched. Eddie squealed, and she realized she was gripping his hand too tight. She deliberately let go.

"My colleague is called Lisa Burdock." Dexter seemed to be trying to say more. Then he turned on his heel and walked back, over the ladder to the sub.

Mike Wetherbee was grinning. "The son you abandoned for the stars. Well, well."

"Shut your fucking mouth, Doctor." Kelly, heavy with gravity, bewildered, realized she was in danger of collapsing, right here. Well, that wasn't going to happen. She patted Eddie's head, took his hand again, and stepped forward. "Who's going to help me over that ladder?"

The rain hardened, becoming torrential.

To get inside the sub Kelly had to climb down through the conning tower into a narrow well with handholds stapled to the wall, penetrating further down into the hull than she'd expected. There was a stink of metal, electrics, gasoline and urine.

She emerged into a spherical compartment a few meters across, with a simple pilot station set before a bank of screens. Fat windows pierced the sphere's hull, mostly looking down into murky blue water. Mesh partitions had been laid down to make a flat floor, with the volume underneath used as storage space for loose equipment and air tanks. Lisa

Burdock was laying down fold-out couches. Kelly sat gratefully in one of the couches, hiding the weakness in her legs, back, neck. Dexter started handing out blankets and thick padded coats, though the sphere was hot and cramped. Eddie had to be carried down, passed from hand to hand, as the handholds were too far apart for him. But once down in the spherical chamber he seemed to brighten up.

As soon as they were all in their couches, Dexter slammed closed the hatch. With a gurgle of water filling the surface tanks, they sank immediately. Kelly had a stomach-churning sense of the drop.

The design of the sub was indeed based on that of the *Trieste,* a classic deep-dive vessel which had reached the ocean's extreme depths nearly a century before. When the flood had begun, Thandie Jones had made many exploratory dives in a rebuilt *Trieste,* its components dug out of various museums by Nathan Lammockson. Now this new sub was one of a fleet of ferries capable of reaching the ocean floor. "She was constructed in Jackson, Wyoming," Dexter said. "A long way from the ocean back then. But when the flood came in '43 she just floated off." He rapped his fist on the metal wall. "This is our pressure hull. The rest of the sub's volume is mostly taken up with flotation tanks, full of gasoline, pretty much incompressible even at extreme depths; conventional air tanks would just crumple, though we do have those for navigation close to the surface. We have hoppers of rocks we can dump if we need to ascend quickly, though mostly we abort down to the Ark in such contingencies. More likelihood of help there than up top."

Thandie said, "You got any coffee in this tub?"

Masayo had strapped Eddie loosely into a couch, but the boy soon clambered out and started crawling over the floor, poking his fingers through the mesh.

Dexter watched him curiously. "We don't carry many little kids on these ferries, as you can imagine. He looks like he feels at home."

"He was born in a box," Mike Wetherbee said. "This is what he's used to. The safety of confinement." He breathed a deep breath. "And the peculiar, comforting staleness of recycled air."

There wasn't much conversation after that. Dexter handed out coffees.

Within minutes the ocean beyond the windows was growing dark. Thandie had told Kelly that little light from the surface seeped deeper than a hundred meters or so. Kelly heard the hull pop and bang, creaking as it adjusted to the increasing pressure of the water. How strange it was that she had spent two decades inside hulls intended to contain breathable air against a vacuum, and now the situation was precisely reversed, she was inside another hull surrounded by water clenching like a fist.

She looked at her companions. Thandie lay back in her couch, a blanket tucked up to her chin, her eyes closed. Mike Wetherbee seemed quietly interested in the engineering. Masayo kept his eyes on Eddie, who sat on the floor happily fiddling with the mesh partition. Lisa Burdock sat facing the passengers, saying nothing. Kelly realized, in fact, that the girl hadn't said a single word. She was a creature of Ark Two, evidently, perhaps educated all her life for a single purpose, and now was not truly interested in anything else—not even returned star travelers. Kelly wondered if as a Candidate she had once been just as monomaniac.

And Dexter concentrated on his controls. That was his job, but Kelly was pretty sure he was using his absorption in his tasks to avoid any conversation with her, or indeed with Masayo and Eddie, his half-brother.

She was guiltily relieved. She definitely needed time to come to terms with the situation. Although she had always said that part of her motive for coming back to Earth was the child she'd left behind, in her heart she hadn't really believed that she would ever find him again. It hadn't occurred to her that if her father had constructed Ark Two as some kind of haven for himself, it was likely that he would take his grandson in there with him. She'd never even imagined Dexter growing up, she realized now. In her head he had always been the two-year-old she had kissed goodbye that last morning, sneaking out of his bedroom before he woke up to know she was gone, and then running for her transport to Gunnison. It was as if Dexter had died, not that she'd abandoned him.

Well, she was trapped with him now, committed to whatever confrontations and conciliations lay ahead.

As the dive continued the air temperature dropped steadily. Dexter wiped condensation from the control surfaces with his sleeve. The adults bundled into the thick coats Lisa and Dexter had handed out. Eddie said he didn't need a coat, but Masayo draped a blanket around his thin shoulders. A little later the boy started to slow down, and Masayo lifted him onto his lap and wrapped him up inside his own coat, and let him nap.

In the sapping, damp cold, in the humming, comforting calm of the submarine, despite the kilometers of ocean water piling up over her head, Kelly felt oddly safe, reminded of the Ark.

Maybe she slept.

She was jarred awake by a buffeting, a whirr of engines. Lisa pointed at one of the small windows, beyond which lights moved in the dark.

Kelly got out of her couch, stiff and cold, and bent down to peer through the plug of glass. She saw spheres set out on the ocean floor, fixed by cables and illuminated by floods, gleaming like some industrial facility. The spheres touched each other, kissing at the circular interfaces that connected them. The spheres all had paintwork on their hulls, the Stars and Stripes, a bold UNITED STATES, and that triangular Ark Two logo. Another submarine like their own hovered over the facility, tethered by loose cables.

They were floating over what looked like a road, and a hummock in the dirt that might once have been some kind of vehicle. But ocean-floor silt lay everywhere like a murky snow, and strange fish and crabs worked their way over broken tarmac, pale pink and white in the sub's lights. A fence of wire mesh stretched off as far as she could see, picked out by the sub's own spotlights, broken by what looked like watchtowers.

Dexter tapped a key. A screen filled up with a human face, broad, gnarled, and a harsh voice rasped, "Ferry Three, you have permission to dock. And you passengers, you are now twelve point four kilometers beneath the waves, deeper than any point on the ocean floor before the flood started. Welcome to Ark Two."

Kelly stared. "Dad?"

Edward Kenzie glared. "That you, Kelly? I knew you'd screw up. I'll see you when you come through regularization. Ark out." The screen flickered and filled with blue.

81

"Regularization" turned out to be a lengthy process. Everybody who had been "up top," including the crew of the ferry, was put through pressure equalization, which involved sitting in a kind of airlock for a couple of hours while medics took samples of blood and tissue from their nostril linings, and gave them basic medical checks. Dexter said the purpose was to ensure they didn't carry any unfamiliar bugs into the Ark itself. The airlock itself showed more similarities to Ark One: the scuffed metal surfaces, the door handles polished smooth with use, the faintly scarred glass of the thick portals. Like Ark One, this was another old machine.

Beyond the processing chamber was a junction of metal-walled corridors. Here, Mel Belbruno met them. He was standing to attention when the airlock door opened. But when he saw Kelly he broke, ran forward and hugged her. "My God. I never thought I'd see you again."

"Well, you weren't supposed to." She held him at arm's length. He had bulked out with age and was losing his hair, but above his thickened neck was a very familiar, slightly anxious face. He was dressed in a coverall like the others, but *smart,* his trouser legs looked as if they'd been ironed. "You look good, Mel. You always did look like you belonged in uniform."

"We've all read your log. What an incredible adventure. I always did envy you. The sights you saw, the places you went—"

"We'll talk about Holle. We'll make time."

"I'd appreciate that."

"She did well, Mel. Very well. And she didn't find anybody else. Or not as far as I know, up to the Split. It was only ever you."

He nodded, his mouth tight.

"Mel, my father—"

"He's asleep right now. He's ninety-four."

"I know how old my own father is," she snapped.

He flinched. "I'm sorry. Look, he wants to see you, but he needs a lot of downtime. Let me host you for a while. You want to rest, sleep, eat?"

"I feel exhausted just standing here. If you'll let me lean on you, why don't you show us around?"

"Sure." He glanced at the party, including Eddie, who held his father's hand. "And this is Eddie? We have a playroom for the kids."

"You have children down here?"

"We're in it for the long haul. Lisa, maybe you could take Eddie—"

"No," Kelly said. "Sorry, Mel, I've a better idea. Dexter, why don't you take him?"

Dexter faced her. "Why would I want to do that?"

"Because he's your half-brother."

His expression was blank. "Grandfather said you were like this. Manipulating." He looked down at Eddie, who for his own unfathomable reason smiled. "But I guess it's not his fault. Come on, kid. We'll have to make sure the other little ones don't play too rough, I think you're probably a bit more easily broken than they are."

"I'll come too," Masayo said.

Eddie took Dexter's hand. "My name's Eddie. What's your name?"

"Dexter. I'm Dexter." They walked off together, with Masayo following.

"Families," Mike Wetherbee said, sneering.

———

Mel asked, "Are you ready?"

He let Kelly take his arm and walked her down the corridor. Mike, Thandie and Lisa followed. Mel kept his pace slow, as if they were very elderly, very frail, but distinguished visitors.

They climbed a metal stair, and followed a corridor that stretched around the circumference of one of the big spheres that comprised this habitat—spheres which, Mel said, the inhabitants called "tanks." The light cast by fluorescents was bright and harsh. Doors off the corridor were labeled with the names of facilities like air management, water filtration, biomass processing, medical isolation, geothermal power. Evidently this particular tank housed core technical functions.

They walked past a robust decompression chamber which, Mel said, also served as an emergency inner refuge in case of a pressure breach. "Which we call storm shelters, which is wrong every which way, but it's a bit of space program terminology we picked up from Gordo. The other tanks are more open than this. We have big communal spaces, an eating hall, an amphitheater. And factories, a big hydroponics plant—although we mostly rely on produce from the sea—and major laboratory facilities, particularly biological. Our power comes from geothermal heat, the energy of the Earth itself."

Mike asked, "How many are you?"

"Around a hundred, including thirty kids under eighteen or so. We're about the same size of community as Ark One, with about the same habitable volume per head as you guys had. Although in free fall I guess you could make more of your space. We're a human colony in the abyss."

The outer wall, subtly curved, was punctured by thick windows set in tapered frames that, Kelly surmised, offered protection against blow-ins. They paused by one window and looked out. The external lights' glow spread only a little way into the dark. Kelly saw gleaming arcs, the walls of more tanks. More of those crab-like creatures scrabbled in the ooze, and a fish swam by, bony and angular. Kelly reminded herself she was twelve kilometers down, as deep as any oceanic trench on Earth before the flooding began. Something else moved across the ooze. It was a robot, low, like a table, with articulated legs and a camera cluster and a manipulator arm like a cut-down version of Ark One's. It crawled out of her view, intent on its own unknown business.

"The waters are still rising," she said. "These hulls must have a maximum crush depth."

Thandie said, "Even at the current depth they're withstanding a ton per square centimeter. But they're overdesigned. Should be able to tolerate an ocean depth of a hundred kilometers, the maximum theoretically possible. In fact it looks as if the flood will top out at around eighteen kilometers above the old mean, well below that upper bound. And as this area was around two kilometers high before the flood, there won't be a problem."

Mike asked, "Why is a hundred kilometers the maximum?"

"Above that limit the pressure is such that water solidifies into a form of ice. No world with similar gravity to Earth's could have an ocean deeper than that, although the precise freeze depth depends on surface temperature and thermal mixing . . ."

Mel said, "When we came down here the topping out at eighteen klicks wasn't yet apparent. We thought we might finish up entombed in exotic ices."

Kelly gazed out into the dark. "This place was a couple of kilometers high, before the flood. Where are we?"

"Wyoming," Mel said.

Thandie said, "Yellowstone Park, to be precise. Did you ever come here, Kelly? Geysers and mud spots and steam vents, and car parks and pine trees, and tourists at the railings around Old Faithful. You were born after such things as tourists existed in the world, but you might have been brought here for a training expedition. No?"

Mel stood with Kelly and peered out. "Edward Kenzie and Gordo

Alonzo brought me here in '44, right after we had to abandon Alma. I didn't even know this place existed, even though Ed had devoted years of his life to it."

"Nor did I," Kelly said with feeling.

"Ark Two was also intended as a last refuge for the President of the United States and his administration. President Peery never made it. I believe it's a long time since we had formal communication with any government. I don't even know who the President is, now. We kind of like being left to run things ourselves, I guess."

Thandie said, "I do know a LaRei consortium began the construction of this place back in the 2020s, when they also started serious work on Ark One, long before the flood waters got here. They used the grounds of the old Yellowstone Volcano Observatory. They built these tanks right out in the open, and waited for the waters to close over them. Built the submarine ferries over in Jackson, and let them float off too."

"The floods came in '43," Mel said. "By then the eye-dees had found this place and were besieging it. That didn't stop even when the waters came; the eye-dees just took to rafts and carried on. When I was brought here in '44, in the evacuation from Alma, the big domes were already just about covered by the water. We were lowered down from the choppers to hatches in the roofs. The first weeks were scary, Kelly. Even when the waters rose up above us, the eye-dees could still dive down to get at us. They used limpet mines, and managed to wreck one of the domes. That was the incident where Gordo Alonzo got himself killed. But the water was rising three hundred meters a *year* by then. That's a meter a day. We watched those eye-dees being lifted on the breast of the sea up and out of sight, until they were too far above our heads to bother us. Then it got darker and darker, until after about three months the sun was shut out altogether. Incredible times."

Kelly tried to stay composed. "And what about Don Meisel?"

He looked at her, surprised. "He stayed at Alma to the end. Protecting Mission Control. That's the last place I saw him; I made it out, he didn't. You didn't know?"

"Nobody told me." Mike Wetherbee was watching her, waiting for her to crack. She forced a smile. "So why Yellowstone, Thandie? What's here?"

Thandie said, "This park contains half the word's geothermal features. Two-thirds of the world's geysers, in fact. I think your father and his advisers dreamed of surviving down here, and living off geothermal heat and the produce of black smokers. And I, and others, argued for a major seismic monitoring facility."

Mike frowned. "What's a black smoker?"

"A drowned geyser," Thandie said. "Heated water escaping from the depths, eventually building up chimneys like smokestacks. You found them in the deepest oceans, in the trenches. And each of them attracts life, extremophile bacteria—that is, lovers of heat and salinity and extreme pressure—off which feed the crabs and the fish and the worms. A whole food chain fed by the Earth's inner heat, and entirely independent of sunlight, which, you'll notice, they don't get much of here. And, Ed Kenzie's idea is, maybe people could live off *that*. Also you'd have access to the seabed and related resources which wouldn't be available from a raft on the ocean surface. You could mine for metals and oil and such."

Kelly said, "And the seismology?"

Yellowstone was such a geologically active area because it sat directly over a mantle plume, a hot spot, a fountain of rock flowing like liquid up from the Earth's deeper core.

"There's actually a supervolcano here," Thandie said. "It's erupted several times in the past—the last more than six hundred thousand years ago. Some of us theorize that the shifting weight of water over the land might trigger a new eruption, which is actually overdue. Which is why we wanted a station here. Even before the waters came there was evidence of uplift, for instance Old Faithful turned off in 2039.

"They've also been running seismic tomography surveys, studying rock flows in the deep mantle. We're still working on theories of why all the subterranean water should have been released just now. It may have something to do with human activity or it may not. Perhaps it's because of the configuration of the continents. They slide around, you know, granite rafts drifting on the mantle, and every few hundred million years or so they coalesce into giant supercontinents. This is called the chelogenic cycle. The supercontinents are like vast lids that block Earth's heat flow, the way Yellowstone traps the heat of the mantle plume. Eventually that heat causes the supercontinent to shatter, and the bits go spinning away. Now the last supercontinent, Pangaea, broke up two hundred and fifty million years ago, and the next formation event is another two hundred and fifty million years off in the future. So we're at a midpoint, and maybe the mantle currents are adjusting somehow to this unique moment. *We* might be entirely irrelevant . . ."

Kelly saw that Thandie had lost her focus. She was talking to herself, receding into a mist of speculation, forever unprovable.

Mel was staring out of the window. "It was incredible to watch the life forms come and go. I mean, in the park there used to be grizzlies and wolves and herds of bison and elk, as well as vast forests. As the water closed over us, we just knew they were drowning, all of them. What's that phrase from Genesis about Noah's flood? 'All in whose nostrils was the breath of life, of all that was in the dry land, died.' But then, you know, we got recolonized, by all the strange creatures that live off the smoker chemicals. Giant worms and shrimps and crabs, and sea cucumbers, and xenophyophores—just single cells, the size of your hand. Incredible things."

Thandie said, "But there was an extinction event even for the creatures of the abyss. The deep trenches were so profoundly physically separated from each other that each trench had its own unique biota. When the flood came they mixed up and competed, and some went to the wall."

"There are critters out there that bore into wood," Mel said. "Clams, worms, crustaceans. They used to rely on the fall of wood from the continents to the seabed. Now they got a whole sunken forest to eat. Those guys are in hog heaven, all around us . . ."

Kelly caught Mike's glance. Buried in their steel tanks at the bottom of the ocean, Mel's people had become introverted, self-obsessed. Strange even by the standards of star-travelers who had spent eighteen years in a converted fuel tank. Kelly touched Mel's arm. "Maybe I could see my father now."

He seemed to come to himself, as if waking from a dream. "Sorry. Yeah. I'll take you to him and see if he woke up yet."

They walked on around the curve of the spherical tank, past window after window that revealed the endless dark of the ocean.

82

Edward Kenzie met his daughter in a storm shelter, a reinforced room right at the heart of one of the tanks. This room was evidently used as a kind of boardroom, for the walls were paneled with wood and a big triangular pine table dominated the floor. It was even carpeted, with a thick pile woven with the wedge-of-Earth symbol of Ark Two.

Edward Kenzie's heavy bulk was stuck in a wheelchair, and his head, entirely hairless, was covered in liver spots. He wore a business suit complete with tie tightly knotted around his neck. He permitted Kelly to kiss his cheek, and he gazed upon his second grandson, Eddie. He showed no signs of recognition, still less of joy. His massive presence in the chair frightened Eddie. The boy cried and clung to his father Masayo, who, as an illegal boarder of Ark One, Edward wouldn't acknowledge at all.

That was it for the family stuff. After that, everybody but Kelly, Edward and Dexter was excluded. They each sat at the center of one of the table's three sides. The silence stretched.

"I feel like I'm on trial," Kelly blurted.

"Ha!" Edward snapped. "That was always your way. Get the first word in and take control, right? Well, this isn't a trial. Tell you who should be on trial, that boyfriend of yours and the other illegals who robbed the Candidates and others of their righteous places on Ark One."

"It wasn't Masayo's choice. Anyhow what's done is done, and even you and all your bitterness can't change that, Dad."

"Bitterness? Is that what you think this is about?"

"Where do you want to start?" She glared at them both. "How I betrayed you, Dexter, by leaving Earth? Or how I betrayed you, Dad, by coming back?"

Dexter was red-faced with anger of a more confused kind. Kelly saw he must have fantasized about this situation, about having some kind of confrontation with the mother who had left him behind. Now she was here, he couldn't find the words.

"He lost his father too, you know," Edward said. "Don Meisel died at Alma, after—"

"I know! I know."

"Good job this boy had me to save him, don't you think?"

"Oh, don't preach at me, you old fraud. You know that if I hadn't volunteered to go back into the selection pool you'd have ordered me to. It was all about the mission. It always was. I was the best Candidate they had, I topped every assessment scale for years. In flight I was a competent commander. I even formed liaisons, I was ready to have more kids and fulfill my obligations regarding the gene pool."

"Yeah. You always had your fan club, superstar. Well, your great days are in your past, if you ever had any. And now here you are with nowhere to go and nothing but a squalling brat by some renegade. So let's talk about the mission. What went wrong?"

"You read the logs. You know what happened. I did what I had to do."

"Horseshit."

"It's true. In my judgment Earth II wasn't a viable option. And going on across another three decades to another hopeful case wasn't viable either. Coming back was the only choice."

Edward thumped the desk with his bony fist. "I say again, horseshit! I know you, lady. I force-grew you like a greenhouse tomato. I know your strengths and your flaws. Yes, you were by far the outstanding Candidate, you always were. You had brains, athletic abilities, leadership skills, charisma. Hell, you even had a good body and a face to match. But you had a flaw, one deep flaw, and that's your damn pride. You weren't going to accept being forced out by Wilson Argent. That kind of thing doesn't happen to Kelly Kenzie! So instead of applying your skills to some other aspect, you fucked over a multibillion-dollar mission and wrecked mankind's best hope of long-term survival in the process. And no justification about the good of the crew or the viability of the mission or how you longed to see your lost little kiddie again is going to wash with *me*." He was shouting now, his voice shrill, his body immobile. "You'd rather have led your crew to hell than follow Wilson or anybody else to paradise. So you fell to Earth, like Satan."

"You made me what I am, Dad, with your pushing and your lies. You never even told me this place existed! My flaws are your flaws."

Dexter said, "And did you make me, Kelly?"

Kelly felt a stab of shame that, in the heat of her confrontation with her father, she had briefly forgotten that Dexter was even in the room.

Edward snorted. "Christ. Look at us, the three of us stuck in a metal box at the bottom of the fucking sea, arguing like shit. What a family."

The door opened. Masayo stood there apologetically, holding Eddie's hand. Thandie was at his side. Masayo said, "I'm sorry. He missed his mom. I think he's a little scared."

"Come here, sweetie." Kelly held out her arms. Eddie ran to her, and with a boost from Masayo she lifted him up onto her lap.

Edward watched, his heavy, frog-like face unreadable. His burst of anger seemed to have exhausted him. "Well, at least you had the sense to come home, to the safest place there is."

Kelly said, "Safe?"

"Sure. The last refuge. That's the point of this place. Earth has had hard times before, so the brainiacs like Thandie Jones assure me. In the early days of its formation, when it was battered by moon-sized impac-tors, life always retreated to where it was safest. *Down and in.* You know there are life-forms down there in the deep crust that eat silica from the rocks and live off the mineral seeps and the heat, that have been there since the beginning. So now here we are too, living as best we can, off the fish and the black-smoker ecologies.

"But this Ark is only a way station. In the longer term we should fol-low the life into its deeper retreat. I'm talking about a merger, of human DNA with extremophiles. I'm talking about sending prokaryotic bugs laced with the substance of humanity down into the deep hot biosphere, and maybe even beyond. It will be like the great endosymbiotic mergers of the past, where we took organelles like mitochondria within the sub-stance of our cells. The essence of humanity sinking into the Earth, where a new genesis event will take place, in a hot Eden. At the heart of the Earth is a core of iron the size of the moon. Maybe our descendants will build cities on the surface of that inner world . . ." He fell silent, his rheumy eyes watering. He dug out a handkerchief, dabbed his eyes, blew his nose, and then coughed, his bulky frame making the wheelchair shud-der. "That's the vision." He was silent again.

Then he began to snore.

Thandie murmured, "The sub's ready to take you up, whenever you are."

"We should wait until grandfather wakes," Dexter said.

"Yes." Eddie was falling asleep too. He wriggled on Kelly's lap, trying to get his head comfortable against her belly. His weight, drawn by the pull of Earth, was huge, precious. "Yes, we'll wait."

Kelly wondered where Holle and Wilson and Venus were, right now.

Six

2068–2081

83

Steel Antionadi waited for Max Baker by the wet farm in the base of Halivah, as far down-pole as she could get from Wilson and his thugs. Nobody was around. Nothing stirred except the green things growing in their glop tanks.

She looked up along the length of the hull. She could see up-pole all the way to Wilson's nest in the dome. In the middle of the day it was bright, the arcs glowing warmly, and people came and went, old folk and kids, and babies gurgling in the air. A work party had taken out the equipment racks from Deck Six and was scrubbing the walls in a spiral pattern.

All this was background to Steel. What she looked for was other shippers like her, shipborn, where they clustered in their little territories, marked by scratchy graffiti signatures on the walls. To her they stood out against the hull's drab background like stars against the black sky. Every so often you would see one of them glare down at you, making eye contact like a zap from a laser beam. There was information in the way they clustered, information in the way they looked and laughed. Nobody much older than Steel even saw any of this going on.

Max Baker came swimming down. Slim and supple, he was good in the air, and he showed off for her, staying away from the guide ropes and handholds, letting the friction of the air slow him down. He was fifteen, she twenty-three. He somersaulted and landed neatly on a T-stool beside her. "Got 'em," he said without preamble.

She glanced around. Wilson said he had taken out the cameras, but everybody knew there were cameras and spies. But Wilson didn't watch the wet farm because shippers didn't work here mostly, and what he liked to watch was shippers, especially the younger ones. Still, she whispered. "The caps. You got enough?"

"Yeah. Exterior store."

He was talking about explosive charges intended for such uses as blowing hatches in emergency evacuations, or separating the shuttles from the hull's main body.

"Hid?"

"Yeah." He glanced up at Wilson's nest in the dome. "*He* won't see them."

"You sure you want to do this?"

He looked back at her, thoughtful, conflicting feelings visible in his face. She could see he was trying to big up in front of her. Well, they had had a relationship. There were so few of them on the hull that everybody had done some kind of fooling with everybody else, on a spectrum of warmth all the way from best buddies to moms 'n' pops. Every gradation of love and friendship had a name. There were even more names for kinds of enemies. With Max she had got as far as feelie-friends before they backed off. He was too young, or she was too old. Being with him reminded her of her time with Wilson, but sort of upside down, for with Max *she* had been the old one. Anyhow she liked Max, and respected him. She didn't want him to get himself killed, which was a strong possibility if they went ahead with their plan.

But he shrugged. "He's got Terese. Wilson. Cold-fucking her. That's not right."

She knew that even the shipborn word, cold-fucking, wasn't appropriate for what Wilson was doing to Max's twin. He was using Terese just as he had used Steel, before she grew too old for his taste, her bones too long, her breasts too big. It was a word Max was using for comfort, a lie he told to himself. That was Max's motive. Hers was deeper.

She grabbed his arm. "We'll do this, end the lies."

He nodded, anger and fear warring in his expression. "When?"

"You'll know."

84

A single gunshot in the night.

Holle sat bolt upright in her bunk, her blanket floating around her in the dark.

A gunshot. A sharp, percussive crack. It was unmistakable. She'd heard enough gunfire in the final years on Earth, but none since the chaos of the launch itself. She'd always suspected that the weapons confiscated from the illegals all those years ago had ended up cached somewhere. By Wilson, probably; he was the kind who would have thought ahead, even back then.

A gunshot in a pressure hull. She forced herself to stay still, to sniff the air, to pay attention to any popping in her ears, to listen for a breeze— any of the signs of a hull breach, of the loss of the air she and her team kept cycling around the ship all day and every day, every molecule of it having passed through human lungs ten billion times, the air that kept them alive. The inner hull was coated with self-sealing compounds, and ought to be able to withstand a single bullet hole. But how likely was it that only one shot was going to be fired today?

Then she heard shouting, a kind of chanting. "Break—out! Break—out!"

She closed her eyes for one heartbeat.

She had always known this day would come. She was forty-nine years old, and, enfeebled by confinement and zero gravity, felt and probably looked older. She didn't want to face a revolt of the young, however inevitable it was. Maybe she could just lock herself in here, burrow down under the blankets, listen to her Angel and think about her father, and wait until Wilson and his thugs sorted out the mess.

But she couldn't hide. Somebody was letting off a gun inside the pressure hull—*her* hull. It had to be stopped.

She moved, grabbing coverall and boots, dressing quickly. She pulled her Snoopy hat over her head, and tried to make contact with Wilson, Venus, anybody. But there wasn't even static.

It was Steel Antoniadi who had the gun.

When Helen Gray emerged from her cabin it was 0400. The big arc-light panels glowed a dim orange, casting just enough light so the watch crew could see.

And Steel was waving a gun around. Steel was in shadow, but the orange light glittered in her eyes, and reflected from the gun's metal shaft. The evidence of the one shot she'd fired so far was a crease in the padding that swathed the fireman's pole. It was an incredible sight. Helen, twenty-six years old, had never even *seen* a gun before, outside archive pictures, HeadSpace simulations. Now, anchored with one hand to a guide cable, here was Steel, one of Helen's oldest friends, holding the ugly black thing above her head. And Steel was shouting, rhythmically. "Break—out! Break—out! It's time, time, our time!"

Helen glanced up. Beyond the fireman's pole with its string of ragged cabins was a wall of steel that sliced off the upper section of Halivah. Wilson and his henchmen and their catamites now occupied the hull's upper four decks, barricaded off from those they governed by layers of mesh-floor partitions. It was dark up there, a mass of shadow, and there was no movement, no sign of any of Wilson's people coming down to take control.

But other crew did come, and were already gathering around Steel— the younger crew, the generation of shipborn. The youngest Helen saw was Max Baker, aged fifteen, brother of Wilson's latest lover. Steel herself was probably the oldest, at twenty-three. One woman, Magda Murphy, came swimming up with a baby in her arms, a fractious child, tired, a second-generation shipborn. Only Steel had a gun, but the others were armed with spanners and wrenches, knives, bits of piping. They belonged to different clans and gangs, as Helen could tell from their tattoos and dyed hair, coming together for this climactic moment.

Steel laughed as they gathered around her. When she opened her mouth you could see the gaps in her teeth, a legacy of the beating Wilson had given her when he'd finally thrown her out of his bed. Steel had clearly planned all this. Planned this moment, put together this ragtag rebellion, uniting the warring factions, entirely out of sight even of Helen, who thought she knew most of what was going on in the hull.

Helen was bleary with sleep, confused in the dark. This had to stop, before people got hurt—or worse. She pushed forward. "Steel!" she hissed. "What the hell are you doing?"

"Ending it," Steel said, loudly enough for the rest to hear. "Ending this farce!" She was wild, manic, her gestures uncontrolled.

Helen considered grabbing her arm, then looked at the gun and thought again. "What farce?"

"We're wasting our lives in this tank, our whole lives. Whatever this mission is, whatever it's for, *we're* just prisoners." She gestured at the woman with the baby. "Now we're having children of our own, more babies born into this cage. Do we want our kids taught the way we were? Do we want them to be *punished* for being smart?"

There was a rumble of support, and some of the crew hefted their weapons.

Helen understood the resentment. She was one of this middle generation herself, a generation for whom the ship was turning out to be a prison. She would be nearly forty when, if, the ship got to Earth III—old! Her life half used up, her youth gone. But she also understood that now they were under way, there was no choice but to go on. That was the hard, inhuman truth.

Now she did grab Steel's arm. "Steel, for God's sake, you'll get us all killed. We're in a spacecraft seventy light-years from Earth. It's not big enough for a revolution!"

Steel shook her off. "You've swallowed the lies," she said coldly. "You and those other fools who let Venus Jenning fill your head with rubbish. You go back to your cupola and your telescopes and your learning, you're a traitor to your own kind—"

"What lies? You can't mean the rubbish Zane talks."

"Rubbish, is it? You think you're a scientist, don't you? What's more likely, that we're in a spacecraft hurled between the stars, or we're in some HeadSpace tank in Denver or Alma or Gunnison?" She waved her hand. "They're out there, standing behind walls of glass, making notes, watching us the way we watch the plants in the glop tanks—looking on our useless lives, and they're *laughing* at us. And when our children start to grow, the prettiest and brightest will be picked out by Wilson's men. Taken up there to his palace of shit. Are we going to bow down to that? Are we?"

That, Helen suspected, was what this was all about, whether Steel realized it or not. This was Steel taking revenge on Wilson for the way he'd treated her.

But whatever Steel's real motive, she was hitting a raw nerve. The ragged chanting started again: "Break—out. Break—out." The crew were agitated, fired up, shouting, and they shook their blunt tools and bits of pipe. Helen shrank back, fear clenching her gut. And, as Steel waved her gun to lead them, the mob started to move, pulling themselves up toward the bridge.

Helen looked around. She thought she saw her mother at the hull's other extreme, by the hydroponic beds near the base. She swiveled in the air and threw herself that way.

With an audible hum the big arc lights flickered to their full brightness, and the hull was flooded with their glare.

On Wilson's bridge, as he called it, it had been Theo Morell who had pulled the big emergency handle that had fired up the arc lamps. Clinging to the fireman's pole he drifted down to the floor, cleared blankets and rugs out of the way, and tried to peer through the protective layers of mesh partitions to see what was going on.

This "bridge," in the hull's nose, was like a big domed room. Its walls had been draped with blankets and rugs, hand-made by the crew from scraps of worn-out uniforms. Wilson and his inner team had their own private sub-cabins, lashed to the floor and wall brackets. Venus had once said this was like Genghis Khan's yurt. On a rack attached to the fireman's pole were the remains of last night's feast, plates sticky with the remains of a mushroom risotto, an empty bottle of rice wine. Clothes, discarded carelessly, drifted in the air, and the private lavatory had its door open, and a fetid smell hung around it. Ordinarily the mess would have been cleaned up by servants, a detachment of the crew coming up through the floor hatches, before Wilson woke to begin his day. But—Theo checked his watch, it was only a little after 0400—nobody would be cleaning up tonight, or doing any more sleeping.

As the noise level rose Wilson's men started to push their way out of their cabins. There were four more aside from Theo and Wilson, all men, all about Wilson's own age of forty-nine, all illegals. They were all naked or dressed only in shorts, as Theo was. Other faces peered out of two of the cabins behind them, small, frightened, one boy, one girl, both about fourteen. Theo wasn't sure of their names.

Jeb Holden pushed his way over to Theo. "What the fuck you doing, soldier boy? Why you turn the damn lights on?"

"Didn't you hear the gunshot, asshole?"

"What gunshot?"

Theo heard a rumbling of voices, that distant chanting. "Break—out—break—out . . ." Not so distant anymore. He peered down through the mesh, and glimpsed some kind of group climbing up the fireman's pole, around the dangling cabins, toward the barrier. Steel Antoniadi was in the lead. Some of them were just kids. There was Max Baker beside Steel. Theo knew Max's twin sister was in Wilson's bed right now.

"Break—out—break—out—"

Jeb snapped, "What the fuck?"

"Just kids," Theo said, uneasy.

"Kids with fucking weapons. Steel's got a gun." Jeb lay flat on the floor and yelled through the mesh, his spittle splashing against the metal. "Steel, you fucking whore! This all because Wilson passed you over to the Pig, isn't it? Steel, you worn-out slut, put that fucking gun down now!" A descendant of Iowans, Jeb had actually been born on a raft, but when he was fourteen he had fought his way onto dry land and joined a local militia to fight off those who might have followed him. Then luck had left him in the right place at the right time to steal a place on the Ark, when it launched from Gunnison.

Steel and the rest were only a couple of meters beneath the floor now. She pointed her weapon at the partition. "The game's up, Jeb, you bastard. Open up the floor or it will be the worse for you."

"Oh, will it?" He laughed, and he spat at her, but most of the gob of phlegm stuck to the mesh, and Theo could see his fear in the way he clung to the partition, his fingers locked in the holes. "Whore! Fucking whore." He threw himself away from the partition and looked around. The others, including Dan Xavi who the catamites called "the Pig," were pulling on their pants. "Where's Wilson?"

"Right here." Wilson came floating out of his own cabin. Theo stared, amazed. Wilson already wore a cooling garment, and he was pulling the heavy outer layers of a pressure suit around him. Behind him Terese Baker, fifteen, skinny, was wrapped in a blanket, looking around with wide eyes. "Shit," Wilson said, "I don't fit in this suit anymore. I'm a fat bastard." He laughed.

Jeb's jaw was slack. "Boss—where are you going?"

"To the shuttle. Ride out the storm. Best thing—remove the focus, take away the prime target—you can see that. I always saw this day coming, even if you didn't. Call me when you've got the situation under control."

Jeb's fists bunched. "And how the fuck do we do that?"

Wilson reached back into his cabin and pulled out a sealed metal box.

He snapped, "Five seven four—open." The lock opened with a click to reveal a set of handguns. "Been keeping these since the roundup after we launched. Not much ammo, however. And we're one gun down. Probably stolen by that bitch Steel. Smarter than she looked." He shoved the box toward Jeb; the guns spilled and drifted in the air, rotating slowly. "Deal with it. Minimum bloodshed. Remember we need those fuckers to keep the ship going. Make an example of Steel, however." He had his suit intact now, his helmet over his head, his faceplate open. With a gloved hand he pulled a rug off the wall to reveal an airlock. He tapped at a pad, and the lock's inner door swung open. Beyond, Theo saw the bare interior of one of the hull's two shuttle gliders, lights snapping on.

"Break—out—break—out—"

Wilson paused at the lock and looked around. "I guess that's it." He glanced back at Terese, who stared at him wide-eyed. "Ah, the hell with it." He grabbed her arm and shoved her through the lock into the shuttle, a tangle of bare limbs. Then he followed head first, wriggling a bit to get through the lock, until his booted feet disappeared. The lock door swung closed, and a red warning band lit up.

"I don't believe it," Jeb said. "He's going to cast off! He could have taken us with him, the prick—"

"Not unless he wanted to lose the hull for good," Theo said. "Here." He plucked guns from the air and passed them around to Jeb, the others. He snapped a clip of ammunition into his own weapon. "I don't know what they'll try to do. Smoke us out, maybe."

"Let's shoot that bitch Steel through the head."

Theo tried to think. "Yeah. It might deter the rest. But we can't afford to go putting bullets through the hull. Suppose we spread around the rim of the floor. If we drop through the hatches, say three of us together—fire inwards at Steel—"

There was a roar like thunder. Theo glimpsed blinding light, billowing smoke. The floor opened up like a flower, metal panels hurled into the open space of the bridge. Dan Xavi was caught full in the chest by one panel and was flung back.

Theo heard screaming, like a child, but it was muffled. A ringing sound filled his head. He was stunned; he drifted, unable to move his legs, his head.

Then they came boiling up through the broken barrier, Steel, Max with his wrench, others. Eager hands grabbed Theo, pulled the gun from his hands, and dragged him down.

85

Under the silent stars, Venus was poised in space, inside the warm, clean bulk of her pressure suit, her booted feet strapped to the mobile servicing system, the manipulator arm. She'd been working on basic maintenance of the insulation blanket that, faded, pocked and worn, still coated the bulk of the hull.

She preferred to go EVA only during the night watch. During the day, when Wilson and his boys were awake and active, it paid to be inside the hull and alert. She sometimes thought that the only real purpose she and the other seniors served was to act as a buffer between Wilson and the rest.

Now she ordered the arm to lift her up and away from the ship. As she rose she took a good unencumbered look at the star field that slowly shifted around the ship, and the telescope platforms that still hovered around the hull, faithful companions. Even seventy light-years from Earth, twenty-seven years since the launch from Gunnison, the constellations hadn't changed drastically. But you did get a sense of motion if you knew what to look for, that faint blueing of the stars ahead of the hull, and of course that eerie disc of emptiness that endlessly pursued them, which Zane creepily called the mouth of Ouroboros.

She surveyed the ship laid out beneath her. Her gaze followed the arm down from her feet along its articulated length to the heavy ball-and-socket joint that attached it to the hull. She studied the ugly, stubby tank of the hull itself with its blankets and sensor platforms and airlocks, the Stars and Stripes ever more faded on its flank, the two remaining shuttle gliders like pinned moths, and the cupola, her own domain, glowing jewel-like near the base. She liked to make this kind of eyeball inspection from time to time, just to see if there was anything obvious the automated systems had missed. And it could happen, especially a multiple fault, such as a leak of some propellant in the precise spot where the pressure sensors were down. The longer the mission went on and as the systems aged—they were now far beyond the Ark's design envelope—the more such low-probability situations were likely to crop up. It was a habit she had picked up during training sessions with Gordo Alonzo, a seasoned astronaut. Never did any harm to walk around and kick the tires, he used to say . . .

She saw a kind of ripple around the belly of one of the shuttles— shuttle A, up near the hull's blunt nose. She'd seen this often enough in simulations. It was a sign of latches releasing, catching the ship's flood-lights as they opened. Then the shuttle shuddered, and with a kind of wrench, as if it was having trouble coming unstuck from a docking interface that hadn't been broken in decades, it lifted up and away from the Ark. Small attitude rockets squirted sprays of exhaust, fans of crystals that dissipated in the dark.

All this in utter silence.

Venus, shocked, tongued the switch on her comms unit. "Halivah, Jenning. Somebody just launched a shuttle. Control, what's going on in there?" If this was some kind of exercise, she ought to have heard about it. Damn it, she was *out here;* if the shuttle snagged on the manipulator arm it could be disastrous. But what kind of exercise would necessitate a physical undocking, such a waste of thruster fuel? They had lost enough to leaks already.

No reply. She tried to recall who should have been on overnight watch tonight. More disturbingly, she didn't even hear the usual hiss of static. There was a backup. She pulled a toggle from her belt and plugged it into a socket on the arm. This was an alternative comms channel passed through the arm's own cybernetic control circuitry. "Halivah, Jenning. Some asshole just launched shuttle A. Are any of you even aware that I'm out here? Halivah, this is—"

"Venus?"

"Holle? What the—"

"Thank Christ you called in. Listen. All hell is breaking loose in here. Steel Antoniadi, some of the young ones—they lost their heads. They're taking on Wilson."

"Shit." She'd always known this day would come; it was typical of her luck to be out of the Ark and unable to deal with it. "I'll come back." She reached for the manual arm control.

"No. No, Venus—*stay out there.* I think we might need you. I—"

The line went dead.

Venus toggled the comms switch with her tongue, fiddled with the plug in its socket in the arm. "Holle? Holle!"

Holle pulled off her comms hat. "Damn it, they cut the fiber link too. They know what they're doing."

Grace said, "Maybe you said enough."

"Break out, break out. Helen, you're sure that was what they were chanting."

"Yes!" Helen snapped.

"I think they're coming out of the nose," Grace murmured, looking up.

Helen, Grace and Holle huddled close together, here on Deck Fourteen, just above the hydroponics banks. This was the base of the hull, about as far as you could get from the bridge. Looking up along the length of the hull Holle could see the smashed-open bridge, still full of a pall of black smoke. Bits of broken floor partitions wheeled around the hull. Some of the crew were still in their cabins, strung out along the pole, peering out in bewilderment. Others were streaming away from the chaos in the nose of the hull, away from the smoke. People cried warnings, a sound like gulls, she thought, an odd fragment of memory surfacing amid the shock. Holle wondered how many had been deafened by the tremendous bang of the explosive charges that Steel had used to smash open Wilson's barricade, a noise that still seemed to reverberate from the walls of the battered hull.

"I wonder where they got the charges from," she muttered. "Maybe explosive bolts from the docking hatches, the emergency-separation stuff. But how did they get it inside the hull without sounding the alarms? And where—"

"Here they come!" Grace yelled.

Whatever small war had gone on in the hull nose was evidently concluded. Steel and her party came down out of the smoke, clinging to dangling cables and wall handhelds. They were all blackened, their clothes shredded; some of them looked injured. But that gun in Steel's hand was clearly visible. She waved it around, triumphant.

And they had prisoners, men held by their arms and legs and hair. Holle tried to count them. Naked, bloodied, the men all looked the same. There should have been six up there, Wilson and his five "advisers," his five closest thugs. She counted three. One might have been Theo; none looked like Wilson. They weren't resisting.

Steel seemed to be directing them down toward a particular equipment rack on Deck Seven or Eight. Some of the rebels had gone on ahead to move the rack, exposing the curved wall behind it. It looked to Holle as if some kind of work had been done on that hidden section of wall, behind the rack. Now a couple of Steel's people started to pull away a mesh covering, and turn screws in the panels.

Holle understood immediately, and saw that Helen had been right about what they intended to do. Holle hadn't believed it. "No," she breathed. "There's no water tank behind that section. Just the fuselage. No, no—"

One of the captured men started struggling, screaming. Maybe he had figured out what was happening too. It might have been Dan Xavi, the one the mistreated children called the Pig. He almost got free, and the rebels fell on him, clustering like flies around a wound. Somebody got Xavi around the neck. Another got hold of his arm and did a kind of somersault, so the arm was twisted, breaking with a sharp snap. Fists slammed into his mouth and nose and eyes, and Xavi's screams were choked by a bubbling noise.

"They've lost it," Grace said. "They're going to kill him."

"He doesn't matter," Holle said. She was still watching the rebels patiently removing screws from that wall panel. "It's our fault. My generation. Wilson, you prick, you couldn't control yourself. And you madman, Zane, look what you've done! OK, OK." She made an effort to calm down, to think. There might only be seconds left. "We have to get people to shelter. Somewhere airtight."

Helen said, "The cupola. The shuttles—"

"Not shuttle A. Venus said somebody launched it, it's gone. Wilson, maybe. Shuttle B, and the cupola. Get everybody in there, one or the other. Everybody who will come." But the rebels wouldn't come, no matter what she said. "And get Zane. Don't forget Zane. Move, move!"

Grace cast one despairing glance at Helen. Holle saw a lifetime of love and helpless anxiety compressed into that one expression.

Then the three of them scattered, launching themselves toward knots of bewildered people.

The rebels shoved Jeb Holden and Theo Morell up to the curving wall, behind the detached equipment rack. Theo could see what they were doing, removing screws that secured some kind of temporary panel there. Jeb was weeping steadily. Tears and snot scattered in the air every time he shook his head. Dan Xavi was already dead, Theo could see. Blood-smeared rebels hovered around his twisted body.

And they were opening up the hull.

Theo struggled against the grip of those who held him. He couldn't help it. But they only held him tighter, and some bastard launched a barefoot kick into his ribs. It was one thing he'd learned today, that this new generation who had grown up in microgravity were a hell of a lot better at fighting in it than any of Wilson's men. They seemed to have an instinctive grasp of how to use their bodies: how to pivot in the air, when to grab something to push against so they could punch you or kick or head-butt or barge.

He gave up struggling, and shook his head to clear it. Think, Theo! If you don't think now you're not going to get the chance to work it out tomorrow.

"You can see what we've done," Steel said. "What we're ready to do. Today's the day, Theo Morell. Today's the day we expose the lie. Today's the day we break out of this stupid sim tank, and then—"

"And then what? Even if you're right—what do you think you are going to do, Steel? Take over Denver? Build a raft? Oh, God! This is crazy."

There was a flicker of doubt in Steel's eyes. Maybe she hadn't actually thought it through that far, not past her fantasizing of this moment of rebellion and revenge. But she was full of momentum. "At least *this* will be over," she said. "The lies, the wasted lives."

"I remember Denver flooding," Jeb Holden said, and he coughed, spraying blood and snot. "I remember Gunnison and Alma. I remember how I fought my way onto this ship. Broke my knuckle on some fucking Candidate's face. I remember the launch, all those fucking bombs. It was real! Can't you stupid kids just listen—"

Max Baker silenced him with a slam to the head with his heavy wrench. Jeb went limp, floating.

They had got the last screw out. Now, Theo saw, that plate was held in place only by the pressure of the air within the hull. Since the launch they had all, including illegals and gatecrashers, been trained for decompression accidents. Theo knew that a hole the size of that plate, around a meter square, would drain the hull of its air in seconds—twenty seconds for the pressure to reduce to a tenth nominal, another twenty seconds for it to reduce by another factor of ten.

Steel stared into his face. His reaction seemed to mean as much to her as the reality of the moment. "Are you ready, Theo Morell? Ready to face your controllers?"

He tried to dredge up something to say, to stop this, at least to stall her. "You've won, damn it. You've beaten Wilson. Isn't that enough? We can put the ship back together. We can talk about how we go forward, how we live together . . ."

Steel just laughed. Max took a jemmy and slid the edge under the loose plate. He braced himself on a bracket, ready to use his weight to pry it loose.

Theo looked at them, at Steel with her battered face, at fifteen-year-old Max Baker, at Magda Murphy, who even now held on to her baby. They could all be dead in seconds. "Steel, for God's sake, I swear, I swear by my life, my mother's—nobody's lying to you. Not about this. The ship is real. If you take that hatch off you'll kill us all."

Steel began to say something.

But Max roared, drowning out any further talk, a lifetime of confinement and frustration redeemed in a single moment, and he slammed his body down on the jemmy. The plate flew back.

The decompression was an explosion, a deafening thunderclap.

Theo saw the loose plate whirl like a leaf and fly out through the hole in the wall. There was a tearing in his lungs, and a powerful pain in his ears, as if iron splinters were being driven into his head, and he remembered to open his mouth wide. People squirmed around him, but their screams were snatched away on the howling wind.

He faced the hole in the wall, a hole in the world, and the wind shoved him in the back. He saw the stars with his naked eyes. Even now he might have a chance, if he could hang on until the air was gone, the wind subsided, and find a pressure suit before he blacked out. But strong hands grabbed him and pinned his arms to his side and shoved him out, bodily.

He spun slowly. He saw the ship's outer wall with its pocked insulation blanket, and the brightly lit hole, square and neat, receding from him. Suddenly he was beyond the wall—*outside the hull,* naked. A kind of fight was going on, people climbing over each other to stay inside the hull. But they were tumbling out after him. Theo saw a child, writhing, helpless in space.

He was cold. He couldn't see anymore. The pain in his chest was agonizing, tearing, burning. He thought of his mother.

Something burst inside his head.

The decompression wind was already dying. The thinning air dumped its water vapor in a mist that pearled in the glow of the arc lights.

Holle kept her mouth gaping wide. The gases in her belly swelled agonizingly before escaping in an explosive fart. She knew she had only seconds of consciousness—ten seconds maybe, less given the way she was using up her oxygen in an adrenaline-fueled burst of action.

She looked around. She had thrown herself in among the rebels, and even before the hull breach she had started shoving them down toward the airlock to Shuttle B. Now those left here were drifting, convulsing, going limp. Frost formed over their mouths and noses, and their flesh swelled as water turned to vapor in their blood and tissues. Even now they could be saved. But Holle could not save them all.

One more.

She saw Magda Murphy, stranded away from the walls, the handholds. Magda had her mouth wide open, the way they had all trained for this contingency. Magda was straining toward her baby, somehow she'd let go of her, but she was out of reach. Astonishingly the baby was still alive, apparently still conscious. Holle saw her flex her tiny fingers.

Holle could reach either Magda or the baby. Not both. An instant choice. Magda could have more kids. She grabbed Magda, plucking her out of the air. Magda struggled feebly, reaching for the kid. Her vision fogging, her flesh crawling with pain, Holle hauled the two of them down to the shuttle lock.

This would never happen again, Holle promised herself. Never.

86

From her perch on the manipulator arm Venus saw the detached panel come tumbling out, and then bits of garbage and a spray of mist, and bodies that wriggled like landed fish. She was glad she was too far away to make out who it was, especially the children.

All this she saw from within the warmth of her suit, the hum of her life-support fans in her ears, immersed in her own slightly musty smell. She considered diving down there to help, maybe detaching herself from the arm and using her SAFER jet pack to plunge in among the tumbling people, wrestle them back into the light through that hole. But it would be a futile gesture. Even if they were not already dead there was no air in the hull, no way she could get them into shelter in time. And she'd probably just doom herself. Best to wait and then descend on the arm, and enter the hull in her suit, and see who was left to save.

If anybody. The thought hit her that *nobody* might have survived, nobody but her. That she might soon be crawling back into a hull become an airless tomb, alone, seventy light-years from Earth.

There was a sparkle of light in the corner of her eye. It was the shuttle, blipping its attitude engines. She felt an immediate stab of relief. Of course she wasn't alone, at least somebody had survived in the shuttle. Now it must be maneuvering to dock with its dedicated port once more.

But she saw, shocked, that the vernier blips were pushing the shuttle *away* from the hull. The motors fired again and again, and exhaust products pulsed out of their tiny nozzles in brief fountains. But each tiny thrust was the wrong way; the shuttle accelerated away from the hull and toward the stars.

No, not to the stars. To the warp bubble. And Venus saw it. The shuttle had been sabotaged, the control circuitry reversed. Sabotaged purposefully to send whoever was hiding out inside it into the bubble wall.

At last whoever was aboard got the message. A new constellation of pulses shone around the rim of the shuttle, its stubby wings. You want to fly *down*, you used the controls that should take you *up* . . . But it was too late to kill the momentum already built up.

A figure in a pressure suit came squirming out of an airlock. Once free of the shuttle, it was propelled forward by a kick from a SAFER backpack. She recognized the suit, from the ident markings on the leggings. It was Wilson Argent's.

It took long seconds for the warp tide to crumple the shuttle hull, like an invisible hand crushing a paper toy. When the pressure cabin gave way the atmosphere gushed out in a dazzle of water-ice crystals. A single body drifted in space, naked and slight, before falling into the warp barrier to become a bloody comet.

87

"It's OK. Not long now, honey. We'll get through this. It's OK. Just hold my hand . . ."

"Oh God. Oh shit. Why did this have to happen why now? Why today? I can't believe this is happening to me. . . ."

"I want Billy-Bob! Dad, I want my Billy-Bob! You wouldn't let me go back for him . . ."

There was nothing Holle could do, not until this shuttle was unpacked. She estimated there were forty people crammed in here, shoved in by herself and Helen Gray, forty in a cut-down one-use-only minimum-mass landing glider meant to take twenty-five tops. She could barely move because of the people around her, people pushing against her back and belly and pinning her legs, their bodies around her head. It was a crowd in three dimensions, people shoved up against each other every which way.

And of those forty, many, ten or fifteen, had been seriously injured. People had grossly swollen limbs, hands, feet, faces. A little boy cried out, over and over, that he was blind. One woman was coughing up sprays of blood in huge racking convulsions, her lungs obviously torn; the people around her were trying to shove her through the crowd toward a wall, to keep her from covering the rest with her blood and snot and phlegm.

A screen on the shuttle's control console, relaying an image from a camera in the airlock, showed Venus, an alien figure in a bright white spacesuit *inside* the hull, in an environment of cabins and food packets and drink cartons and drifting toys, laboring to make Halivah habitable again. They were lucky Venus had been out of danger. Holle made a mental note. From now on there had to be somebody in a pressure suit at all times, a faceplate snap away from independent life support.

Until she could get out of here Holle could do nothing but endure. She tried to tune out the weeping and the rasping breaths.

"If I get my hands on the asshole who thought it was a good idea to take off a fucking hull plate I'll rip out what's left of their lungs with my bare hands . . ."

"It's OK. He's fainted, that's all. I didn't notice, he can't fall over in this crowd. He's just fainted. As soon as we're out of here he'll be fine."

"No, you're wrong. This man's dead. Jay's dead! Look at him!"

"I can't see! Dad, why can't I see?"

There was a hammering on the shuttle hatch. Holle glimpsed Venus through the thick window, clumsy in her stiff pressure suit, hauling at the handle.

The hatch opened. Holle felt her ears pop, and she had a spasm of fear about more air loss, but the pressure drop was only slight. The people closest to the hatch immediately started to spill out, with gasps of relief. Once out they turned and helped Venus pull out those who followed. Soon there was a cloud of bodies drifting away from the hatch, in pairs and threes.

As soon as she could move, Holle shoved her way ahead of the rest. It was an immense relief to reach the comparatively open space of the hull, to stretch her arms and legs wide, to breathe in air that smelled clean if faintly metallic, air straight from the emergency reserve tanks.

She looked around. Venus had backed off to the fireman's pole, where she had tethered herself and was dismantling her pressure suit. Helen Gray was at the shuttle lock, supervising the evacuation. Holle glanced along the length of the hull, and saw that a similar unpacking was going on at the lock that led to the cupola, another fan of weary, injured people working their way out into the open air. Grace Gray was screening those who emerged, and gently diverting the injured.

A baby floated by. Naked, its skin so swollen it had become twice its size, it was obviously dead. Holle couldn't recognize it, didn't know if it was Magda's baby, the baby she had failed to save. For a second she froze, guilt and doubt and a kind of hideous self-consciousness pressing down on her.

"Holle."

Venus, down to her cooling undergarment, was watching her steadily. Venus who'd known her since she was a kid, Venus from the Academy. Holle pushed her way over and grabbed on to a handhold. "You OK?"

Venus laughed. "Me? Hell, yes. Just another EVA for me. What happened in here?"

"A rebellion of the shipborn."

"They smashed open the hull. It's a miracle you weren't all killed. What was it, some kind of suicide pact?"

"No," said Helen Gray. She came drifting over from the shuttle lock to join them. "I think they were trying to tunnel out."

"*Tunnel out?*"

"Out of the sim . . . It was all those ideas of Zane's."

Holle said, "We never took this stuff seriously enough. Bloody Zane. Well, we took it to Wilson often enough, and he didn't listen, and it cost him his life."

"Maybe not," Venus said. "I saw shuttle A. It detached from the hull, actually undocked. This was before the pressure hull blew out."

Holle shook her head. "Typical Wilson. He probably had that move planned for years."

Venus described the sabotage she suspected. "The shuttle was wrecked. But I think Wilson might have survived—I saw him bale out, or anyhow somebody in his pressure suit. If his SAFER holds out he's probably back at one of the locks already."

But Holle was only half-listening. "You say the shuttle was destroyed."

One of their two shuttles, gone just like that. All because of Wilson and his incompetence and craven selfishness.

Venus was grave. "We'll have to figure out how to get by without it."

That baby corpse drifted across Holle's eyeline, buffeted by stray breezes in the new air. The loss of a shuttle didn't matter a damn if they couldn't get through today.

Helen touched her arm. "Holle? I think my mother's getting overwhelmed. I'll go help her."

Holle nodded. "I'll come with you. Venus, can you handle the rest?"

For one second Venus held her gaze, and Holle could see the challenge in her eyes. Suddenly this was a key moment, the start of a new chapter. Who was Holle to be giving the orders? But Venus backed off, subtly. "Sure. What 'rest'?"

"Get together a work crew. We need to nail down the basic systems. Ensure the integrity of the hull around that patch. The explosive decompression might have caused some flaws elsewhere. And check over the ECLSS systems. The hydroponic beds—"

"They ought to be OK," Helen said. "The plants can stand an hour or so of vacuum; the loss was only a few minutes."

"All right. Check them anyhow. What else?"

"How about positioning?" Venus said. "We just had an air rocket venting out the side of the hull. The GN&C systems should have compensated, but I don't know if the verniers fired to push us back."

"If they did, I didn't hear. Check it out. We don't want to drift into the warp wall."

"We'd better have somebody ready to meet Wilson if he does come back."

Holle shrugged. "Cuff him to a stanchion. We'll deal with him later. Venus, anything else you can think of, just handle it."

Venus was down to her underwear. "I'll grab a coverall and get on it."

"OK. Oh, and Venus—" She moved closer to her, and murmured, "Get a party and do a sweep through the hull. Collect the dead. These drifting corpses. Shove them somewhere out of sight for now, up on Wilson's bridge, maybe. And log the survivors. Come on, Helen. Let's go help your mother."

88

The crushing in the cupola had been even worse than in shuttle B. People were emerging clutching their ribs and struggling for breath, and one couple were holding a limp little boy, desperately pummeling his chest and breathing into his mouth.

Among these drifting survivors was Zane, looking cowed, frightened. Holle felt a surge of savage anger. She wondered which of his alters had come out to help him cope with this crisis he had done so much to trigger. And there was Jeb Holden, one of Wilson's closest associates, a brute of a man now naked and blood-smeared. He pulled away from the rest, evidently looking for a blanket, something to cover his body.

Grace, hanging on to a handrail, was trying to get the apparently unharmed to help her, while she sorted the rest into rough groups according to their injuries. Her coverall front was sprayed by blood and bits of grayish flesh. Chunks of somebody's lung, Holle suspected. Grace was functioning, but she looked bewildered. Holle always had to remind herself that Grace wasn't a doctor, even though for sixteen years since the Split she had been trying to fill the hole left by Mike Wetherbee.

Holle grabbed Helen's hand, and they dived over to Grace's side. "Grace, we're here. Tell me how we can help."

Grace looked at her vaguely. "There were around twenty in the cupola. Twenty! I thought we'd all die in there. I estimate twelve seriously injured."

Holle nodded. "OK. We had about forty in shuttle B, many injured . . ."

She didn't have to complete the arithmetic. Since the Split the crew's numbers had grown, minus some deaths and plus several births, grown in an unplanned way that would have horrified the social engineers back in Denver. A total of around sixty saved in the shuttle and the cupola together meant they had lost several lives to the decompression. And, glancing around the hull, her first estimate was that maybe a third of the survivors were wounded. A third of the crew of a half-wrecked ship, incapacitated.

One step at a time, Holle. "What about the injured?"

"Some crushing from the crowding in the cupola. The rest, what you'd expect from exposure to vacuum. Cases of hypoxia—we may see some brain damage. There are cases of temporary blindness from neurological effects. A few cases of the bends, caused by air bubbles in the bloodstream. I'd recommend using the cupola as a high-pressure chamber to relieve those symptoms."

"Do it."

"The ebullisms—the swelling, caused by the vaporization of water in the tissues—ought to subside in a few hours. They look worse than they are, mostly. Some internal injuries due to gases trapped in the bowels. Damaged eardrums. Anybody with any congestion or catarrh will have suffered. We've also got injuries relating to the explosion at Wilson's bulkhead. Blast injuries, burns, broken bones, hearing loss—"

"There must be damaged lungs."

Grace nodded. "Two in this group."

"Yeah," Helen said. "More in the shuttle group."

All the crew, and every shipborn child since before they could walk, had been trained to open their mouths wide in the event of a decompression. Try to hold your breath and the expanding gases in your lungs just ripped apart your delicate pulmonary tissues and capillaries, and then trapped air was forced out of the lungs into the thoracic cage, from where it could get directly into the general circulation through ruptured blood vessels. The final result was massive air bubbles moving through the body and lodging in the heart and the brain. But, despite all the training, some people always followed their instincts to hold their breath when the crisis came.

Grace said, "We're going to have a host of cases of bronchiectasis. Damaged lungs. You're left vulnerable to infection for the rest of your life. I'm concerned about our stock of antibiotics."

"We'll figure that out."

"Some are worse than that," Grace said bleakly. "I don't believe there's anything we can do for them. I don't think even a medic with the proper training could—"

"It's OK," Holle said. "We'll deal with this. Helen, go round up some volunteer paramedics. You know who to ask." As Helen pushed away, Holle spoke quietly to Grace. "We need to set up some kind of triage system. Three priorities," she said, thinking aloud. "First, those who will recover but need immediate treatment. The burns, the bends victims. Second, those who will recover in time with minimal attention. People with swellings, this temporary sight loss you talked about."

Grace looked away. "And third—"

"Those who won't survive. The ripped lungs. We'll put them some-where. Hell, we'll put them in the shuttle, away from the rest."

"What do we tell them?"

"Lies. We'll have Helen or one of her volunteers round up lovers, parents, whatever."

"I can't operate like that."

"That's OK. You don't have to. I'll stay with you. You just indicate to me which category each patient is in. I'll do the rest." She listened to the words coming out of her own mouth. Could she really do these things? Well, she must, so she could.

"Holle, there's one more thing. Steel Antoniadi. She survived. She's still in the cupola. Everybody knows she led the rebel attack. I thought it was best if she stayed out of sight."

"Good thinking. I'll talk to Venus about that, about keeping her safe somewhere—"

There was a tap on her shoulder. "Holle."

She turned.

The punch in the mouth was hard enough to send her sailing through the air. Somebody fielded her, and she grabbed a handhold and shook her head to clear it.

It was Magda Murphy. Her arms and hands were swollen; that punch must have hurt her own fist like hell. Magda came up against an equipment rack on the wall, spun in the air, and used her booted feet to kick off and throw herself at Holle again. Somehow Grace Gray got in the way. She grabbed Magda around the waist, and the two of them, deflected by Grace's momentum, drifted away.

Magda pointed at Holle and screamed, "You left my baby to die! You left her to die! All you had to do was reach out—" She struggled, but Grace held on tightly. The strength went out of Magda, and she broke down into wretched sobbing. "I'll never forgive you for saving me rather than her, Groundwater. Never."

89

Three days after the blowout, with the situation in the hull moderately stabilized, Holle led Grace and Venus to the cabin Wilson had been assigned, on the fireman's pole at around Deck Eight. He had been confined here the whole time since he had emerged from the airlock in his pressure suit, having abandoned shuttle A and Terese Baker to their encounter with the warp bubble wall.

Holle pushed her way in without ceremony. The others followed. Holle lodged herself into a corner of the cabin, and let her eyes adjust to the dark.

Wilson just stared as the women came in. He wore a grimy, much-used T-shirt and shorts. He was floating in the cluttered cabin, surrounded in the air by an unrolled sleeping bag, a sponge backside-wiper, a food packet. His muscular legs were drawn up against his chest, and he was holding on to his bare feet with his big hands. The T-shirt bore some kind of logo, a slogan impossibly faded, a relic of Earth, even of the days before the flood. Oddly Holle found herself wishing she could read it, read about some long-ago sports event or rock band's tour.

There was no sign that Wilson had been doing anything in here, no handheld, no books. There wasn't even a lamp glowing; the only light seeped in from the big hull arcs through seams in the walls. His skin looked oily, and he smelled of stale sweat. She wondered how long ago he'd washed, in one of the microgravity showers that she had finally got up and running again. But he looked healthy. He was the only survivor aside from Venus who had not had to live through the decompression.

Wilson and Venus were Holle's colleagues from their long-gone days as Candidates. Now they were all nearly fifty, their bodies heavy, their expressions hard, their hair graying, their skin lined, their souls dulled by the tedious horror of half their lives spent aboard this Ark. She never would have imagined they would end up this way. But Wilson looked the most composed, confident. He even grinned at Holle.

Grace Gray looked intensely uncomfortable to be here.

Holle said, "Let's just start. We can't be overheard, we aren't being recorded. What we say today passes between the four of us, and nobody else."

Wilson snapped, "And what's so special about 'the four of us'?"

"We're the people with power on the ship. Venus with her planet-finding and GN&C. Grace the doctor—"

Wilson jumped in again. "And you, Holle? You're the plumbing queen, right? And me? What power have I got, in this new world of yours?"

"You're the only specialist in the hull's external systems we have. You're also the only Earth-trained shuttle pilot left aboard. So you've got value, Wilson."

"And that's the reason I haven't been thrown out the hatch, is it?"

Venus murmured, "We never discussed sanctions against you, Wilson, not yet—"

Holle overrode her. "Yes. That's all that's kept you alive, Wilson."

Wilson glanced at a smoldering Venus, an increasingly withdrawn Grace. Then he focused on Holle, perceiving she was the instigator here. "I was competent," he said coldly. "I ran this damn hulk for twenty years."

"But you shut yourself off from the crew. You didn't see Steel's rebellion coming, and you had no countermeasures in place when it broke. What kind of competence is that?"

"So if this isn't some kind of trial, what is it?"

"I think it's a *coup d'état*," said Venus, watching Holle.

They were all silent, waiting for Holle to speak. So the moment had come. Holle took a breath, her heart beating hard. She hoped that none of them could see her deep uncertainty and self-doubt. But they surely knew her too well for that.

She knew what she was letting herself in for, by stepping forward like this. She'd seen how Don Meisel had hardened when he was banished out of the Academy and sent to the front line. She remembered what she herself had seen the day she had got separated from her father when they evacuated the Academy, as Denver drowned. She remembered the nightmares that used to wake Mel in the night. She had grown up with the flood, but she had always been protected from the worst of it—the harshness of its human consequences, the cruelty, the arbitrariness of life and death. Now all the protective layers had been stripped away from her, even Wilson's brutal control. And it was her turn.

But she reminded herself why she was doing this. Magda's baby. Those long minutes in the crowded shuttle. Never again, no matter what it cost her personally.

The others were waiting for her to speak.

"I'm taking over," she said. "Simple as that. I don't care what you call it. No elections, no process, no show of hands." She looked around. "Who else is there to do it? You, Wilson? The crew would destroy you the way they ripped Dan Xavi apart. You, Venus? Wilson faced you down once before; you couldn't control him now."

Venus was looking at her as if at a stranger. "And if I did stand against you, would you turn off my air?"

"That's the question, Holle," Wilson said, probing. "So you have control of the air and water. The only way you can use that power is to withhold those basic essentials from the crew. Are you really going to do that? It violates the most basic principles of the Ship's Law we evolved under Kelly, and the Bill of Rights I signed back in '49."

"Yes, it does. But all that matters now, Wilson, is survival. We have to last out thirteen more years to Earth III. Thirteen! We can't afford another rebellion like Steel's. And we can't afford another self-indulgent autocrat like you, sucking up the resources and corrupting the kids."

"And so, instead, we've got you," Venus said.

Wilson laughed again. "I got to congratulate you, Holle. How long have you been planning this? Was it from the beginning, from the launch? Or was it even before then, back when we had to choose an aspect of the Ark's design to specialize in? Maybe even then you saw control of the life support as your way to ultimate power."

"I've been planning it since I was hanging in the vacuum in this fucking hull. That's how long."

"And you'd switch off the air if you had to."

"If it meant saving the majority—yes." She looked at them, one by one, forcing them to meet her eyes. "Unless you have any more to say, this is the end of that discussion."

None of them challenged her. Grace had said nothing at all.

But Wilson kept grinning. "Well, well. Harmless little Holle. The mouse that roared. So what's next on the agenda?"

"Survivability," Holle said immediately.

Venus nodded cautiously. "Go on."

"Since the accident we've secured the ship and its basic systems. Now we need a review and rebuild from prow to stern, fixing what got broken in the blowout. And I want to build in more security against failure modes, even against another hull breach. Design redundancy was compromised after the Split. We need to robustify the ship. Is there any way we can improvise leak-proof internal bulkheads, for instance? And we need a rota of crew with suitable equipment waiting in the refuges at all times, the shuttle and the cupola. Also at least one crew member, maybe two, partially pressure-suited. I want to up the crew training for the case of decompression, and other failure modes like fire and power loss. Wilson, you and I will work on this, figure out some kind of strategy."

"OK. But I remind you that it was sabotage that caused the blowout. No amount of redundancy will protect you from that, ultimately."

"True. But maybe a full restoration of surveillance systems will. Venus, I want you to work with Grace on that."

Venus frowned. "Why us?"

"Because you, Venus, have the technical expertise, and Grace already knows the crew individually as well as any of us; she's their doctor. I want to catch any more rebels before they get a chance to act. Grace, if you notice odd patterns of behavior or unexplained absences from work details or whatever, you come to me."

Grace looked deeply unhappy. She hadn't spoken since they'd come together. Now she said, "If I really was a doctor I'd say that violated patient confidentiality."

"Well, you're not really a doctor, so that's not an issue. Oh, and do something with Zane."

"Like what? Cure him?"

"No. There's no hope of that. Abandon the therapy program, except for some kind of monitoring. We need Zane's expertise. But keep him away from the crew, the younger shipborn."

"How? Shall I keep him in a cage?"

"If you have to."

Wilson said, "So what else?"

"We're short of resources. We lost a lot in the trauma—the blowout, the explosion, the fire on your bridge. We were already under strain; after the Split our recycling loops were cut in half. Now we're going to have to aim for a much tighter closure of the loops. Really, we need to achieve one hundred percent from now on. And that's going to begin with the disposal of the dead from the blowout."

"We've buried dead before," Wilson said. "Over the side, and out to the warp bubble, and *poom.*" He spoke flippantly, but handling their occasional "space burials" had always shown Wilson at his authoritative best. With due ceremony the bodies were sent out of the airlocks, accompanied by Wilson's intonation of the old US Navy's service: "We do now commit this body to the deep . . ."

Holle said, "Sure. But things have changed, Wilson. We've always encouraged people to think of recycling the dead through the ECLSS systems."

Wilson grinned blackly. "Feeding loved ones into the furnaces chunk by chunk."

"Do you know what percentage did that so far? Less than twenty percent."

Wilson shrugged. "It wasn't something I wanted to make a stand on."

"Well, now we need to reclaim every drop of water, every scrap of organic material, and that includes corpses. We need to work out some variant of Wilson's funeral procedure to honor those who give up their bodies to the furnaces. Make it clear that the greatest contribution you can make to the Ark is to keep it running for those who outlive you."

"Have people will it," Venus suggested. "Before they die. Lodge it in the archive. That might reduce the conflict after death."

"Good idea. And Grace, you may need to work on some education program about reducing the taboo of consuming the remains of the dead."

"That won't be hard for the shipborn," Grace said. "They've grown up knowing that every sip of water they take has already passed through other people's bladders a zillion times. They don't have the same hang-ups as the older crew. *We* will be the problem. I'll look into it."

"You need to think about the refuseniks," Wilson said. "There will always be some."

"They won't get the choice," Holle said flatly. "OK. Then there's the question of punishment for the actions leading up to the blowout."

"Ah." Wilson sat back and folded his arms. "So this is some kind of trial after all."

Holle shook her head. "No. Listen, Wilson, you're indispensable. But you are going to have to survive in this ship, and it's a damn small place. I'm not putting you on trial, you won't be formally punished. I won't even criticize you in public. You need to make some kind of recompense of your own. Find ways to apologize to the kids you hurt, and their families. That's up to you."

Wilson nodded. "Well, that's pragmatic."

Grace said, "If we aren't punishing Wilson—who?"

Venus said, "I'm guessing Steel Antionadi."

Holle nodded. "Right. For the crime of a rebellion that nearly killed us all. We have to make an example of her."

Wilson grinned again. "Why not just say it straight out? You're going to execute her."

Grace laughed nervously. But Holle kept her face expressionless.

Venus gasped. "Are you serious? Holle, the kid was abused by this gorilla here, she had her head filled with rubbish from Zane—what chance did she have? Her crime was our fault, our generation's."

Grace said, "And to execute her—in Walker City we had crime, we had rape and murder. But we rejected capital punishment, the mayors did. We were too small a society for that. Each of us would have been too close to the executioner, each of us would become a killer. And compared to this crew, we were a mob. Everybody will be tainted by this."

"Good," Holle said.

Venus said, "Besides, Holle, you said we can't afford any more losses. Steel is one of the brightest of her cadre. Even if you consider the rebellion, she showed vision, leadership, planning, even a kind of military skill. She managed to unite all those teenage gangs. And she was thorough. She cut the comms links, including the backup. She sabotaged the shuttle. All in complete secrecy—"

"I don't want leadership," Holle said. "Not among the shipborn. I don't want vision, or idealism, or curiosity, or initiative. I don't want courage. All I want is obedience. It's all I can afford, until we're down on Earth III and the day comes when we can crack open the domes and let the kids just walk away. Yes, she's the best of her generation, and that's why she's such a danger. We have to make the process as public as possible. In fact that's the point. But in the end, yes, she'll die. Grace, I'll expect you to make recommendations on how we do that, fast and painless."

Wilson blew out his cheeks. "Wow! You really have been thinking this through, haven't you?"

Venus shook her head. "I don't know what to say."

"Then don't say anything. Just accept my verdict."

"I can't believe we're having this conversation. I've known you almost your whole life, Holle. Now you're imposing a regime of total surveillance backed up by total power. Is this *you*?"

Holle faced her. "Remember all those theoretical debates, back in the Academy? About the conflict inherent in a situation like this between human rights and the need to sustain life itself? The truth is, no matter what system we tried, we were always going to fail in the end. The only way we can survive now is to impose total control from the center. And the only right the crew have left is the right to a chance of surviving the journey."

Grace murmured, "Maybe Holle's right. It's not our fault. Nobody should be made to endure a journey like this. Nobody should condemn a generation of children to grow up in a cage."

"It was necessary," Venus said. "Or so the mission planners thought."

And maybe, Holle thought, clinging to Grace's words, the crew would be able to forgive her.

"Well," Grace said. "This has been—eye-opening. So is that all?"

"For now," Holle said. "Let's get to work."

Without another word, and apparently with relief, Grace arrowed out through the hatch, with an unconscious skill born of decades in free fall.

Wilson prepared to follow. "Have to admit I never saw this side of you either, Holle. Shame it didn't come out earlier. We'd have made a great team."

When he'd gone, Venus lingered for a moment. "I guess the others didn't pick up on our long-term problem."

"What problem?"

"The loss of shuttle A. I don't have any solution to that. Do you?"

"No," Holle whispered. "No, I don't."

Venus nodded. "Well, it's a long way to Earth III yet. We've time to figure it out. As for the rest—" She looked at Holle for long seconds, as if she'd never seen her before. "Ah, the hell with it." She floated up out of the cabin after the others.

Holle was left alone in Wilson's cabin. She sat still. Then she folded over on herself, hugging her knees. She dared not cry for fear that she might be overheard.

90

May 2078

Helen Gray brought Zane a present. Wrapped roughly in a sheet of insulating foam, it was a block of frozen urine, elaborately sculpted into a bust, a human head. The artist intended it as a memorial to the dead, to mark a decade since Steel Antoniadi's Blowout Rebellion.

In the gloom of his cabin, Zane hefted it, cupping its cheeks in his stiff, liver-spotted hands. The glow from the cabin's single lamp shone through the ice, picking out its dark golden color and highlighting bubbles and streaks of other fluids within. Zane said dryly, "I do like the way the light catches piss ice, if you display it right."

This was Zane 3, Helen tentatively decided, the determined amnesiac who remembered nothing before his own awakening after the launch from Jupiter. She was glad Zane 3 was out today. Though his mood was often black, and though Zane had been a pariah for ten years since his conspiracy theories fueled the Blowout, Zane 3 was a rounded person with a unique perspective of his own, while Jerry was competent but hollow, a bluff, arrogant bully. According to Holle and Grace, who had long since given up their attempts to reintegrate Zane, there was evidence of other alters orbiting inside Zane's head now, spun off at various crises to take away more distress from the core personality, alters with names like Leonard and Robert and Christopher. The only objects of interest on the Ark were other people. Zane 3 might be nothing more than a fragment of a disintegrating mind, but he remained one of the more interesting people on the ship.

"It's well made," he said now, turning the urine head over in his hands. "If the features are exaggerated. These features, the big eyes, the mouth, the nose. It's like a puppet head."

"Bella used other bodily fluids to highlight internal structures. Look, you can see that string of blood . . ."

"Not too anatomically precise."

"It's fanciful, meant to represent the mind, not the body."

"Yes. You can see the expression she's trying to capture. Curiosity. Doubt, maybe. How old is this Bella?"

"Eighteen."

Bella Mayweather was of the generation who had come of age in the decade since the Blowout; only eight years old at the time of the rebellion, she likely had only blurred, nightmarish memories of those events themselves, and had grown up under Holle Groundwater's tough-love rule.

"Eighteen years old," Zane said, turning the head over in his hands. "Shipborn art does fascinate me. So does their culture, the language they seem to be evolving. The way they flock like birds in microgravity. You know, the one thing I've learned above all on this cruise to nowhere is about the resilience of the human spirit. We go on and on, decade after decade, and each new year is worse than the last, each subsequent cadre of kids growing up in even worse conditions than those before. Now we have nothing left to give them, not even any raw materials for art. And yet they manage to express themselves anyway. Their sculptures of frozen piss, and their paintings of blood and mucus on the walls of the ship, those elaborate tattoos they wear, their endless songs. All evanescent, of course."

"Yes. Even this head will have to go into the hoppers in another few days. The image will be stored in the archive, but . . ."

But even Halivah's digital archive, stored on radiation-hardened diamond-based chips, was running out of room. Half the capacity had been lost to Seba at the Split, and the rest had only been intended to record a voyage of a decade or less. As Holle sought new capacity, for instance for the revival of the HeadSpace booths she had ordered, the institutional memory stored in the archive had been "rationalized," and whole swathes of it dumped.

Zane said, "This is the sort of thematic resonance which underpins my so-called conspiracy theories. You see the same themes expressed over and over at different levels in our little world, which is evidence of artifice, of deliberate if clumsy design. Thus we are all trapped together in this hull like racing thoughts in a single skull, just as I and my alters are trapped in my own head. And now the Ark's electronic memory is being wiped out, megabyte by megabyte, library shelf by library shelf. Will the Ark wake up one day not knowing what it is, just as I did at the start of the voyage? Maybe there's nobody here but me," he said suddenly. He looked at her. "Maybe you are just another alter, spun off to save me from loneliness. Maybe there's only me, alone in this empty tank, while the observers watch me going steadily crazy."

Helen shivered. As with so many of Zane's visions there was something authentic in this latest speculation, this latest bizarre hypothesis. After all, even though at thirty-six years old she was among the very oldest of the shipborn, she couldn't remember Earth herself. Intellectually she believed that the stars were real, that Earth was real, that there really had been a flood that had drowned a planetary civilization, and that in only three more years they would reach Earth III. But it was a matter of faith, for her. And there were people like Steel Antoniadi who had been born, lived and died on the Ark without ever experiencing anything outside its hull. What difference had it made to them if it had all been real or not?

Listening to Zane's theorizing was like listening to a horror story, giving her a kind of pleasurable scare. But, since the Blowout, listening to Zane had been against ship's rules.

"This is why none of the kids are allowed to come and see you, if you talk like this."

"Ah, the children. I am still the ship's bogeyman, aren't I? But I do miss those dream-sharing sessions we used to have." He glanced at her belly, where her coverall showed a slight swelling. "You've another coming yourself?"

She smiled. "We just got in before the deadline. Holle wants a moratorium on conception from here until Earth III. She doesn't want us landing with newborns aboard."

"That makes a certain paranoid sense. A little sister for Mario?"

"Actually a brother."

"Another boy for Jeb. That will please him."

"I guess," she said indifferently. Jeb Holden, formerly one of Wilson's bruisers, had not been her first choice as father to her children—and nor, she knew, had she been his choice. After all he was about Zane's age, nearly sixty, much older than Helen. But Holle had encouraged everybody to get busy producing babies, following some demographic logic of her own, and the ten years since the Blowout had seen a whole new crop of infants growing up, second-generation shipborn. Helen could hardly stay aloof. "Just remember," Grace had said with a strained smile, "I didn't get to choose your father either. And nor did my mother have any choice about the man who fathered me." Grace had hugged her daughter. "But we didn't turn out too bad, did we?"

"Jeb's OK," Helen told Zane now. "He came from a good family, I think. We named Mario after his own father, a farmer who died in an eye-dee flash war, which was how Jeb ended up fighting for his life on a raft. Wilson was a bad influence on him."

"And what are you going to call the new addition? What was your father's name—Hammond?"

Helen smiled. "My mother won't hear of that. We're thinking of calling him Hundred. Because when he's born we will just have completed a hundred light-years from Earth."

He groaned. "These made-up shipper names! I can't abide them."

She drifted to the door. "I need to go. You can keep the head for a few days. Don't let it melt."

"Oh, believe me, I won't." Zane stared into the eyes of the sculpture, as if seeking answers there.

She felt an odd impulse to hug him. But with Zane you couldn't be sure *who* you were hugging. "You're very valued, you know."

"Oh, really?"

"You're still the authority on the warp generator. We need you."

"No," he said. "Come on. You know as well as I do that our flight to Earth III, regarding the warp mechanics, has been programmed in from launch."

"But if the warp failed in flight—"

He laughed. "If that happened it would most likely kill us all in an instant. No, my usefulness ended the moment the warp bubble successfully coalesced at Earth II."

"You're useful to me, if you want to put it like that. I enjoy our talks."

"You're very kind. But as your children grow, when you reach Earth III and you start the great project of building a new world—" He seemed to come to himself. "I'm fine. You go back to your little boy. Go, go!"

91

"It was the ruins on Earth II that were the clue," Venus said softly. "I mean, think about it. The first world we come to, the first exoplanet ever visited by humans, and we find ruins, traces of some civilization long gone. The principle of mediocrity dictates that there's no such thing as coincidence; you must expect that what you discover is average, typical. So, find one world with ruins and you'll find more . . ."

They were sitting in the cupola, Venus holding court with Holle and Grace. Venus spoke softly, and the others followed suit. Somehow, even after all these years, the subdued twilight of the cupola was a place where hushed voices seemed the right thing. And even now Venus was mean with the coffee, and Holle tried to resist asking for another cup. They huddled together, their three faces softly lit by the light of Venus's screens, while the stars hung like lanterns outside the big windows. All three of them were around sixty or older, their hair roughly cut masses of gray, their faces lined, their bodies solid and stiff, nothing like the slim, smooth-faced girls who had boarded the Ark all those years ago. And Holle knew that she had aged most of all.

All the way from Jupiter, Venus and her slowly changing cast of trainee astronomers and physicists had studied the universe through which they traveled, from a vantage point unique in all mankind's history. And, having sifted nearly four decades' worth of data, Venus had come to some conclusions, and had come up with a deeper theory of life in the universe than had been possible for any earthbound astronomer.

"It's remarkable that mankind discovered life in the universe, through the analysis of data from the planet-finder projects, just at the moment civilization was falling apart because of the flood. What a tragedy that was! But all we found was mute evidence of atmospheric changes, such as the injection of oxygen and methane, a glimpse of what looked like photosynthetic chemicals. You don't need intelligence to produce such signatures. But it was intelligence we wanted above all to find.

"But, despite decades of listening long before the flood came, and an even more careful survey from the Ark in the years since we launched, we've found nothing. Heard nothing, not a squeak. I might say we've not just been looking for radio and optical signals but city lights and industrial gases, and evidence of more exotic objects, Dyson sphere infrared blisters, wormholes, even warp bubbles like our own.

"And yet we do see traces of their passing. Well, we think so. Even when there aren't actual ruins, obvious traces. You recall how the Earth II system was depleted of asteroids? We've found other depletions, anisotropies—differences in concentrations of key materials between one side of the sky and another. Even the solar system had some odd deficiencies, for instance of neon and helium, that we couldn't explain away with our models of planetary creation."

Holle asked, "So what are you suggesting? That somebody came by and used up all the good stuff and moved on?"

"That's exactly what I'm suggesting. And why do we find this? Because, I think, the Galaxy is old . . ."

As the Galaxy formed from a vast, spinning cloud of dust and gas and ice, embedded in a greater pocket of dark matter, the first stars had congealed like frost.

"In the primordial cloud there wasn't much of anything except hydrogen and helium, the elements that had emerged from the Big Bang. Those first stars, mostly crowded in the Galaxy's center, were monsters. They raced through fusion chain reactions and detonated in supernovas, spewing out metals and carbon and oxygen and the other heavy elements necessary for life—at any rate, life like ours. The supernovas in turn set off a wave of starmaking in the regions outside the core, and those second stars were enriched by the products of the first." She mimed a cage with her hands, slowly expanding. "So you have this zone of intense activity in the center of the Galaxy, and a wave of starmaking washing outwards, with metals and other heavy elements borne on the shock front. That starbirth wave finally broke over the sun's region maybe five billion years ago, and the Earth was formed, and so were we.

"But Sol is out in the boondocks, and was born late. The Galaxy's starmaking peak was billions of years earlier. Most stars capable of bearing planets with complex life are older than the sun, an average of two billion years older. That's half the Earth's lifetime—maybe four times as long as it has been since multicellular life emerged on Earth."

Grace asked, "And you believe this is why we see no signs of intelligence?"

Venus shrugged. "We're latecomers to the party—like the gatecrashers on the Ark. *They* were most likely to emerge billions of years before us. What happens to a culture after billions of years? Most likely they die out, right? Or maybe they migrate. Me, I'd head for the Galactic core. That's where the action is, the crowded stars, the energy." She glanced out of the windows. "The energy of starlight is thin out here, a millionth the strength of sunlight at Earth. Which is why the Ark is not equipped with solar panels. In the core you could just coast around in the starlight, lapping up all that free energy falling from the sky. It must be like a city in there, hot, crowded, dangerous. Whatever, after a billion years, they're nothing like us, and they're not *here*."

Grace asked, "So where does that leave us?"

"Alone," Venus said firmly. "If we expected to come out here and join in some kind of bustling Galactic culture, it ain't going to happen. We seem to be young, in a very old Galaxy. We're like kids tiptoeing through a ruined mansion. Or a graveyard. 'Go on through the lofty spaces of high heaven and bear witness, where thou ridest, that there are no gods.' That's Seneca—*Medea*."

Holle said, "You always were pretentious, Venus."

Venus grinned. "Sorry."

"I sometimes wonder why we care," Grace said. "I mean, why would we long to find minds on other worlds? Gary Boyle used to say that we are lonely because of our evolutionary history. Our ancestors were hominids, just one species in a world full of other kinds of hominids. There are many species of dolphins and whales; *they* aren't alone. But our cousins all went, we out-competed them. We're not evolved for a world where the only minds are ours. We're lonely but we don't know why."

Holle considered. "Well, if all this is so, it's up to us not to fail. On the Ark, I mean. If Earth has gone, if Earth II fails, we may be the only receptacle of high intelligence left in the Galaxy."

"Quite a responsibility," Grace murmured.

"Especially as we're dumb as shit," Venus said. "I mean, we can't even last a few years in this tin can without turning on each other."

They were silent for a while, and Holle wondered grumpily again if Venus would ever get around to offering them that coffee refill. She said at length, "You know, I sometimes think we were terribly ill-equipped, the Candidates. We spent our whole lives training for this mission, but we weren't rounded. I mean, for instance we never even read any *books*—no books that counted. Do you remember, Venus? I liked historicals, tales of a vanished past. You liked old science fiction about vanished futures. We never engaged with the world as it was unfolding around us, not even through fiction."

"Nobody was writing novels about the flood," Venus pointed out.

"They were all too damn busy. More to the point, Holle, you and I never had kids, before or after we left Earth."

Holle shrugged. "True. I sometimes think I never got over Mel. And then there was that strange business about Zane. After that, I always felt I had too much to do."

"Yeah. As for me, my students are my children."

"Those are excuses," Grace said gently. "You were Candidates. You were brought up knowing it would be your *duty* to have children, to pass on your genes. But you didn't. On some level you both deliberately chose not to, for whatever reason."

"Maybe I was scared," Holle said. "Scared to make that kind of commitment."

"To have kids and to know you couldn't save them."

"Something like that."

Venus said coolly, "I wonder if you could do the job you're doing now, Holle, if one of your own kids was affected by your decisions. Living in your water empire."

"I don't know," Holle said honestly. "I think Kelly Kenzie could have done it. She was always the best of us, wasn't she? Before the Split she was hooking up with—with—"

"Masayo Saito."

"Yes. She intended to have kids with him. Maybe she has by now. And if not for the Split, maybe she'd have had kids with Wilson. Either way she'd have been able to keep on functioning as a mother, I think."

"And she'd have kept Wilson in check better."

"Yeah. She'd have done a better job than any of us."

"You can only do your best," Grace said to Holle. "Kelly isn't here; she's long gone. All we can do is keep on until the end—"

An alarm went off, a faint buzz, one of Venus's screens flashing red. She turned and tapped a key. "Oh, shit."

Holle leaned forward. "What?"

"It's a suicide note. From Zane. He says he doesn't want to be a, let me see, 'a useless drain on resources.'"

Grace shook her head. "That's Zane 3. He's done that before, the other alters overpower him."

"This is signed by a committee. Jerry, Zane 2, Zane 3, somebody called Leonard and Christopher and—"

Grace unbuckled and clambered out of her couch. Venus was already opening the airlock hatch.

92

Helen Gray sat on hot, prickly sand.

The beach, textured by dunes and wave marks, stretched off as far as she could see. Before her was another semi-infinite plain, a sea that reached to a razor-sharp horizon. The sky was a blue dome, and in it, directly before her, was a star—no, the word was "sun." It was a disc of light just like the hull's arc lamps. It warmed her face and dazzled her eyes, and scattered highlights on the sea and cast a shadow from the child playing before her.

Mario, four years old, dressed in a baggy old adult's T-shirt, paddled in the surf. He squealed every time the water lapped over his toes. He looked quite at home. But his walk along the beach was clumsy, a babyish scrape at the ground. You had to walk in these planetary sims, that was Holle's rule, the kids were going to have to walk on Earth III and this was where they would learn how, and the HeadSpace suit constrained you to do just that. But the sim could not simulate the effects of gravity, and so the whole experience was incomplete.

Further along the beach sat another parent, Max Baker, with another child, five-year-old Diamond, the little boy Max had fathered with Magda Murphy. Max was talking steadily to his son, encouraging him to race and splash. Helen liked to see Max being like this. It had taken a lot for him to get over the loss of his twin sister during the Blowout, and Magda the loss of her baby. Like herself and Jeb, Max and Magda were parents if not lovers, but they seemed to have found consolation in each other's company. Magda had even had a second child with Max, a one-year-old girl called Sapphire. Maybe later Diamond and Mario could play together.

The detail of this HeadSpace sim was good. The waves on the sea's surface and the froth where they broke, generated by simple fractal routines, were convincing enough, or so Helen's mother had told her. Each individual grain of sand cast a shadow. She could even feel the sand under her bare legs, gritty and sharp—more fractal processing. But to a trained eye it wasn't hard to see the virtual's limitations, such as differing shades in the blue sky delineated by straight-line boundaries, as if it were constructed of huge panels. Grace, who had actually stood on genuine beaches on Earth, pointed out the lack of such features as clouds in the sky, and seaweed and jellyfish in the ocean, and seawrack on the sand—and, she had observed dryly, raft-loads of eye-dees crowding out as far as the eye could see. The HeadSpace booths were aging technology, and the processor capacity devoted to these sims was restricted.

But, wrapped up in their virtual suits in their separate HeadSpace booths, sharing this virtual sky, the children could wrestle and race and splash in the water.

All this was Holle's idea. She had also reinstated sports tournaments, like wrestling and sumo, young bodies stressed against each other in weightlessness, programs designed to build up muscle mass and bone strength to cope with the gravity field of Earth III. Holle didn't want the crew spilling to the ground like babies, baffled and terrified by such basic features as an open sky.

It seemed to be working. Mario, playing, wasn't fazed by the fact that you couldn't turn down the sun or turn up the wind. But sometimes Helen wondered if something unique was being lost as the mission approached its terminus, a culture born of necessity over forty years in the ship's dark corners, with its own furtive art and language and style. The tribes of half-naked, elaborately tattooed children had to be taught the word for "sky" by being taken into a HeadSpace booth and shown the referent. But the shipborn had evolved forty new words for "love."

Besides, Helen herself hated the sims. She too was a shipborn, and maybe it was too late for her to adjust to the openness of a planet. But landfall loomed ahead like the date of her own execution—even though she relished the challenge of piloting a shuttle down to the new world. So as little Mario played his way through his allotted time she endured the openness, the sunlight on her bare arms, the lack of the comforting enclosure of scuffed metal walls. And she clung to faulty details, the lines of broken shade in the sky, as reassurance that none of this was real, and she could come to no harm.

She was relieved when time was up and she called Mario back from the edge of the sea.

93

Once, just once, as Venus drifted in the dark of the cupola, she picked up a strange signal. It appeared to be coherent, like a beam from a microwave laser. She used her space-borne telescopes to triangulate the signal, determining that it wasn't anywhere close. And she passed it through filters to render it into audio. It sounded cold and clear, a trumpet note, far off in the galactic night.

If it was a signal it wasn't human.

She listened for two years, all the way to Earth III. She never heard it again.

She said nothing about this to Holle and the others.

94

July 2081

Venus brought Thandie's old crystal ball out of storage one last time, and set it up at the heart of the hull, mounted on a strut attached to the fireman's pole. Holle drifted beside her, clinging loosely to the pole, two solid, competent women in their sixties, side by side.

Helen Gray, clinging to a strut that had once supported a deck partition, glanced around as the crew settled into their places, all around the hull. People clung to guide ropes or handrails every which way up, unconscious of their differing orientations after so many years without gravity, and they made a shell of faces all turned toward Venus. Save only for the crew on watch in the shuttle and cupola, everybody was here, all chores suspended for the day, and there was a buzz of conversation.

Helen spotted her mother. Grace had her grandson, two-year-old Hundred, with her today; the little boy seemed fascinated by the whirling of the crystal ball. And there was Jeb, with seven-year-old Mario sitting on his shoulders. Close by was Mario's best friend Diamond Murphy Baker, a year older than Mario, with his own parents, Magda and Max, and little Sapphire. Helen was struck how many children there were, the final shipborn. But the survivors of the original crew, those few who remembered Earth, were here too, like Venus and Holle, work-hardened sixty-somethings, and Cora Robles, now a contented grandmother. Wilson Argent hovered up near the apex of the hull, within the charred walls of what had once been his palace. Still a big man at sixty-plus, his hair snow white, he was alone; even now people were generally in awe of him.

If only Zane was here, Helen thought suddenly. She'd scarcely thought of Zane since his suicide three years back. For all his problems he had always achieved everything that had been asked of him. When they got around to building the statues on Earth III, Helen promised herself, there would be one for Zane Glemp, alters and all.

Now Venus seemed to be ready. She didn't call for order but just looked around. She had always had a kind of natural command, Helen thought. Everybody quietened down quickly, save for the piping voices of a couple of the children. Venus touched her crystal ball. The whirling screens spun into invisibility to reveal a glowing pink-white sphere, a star small as a pea, with a single visible planet, one side illuminated by the star, the other in darkness. The hull's big arc lights dimmed.

The session was suddenly so like Venus's report on Earth II, when Kelly had challenged Wilson, provoking the Split. It was so long ago, Helen had only been nine years old and now she was a year away from forty, but she remembered its drama distinctly. The hull, a battered, half-burned-out wreck, was all but unrecognizable from the bright, clean ship of those days. Now it was more like a cave, with its charred walls and worn equipment racks and panels covered with the gangs' graffiti scrawls. And yet the green plants still grew in their hydroponic beds down on the lower deck, and Holle's pumps and fans still hummed as they cycled air and water through the hull's levels. Like the worn-out crew, Halivah had done its job.

Venus began: "Well, we got here."

There was a spontaneous storm of applause. Helen saw little Hundred happily clapping about something he couldn't possibly understand, his grandmother's hand on his shoulder to stop him drifting off into space.

Venus turned to her display. "Here is your new sun, the M-sun. These images have been assembled from observations taken from the cupola and the free-floating space telescopes." The view panned in on the star, so that the pea-sized image swelled up to the size of a basketball. "It's a red dwarf star, an unremarkable member of the constellation Lepus, not even visible to the naked eye from Earth. We are a hundred and eleven light-years from Earth, yet the star is not unlike the closest star of all to Earth, Proxima Centauri—though it has twice Proxima's mass, about a fifth of a solar mass. And it's small, about a quarter the sun's diameter. It would fit into the Earth-moon system, in fact, with one edge brushing Earth, the other the moon. It's of the stellar type M6." She pointed at snakes of yellowish light that crawled across the star's surface and reached up in spindly arches. "You can see it's active. We can expect solar storms—lots of auroras. In fact it was a lot more active when it was younger, but it's pretty quiescent now. There is no significant ultraviolet component in its light, for instance, unlike Sol. It will be a safe and stable sun—and it will outlive Sol a hundred times over."

"And it's white!" somebody yelled.

"Yes," Venus said, and she grinned. "Its spectrum peaks in the infrared, but there's enough light in the rest of its spectrum that close up it will saturate your eyes' receptors, and will look white."

"So much for Gordo and Krypton," Wilson called down.

"And here is Earth III."

The viewpoint panned back so that the pinpoint planet swam back into view, and then zoomed in. Everybody had had a chance to glimpse the new world through the cupola windows, to see an unfolding panorama of lakes and mountains and seas passing under the orbiting hull. But this was the first time they had been able to inspect the planet as a whole. There was another burst of applause, but it was muted, Helen thought. For Earth III looked nothing like Earth.

There was an ocean at its subsolar point, where the M-sun would be directly overhead. Further away continents could be made out, fractal shapes against the ocean's face, wrinkled by mountain ranges and incised by river valleys. But unlike the gray-green of Earth's continents seen from space the land was eerily black. And there was a kind of banding effect across the planet, concentric circles with different textures as you looked away from that oceanic subsolar point, so the sun-facing hemisphere looked like the targets they used in the kids' microgravity archery contests. All this was obscured by a thick layer of atmosphere, with banked clouds at the higher latitudes, and haze as you looked toward the horizon. The shadowed side of the planet, the night side, was entirely dark save for lightning crackles. At the antipode to that subsolar point Helen saw the pale gleam of ice, illuminated by the faint light of the distant stars.

Huddling for warmth, Earth III orbited so close to its parent star that tides had long since massaged its rotation so that its day equalled its year, and it kept the same face permanently turned toward its sun. One side was in perpetual light, the other in unending darkness, save for the star-light. But even the side of perpetual day was so cold that glaciers draped equatorial mountaintops.

Maybe it was habitable. It was not like Earth. That was the basic truth that was driven home to Helen even as she first examined these images, even as Venus began to describe the new world.

Venus said, "Earth III is the innermost planet in its system, but there are other planets further out. More Earths and super-Earths. Not as easy to colonize as Earth III, but they're there for our descendants—new homelands just waiting in the sky for them, off in the future.

"We looked for planets in the habitable zones of stars, that is the or-bital radius where liquid water is possible on the surface, and that's just what we found here. You can see the oceans. But this M-sun is a lot dim-mer than Sol, so Earth III has to be closer in to its parent, only about ten million kilometers out—much less than the orbit of Mercury. The year is different, of course. Earth III's year is just fifteen of our days long. The stars will shift quickly in the sky. But there is no 'day,' and there are no seasons. From the ground you will never see the sun move from the same position in the sky. And it's cool. Even at the subsolar point you'll only get about sixty percent of the radiant energy as you'd receive from the sun, on Earth. If you're on the night side you never see the sun at all." She pointed. "There's an ice cap at the point of deepest shadow, as you can see. It gets pretty cold back there.

"You might wonder why the air doesn't all freeze out on the dark side. It doesn't work like that; the atmosphere is thick, full of greenhouse gases injected by volcanoes, a blanket that transports heat around the world. Also you have the planet's own inner heat, which is greater than Earth's. The climate is stable. It's just different.

"And Earth III is larger than the Earth—that's the most basic fact about it. It's an exoplanet of the kind the planet-hunters called a super-Earth. It has around twice Earth's mass, and maybe twenty-five percent higher gravity. That will feel hard, but you'll soon muscle up, and your children will grow up stockier than you are and won't even notice.

"More planetary mass is *good,* and it's one reason we selected this world. More mass means more inner heat, a thinner crust, plate tectonics, a spinning iron core. That core produces a healthy magnetosphere, so there is plenty of shelter from radiation, both from the M-sun's flares and from cosmic radiation. And you can see the evidence of the plate tectonics for yourself. Lots of mountain-building, and active volcanoes." She pointed to the horizon. "See the layer of dust and ash up there? Volcano smog. Plate tectonics keep a world young. The good news is that this world, being more massive, will keep its inner heat longer than Earth. Earth III will *stay* young, long after Earth itself has seized up and turned into a bigger copy of Mars.

"And there is life here. We knew that from the spectroscopic studies we did of the atmosphere from light-years away. There is photosynthesis going on in the oceans. On the continents, you can see there are bands of different vegetation types working out from the subsolar point, adapted to the lower light levels. We think we've seen living things even in the twilight band, around the rim of the daylit face, at the terminator. Like trees maybe, straining up so their leaves can catch the last scraps of light. That's something for you to find out, some day."

She looked around, an earnest, exuberant woman, testing to make sure they understood the nature of this gift she was presenting to them. "So you have a sun that will last a hell of a lot longer than Sol, and an Earth that will stay young too, and more worlds to explore. We couldn't have found a better refuge for your children, for mankind, stretching off into the distant future.

"This is the Ark. After a voyage of forty years, here is your Ararat." She stepped back.

But she was met by silence, and blank looks. Perhaps the world she had given them was simply too strange.

Then Holle came forward, her face tough, determined, her eyes sunken. Everybody was silent and stock still, save for a few wriggling children. Even little Hundred seemed to be paying attention. Holle's grim expression was racking up the tension. Helen suddenly realized she had no idea what Holle was about to say.

"Thanks, Venus," Holle said. "So much for the good news. Now we have to talk about landfall. We have a problem."

95

"Most of you don't even remember how the Ark was when it was launched. There were two hulls, called Seba and Halivah. And we had four shuttles, each capable of taking around twenty-five people down to the target planet. We launched from Earth with under eighty crew, a bit less than the design limit. We figured that we would have plenty of capacity in the shuttles, even allowing for a few births along the way.

"But it didn't turn out that way. You all know what happened. We got to Earth II thirty years ago, and split up. Seba went back to Earth, taking one shuttle with it. We used another shuttle to land the colonists who opted to stay at Earth II. That left two more, for us to take to Earth III— but we lost another on the way, during the Blowout." A few of the older people glanced at Wilson, who hung defiantly in the upper section of the hull.

"So we arrived here," Holle said, "with just one shuttle. The shuttle is basically a twenty-five-seat glider; it's only equipped to make one trip, one descent to the surface. The design was like that to save weight. It can't take off again and return to the hull . . ."

Helen's anxiety tightened. She had known there was a problem with shuttle capacity since the aftermath of the Blowout. But back then landfall had been years away. Holle, tough, autocratic, always kept a lot of her decisions and deliberations secret. Helen had trusted Holle to come up with a solution in time. Now, it seemed, that trust might have been misplaced.

"I'm sorry," Holle said bluntly. "We tried everything we could think of to improvise some other way of getting down to the planet's surface. The trouble is that heavy gravity, the thick atmosphere. There will be a ferocious frictional load as any entry craft dumps its orbital energy. The shuttle is designed to cope with that; it has a properly engineered heat shield. Nothing we could lash up comes close to that capability." She paused, and there was silence, save for a baby's sleepy murmur. "You need to understand clearly. We got you here. We came all this way, and some of you will walk on Earth III. But I can't take you all down to the surface."

"And what of the rest?" somebody shouted.

"I'll stay with you," Holle said immediately.

"You'll stay with us to die? Is that the deal?"

"Nobody's going to die." Venus pulled her way forward so she was beside Holle. "We just won't leave the ship, is all. We will go on. The ship is still functioning, it has water, air, power. And we can still use the warp generator—"

"Zane's dead."

"We can trigger the warp bubble without Zane." Holle forced a smile. "We can go wherever we want."

Max Baker drifted forward. "Some are going to make landfall, some will stay here. Twenty-five of us will go down, I guess. Who, Holle? How will we decide? Is there going to be some kind of ballot?"

"No," Holle said firmly. "We don't have that luxury. We have to get this right. I'll decide—I *have* decided."

A kind of collective murmur ran around the hull. Holle always stuck to her decisions, and implemented them in every last detail. Everybody old enough to understand what was being said knew that their fate was already determined.

Holle's expression softened. "And you're wrong about something else, Max. The number's not twenty-five. Twenty-five's not enough. I went

back over Project Nimrod's original design documents. Twenty-five individuals don't provide enough genetic diversity for a viable human colony.
Well, we found a way to take more than that. We think we can carry
about forty. That still might not be enough, but it may be the best we
can do."

Max snapped back, "How?"

"We rebuild the shuttle's interior. We install new couches . . . Max, *we
take children*. That's how we fit in forty. It will be a ship full of children,
with three adults to manage the landfall and help them through the first
years." She looked around. "That's why I've been encouraging you all to
have kids these last years, frankly. I always feared it might come to this, if
we didn't find a miracle solution to the shuttle issue, and we haven't."

Helen could feel the tension rise in the hull as Holle's basic logic
sunk in.

She kept talking. "I've selected a list of children from the ages of two
up to fifteen. Thirty-seven of them, most of them ten and under. No
siblings, to maximize diversity. And no relation to the adults. There will
be no mothers, fathers, brothers, sisters. Just as when we launched from
Earth, in fact." She glanced around. "You older ones, I picked you carefully, it's going to be hard for you. You'll have to help the adults manage the little ones as you establish the colony. The shuttle is full of gear
to help you get through the first months: inflatable habitats, freeze-
dried food packs. But it will be tough work. There will be ground to be
cleared, and—"

Max challenged her again. "You're sending very young children away
from their parents. It's inhuman."

"Of course it's inhuman," Holle said steadily. "Everything about this
mission is inhuman."

Magda pushed forward. "You have no kids of your own. You're only
half alive yourself. That's how you come up with cruelty like this."

Holle, flinching, took a breath. "I'm sorry it's come to this, Magda. I'll
announce the full list later. I'll speak to the parents individually first. But,

look—your Sapphire is on the list. She's the youngest in the shuttle crew, she'll be the youngest person in the whole world. Think of that—"

"You murderous bitch, you won't take another baby from me!" Magda threw herself away from the wall. There was an eruption of shouting, of anger, people grabbing at Magda.

Holle waited by the pole until the commotion had subsided. Then she said clearly, her amplified voice booming, "The adults."

Again she was the focus of attention, in silence save for Magda's wretched sobbing, and the thinner cry of an upset child.

Holle said, "These three have to be the core of the first days, weeks, months—a core of expertise, and of discipline until the older children can take over. I've selected them for necessary competences, and, with one exception, for experience of Earth. I don't want everybody on that shuttle to freeze the first time they step through the hatch and onto a planet.

"So, first: Jeb Holden. I know you don't all love him. But he came from a farming background. He saw a hell of a lot of the world as an eye-dee and then a Homelander. Nobody else aboard has that breadth of experience. So, Jeb goes."

Helen, shocked, looked for Jeb. He had taken Mario off his shoulders and was staring at him, immediately realizing the implications of Holle's choice. *No parents,* Holle had said. If Jeb was sent down to the ground, Mario and Hundred would be left aboard the ship. Jeb looked stricken. He was a good father, for all his faults; this was going to be terribly hard for him. But at least Helen would have the children, she thought with a stab of savage, selfish relief. At least she would be here with Hundred and Mario, on the Ark.

"Second," Holle said now, "we need a shuttle pilot. If those few minutes of the descent go badly, none of the rest matters. And though we've tried to train up replacements, we only have one experienced flier. That's Wilson Argent."

Wilson looked dumbstruck. There were howls of protest.

Max turned on Holle again. "He's the man who raped my sister and left her to die! He's the man who took the damn shuttle to save his own skin, that created this mess in the first place. Now you're giving him the planet, him and his thug Jeb—"

"He's the only pilot, Max. That's all that matters. There's nothing remotely fair about this process."

Wilson drifted in the ruins of his palace. "I'm sorry," he said, his voice barely audible.

"Finally," Holle said, "I chose one shipborn, of the middle generations. Somebody who can empathize with what the youngsters are going to have to go through to adjust to life outside the ship, yet is old enough to offer perspective, some kind of guidance. Somebody who has some piloting training to back up Wilson. She has family bonds to one other on the shuttle crew, though not genetic. Maybe that will help stabilize things in the early days. And she's somebody you respect, I know that.

"I'm sending Helen Gray."

Everybody turned to stare at Helen. For a long heartbeat she couldn't understand what Holle had said, the implications.

Then she hurled herself across the hull, looking for her children.

96

August 2081

Helen and Jeb spent one last evening with the children, a normal routine at the end of a final day of chores and schooling. There was supper and cleanup, and a complicated zero-gravity basketball game for Mario with his father, and story-reading from his mother's handheld for little Hundred.

Helen suspected that seven-year-old Mario knew what was going to happen, but if he did he was being brave for the sake of his little brother. Even Hundred wasn't quite himself that evening, but he played gamely, and gurgled when he was tickled as he was dressed for bed. Then they all piled into the parents' big sleeping bag, suspended across the interior of their cabin where it hung on the fireman's pole, and Jeb and Helen held the children until they slept.

When they gently disentangled themselves, Mario stirred. He opened his big eyes and looked at his father, who was pulling on his T-shirt and shorts. He whispered, "Am I in charge now, Dad?"

"You're in charge, big guy."

Mario just smiled. "I'll look after Hundred."

Helen couldn't bear anymore. She pushed out of the cabin into the dim light of the hull's night watch.

Her mother was waiting outside. Grace looked gaunt, old. But she hugged her daughter. "I'll go climb in with them," she whispered. "So there'll be somebody there when they wake."

"Thanks," Jeb said gruffly.

"It's going to be strange for you, Mum," Helen said.

Grace shrugged. "I was a hostage. Then I was a princess. Then I was an eye-dee, a walker. Then I was a sailor. Then an astronaut, and a doctor. Now I'll be a grandmother, full time. I'll adapt." She released her daughter. "We've said all there is to say. Go now, it's time." She pulled herself inside the cabin.

Helen wasn't crying; she seemed to have done all the crying she was ever going to do in the month since Holle had announced the split of the crew. But she couldn't speak at all. Passively, she let Jeb take her arm and guide her up through the silent hull.

At the open hatch to shuttle B, the forty crew were being suited up. The older children, wide-eyed and subdued, helped sleepy youngsters into their suits. The lightweight pressure coveralls they were to wear during descent were just flimsy shells of polythene, enough to protect them if the cabin lost pressure. They had been stored in a locker for four decades, and, unusually aboard this battered old hulk, smelled *new*. They even had AxysCorp logos on their chests, cradled Earths. With spares there were plenty to go around, but they had been cut down to fit the smaller children, and turned into simple sacks to contain the very small ones. The shuttle launch had been timed for the night watch, when the children, drowsy with sleep, might be more easily handled. Perhaps they could be loaded aboard the shuttle and thrown down to the new world before they woke properly and realized they had lost their parents forever.

Helen, her mind blank, found her own suit, shook it out and pulled it on.

Venus and Holle approached. Holle looked tremendously sad, Venus frankly envious.

Holle said, "Wilson's already aboard, checking over the systems. I—here." She handed Helen a small stainless-steel sphere. It was a globe of Earth III, a product of the Ark's machine shop. "We did the same at Earth II, I don't know if you remember that. We put them in the kids'

packs; something for them to find. I wanted to give you yours personally."
Impulsively she hugged Helen. "I'm sorry I put you through this."

Helen shoved her away. "You can never be sorry enough," she said
fiercely.

Holle just soaked this up, as she had soaked up all she had done for
the sake of the crew, the mission, since the day she took over from Wilson.
Maybe, in the end, that was Holle's role, Helen thought, not leadership
at all, just a receptacle for all the guilt at what had had to be done so the
rest could survive. Nevertheless Helen felt a stab of renewed hatred.

Venus came forward and fussed over the seals on Helen's suit. "Don't
forget, it will be damned cold down there. The next generation won't
notice, but you will. Wrap up before you crack that hatch." She moved
back, her eyes brimming. "Christ, I'll miss you. You were the best student
I ever had. Pass your learning on to the kids. You're not to slip back to
the fucking Neolithic, after coming all this way."

"I will. What about you, Venus? What's next?"

She glanced at Holle. "Well, we have a plan, of sorts. As soon as we
pick up the beacon that says you're safely down, we'll send messages back
by microwave laser to Earth, Earth II. Then, in a hundred years or so,
anybody who's listening will get the good news.

"Then we have this plan to go exploring the system of this M-sun."
She snapped her fingers, click, click. "Little bitty warp jumps, from planet
to planet. Zane would have loved working all that out. We'll send you
back the results, surface maps, internal structures, whatever we find out.
Keep that radio receiver functioning. It will be a legacy for the next generation, when they're ready to go exploring, yeah?"

"And then?"

Venus spread her arms. "Hell, the sky is ours. We'll just explore some
more. Maybe we'll find Earth IV and Earth V and Earth VI. We'll laser
back, we'll tell you what we find. Or maybe we'll come back and beat
the light and tell you ourselves. Go," she said, her voice suddenly gruff.
"Go now before they close the damn hatch and leave you behind."

Most of the kids were already aboard. Jeb glided through the hatch.

There was no reason to stay. Helen swiveled in the air and dropped down herself, feet first. The pressure garment felt odd, too clean, and it rustled when she moved.

Once inside the shuttle, she looked back. Holle's face, full of remorse and suffering, was the last she saw of the Ark. Then Venus closed the hatch.

97

The layout of the little craft was simple. The cramped, tubular cabin was packed with rows of seats, improvised from Ark gear and jammed in among the original design's twenty-five couches. Two seats sat proud of the rest, up in the nose before a rudimentary instrument console and scuffed panoramic windows. Wilson was already in the left-hand seat, running over systems checks, and Helen made her way to the right-hand seat. He handed her a Snoopy comms hat, and she pulled it on.

The shuttle was an automated glider, essentially, with the characteristics of Earth III's atmosphere and gravity profiles programmed into its onboard computer. It was smart enough to avoid such obvious obstacles as oceans and rock fields and snowbanks, and indeed was capable of flying itself all the way down to the ground. But in the design offices back in vanished Denver it had been recognized that you'd likely need human control over the first unpowered landing on an entirely alien world. A few hundred meters up was the point where Wilson would come into his own; that was the reason this despised sixty-two-year-old was aboard the shuttle, while Helen's own children were left back aboard the Ark. Helen was the nearest thing available to a copilot. But she had never even flown as a passenger in an atmosphere before, and she prayed the rudimentary skills she had picked up in her training, and from working with Wilson in HeadSpace sims in the last month, would not be called upon.

As she buckled in she glanced back over her shoulder. The kids were packed in, their orange pressure garments bright. The few older kids, the fourteen- and fifteen-year-olds, were dotted around among the rest. The ten-year-olds looked scared, but the infants were mostly sleeping, in the shuttle's warm humming atmosphere. Helen saw little Sapphire Murphy Baker, the youngest aboard at four years old, holding the hand of an eight-year-old. Jeb sat at the back, in theory watching over the kids and ready to intervene in case of any crisis. Seeing Helen looking, he waved. She tried to smile, but the desolation in his face was clear.

This was how they were going to colonize a new world, with a pack of children and three adults, and a hold containing a nuclear generator and seed stock and tools and a couple of blowup hab modules, and broken hearts.

"We must be insane," Helen murmured.

"Those who sent us from Earth were insane." Wilson glanced over at her. "You ready?"

"As I'll ever be."

He flipped a switch, a heavy manual toggle. "Well, that's it. I've initiated the automated program. Now this baby will fly itself all the way down, all but. Here comes the first mission event. Three, two, one—"

Latches rattled, and attitude thrusters banged around the shuttle's exterior. Helen felt a pull in her stomach. Some of the sleeping children stirred and moaned.

"We cut away from the Ark. That's it, we're flying solo. Better get used to that acceleration, we'll be facing a lot of that this morning."

"Solo now and for the rest of our lives . . . wow." She felt a slight dizziness, her inner ears telling her they were spinning on their long axis.

"That's the inspection spin. Just giving Halivah a chance to check that the heat shield tiles haven't fallen off in the last forty years."

Venus Jenning's voice crackled from a speaker. "Shuttle B, Halivah. Looking good for descent, Wilson."

"Copy that. Thank you, Venus."

The spinning stopped. Helen looked out of the window. They were somewhere over the night side of the planet. They were flying backward, with their heads to the stars and the new world unfolding beneath them, utterly black save for a purple flaring of storms and a sullen red glow that looked like a huge volcano caldera. The idea was that they would enter the atmosphere over the night hemisphere, and their entry trajectory would bring them swooping around the world's curve to land on the side of permanent day.

Wilson glanced over his shoulder. "Everybody OK? Next it's the retro rocket. It will feel like a kick in the back. Nothing to worry about. Three, two, one—"

The cabin was filled with noise, a guttural crackling roar like an immense fire. It was indeed a kick in the back. Helen felt it in her lower spine and neck and legs as she was pressed into the padded couch, and the shuttle seemed to swivel until it was as if it was standing on its tail, and she lying on her back. The retro system was a rocket pack bolted to the rear end of the shuttle, designed to shed the velocity that kept the ship in orbit alongside the Ark, and let it fall into the air of Earth III. Now, after lying dormant for forty years, it had fired up for its one and only burn.

Wilson called, "Three, two, one—"

The retro died as sharply as it had opened up, and Helen was thrown forward. More of the children were awake now; with the rocket's roar gone she could hear them crying in the sudden silence.

Another clatter, and a snap as if something had slapped against the hull. Wilson called, "Retropack jettisoned. One of the straps caught us. Checking the burn. I got nine zeroes on three axes, perfect." He was grinning, Helen saw, enjoying the ride for its own sake. "We're no longer in orbit, baby, we are committed to Earth III."

The shuttle was now unpowered save for small attitude rockets, and these fired in bursts, a series of pops and bangs. The shuttle swiveled around a vertical axis until it had its nose pointed in the direction of its descent. As it swept through this maneuver Helen glimpsed the Ark, just briefly, a battered pockmarked hull with the lashed-together warp assembly attached to its nose. It looked all but worn out. She twisted her neck to follow it as it crossed her window, but it was soon gone, swept out of sight by the shuttle's rotation.

Now the shuttle tipped up so it was flying in belly first. Its design was based on the old NASA space shuttle; the fat heat shield on its belly would hit the atmosphere first.

"Enjoy the zero G," Wilson murmured. "Not much of that left now."

"Or the stars," Helen said. "Astronomy will be tough down there."

"We'll find a way . . . Bingo." A new panel lit up on the console before him, bright red, labeled "0.05 G." "Here comes the deceleration. Damn, we're high up compared to an Earth entry. This air is *thick*."

She felt the first tugging of deceleration in her gut, a kind of shuddering as the first wisps of atmosphere grabbed at the hull, and then a more steady drag that pulled her down into her seat. There was a faint glow beyond the window now, like the first flickering of Halivah's arc lamps in the ship's morning. It was the air of Earth III, the first direct human contact with the planet, air blasted to plasma, its very atoms smashed apart by their passage. The glow quickly built up into a kind of tunnel of colors, lavenders, blue-greens, violet, rising up above the shuttle. Sparks flew up around the ship, burning, flickering as they died.

"Insulation blanket." Wilson had to shout; the shuttle was starting to shudder, the fittings rattling. "Burning up and taking away our heat with it. It's supposed to happen. I think." He grinned coldly. "Pretty lights."

Helen didn't try to reply. The glow outside built up further and the weight piled on her in jerks, in sudden loads, surely already exceeding a full Earth gravity. She could hear the children crying. It will get better, she told herself, it will be easier than this. But the weight would never lift off her shoulders, not ever again. She was committed to the descent, bound to the planet with no way to return, ever. She would never see the hull, never hold her children, maybe never even see the stars again. Her eyes blurred, the tears coming for the first time that morning. But still the weight built up, and the light outside intensified, the colors merging into a white sheet that filled the cabin with a brilliant silver-gray glow. The experience was utterly unreal. She could see nothing but that celestial glow, and had no sense of falling, nothing but this monstrous, shuddering weight.

Wilson whooped. "This is what I call flying! We must be lighting up this fucking planet like a comet."

Then, quite abruptly, it eased. The weight load on her shoulders, though still heavy, was steady now. The plasma glow faded, the last wisps of it dissipating like glowing smoke, to reveal a pale pink sky littered with brownish clouds.

The clouds were *above* her, Helen realized.

The shuttle shuddered. Wilson worked a joystick before him, experimentally. "Aerosurfaces are biting. This thing actually flies. Jesus, I'm beginning to think we might live through this." He glanced at Helen. "You understand we're inside the atmosphere. We're not falling, we're gliding, flying. And that pull you feel isn't deceleration—"

"Gravity."

He grinned. "Authentic planetary gravity, pulling on your bones for the first time since you were in the womb."

It wasn't as bad as the peak deceleration, but she was still so heavy she felt she could barely breathe.

A speaker crackled. ". . . Halivah. Shuttle B, Halivah. Can you hear me? Shuttle B, this is Halivah—"

Wilson snapped a switch. "We're out of the plasma sheath. My God, Venus, what a ride!"

"We saw you. We still see you, in fact. I'll let you fly your bird. Let us know when your skids are down on the ground. Halivah out."

"Copy that. Let's see what we got." Wilson pressed his joystick forward, and the shuttle's nose dipped.

The world tipped up, revealing itself to Helen for the first time. The land below was dark. They were still so high the horizon showed a curve. The sky was a deep, somber shade of red, but it brightened as she looked

ahead toward the horizon. And there she saw an arc of fire, a vast sun lifting above the curve of the world, the M-sun that illuminated this super-
Earth. Now, near the horizon, she saw a chain of mountains whose peaks
caught the light, shining like a string of lanterns in the dark. She remembered what Venus had said, about the possibility of organisms like trees
straining up out of the shadow of the twilight band to catch the fugitive
light.

The shuttle dipped sharply into the thickening air. This world's dense,
stormy atmosphere was turbulent.

The events of the descent unfolded rapidly now. The world steadily
flattened out to become a landscape. That sun hauled its bulk wearily
above the horizon, huge and distorted into a flattened ellipse by some
atmospheric effect. It was white, tinged faintly pink, scarcely red at all.
The little ship crossed the mountains with their brightly lit summits, and
they flew over the terminator, the unmoving boundary of night.

As they fled over sunlit ground a panel on the console lit up with an
animated map, based on observations from the orbiting Ark. Helen peered
down. The ground was rocky, a continental shield, wrinkled with mountains and cracked by huge crevasses. Much of it was coated with old, dirty
ice that gleamed pinkly in the sun's low light. She had studied sims of
Earth landscapes from the air, recordings made before the flood; this was
something like flying low over the Canadian Shield. She made a mental
note to report that impression back to Venus.

"Shit," Wilson said. He grabbed his controls, left hand for translational
control and the right for attitude, and hauled, overriding the automated
systems. The shuttle obediently banked right.

Helen looked ahead. A vast volcano, almost like Olympus on Earth II
but more compact and clearly active, sprawled ahead of them. She could
see wisps of some dark gas escaping from the complicated multiple cal-
deras at its summit.

Wilson said, "We don't want to fly through a pillar of lumpy hot air,
or into the volcano's side, though I trust the shuttle not to do that."

The shuttle sped past the flank of the volcano. Looking down Helen saw patches of black, sheer darkness like blankets of plastic, clinging to old lava flows.

"More mountains up ahead," Wilson muttered, eyes fixed, the flaws in his stubbly flesh picked out by the glow of the low sun.

The approaching mountains were a multiple sawtooth chain, dead ahead, a geological system hundreds of kilometers deep. They were silhouetted from Helen's point of view. She compared the view with the animated map on the console, which showed a dotted red line and a cartoon shuttle swooping over a jagged mass. "They're right where they should be, Wilson."

"Good. And so are we. In which case we should come on our landing site soon."

The mountains swept beneath their prow. Their flanks were gouged by glaciers, ice glowing pink-white on the rock. The parallel ranges fell away, dissolving into foothills, themselves young and sharp-edged. Now ahead of them lay a plain, barren and strewn with rock, with a sheet of ice beyond it, the surface of a frozen lake. The shuttle dipped sharply, heading for the lake, its destination obvious.

"Right on the nose," Wilson said. "That lake's the nearest thing to a natural landing strip we spotted. I hope everybody's still strapped in."

Helen glanced over her shoulder. The low sun shone straight into the cabin, bathing the children's faces with its eerie pinkish light—eerie now, but maybe in a couple of years they'd get used to it. The children sat slumped in the gravity, though they mostly seemed awake. Some were crying, and others looked as if they had soiled themselves, or been sick. Helen forced a smile. "Not long now. Just hold on—"

The shuttle dropped sharply. She gasped, fearing she was falling.

"Sorry," Wilson muttered. "Air pocket. This damn air is just as thick as we thought, but lumpier, more turbulent. A real stew. Here we go, initiating final descent sequence." He tapped a switch, and gripped his controls hard. Now he and the autopilot were sharing the flying of the shuttle between them, though Wilson always had the casting vote.

There was a clatter from beneath her feet, and a roar of air.

Alarmed, she asked, "What the hell's that? Has a pump broken?"

Wilson just laughed, without taking his eyes off the scene outside the window. "The landing gear just dropped. And that's no busted pump, that's the wind, baby. Here we go. Coming down fast now . . ." He fell silent, watching the fleeing landscape, tracking monitors that showed his speed and altitude and rate of descent. The shuttle shuddered again as its aero-surfaces bit into the thick air.

They passed a last chain of hills. They were already beneath the summits of the highest of them, Helen saw. Then the shoreline of the frozen lake fled beneath their prow, its edge marked by parallel bands in the ice, as if the lake had melted and refrozen repeatedly. Evidence of volcano summers; every so often, Venus had advised her, a big enough eruption would inject so much carbon dioxide into the air that the temperature globally would climb, maybe for years. She wished Venus were here, talking her through this, holding her hand.

The shuttle shook again and dropped some more. Now they were flying very low over the lake. In the light of the sun Helen could see detail, rocks and scraps of ice scattered over the surface, fleeing beneath the prow.

Wilson muttered, "Nothing's ever so smooth as it looks from space. As long as we miss those itty-bitty rocks with our skids, we'll be fine. Coming down easy now. A hundred meters up. Eighty. Sixty. Woah—" He hauled on the translational control and the shuttle banked sharply right. Helen saw a field of ice boulders that had been right in their path. When he had the shuttle pointed toward a clearer track, Wilson released the control, and let the automated systems level the bird up again. "That was close."

Helen pointed dead ahead. "We're kind of near the shore." Beyond which more hilly ground rose up, looking rough and rock-strewn, and mottled with that strange black color.

Wilson grinned. "Maybe, but we only get one pass at this, girl. Let's hope we got enough room." A monitor chimed; the radar altimeter showed they were only ten meters up. "Here we go . . ." He pressed the handle forward gently. The lake lifted up to meet them.

The skids hit the ice. The shuttle rattled and skipped back up into the air, and Helen clung on to her couch. The shuttle dropped again, and bounced, and then she heard a squeal of metal as the skids scraped along the ice sheet. There was another bang, and Helen was thrown forward against her restraints, as if some great hand had grabbed the rear of the craft.

"Chutes deployed!" Wilson called. "Wow, what a ride this is."

With the parachutes dragging at the thick air, the shuttle soon slowed. The last few meters, as the skids bumped over every rock and ice block in their path, were jarring. Then the shuttle swiveled through a few degrees, and slid sideways for another dozen meters, before coming to a halt.

Wilson punched a button. "Chutes jettisoned. First job is to collect the silk, we're going to need it later . . ." He looked stunned. He tapped his microphone. "Halivah, shuttle B. We're down, down in one piece. Yeah! We're down," he repeated more quietly, and he looked over at Helen. "Now what?"

98

The shuttle's exit ramp was simple, a section of the hull that would fold down to the ground, lined with a corrugated surface for traction.

Helen, Jeb and Wilson stood by the closed door. They wore thick-lined bright green overcoats, and gloves and hats, and face masks connected to filter bottles. A few of the older children were with them, all in coats and masks, while the rest waited in the main cabin. Jeb, awkward and panting, was carrying little Sapphire Murphy Baker in his arms. The girl's face was almost entirely hidden by her mask. They were all hanging on to rails, supporting their unaccustomed weight. Jeb and Wilson had at least grown up in Earth gravity; Helen had only known the hull's fractional gravity and that not for thirty years since the Split, and the one and a quarter G felt crushingly heavy. But she stood, determined.

"So," Wilson said, his voice muffled by his mask. "Everybody set?"

"Do it," Helen murmured.

Wilson pulled a lever. With a hiss of hydraulics the hatch gracefully yawned down to the ground. Cold, sharp air washed into the shuttle, and a pale pink light drowned out the glow of the artificial lamps.

Wilson glanced around. "Nobody dead yet? Ready for the EVA?"

Helen snorted. "An EVA which is never going to end, Wilson."

"I guess not." He led the way out of the hatch.

They all walked cautiously down the ramp—cautiously as they encountered the new world, and cautiously because Helen wasn't sure she even remembered how to walk. Jeb carried little Sapphire, who looked around wide-eyed.

They were looking straight toward the sun, which hung huge in a pink-brown sky. It was maybe forty times as wide as the sun's disc as seen from Earth, but you could look directly at its pale glow without blinking. The hills at the edge of the lake rose up, coated with streaks of black, their shadowed faces thick with frost. Shapes like stocky trees, squat and dark, pushed up from the hills' flanks.

Helen felt a deep, gut-wrenching fear to be walking out of the shelter of the shuttle like this, to enter openness, infinity, to be for the first time in her whole life not contained within a hull. This was *not* like the Head-Space sims, she thought; in the end they had been no real preparation. And yet she kept walking, one foot in front of the other, down the ramp after Wilson. She was evolved for this, she told herself. The kids were young; they would adapt.

They paused before they got to the base of the ramp.

"I think I see open water over there," Jeb said, pointing. "See, in the valley between those hills? Like a river, feeding the lake."

"I can't see," Helen said. She had trouble focusing on the middle distance. But then she'd only ever had to look at things within the hull, or at infinity, nothing in between. Maybe her eyes would adjust.

"We can always move closer to the subsolar point if we want," Wilson said. "The shuttle is designed to break down to build habitats, sleds. We might try to get to the ocean. It's not far, fifty klicks."

Helen, new to planets, didn't want to sound foolish. "You think those tall things are trees?"

"If they are, their leaves are jet black," Jeb said. "And so's that grassy stuff at their feet."

"Well, that makes sense," Helen said. "The M-sun's light isn't like Earth's. It peaks in the infrared. Photosynthesis here needs to be efficient, absorbing as much of the spectrum as it can consume. Hence it looks black."

Jeb the farmer's son asked, "So you think we really can grow crops here? It's all so strange."

"Hell, yes," said Wilson, and he waved a gloved hand. "In the long term there are all sorts of advantages to a world like this. That sun's never going to move from where it is in the sky."

"It's always morning here," Helen murmured.

"Always morning. We can set up mirrors to concentrate the light. Later, when we get back off planet, we can throw up strings of orbital mirrors to focus the light on our farms, even start lighting up the far side and melt that damn ice cap."

Helen smiled behind her mask. "One step at a time, Wilson."

"I think I smell sulfur," Jeb said.

"Volcano air," Wilson said.

Helen took another step, toward the base of the ramp. It had cut a shallow groove in the ice, which was gritty and littered with small rocks and a thin ash, maybe from some volcanic event.

On impulse Jeb kneeled down, cautiously, and set little Sapphire down on the ramp. Sapphire, the youngest of the crew, too young to know she had not yet learned to walk, tried to stand up, and fell flat on her backside. But she just rolled over and got up on her hands and knees and began to crawl, a bit unsteadily, but purposefully.

And she crawled right off the edge of the ramp and onto the ice of Earth III. She squealed at the cold, and then poked her gloved finger into the groove the ramp had made. Helen felt regret, a deep, visceral stab, that her own children couldn't come running down this ramp and join her.

"Look up," Wilson said.

Helen straightened up. There, crossing the tall red sky, was a star, ruby-bright, tracking steadily toward the M-sun. It was Halivah, the only moon of Earth III. And as Helen watched, straining her eyes, the sky puckered, and the Ark was gone.

Afterword

In recent decades our understanding of how an interstellar voyage might be achieved, and of the possible destinations of such a voyage, has been transformed. See for instance *Interstellar Travel and Multi-Generation Spaceships*, ed. Yoji Kondo (Apogee Books, 2003). This includes a new study on the size of viable human populations. A recent review of possible interstellar travel technologies is *Centauri Dreams* by Paul Gilster (Copernicus Books, 2004).

The science and technology of the "warp drive," deriving from the seminal paper by Miguel Alcubierre (*Classical and Quantum Gravity*, vol. 11, L73–L77, 1994), is being developed by a community of researchers who came together for a seminar which I attended at the British Interplanetary Society on 15 November 2007, and which is documented in *The Journal of the British Interplanetary Society*, vol. 61 no. 9, September 2008. The journal contains a paper by Obousy et al. (pp. 364–69) outlining the notion of manipulating higher dimensions in order to inflate spacetime. The idea of reducing the energy required by shrinking the "warp bubble" is extrapolated from a paper by C. Van Den Broeck (*Classical and Quantum Gravity*, vol. 16, pp. 3973–79, 1999). For references on the optical effects of a warp field see a paper by C. Clark et al. (*Classical and Quantum Gravity*, vol. 16, pp. 3965–72, 1999) and a dissertation by D. Weiskopf ("The Visualisation of Four-dimensional Spacetimes," University of Tubingen, 2001). The theoretical and engineering obstacles to creating a warp-drive starship remain huge, however.

The astonishing Cold War dream of interplanetary travel powered by nuclear weapons is documented in George Dyson's *Project Orion* (Holt, 2002). Revolutionary designs for high-energy "plasma accelerators" are being considered by the US Department of Energy (see *New Scientist,* 3 January 2009).

The portrayal here of the prospects for intelligent life in the universe is drawn in part from my participation at the "Sound of Silence" workshop hosted by Arizona State University in February 2008, and the IAA Symposium on "Searching for Life Signatures," September 2008, in Paris. A recent review of "exoplanets," the newly discovered worlds of other stars, is *The New Worlds* by Casoli and Encrenaz (Springer-Praxis, 2007). The argument that most stars in the Galaxy that harbor complex life will be older than the sun was developed by Lineweaver et al. (*Icarus,* vol. 151, pp. 307–13, 2001). The "starshade" telescope concept was devised by Cash (*Nature,* vol. 442, pp. 51–53, 2006).

The dynamics of extraterrestrial human societies is explored in, for example, Charles Cockell's "An Essay on Extraterrestrial Liberty" (*Journal of the British Interplanetary Society,* vol. 61, pp. 255–75, 2008).

The biblical quotations are from the King James Bible.

Any errors or inaccuracies are my sole responsibility.

Stephen Baxter
Northumberland
April 2009